Amantarra

Richard J. Galloway

Published by: Richard J. Galloway

Richard J. Galloway asserts the right to be identified as the author of this work.

www.richardjgalloway.co.uk

ISBN: 978-0-9573257-4-6

In fondest memory of my father Ron Galloway, 1932-2012

ACKNOWLEDGMENTS

Thanks to Angela and Claire for test-driving this book and to Paul and Francis for their promotion efforts. Amantarra would not have been created but for the support and encouragement they have given me.

1
VALHEEL

Artullus sat in the Great Library of Valheel. The vast domed room was almost empty save for a few who sat at the long tables in isolated silence. On the table in front of each was a flat console rather like the ink blotters of old. Three dimensional images floated in the air above them. Artullus removed a clear crystal from the receptacle to the right of his console and the images in front of him vanished immediately. The crystal fitted into the palm of his hand, he rolled it from one hand to the other several times and then held it up to the light. He turned the crystal slowly as he waited for Amantarra to make her appearance; colours danced in each of the facets. He thought about his time on the high council and the subtle changes he had witnessed over the millennia; changes that had affected friends, colleagues and council members alike. Were he and Amantarra the only ones to have noticed them? He did carry a certain amount of guilt; after all he was the leader of the council when the decision was made to create Valheel.

The light blue walls of the domed circular reading room were lined with crystals identical in shape but smaller than the one which Artullus was holding. Each crystal contained the complete knowledge of any subject you could think of. The Bruwnan had reached the limits of what is technically possible in Euclidean space millennia before their ascension into the ethereal beings they were now; and all of that knowledge, plus history, art and everything else was contained in this one room. Artullus closed one eye and turned the crystal so that he could see only red light and then turned it the other way so that the colour changed up through the spectrum to blue. Behind the crystal Amantarra appeared in the entrance to the library. Artullus placed the crystal on the table in front of him and waved to her.

'Amantarra, it is good to see you,' he said as his daughter arrived at his side.

'Thank you father, and how goes your research into the history of Bruwnan technology?' Her question had a slight air of amateur dramatics about it, as if it had been said for the benefit of other ears.

Artullus picked up the crystal from the table as Amantarra sat next to him. 'It's complete.' He held it up to show her.

'How much did you manage to get on there?'

Artullus looked around to see if there was anyone close by, and then leaned in close. 'All of it,' he said.

Amantarra looked around at the crystals that lined the library walls. 'All of this,' she whispered, 'the whole thing?' She looked amazed.

'It wasn't easy. I had to use some of the same techniques used by the city to store its data, so the sooner it's out of here the better.'

'What about the Primary Key?' Amantarra whispered.

Artullus indicated the crystal with a nod, 'and only here,' he said quietly. 'How go your plans?'

'I have primed the Ja'liem, the humans are ready for the next genetic phase, and I've left a trail of breadcrumbs for Elleria,' said Amantarra in hushed tones.

Artullus sighed. 'It's been three hundred thousand years since I had this conversation with your sister.' Artullus held the crystal up. 'I wish I had managed to send her off with this information. We might have heard back from her then.'

'Saranythia didn't need it; she was always the clever one.'

Artullus shook his head. 'I fear for her, she was always far too adventurous.' He was silent for a moment, lost in his thoughts about Saranythia. 'Whatever she was trying must have failed.'

'As soon as it is possible for me to do so I will seek her out.'

Artullus nodded his thanks. 'Amantarra,' he handed her the crystal; 'it's time.'

'How many are left?' asked Amantarra.

'Difficult to tell, the city's sensors are being fed false information, but I've analysed the energy flows and by my estimation there's only a few thousand of the original ascended left.'

'Then now is the time,' said Amantarra.

Artullus reached into his pocket and produced a ring. 'You'll need this,' he said, as he handed it to her. 'It uses the same technology as the weapons the Guardians of Valheel carry. Initially it will disrupt the protective field around the Node Zero allowing you to access it directly. Once the ring is fully interfaced, it will change the operating parameters of the Node allowing a reversal of the energy flow. The Node will be very vulnerable once you have removed the protective field and it is vital that it receives no shocks until your task is complete.'

Amantarra placed the ring on her finger and held it up so that the light caught the single large red stone.

'Good luck Amantarra. I'm going to leave Valheel so that the plan cannot be extracted from my Avatar. If you are successful and you have enough time to complete your work, then we will meet again. If not, then this will be our final goodbye.'

They stood and embraced. Amantarra sat back down and watched Artullus make his way towards the exit. He waved from the doorway and then left, heading for the portals on the plaza which were the only way in or out of the city. She sat for a moment mourning the absence of her father and contemplating the implications of her next move. Amantarra looked at the crystal in her hand and then surreptitiously placed it in her pocket. She stood and made her way towards the rear exit of the library. In a few moments, as the crystal left the library, the alarm would sound.

Behind her the blue door to the Great Library of Valheel stood open. The low chiming of an alarm could be heard coming from inside. Amantarra was running from the door towards the entrance of one of the arcades that led to the Blue Plaza. She reached the entrance to the arcade and a quick look confirmed that it was empty, Amantarra slipped round the corner.

The glass roof of the arcade was supported on arched metal columns that met in a point at the top, making it look like the ribcage of some enormous dead beast. Amantarra ran quickly but cautiously along the arcade towards the circular plaza at the base of one of the centroid towers. This is too easy, she thought. As she neared the end of the arcade she slowed, moved closer to the wall and hid behind one of the columns.

She felt the lump the crystal made in her clothing: so much time; so much knowledge; so much dangerous knowledge. The data it contained had not been easy to collate. Artullus had risked a lot to compile this knowledge and she had never dared believe that it would ever be completed.

3

She chanced a peep around the column. The arcade was still clear. Amantarra sprinted to the next column. She was now only two away from the arcade exit. Again she looked around the column and out across the plaza.

There were two of them.

They had just appeared around the side of the blue centroid tower in the centre of the plaza. She pressed her back into the column and closed her eyes.

Seconds passed.

Opening her eyes, she looked up and through the glass roof of the arcade at the towers of Valheel that arced overhead. The city of Valheel was built on the inside of a sphere some two kilometres in diameter. At the centre of the sphere was a spherical chamber which housed Node Zero, Amantarra's next port of call. And the only way to reach Node Zero was up one of the four centroid towers; red, green, yellow or blue. She both hated and loved the geometric purity of the city; if you drew a straight line between the bases of the centroid towers it would form an equilateral pyramid. There was purity in that, which Amantarra liked; but she hated what it represented. To her it meant constraint, and she mourned the passing of her people's ability to think creatively. She studied the buildings on the other side of the sphere, from her current position she could see the base of the red centroid tower with its circular plaza and four arcades identical to the one she was in now. The smaller buildings and towers that made up the city looked like toys on the far side of the sphere. The light issuing from their windows was steady, unhindered by atmospheric disturbance; Valheel had no atmosphere; the city and its inhabitants were constructed of pure energy. Strange, she reflected, why is it that as ethereal beings, we have the need to set these boundaries for ourselves, constructing virtual cities and, she looked down at her body, shells for our consciousness. Perhaps leaving our corporeal existence was a mistake, one which will always haunt us.

Amantarra breathed out slowly in a silent sigh of relief. They hadn't spotted her. Now she had another problem. They were between her and the base of the tower. She contemplated a new route. Whichever way she went it would take longer, and the longer it took the greater the risk of detection. Perhaps the guards' would make their way down one of the other arcades. Intelligent though they were, they did not possess an independent conscious, they were not Bruwnan or even Radgarc; they were constructs of the city itself, Avatars, known to all as the "Guardians of Valheel". Which was a bit of a joke, there was nothing to guard against. No, as far as Amantarra was concerned they were there to suppress.

The column in front of her rang as a pulse of energy struck it; she looked down from the glass roof at the impact point. A small round section of the metal had been replaced by a green grid of construction lines which in turn rendered into glowing orange hot metal. Amantarra remained still behind her column. This is taking the virtual boundaries too far, she thought. Weapons! Beings that do not need physical form do not need boundaries, never mind weapons to enforce them. The weapons did not kill. They couldn't; it was impossible to kill a Bruwnan, they'd left their physical forms behind long ago. The weapons disrupted the avatar placing a copy of the occupier's consciousness under the control of the city. That, thought Amantarra, would not be a good thing given what she was about to attempt.

Amantarra risked another look. The two guards were heading her way across the blue paving of the plaza. It wouldn't be long before there would be more coming from the library side of the arcade and she would then be completely trapped. Two more shots struck the column she was hiding behind but did not penetrate.

A volley of five or six wild shots some hitting the far wall, most travelling further down the arcade, but one shot shattering the glass in the roof above Amantarra. She lowered her head as the glass rained down evaporating into a multitude of green construction grids that tumbled and spun in the air turning back into shards as they fell. From the change in trajectory and wildness of the shots, she realised that the assailants must be running to get a better angle on her.

Time was running out.

She shook the glass from her hair and looked up. The entire glass panel had gone and for the first time Amantarra noticed the nicely spaced anchor points that attached the column to the wall. She didn't need to think about it; in an instant she was halfway up the column using the anchor points as handholds. Two more shots, both struck the wall halfway between her column and the next one with some accuracy, they'd obviously stopped running but hadn't got the angle right yet.

At the top Amantarra rolled over the parapet wall dropping down a short distance onto the flat roof. The wide roof curved round to the next arcade, its only feature was a large spire at the halfway point. The distance to the spire was too great; she would never be able to run to it in time.

Two more shots very close. Amantarra's column rang with the impact.

Then she could hear them below; they were in her last hiding place.

'Up,' said a voice.

She could hear one of them start to climb and she tucked herself close into the parapet wall. Perhaps they won't climb onto the roof, she thought, perhaps they'll just look, and seeing no one climb back down.

A hand appeared over the parapet just in front of her, it was holding a weapon. Forget plan "A" hiding and hoping; without thinking Amantarra sat up. In the same movement she grabbed the weapon and pointed it at the guards head. Smooth featureless metal with strips of black where the eyes should be, it was a face that was incapable of showing surprise. Amantarra had always thought that the design of the guardians lacked imagination. The guardian looked from his empty hand to Amantarra's face as if he was trying to work out what had happened. Amantarra looked at her reflection in the black plastic eyes and wondered if the automaton had any concept of the meaning of surprise, or for that matter any inkling of what was going to happen next.

The best form of defence is often attack.

Amantarra pulled the trigger removing the top half of the guards head leaving only the un-rendered green construction grid outlining his cranium; and true to the rules governing the city his avatar immediately shutdown, falling onto his climbing comrade and knocking him to the ground. Amantarra leaned over the parapet and finished the job with a shot to the chest of the second guard as he sprawled on the ground.

She quickly slipped back over the parapet and down the side of the column. As she reached the ground the shattered glass vanished and the roof reappeared as the system automatically cleaned up the damage, it wouldn't be much longer before the guards vanished and were reintegrated back into the system. She grabbed the second guard's weapon and with one in each hand, ran to the arcade exit. She scanned the plaza; there were no more guards. Head down she sprinted towards the domed structure at the base of the tower which housed the distribution crystal.

She was about three quarters of the way across when an energy pulse whizzed past her. She immediately jinked left, left again and then right. Several more shots, that were close, but not close enough, impacted on the wall of the tower in front of her. She'd suspected there would be more guards approaching from the other end of the arcade and apparently they had now arrived.

The base of the tower was set slightly below the plaza. Amantarra crouched at the base of the short flight of steps that led down to it and returned fire. There was no way, she thought, that she would be able to hit them from this range, but at least it would delay their attempt to cross the plaza. The shots did stop them; they knelt in the entrance to the arcade and returned fire with considerably more accuracy than Amantarra. She stood and ran, following the curved wall round to the entrance. The guards' shots followed her progress, hitting the wall behind her.

The door to the tower was set back in the wall. Keeping low, she tried the large double doors, they were locked. Amantarra took aim at the lock and fired. It took six shots but eventually the lock evaporated back to the underlying green construction grid. Amantarra went partway back up the steps, took careful aim and let off three more shots towards the four guards who were just venturing out of the arcade. Unbelievably, and more through good luck than skill, she actually managed to hit one of them. The other three guards dropped low to the ground and returned fire. Amantarra was about to turn and go inside when she saw another figure appear in the entrance to the arcade. It was unmistakably Tyrus, Valheel's Enforcer.

Tyrus raised his arms straight above his head and a large ball of blue white energy formed between his hands. Throwing his arms forward he hurled the ball in Amantarra's direction. As the energy rapidly crossed the plaza it passed through one of the guards destroying him completely. Amantarra dropped and rolled down the steps as the ball of energy struck the wall to the right of the door causing a large section of it to vanish leaving only the green construction grid.

Amantarra did not wait for a second shot; she was already pushing the doors open and making her way inside. She was in a short corridor. To her right was the top of a flight of stairs that disappeared down into darkness. Ahead there was another set of double doors, Amantarra ran to them. The doors weren't locked and she pushed them both open to make a grand entrance.

Inside, the curve of the domed roof ran around the perimeter of the circular chamber. It terminated at its highest point with a circular hole which was the base of the centroid tower itself. There were no columns or any other supporting structures for the tower. Nor were there any intermediate floors in the centroid tower, it was clear all the way to the Node Zero chamber. In the centre of the floor a pure white beam of energy from Node Zero a kilometre above, terminated its journey on the facetted surface of a clear crystal set on a low, wide plinth. From here, the energy was distributed to this quadrant of the city. It was where the essence of the Euclidian universe met the virtual existence of the city of Valheel; without this energy stream, and the ones from its three siblings, the city would not exist. Surrounding the plinth were four long curved benches that looked like they were made from black marble. Amantarra couldn't believe that anyone would want to sit and stare at the energy stream, but obviously that was what one of the designers had imagined. Cantilevered out from the wall of the wide circular tower was a spiral staircase that wound its way up to the Node Zero chamber. The last section of steps descending from the hole in the roof to the chamber floor seemed to float in the air without any visible means of support. The entire length of the tower was illuminated by the energy beam making the blue walls and staircase glow.

The tower itself was translucent and she could see the yellow zone of the city above her as she started to climb. It was a long way up, but it was the only way. At least her body would not get physically tired. She was about five turns up when a pulse of energy flew past her. The shot struck the underside of the stairs above her leaving black radial burn mark. Amantarra kept running; the more time they wasted down there, the longer she would have in the chamber. She could hear raised voices; it was Tyrus voicing his concerns over using a weapon this close to the beam.

Amantarra had climbed another two turns before she could hear them on the stairs below her. She could always wait and pick them off as they drew closer, knowing that they probably would be reluctant to return fire. She dismissed the idea; having them closer was the last thing she needed, and she couldn't risk one of Tyrus' fireballs. And so the climb continued. Amantarra, free from the fear of ambush, unlike her pursuers, managed to increase her lead.

Twenty minutes later Amantarra arrived in the one hundred metre diameter sphere that was the Node Zero chamber. Node Zero itself dominated the chamber, almost filling it, there was a gap of only ten metres between the rounded totally black multifaceted crystal and the curved floor of the chamber. Each centroid tower was capped with a series of arches like those making up the arcades' far below, they terminated around a ring through which the energy beam from Node Zero passed as it started its journey down the tower.

One of the facets was perfectly aligned with the ring at the top of the arches. The chamber resonated with a slowly changing harmony as the energy levels in each beam rose and fell. Energy, Amantarra needed a lot of it, but she also needed to store it, because what she was about to do would cut her off from the source for a long time.

The Bruwnan had left Euclidian space half the age of the universe ago. They moved their minds to a different set of dimensions where they fabricated this city, this reality. A reality built on rules applied by an artificial intelligence and sustained from energy derived from living organisms. This meant that the Bruwnan were not divorced from the Euclidian universe, they were completely dependent upon it. Without it they were just thoughts in the void. They had constructed a network of thirty trillion nodes to concentrate enough energy to construct the city of Valheel where they could condense their consciousness into shadows of their former physical forms. The Bruwnan could no longer have any tangible presence in the Euclidian universe, but they didn't need it because they had tools to exercise their influence there.

Amantarra wasted no time, and tucking the weapons into her belt climbed one of the arches to reach Node Zero. At the top of the framework she made herself as comfortable and secure as possible by wrapping her legs around the metalwork. Node Zero was just above her; she tilted her head back and looked into the crystal. There was no surface reflection, there couldn't be, the Node was not an object it was the interface between all the dimensions the city operated in and Euclidean space time.

Amantarra reached into her pocket with her ring hand and produced the clear crystal. Raising her hand she pressed the red stone on the ring against the surface of the Node. The black crystal felt cold to the touch like polished granite. Moments passed and nothing happened. Amantarra was just beginning to doubt if the ring was doing anything when the stone changed from red to green and her hand started to slip below the black surface. Amantarra pushed harder, forcing her hand and the clear crystal she was holding into the Node.

The consistency of the Node had gone from granite hard to treacle. She could feel the vibration as the energy from thirty trillion worlds coursed around her hand. There was a slight flickering of the light levels as some of the energy was diverted away from the city, back into the Euclidean universe where it had come from, and into a construct of Saranythia's design. She could sense the mass growing, but mass soaked up a lot of energy and it would take several minutes to complete at this transfer rate.

Three guards arrived at the top of the tower. At first they couldn't see where she was and made their way towards the tops of the other towers to see if she had started down. Amantarra watched until finally their legs became obscured by the curved outline of Node Zero.

It was several minutes, several precious minutes, before they reappeared at the base of the framework.

'There,' shouted one of the guards.

They levelled their weapons at her, but lowered them when they saw that the force field had been penetrated; it was just too dangerous to use them in this place with this much energy about.

Amantarra pushed her hand further into the crystal and the lights visibly dimmed throughout the city, plunging some of the buildings into darkness momentarily. Lowest down the pecking order for energy, for a split second the guards were replaced by green construction lines as the city adjusted to the drop in power. Amantarra used the opportunity to retrieve one of the weapons from her belt. The guards looked around the chamber as if that held the answer to the dropping light levels. Amantarra could sense the increase in the growth rate of her construction. Shouldn't take too long now she thought.

'What are you doing?' one of the guards asked.

Amantarra did not answer; she just closed her eyes and concentrated.

Even with her eyes closed Amantarra could sense him as he arrived at the top of the stairs. Tyrus, Valheel's Enforcer. To Amantarra he was the epitome of the rot and corruption that centred on the council and reached out now to infect every aspect of the Bruwnian existence.

The guards stepped back as he approached.

Tyrus calmly took in the scene. Looking from the weapon Amantarra was holding, to the hand she had embedded in the black crystal.

'Remove your hand from the crystal,' said Tyrus calmly.

Amantarra opened her eyes and looked at him. He was smiling at her with one of those self-confident little smirks that the really annoyed her. She hated his arrogance. Amantarra raised her eyebrows as if to say "yes, can I help you?" He was a servant of the Bruwnan after all; and again she found herself questioning why the council had given the avatar such power. It was way beyond anything the Bruwnan themselves had.

'Remove your hand from the crystal,' repeated Tyrus. There was more impatience in his voice now, Amantarra relished it. She smiled at him to try and annoy him some more.

'When you have removed your hand, you can tell me what you are doing.'

He hadn't expected her to comply and was doubly surprised when she did and the lights suddenly brightened. The clear crystal and the ring were no longer present. Amantarra used the distraction of the light levels to retrieve the other weapon from her belt and pointed both of them at Tyrus. Amantarra knew that if she did fire at him, he would only reappear again a short while later, but the temptation to annoy him was quite strong. She decided not to fire, mainly because she wanted him to witness her next move.

'Don't fire in here idiot; you might hit the node!'

"Idiot", thought Amantarra, this servant is out of control.

'Really, that's strange,' said Amantarra pointing one of the weapons at the black crystal; 'because hitting the node is exactly what I want to do.'

Tyrus opened his mouth to speak as Amantarra fired.

The city and its avatars vanished instantly casting the Bruwnan out into the void. In that brief moment of nothing there were voices, Bruwnan voices, the complaints of the city dwellers as they were cast out. And then they were gone. She thought about them for a moment, but didn't dwell on them for very long. It would be an age before a new Node Zero was constructed and Amantarra had work to do; and a new home to occupy.

2
EUCLIDEAN

Of the billions of planets in the millions of galaxies that Amantarra controlled, this one had always been her favourite. In the centre of a vast continent sized jungle of massive silver barked trees, there was a hill shaped like a truncated cone. No trees grew on the hill which had an artificial symmetry about it that made it look completely out of place in the forest. Its slopes were covered in long golden grass which blew in the wind that swirled around its upper levels forming ripples that ran round and round across its surface. The top of the hill was flat, and whether by design or coincidence, was level with the top of the surrounding forest canopy. The centre of the hilltop was occupied by a large, white, domed building; which in construction resembled the Great Library of Valheel. It was the only building on the planet.

The building had a single arched entrance with heavy metal doors. Standing with her back to the doors stood what appeared to be a female Bruwnan; which was strange, as the Bruwnan had not existed in this form for half the age of the universe. She was looking out across the tops of the trees studying the light and dark contrasts in the canopy as the orange light from the setting sun streamed in from her left.

Although very similar to humans, the Bruwnan, particularly the females, were tall, slender and graceful in their movements. Her skin was almost pure white with just a hint of pale blue; it reflected the orange light as the sun disappeared slowly down behind the trees. She had her long blue hair tied back into a pony tail; it moved along with her flowing white clothes as the wind revolved around the domed building. Sapphire blue eyes set above a small flat nose glinted with a certain amount of excitement in the setting sun. To the right of the sun, just visible in the orange sky were the crescents of two of the three moons. The third moon to Elleria's right was almost full in the fading blue half of the sky.

Elleria was Amantarra's Radgarc, and when she needed to take physical form to perform her duties she occupied a Bruwnan shaped shell of Saranythia's design. The shell was a facsimile of what the Bruwnan had once been. It was Bruwnan shaped and had five senses, but there were no internal organs, the shell was hollow and only lasted a short while, its only purpose was to provide a physical vessel for Elleria's consciousness.

Every Bruwnan owned a Radgarc, every Bruwnan had created one; they managed the energy flow into the city of Valheel from the Nodes created by each Bruwnan. In Elleria's case she managed all of Amantarra's Nodes. Radgarc's differed from the Bruwnan in that they could take physical form in the Euclidian universe and they drew their energy directly from the Nodes they managed; they were not tied to Valheel for their energy as the Bruwnan were. Tyrus drew his energy directly from Node Zero making him very powerful indeed, but then he was an Enforcer, the defender of Node Zero, his role was to protect not to manage.

Managing Nodes was interesting enough, but the best part of all, the part Elleria always looked forward to, was the activation of a new Node, because that meant she could take physical form for a day. And today was an extra special day, because the activation was going to take place on an extra special planet. Amantarra had spent longer developing the life here than she had on any other planet that Elleria knew of. It was the only planet that Amantarra had encouraged Elleria to visit with her as she developed that life. Elleria had visited as often as she could; but not as often as Amantarra, who had in the past, often spent years at a time here. Unlike Elleria, Amantarra could not take physical form, the rules of Valheel; Amantarra's power source; denied her the resources to be able to do that. Elleria had no such restriction as she drew her power directly from the Nodes she managed.

Elleria had hoped that Amantarra would be here to witness the activation of the Node and its connection into the network, but she wasn't. She comforted herself with the thought that there was still time; she hadn't yet started the merging process, and it would be a full rotation of the planet before it was ready to connect to the network. Elleria looked down at the small clear crystal in the palm of her hand and then back out across the treetops. Half the sun's disk had disappeared below the trees deepening shadows in the canopy. In the trees closest to the hill there was movement high up in the canopy and although the Ja'liem kept to the shadows Elleria knew they were there. She didn't need to use her Bruwnan senses to detect them, they were always there. The Ja'liem filled the forest in their millions, they were everywhere.

The Ja'liem, as Amantarra had named them, were small black furred primates with a splash of colour. They were short and stocky in stature with short rear legs, broad shoulders and long arms. They walked on all fours, particularly when running through the canopy, but often they could be seen walking upright along the wide branches. Their faces were drawn out to form a bear like muzzle containing large teeth and impressive canines. The males had a single purple stripe that ran from between their eyes, over the top of their head and down to a tapered point in the centre of their backs. The females had two orange stripes that followed a similar path. Over the millennia Elleria had occasionally glimpsed exceptions to the stripe arrangements, but these were rare events. The exceptions were always large males and they invariably had all three stripes. Elleria had observed; on the two occasions that she'd seen one; that their behaviour was different to the others, they had a calm almost distinguished air about them, and the others were deferent in their presence. The last time she had seen one was over fifteen thousand years ago and at the time she had asked Amantarra about the three stripers, whether they were occasional mutations, or if they were present in every generation but just tended to remain hidden; her reply was; "when the time is right, you won't need to ask the question".

Elleria thought about Amantarra's answer as she watched the Ja'liem gather in the trees around the hill. Although this behaviour was unusual it probably wasn't unexpected, this was the first time Elleria had ever taken physical form on this planet; the creatures were probably just curious. In all her previous visits she had drifted through the forest with Amantarra like a phantom, sensing the forest by measuring the interference between these dimensions and the ones she normally occupied, detecting more detail but less substance. The five senses in the shell she now occupied were quirky but somehow more comfortable; they were similar to the ones the avatars in Valheel received. She breathed in deeply, taking in the smells; felt the wind on her skin, you didn't get that in Valheel; and sound was so much better when you actually heard it instead of just interpreting the pressure waves. This was why Elleria liked activating a new node.

The Ja'liem were starting to make quite a racket and it was then that Elleria realised just how many had gathered in the trees around the hill. In the past, as she had studied the creatures with Amantarra, she'd been able to distinguish a number of their calls, the most common being "hello", "follow me" and "predator". The last one produced the most electrifying response, with the Ja'liem scattering in all directions. The rest of the time they just seemed to be chattering and chirping just for the sake of making a noise, like they were doing now.

In the fading light with the sun just peeping over the top of the trees the creatures were hidden in the shadows, Elleria had to use her normal senses to detect them. Those at the edge of the forest closest to the hill were sitting on the thick branches, packing them out completely and more were arriving at every moment. Pushing the field of her senses further out, the forest was alive with the Ja'liem. Running over the branches, jumping from tree to tree they were all heading for the hill. Elleria was shocked; how did they know I was here? And why would I create such curiosity? She watched a few of them as they ran, leapt and swung, never making a mistake they moved easily through the trees. How often had she wished she could join them, they looked so free.

The sun was a sliver of deep orange just above the forest canopy when Elleria saw him. Sitting directly in front of the entrance to the building flanked on either side by enough space to give at least a dozen Ja'liem a seat, given how crammed the others were, sat a three striper. The three striped Ja'liem sat silent and still while those around him shouted and screamed. He was staring directly at Elleria looking in every way the king of the Ja'liem. Elleria looked back at him, his stare wasn't aggressive, it was more observational, judgemental; and he didn't flinch or look away, he just sat there, waiting.

With a flash of green light the sun disappeared below tops of the trees and the forest instantly fell silent. The effect took Elleria's breath away.

They were all watching Elleria expectantly now.

In the silence Elleria turned and walked towards the entrance to the domed building. She pushed open the huge double doors and entered the Node chamber. The interior of the building consisted of a single large space. The walls and the underside of the dome were white and glowed with an inner light. On the floor in the centre of the space, was a black multifaceted crystal, otherwise the interior of the building was completely empty. The doors closed behind her with a dull thud which rumbled around the circular space, the sound dissipating with each circuit until it was no more than a murmur.

'I am Elleria!' she shouted, listening to the reverberation as the sound rolled around the room, 'and I am Amantarra's Radgarc.' Elleria liked to play with these quirky senses. She liked the way that you only got this reverberation when you stood near the wall of a Node chamber, if you stood in the middle the effect simply didn't exist.

'So Quirky,' she shouted, for no other reason than hearing own voice.

Elleria waited for the sound to die and then walked to the black crystal. The crystal, the top of which reached Elleria's waist, was smaller but of the same dimensions as the one in the city of Valheel; or at least it would have the same dimensions once Elleria's task was complete, at the moment it only had three.

Elleria rested her left hand on the black crystal and held the small clear crystal up in front of her on the palm of her other hand. The small crystal contained the instructions that would turn the large crystal into a Node. The process of merging the two crystals took the same time as it took the planet to spin once on its axis, in other words a single planetary day.

She closed her eyes and started the merging process simply by picturing the two crystals coming together. Opening them again, she watched the small crystal boil red for a moment. When the crystal had cleared again she placed it on top of the black one. Once the merging process had started, both crystals only needed to be on the same planet; but, reasoned Elleria, if you put the small crystal on top of the larger one, then at least you knew where it was.

Elleria turned her back on the Node and walked to the entrance. To the left, the sky outside was flame red as the light from the sun caught the high clouds. The red gave way to a deep blue and finally, to Elleria's right, black where one or two of the brighter stars were beginning to appear. The Ja'liem, still sitting in silence, watched as Elleria stood at the edge of the hill. There didn't appear to be any more arriving and she wondered whether this was the entire population. Nor did the Ja'liem show any sign that they were about to leave. If only, Elleria thought, she knew how to construct a shell; she could become one of them and sit out the day's vigil in their company. She pictured what it would be like, running through the trees. Would she take on more aspects of the creatures if she spent time with them? It saddened her to think that it probably would never happen.

She made her way down the hill towards the floor of the forest. Once there she entered the forest. This was one of the highlights of being corporeal; you got to explore a real world. As she walked around the bases of the giant trees, she could sense that a large group of the Ja'liem had broken off from the rest and was shadowing her as she moved. The three striped one was amongst them. It made Elleria glow with importance.

*

On another world in another galaxy, Amantarra looked down at her new home. Physically it was human shaped, male to be precise, well-muscled and lean looking. Amantarra considered male to be the best option for the construct, given that the social structure seemed to be male dominated. Shape was where the similarities between humans and the construct ended; the vessel Amantarra occupied was solid. Solid and densely packed, in its newly created state the construct weighed just over five hundred kilograms. It was storing a lot of energy, and with Valheel gone she would need it. Over time the mass would diminish as it was converted to energy, the insides liquefying to maintain the bulk, but that time was a long way off.

The increase in the volume of bird song and a golden sky to the east heralded the coming dawn. Amantarra's naked form tingled with goose flesh from the fresh breeze blowing across the plane. It had been a long time since Amantarra had experienced the joy of an additional five senses. Although interesting, Amantarra preferred the Bruwnan method of measuring the interference between dimensions, it was so much cleaner and lacked the disadvantages; he made a mental note that if it didn't improve soon, he was definitely going to turn off the sense of smell.

In front of him, to the south, a grass plain sloped gently to the east; this was bordered on the west by a forest, the trees yellow and orange with autumn's embrace. A thin layer of mist formed a band halfway up the trees cutting them in two. The nights hunters had gone, settled down for the day. Half a dozen deer had ventured out of the forest and onto the plain. They alternated between grazing and watching for predators their heads bobbing down to grab a mouthful of grass and then up again, ears twitching as they chewed. Amantarra watched them as he contemplated his situation. He estimated that he had about thirty thousand years to conclude his experiment before Valheel was reactivated and he wondered if it would be long enough.

The sun peeped over the horizon and the trees appeared to burst into flame as the golden light struck them. The deer looked up and round, startled by the sudden change in light and then relaxed, returning to their grazing.

Behind Amantarra was a cliff face, he could sense his creations as they slept in a cave set into the rock. There were twenty three, a family group, five of them were fully grown males who would not take kindly to waking up to find a stranger in their midst. Amantarra turned to look at the cave entrance, it was low and wide, a narrowing gap under a slab of sloping rock. Large stones had been piled up at the lowest side to reduce the width of the entrance, and the remains of last night's fire smouldered just inside the open portion.

How could he make contact? Amantarra walked to the entrance. They would obviously be alarmed at his presence and he didn't want to dominate by killing one of them, his mission here was not to rule, but to enhance genetically, with some teaching thrown in for good measure. He picked up a stick of charcoal from the fire and made a decision; the smell emanating from the cave was enough to clinch it, and he turned off his sense of smell and set to work.

The flint tipped spear came out first, followed by a head with long black hair tied back with a band of animal skin. It was one of the younger male adults. He looked round the entrance to the right, checking for ambush, and then to the left where he suddenly realised that he'd found it. Yelling he leaped from the entrance; Amantarra could hear replies to the warning from inside. The young male positioned himself behind Amantarra as the other males emerged from the cave; unsure, he held his spear defensively. Amantarra ignored him and carried on working.

The males dressed in a variety of furs and skins formed a semi-circle around Amantarra and bolstered by each other's presence started to shout and jab their spears at him.

Amantarra confused them by continuing to ignore them.

Slowly, as they realised that the perceived hazard was not as high as they had previously thought, and that the stranger didn't seem at all concerned by their threats, the shouts subsided and curiosity took over.

One of the males looked behind, across the plain and then back at the stranger. He said a single word, which Amantarra did not recognise, and the others nodded and agreed. One of the females emerged and gasped, not because Amantarra was naked and the largest male she had ever seen; although that contributed; but because of what he was doing. On cliff face there were deer trapped in the rock, two of them. The stranger's hand worked quickly to trap a third.

Amantarra sighed and wondered how long he had supressed the artistic side of his being, this was so liberating he wished he had done it sooner.

They were all out of the cave now, females, children and the elderly; standing in silence as the image formed on the rock. With the third one finished Amantarra turned and offered the charcoal to the young male who had first emerged from the cave. Not because he looked the most artistic, he just happened to be the closest. He looked round, as did the others, at the oldest female. A matriarchal system observed Amantarra. That could be useful.

The old woman grunted to acknowledge their questioning looks and without any sign of fear she walked towards Amantarra. She moved with difficulty and her progress was slow. The others waited silently. Standing next to Amantarra she looked up him and down; grunted some more as she indicated that he should move out of the way. Amantarra obliged and took a step back away from the cliff. The old woman studied the drawings closely for a few minutes and then turned to face him.

Amantarra thought she was going to speak, but instead she just waved him aside; it would seem that Amantarra was always in the way. Taking a step to the right Amantarra turned and followed the gaze of the matriarch out across the plane. The old woman squinted as she tried to force her old eyes to see the deer there. The others watched her intently.

The old woman didn't like change; it was often the precursor to disrespect. And as she couldn't physically demand respect these days, change was to be avoided at all costs. As far as she could remember, it had been a while since she'd seen a live one; the drawings on the wall were a good likeness. But this was dangerous stuff, where would it all lead, this trapping of deer in the rock. Perhaps she should just send him on his way. But what if he wouldn't go? He was at least a head taller than everyone else here and well-muscled, as an enemy he could cause a lot of damage. And what was he offering? Deer in the rock, well what use was that. Physically he would make an excellent contribution as a member of the tribe. No, perhaps she shouldn't take the risk. And as she started to err on the side of "no change", a new train of thought entered her head. The thoughts were along the lines of; this man isn't a stranger, I've met him before, in fact I've known him nearly all my life, he's just been away for a while. We should welcome him and learn what he teaches. She couldn't think why she hadn't remembered these things before.

'Hah,' she said giving up the struggle to see across the plane.

She turned to the young male and nodded. Winning the support of someone was much easier when you cheated, reflected Amantarra.

The young male stepped forward and took the charcoal from Amantarra.

The process had started.

*

The sun was setting again as Elleria climbed back up the hill towards the Node chamber. She was surprised to see that the Ja'liem where still sitting silently in the treetops. She realised that with the exception of the troop that had followed her, they must have been waiting here all day.

Elleria reached the doors to the Node chamber and turned to face the forest. The sun was just above the canopy, the moons were pretty much in the same places as yesterday. The creatures were still sitting silently. And back where he had been yesterday was 'three stripes'. She turned, pushed open the doors and crossed the floor to the Node.

As she reached the black crystal it momentarily glowed with an inner light. The merging was complete.

'What we have before us,' said Elleria loudly as if addressing a lecture theatre full of students; 'is a completed Node.' There was no echo; the sound seemed dead in the centre of the chamber. 'The Node is now protected by an energy field. A field that only it's Radgarc can penetrate. That's me, by the way, in case any of you were wondering.' Elleria loved the sound of her voice. Not because she felt she had anything important to say, but because she just didn't get to hear it very often.

Placing both hands on the completed Node Elleria tested its status. It was already starting to receive energy from the biomass on this planet and the flow rate was strong. She waited until the Node had finished unfolding back into the other dimensions which it now occupied.

'So far so good,' she said out loud for no other reason than hearing her voice; 'now to connect it to Node Zero.' There were never any problems with Node activation. Closing her eyes she initiated the connection.

Done... Elleria waited for the transmitting signal.

She wasn't getting one. Strange, she thought, it normally only took a few moments.

Elleria waited a bit longer... seconds passed.

This had never happened before. She reset the connection and tried again... nothing.

She checked the crystal, it was merged and the energy it was receiving was starting to build up inside the crystal. The problem must be with Node Zero in Valheel. Elleria was a bit stumped. The only thing she could think of doing was to contact Amantarra.

'Amantarra, there's a problem,' she called into the void.

There was no reply.

'Amantarra, are you there?'

Still, there was no reply.

Elleria scanned the void for Amantarra... she wasn't there, which was impossible; there was nowhere else for her to be. Regardless of whether she was visiting Euclidean space or not, part of Amantarra never left the void. She scanned the void again... there was something else missing. Valheel had gone. No, she thought, that can't be. She scanned the Nodes that she managed; they'd all lost their connection back to the city and the energy was building up inside them. What had gone wrong? Had she caused this? The question worried her. She hadn't done anything out of the ordinary, activating a new Node was routine. She stared at the crystal, trying to think what to do next.

'By now you will have realised that there is something wrong with Valheel,' said a voice behind her. Elleria spun round. It was Amantarra, or at least an image of her. 'For reasons that I cannot go into,' continued the recording, 'I have deactivated Valheel.'

'Deactivated Valheel,' repeated Elleria silently. How do you deactivate and entire city?

'This is a temporary situation and Valheel will rebuild itself, but the process will take several thousand years. Your role in what happens next is crucial and the less you know the safer you will be.' Amantarra sighed and then continued. 'Elleria, there is so much I wish I could tell you but can't, there is too much at stake. I have left you another clue; it's one only you would be able to interpret and when Valheel is restored, you will find it in my quarters. In the meantime disconnect all the Nodes from Node Zero so that they don't reconnect when Valheel is rebuilt. Finally, and most importantly, discuss this with nobody.' Amantarra looked pensive; she lowered her head as the image faded.

'Amantarra,' said Elleria, 'what have you done?'

3
IMMORTALITY

Since Amantarra had first drawn the deer outside the cave on the day that Valheel was destroyed, she had watched the ice retreat and followed the tribes north out of what would become France; hunting mammoth in the spring as they migrated across the vast plains that would become the North Sea. After spending several thousand years in Europe, Amantarra joined more tribes as they made their way east. Visiting every continent on the globe more than once, for a thousand lifetimes Amantarra journeyed, never stopping in one place for more than a few years; always moving on, and constantly changing form.

Amantarra had been all skin colours and both genders, but she generally found it easier to move on as a male. And moving on was the key to staying hidden. You couldn't have the traditional laid in bed, surrounded by family, the priest is on his way, type of death; because being immortal, you would outlast every family member sitting round the bed and would probably get through a few priests as well. No, the disappearance had to be plausible. Sometimes you could just walk off into the sunset, walk far enough and you'd would never be found; and in seventy or eighty years there would be nobody left to find you. This method did sometimes leave a few loose ends and Amantarra tried to avoid it whenever possible. Posing as a travelling merchant or entertainer Amantarra could return to the same villages several times a year for many years, until an apprentice had been trained and Amantarra could move on to new pastures.

There was also aging to consider. The physical process of growing old wasn't a problem, the body; the construct Amantarra occupied was programmed to do that anyway. The problem was that being immortal the body didn't die, it just kept on aging; and given that there weren't many two hundred year old people around, it was wise to change bodies occasionally. So every forty years or so Amantarra would dissolve the construct and use the energy to create a new form.

It was in Laon, Picardie, North-East France, during the October of 1868 when sixty-two year old Pierre Marets, a migrant farm worker; decided that it was time to move on. Amantarra looked in the mirror and the ravaged, baggy eyed, grey stubbled face of Pierre looked back. The next shell Amantarra occupied would need to be slightly modified for the next stage of the plan, not to mention younger and better looking.

Her conditioning of the human race wasn't complete but it was close. Amantarra wondered how much time she had left as Pierre stroked the stubble on his face. From the moment of its destruction thirty two thousand years ago Node Zero had been regenerating. All that Valheel was, all that it had been, was recorded into the fabric of the universe; it only lacked the focus of a Node Zero to reanimate it. From the smallest flicker of energy coaxed down a path of least resistance a new grain was constructed. Other grains followed binding to each other as they sparked into existence to build the intricate structure that reached back into the dimensions of Euclidian space to form a new Node Zero. Once formed the Node would rebuild the city starting with the four rings above the surface of the Node, through which the energy would flow, then the supporting arch structures, the Node Zero chamber, the centroid towers and finally the city itself. It would still be some time after that before the city was complete and fully functional. Amantarra knew this would happen, the destruction of Node Zero had been necessary to buy time, it was just how much time it had bought that was not known.

*

'Bonjour Pierre,' a voice rang out across the square in front of Laon Cathedral as Amantarra crossed it in the early morning. Pierre turned; it was Father Benoît one of the young priests standing in the doorway of the cathedral. Pierre turned towards Benoît and raised a hand to acknowledge the priest. Pierre liked the priest, liked his enthusiasm, his selfless commitment to helping the community and his single minded optimism that one day he would witness a miracle. Benoît had told Pierre of his ambition to witness a miracle in an attempt to gain his trust and lure him into the confessional. Benoît displayed the qualities that Amantarra had been developing in the human race for millennia.

'Salut Père Benoît, ça va?' replied Pierre.

'Pas mal,' replied Benoît as he turned to go back into the cathedral.

"Not bad", it wasn't one of Benoît's more upbeat greetings. Perhaps he was reflecting on the fact that despite revealing his one ambition, he still hadn't managed to get Pierre into the confessional yet. Pierre had insisted that he had nothing to confess, but the young priest simply wouldn't believe him. "The journey of your life is written on you face," he'd told Pierre at the beginning of the year when the priest first arrived at Laon. "Believe me Father, it isn't," Pierre had informed the young priest. And now it was too late; with the season over and the harvest in and stored, Pierre, like all the other migrant workers would be moving on to find work over the winter in the larger towns. At least that is what Amantarra let them believe; when Pierre moved on this year he would not be coming back.

It had taken all day, but the large bonfire Pierre had been building in a field to the north east of Laon was complete. Pierre stood back and admired his handy work. Constructed of old wood and dry straw liberally coated with lamp oil it should produce a nice intense fire. Pierre used a lighted taper made from a rolled up newspaper and lit the bonfire at several points around its base. Within a few minutes the flames were reaching over two metres in height and the roar from them was the only thing you could hear. Pierre took a last look around… there was no one to be seen.

The roaring of the flames stopped abruptly plunging the world into absolute silence as Pierre stopped time. The flames stood motionless like a light sculpture. Pierre placed both his hands into the frozen flame and a moment later stepped forward to stand in the middle of the fire. The intense yellow of the flames faded and Pierre's body crawled with a blue light. The flames, translucent and pale now, quickly faded to nothing. A number of pictures made entirely of light appeared in the air in front of Pierre. Without hesitation he touched one of them and the pictures vanished. Pierre raised his arms and focused all of the energy he had absorbed into a single point. From that single point a sphere grew until it was two metres in diameter. The sphere sang with a very quiet high pitched sound. He took a step towards it and paused. The sound dropped through the octaves to much lower level. Pierre stepped into the sphere and ceased to exist.

Father Benoît had been walking along the lane two fields away when he saw off to his left the flames from the bonfire. Pierre was there, standing next to it. As he walked, his view of the scene was temporarily obscured by a large tree. He wondered why Pierre had built a bonfire so big and decided to have a wander over to ask him. The scene was only hidden for a few seconds, but when Benoît emerged from the other side of the tree both the fire and Pierre were gone.

The tunnel into which Pierre had stepped linked two points in time. Amantarra had selected the maximum jump forward in time of fifty years because she sensed that the humans were almost ready for the next step, and perhaps another fifty years would just about do it. The energy reclaimed from the construct known as Pierre Marets was being used to build another. This new construct would have the capability of reproduction because the next two stages required the production of a human that was traceable across time.

When Amantarra had set off through the tunnel in 1868 she hadn't expected to arrive in the middle of a battle. But now, in October 1918 that same field just outside Laon was the front line. The Germans had held this territory since the beginning of the war, but in the last two months they had been pushed hard by overwhelming allied forces. It was the beginning of the end of the war. The Germans were in full retreat; they were fighting now to stay alive.

Night had almost taken over from dusk, the last of the light showing as a pale blue strip on the western horizon, when William appeared stark naked and beautifully silhouetted just in front of a hastily dug British trench. The German machine gunner reacted instinctively and with an accuracy born of years of self-preservation. William was thrown back into the British trench, the process of constructing his new body disrupted.

'Get him out of here and back to the medics,' a corporal was screaming. The corporal, who had been hoping for a quiet night, didn't need any naked lunatics distracting his men; the whole front had just opened up.

The image of a naked man in the middle of a battlefield haunted the German gunner for years, not the least of which because nobody believed him.

*

26

Field hospital, Notre Dame Cathedral, Laon, Picardie, North East France, October 1918

The war was almost over, but for the men of the medical core and their officer who were stationed just behind "the thick of it", it didn't seem that way; for them, it was business as usual.

Captain Robert Fortesque, the doctor at the field hospital, was slumped in a dilapidated easy chair outside the twelfth century cathedral. He looked up at the oxen that looked down from the twin towers and made a mental note to find out why the cathedral was decorated with life sized oxen.

He hadn't slept for twenty-seven hours, his mind was beyond sleep but he felt should make the effort while the opportunity presented itself. His Sergeant, Billy Fairweather; who hadn't slept for a similar length of time; had complicated the situation by giving the Captain a package from home which, amongst other things, had contained pipe tobacco. And now the Captain couldn't decide whether to smoke a pipe full or go to sleep.

He'd already decided not to read the accompanying letter from Aunt Gertrude as he had difficulty focusing on her hand writing. And besides, she always wrote about the same things; problems replacing the staff that'd joined up to "see off the Bosch", organising church events and so on. Aunt Gertrude's life was nothing if not predictable, and whilst he always welcomed news from England, he did wish that Aunt Gertrude would get out more.

Robert was sat in the small square outside the west front of the cathedral under an impressive rose window. In contrast to the location of the last field hospital he was stationed at, the war had not touched this little part of France.

In the last place the town had been shelled quite heavily and a lot of the buildings were in ruins. Robert remembered the remains of a shop, the sort where the owners lived in the two floors above. The front wall of the building had collapsed exposing the upper rooms, the private spaces of family life laid bare; exposed to outside gaze. To the left of the shop was a café; its broken sign hanging lopsidedly from a wrought iron wall bracket. "Café de Paris" announced the sign; it's peeling paint evoking memories of lost glasses of red wine in the lazy summer shade outside the café. A path, wide enough for two carts to pass, had been cleared up the main street; the rubble piled up on both sides against the broken walls.

Robert shuddered; the late afternoon October sun was pale and there was a chill in the air outside the cathedral. Robert surveyed the peaceful square, remembering holidays in France before the war. Laon at least, remained untouched by the war. Had he once visited this town? Robert couldn't remember.

He looked down at his hands resting on his blood stained apron, his butchers apron as he referred to it, and realised that he'd already filled his pipe with tobacco... he couldn't remember doing it.

*

'Captain,' said Sergeant Fairweather. 'Captain Sir,' he tried again a little louder.

Sergeant Fairweather was a regular soldier who'd joined the Medical Core in 1901 after a two year stint in the Transvaal fighting the Boers. He'd seen the medics work first hand after being wounded and had been interested enough in what they did to ask lots of questions. This had got him noticed by the Medical Officer. Although his interest in the medical side was genuine, Billy had been more interested in the fact that nobody was shooting at the medics. With his wounds severe enough to take him off the front line, he volunteered for the medical core rather than leave the army. Captain Fortesque was the fourth Medical Officer he had served under and the only one he had ever liked. He wasn't a snob like the other officers; he didn't demand respect, he earned it. The Captain had given him a book to read, "Dracula" it was called, said it matched the gothic mood of the place they were stationed in. The Sergeant had read it twice and thought that Captain Fortesque was right; it did match the mood of the place; although he didn't know what "gothic" meant, but he assumed that it had something to do with vampires and the un-dead. But that wasn't the point thought Sergeant Fairweather; the point is how many other officers would have loaned a book to an NCO.

Sergeant Fairweather did not like to wake his officer, not after the last wave of wounded, he wanted to let him sleep on; but he had no choice.

'Captain Sir.'

Robert stirred, he couldn't remember falling asleep and for a moment in the darkness he didn't know where he was.

'Sorry to wake you Sir.' The Sergeant was squatting beside the chair holding an oil lamp close to his face.

In the low yellow light, the enormous moustache, and the strong smell of nicotine and sweat suddenly registered with the Captain. 'More wounded Sergeant?' he said sitting up in the chair.

'Just one Sir; looks bad, machine gun to chest. Strange Sir, but the story is that he just appeared in no man's land out of thin air.'

Robert gave the Sergeant a look that said you're much too worldly wise to believe stories like that.

'You shouldn't believe everything you hear Sergeant.'

'No Sir.'

The Captain stood up, looked curiously at the pipe in his hand, knocked the tobacco out of it, realised that he hadn't smoked it, cursed under his breath and put the empty pipe into his pocket.

'Lead the way sergeant.'

'Yes Sir.'

'What time is it?' Robert asked as they made their way through the stone entrance of the cathedral.

'Nearly eleven o'clock, Sir. I saved you something to eat, but I thought it best to let you sleep.'

'Thank you sergeant,' said Robert, who couldn't remember the last time he ate, but hadn't felt hungry until the Sergeant had mentioned food.

In the Nave all the pews had been cleared out and the wounded lined the floor, some on low beds, some on mattresses, but most on only a blanket. Apart from the occasional cough there was very little noise; most here were too ill to complain about it.

The Sergeant led them through the Nave and round the screen that had been put up in front of the altar.

Robert remembered his school days; altar, from the Latin altaria, meaning; burnt offerings altar. He recalled one of his headmasters "you'll burn in the fires of hell" sermons. Robert wondered what his headmaster would make of the fires of hell if he could see what he'd seen these last few years.

The stone altar was now the operating table, and Robert felt that its current use was more closely related to the sacrificial meaning of the original Latin name. He hated this bloody war. From the position that he viewed it, up to the elbows in blood and entrails, there was no hope. Robert had become a doctor to make a difference; but here, stood at this altar, from which a message of hope for mankind was supposed to be issued, there was nothing he could do to make a difference. Robert felt helpless, all he could do was stop the bleeding and hack off dead limbs. And despite his efforts, in half the cases all he was doing was delaying the inevitable and prolonging the agony. The other half didn't fare much better, blinded, limbless, lungs burnt to hell, they were changed forever; how would they earn a living after the war?

Sergeant Fairweather hung the lantern he was carrying on a hat stand near the altar and lit another.

Laid on the altar was a young man in his twenties, he was naked. There was severe trauma to the chest where he had obviously caught the full force of machine gun fire as the gunner had swept his weapon through an arc. His eyes were closed and he did not appear to be breathing; despite that, the young man's skin looked pink and flushed with blood. Apart from the holes in his chest, the absence of any movement or a pulse, he looked a picture of health. Sergeant Billy Fairweather had taken one look at him and thought him dead; but that was only an opinion, it wasn't a fact until the medical officer said it was.

The sergeant held the lamp he had just lit close to the young man's chest as Robert examined the wounds. There were five bullet holes in an almost straight line and it looked like he'd lost both lungs and his heart.

'There's not much blood,' said Robert. 'And where's his uniform?'

'That's how he came in Sir...' Billy paused; 'Captain, Sir?'

Robert continued to examine the body; but when Billy didn't finish his question he looked up.

'What is it Sergeant?'

'That's what I was saying before Sir, they said he appeared in no man's land close to our lines... from nowhere... and naked, Sir. He fell back into our trench when he was hit. Sir, how can anyone just appear out of nowhere?'

Robert thought his Sergeant looked a bit spooked and wondered when he'd last slept. He decided to give him something to do, to take his mind off this tall tale.

'Get a blanket Sergeant, let's give the man a bit of dignity; it looks like he's laid there ready for autopsy.' Which, Robert thought to himself, is probably fitting.

The Sergeant placed the lamp on the altar and went for a blanket. Robert again checked the man's neck for a pulse; he couldn't get over how healthy he looked... as he suspected, there wasn't one. Robert sighed, another one that couldn't be saved.

The Sergeant returned a few moments later and covered the corpse's lower half.

'Would you hold the lamp again Sergeant,' Robert was fascinated by the fact that there was no blood. He examined the chest wounds more closely. There wasn't a trace of blood, nothing on the skin surrounding the wounds, and nothing in the wounds. Robert placed a finger into one of the bullet holes; there was no blood on it when he removed it.

'Give me a hand to turn him on his side so that I can examine his back.' Sergeant Fairweather placed the lamp on the altar and pulled the young man's shoulder towards him. Robert bent down to examine his back. There were five exit wounds; Robert could see the Sergeants tunic through the holes, but again, no blood. They lowered him gently back onto the altar.

'Nothing we can do for this one sergeant,' said Robert. 'The absence of blood is very curious though, it's almost like someone has drained him of it.' Robert instantly regretted his remark but it was too late.

'Drained of blood Sir? You mean like in that book, Dracula?' said Sergeant Fairweather looking up at the huge stone columns that disappeared into the ink black darkness; which for Billy, now held the watching eyes of a vampire. Sergeant Fairweather hadn't been a nervous man until he'd read Dracula, but now this place gave him the willies.

'Don't worry Sergeant; there are no puncture wounds on his neck,' said Robert gesturing towards the man's throat. The sergeant looked at where Robert was pointing; there were indeed no puncture wounds. Billy exhaled a huge sigh of relief and allowed himself to relax.

'Bonsoir, anything… I can… do?' said an elderly priest in broken English. He had seen the corpse and felt that he was better suited for the current task than the medical officer.

'Father Benoît, I didn't see you there,' said Robert. 'Yes, unfortunately I think you can do more for him than I can. Oui Père, le homme est mort.'

The corpse's eyes flicked open.

'Bloody Hell!' exclaimed the Sergeant jumping back and crossing himself as the corpse lifted his head. 'Sorry father,' he added glancing at the priest and then back at the corpse. Robert opened his mouth but was too shocked to utter a word.

Amantarra was disorientated, the building of this new construct had been disrupted and she was struggling to gather her wits. Slowly, slowly she thought; the body is almost ready. There were two men in uniform stood one either side. One of them had spoken… sworn… "Anglais", thought Amantarra still shaking off the ghost of Pierre. Directly to the front was a priest. Amantarra wondered how bad the construct must look to warrant the attentions of a priest. She recognised him, his build and features were older, but it was unmistakably

Benoît; still here after all these years. Amantarra wondered if he remembered Pierre Marets, but decided that she would not be asking him.

And there was something else; it was as obvious to Amantarra as a brick thrown into still water, the ripples from its activation bounced back and forth, crisscrossing each other through the dimensions making the whole of space, time and beyond ring like a bell. There was a new Node Zero, although it was still weak and the reconstruction of Valheel had not yet started. Fifty to sixty years, that was how long she estimated she had. There was a lot of work to do and a limited time in which to do it. Time to get started thought Amantarra.

'Hello,' said the corpse; 'my name is…' Amantarra paused to recall the name; 'William Godbert.' William propped himself up on his elbows and looked around at his surroundings. 'What am I doing here in the cathedral?' He noted the wide eyed, ashen expressions on the faces of those stood around him.

The officer pointed at William. 'Your chest,' he said.

William looked down.

'Oh dear,' he said.

4
HIDDEN TREASURE

Easter holidays Friday 23rd April 1976

Reginald Scribbins, a small wiry, balding man, known to his friends as Reg, and to the pupils of Penshaw Grove Secondary School as "Captain Cardigan"; was cycling from his house to the school. It was a journey of no more than 200 metres; or as Reg used to joke, "That's just up the road in feet and inches"; but the plain, black, forty year old bike came with the caretaker's job. It was the job's only perk, and Reg certainly wasn't going to waste it.

Over his faded greyish blue boiler suit he always wore a faded greyish green cardigan. Button less, the cardigan billowed out behind him, like the cloak of a superhero; an image that had earned him the nickname he was completely oblivious to. Not that the kids ever called him Captain Cardigan to his face; Reg had a certain amount of implied respect because his broken nose seemed to indicate that he might be slightly intolerant of adverse comment. But that wasn't the case; Reg was a quiet unassuming man who felt that he knew his place in life. And the broken nose, well he certainly didn't get it fighting.

It was 8:30am when Reg glided into the yard at the back of the school. Perhaps glided wasn't the right word, it would be more accurate to say that Reg stopped peddling, and the bike continued to move forward, twitching gently due to the slightly buckled wheels. Planning ahead, Reg applied the brakes early. The brakes groaned, the bike shuddered and twitched with more enthusiasm, but the speed remained more or less constant.

Reg was a man who liked to think the same regular thoughts; it was easier on the brain. For example, whenever he shaved he thought about waxed moustaches and monocles; he didn't have either, he didn't want either. No, Reg thought about waxed moustaches and monocles because of something he had planned to do as a teenager. Unfortunately the closest he came to achieving his teenage ambition, was at the time, a bit one sided; and would in any case have been a big disappointment for Reg, had he known all the facts. Reality rarely lives up to dreams.

Anyway, at about this point in his journey to work, with the bike now twitching violently and trying to throw him off, Reg always had the same thought, and that thought was; that he really must do something about these brakes.

Halfway across the yard, with the brakes full on, enough momentum had been lost for Reg to dismount and trot alongside the bike slowing it down to a walking pace. He stopped outside a dark red door, removed his bicycle clips, and unlocked the entrance to his secret underground lair.

Reg propped the bike against the wall just inside the door and hung the bicycle clips on the handlebars. Then he turned back to the door, locked it, then checked that it was locked, twice, and finally he rattled the door just to make sure. This was Penshaw Grove, you didn't leave anything unlocked. The two metre high steel gates to the yard had been left unlocked a few months back, and somebody had stolen them.

Reg descended the long flight of stairs into the warm darkness of the boiler room. Two large gas boilers rumbled and fizzed as he turned left and through the door at the bottom of the stairs.

He switched on the light, the emphasis here being singular. There was only one. Fixed to the underside of the concrete ceiling, the fitting was cast metal, round, and had been designed to withstand heavy wear and tear and last for… well probably until the end of time. The original glass front was missing; this had failed to live up to the promise of the rest of the fitting. The fitting itself held one bulb; it was a good bulb though, despite being only forty watt. It had been purchased from Woolworths in 1940, which meant that over its thirty-six year lifetime it had given out more light than a typical one hundred watt bulb. They knew how to make light bulbs in those days, despite the war. Makes you think, thought Reg; another of his regular thoughts.

As Reg made his way past the boilers to the old desk in the corner he referred to as his office, he contemplated changing the bulb for a brighter one; but he knew its history, he was a part of that history, and once again, he just couldn't bring himself to do it. Further proof that regular thoughts; as opposed to regular thinking, which was far too creative for Reg; saved a lot of work.

Reg always felt safe in the boiler room. Since his first unofficial visit as a teenager, he'd felt a presence there, a good presence. Some would say that the sensing of presences, ghosts if you prefer, was all in the imagination. Perhaps this was true, perhaps he did only imagine the presence of a guardian angel these days; but there were two factors that tended to indicate the opposite. One, Reginald's complete lack of imagination; and two, his rescue from certain death during his first visit to the boiler room had never been explained.

The floor around the boilers was always swept clean, but the corners of the ceiling were populated with ancient thick black cobwebs, which harboured an unknown and presumably very large species of spiders. Over the desk, a few stray strands of cobweb danced in the convection currents as Reg sat down.

There was very little on the desk in the way of clutter. There was Reg's official clipboard; it was a special magic clipboard, which had the ability to double Reg's importance when picked up. Other items included a pen, a pencil, a tape measure and a big bunch of keys. Last, but by no means least, was an item which represented Reg's only ambition; a coupon for the football pools. Reg filled a coupon in every week without fail; and dreamt of a quiet life in the country sipping beer from a champagne glass; or whatever it was that rich folk drank their beer from.

He picked up the clipboard from the desk, and felt a surge of power. The clipboard contained a list of jobs that could only be done when the kids weren't at school, and it had been written by the headmaster. This affiliation with power increased Reg's importance further, possibly even quadrupling it. Reg held the clipboard so that it caught the light, moved it closer to his face, then away, closer, away; he repeated the exercise a few more times, then gave up, put the clipboard back on the desk and reached into his top pocket for his glasses.

The boilers continued to rumble and fizz masking all other sounds as Reg picked up a pencil and used it to point at each item on the list in turn. There was a pencil line drawn through each item indicating that it had been completed. He stopped at the last item on the list, number eight, the only one not crossed off; Reg tapped the pencil on his chin, thought for moment and then ran a pencil line through the headmaster's copperplate writing. He'd done that task last week before the kids had broken up for the holidays. That was the list complete. What could I do today, he thought? Reg's mind was a blank, but that was nothing new. Then something unusual happened. Reg couldn't decide whether he saw the image of shelves first, or whether he said it out loud first. The important thing was that Reg had had his first idea in years.

'Move the cupboard out of the old music store and replace it with new shelves,' he said out loud. He could have sworn that he heard a whispered reply, which sounded like "yes, now is the time," mixed in with the fizzing sound of the boilers. He shook his head; you could hear all sorts of strange noises when the boilers were on.

Beside the desk was a collection of essential janitorial equipment.

Item one; the emergency vomit kit, which consisted of a bucket of sawdust with a small hand shovel sticking out of the top, a stiff brush and a small dustbin.

Item two; a bigger brush.

Item three; an old shopping bag containing even older tools.

Item four; a mop and bucket.

Item five; a large bottle of disinfectant. Sorry no, scrub that, item five was a large, empty bottle of disinfectant.

Disinfectant was rarely used.

Was disinfectant rarely used because there wasn't any? Another question would be; is the reason there wasn't any disinfectant, because it was rarely used? Reginald considered these to be important philosophical questions, and he avoided thinking about them because they put his brain into a sort of loop, which meant he couldn't concentrate on anything else.

Job nine, his own idea that no one else had thought of; Reg felt his chest swell with pride; may require the use of item three, the bag of tools. Moving cupboards sometimes required the removal of doors.

'Time to get started,' he informed the spiders and anything else that might be listening down here.

Picking up his bag of tools and the keys from the desk, Reg moved with a sense of purpose. It was Friday and he only intended to do this one job today, so the quicker he got it finished the sooner he'd be away.

In the wall between the boilers was another door. The paint was cracked with age and dry heat, the wood was worn round at the corners; but the hinges were oiled and well maintained. Reg opened it, and put the switch down that was just inside, illuminating a chain of equally spaced lights which disappeared off into the distance. The service tunnel which ran under the entire length of the school was Reg's secret rat run, and was the only way to get to the science block in the centre of the playground without going outside. The heating pipes lining one side clicked constantly with the heat. Throughout the tunnel there was always some part of the pipes that was either heating up or cooling down.

Above ground the long school buildings were constructed in a warm brick with sandstone trimmings and window frames. Despite being only two storeys high, the building was twice as high as all the houses in Penshaw Grove. From a distance it looked like an ocean liner sailing on a sea of slate roofs and trees. The school buildings formed a rectangle which was enclosed on two opposite sides by long classroom blocks, north and south; linking these at main entrance end, was the admin block; and at the other end, where Reg's yard was, the sheds. The sheds were just covered spaces in the playground bounded by three walls. They served as shelter when it was "precipitating down"; one of Reg's jokes, it was the only long word he knew. In the centre of the playground was another large two storey building, this was the science block and dining hall. The science block was joined to the sheds by the toilets, making the playground 'U' shaped.

There were a few design oddities, no doubt related to the era in which the school was designed. For instance, the corridors which linked the classrooms, and ran the full length of each of the main buildings were open to the outside. They were, more or less, just covered walkways, with a series of arches opening onto the playground. Amazingly, they had radiators in them, which attempted to heat the corridors in the winter. It was an attempt that was doomed to failure.

The toilets were also open to the outside. An idea no doubt intended to cut down on the smell. This also failed. The toilets however, were not heated. The architect obviously considered this a frippery, and in the winter, they froze; yellow ice covering the floor. When the thaw started, the toilets were the last place you wanted to slip over.

Reg set off down the tunnel with his tools. Halfway down he turned left into another tunnel which ran under the playground passing beneath the science block on its way to the other classroom block.

Reg turned the lights out in the first tunnel and instantly regretted it, because he couldn't find the switch for the cross tunnel. Actually, what would be closer to the truth was that he instantly regretted it again; this was one of those habits that Reg just couldn't seem to break.

The pipes clicked in the darkness as Reg ran his hand down the wall on a voyage of discovery; a hole in the brickwork, a spider's web, a hot pipe bracket and finally a light switch.

Reg decided to leave the lights on when he reached the bottom of the stairs which led up into the science block; he didn't know why he was so conscientious when it came to saving electricity, after all he wasn't paying the bills, not on the wage he got.

Opposite the bottom of the stairs was a steel door, the words "Air Raid Shelter" had been chalked on it. Reg didn't go in there at all; there were too many childhood ghosts. He turned his back on the door and climbed the stairs.

He opened the door at the top of the stairs, the keys jingling as he turned them in the lock, and entered the cloakroom. Then round the corner and up some more stairs to the first floor. At the top of the stairs next to the door to the chemistry lab, was the door to an old store which hadn't been used for a long time. Reg unlocked it and went in; remembering that the last time he'd been in here was ten years ago when he had painted the walls magnolia. Ignoring the shelves full of old brass instruments along the left wall, he went straight over to the cupboard on the opposite wall, and opened it.

Good, it was empty, that's one job less, he thought.

Reg got a good grip and heaved at the cupboard. There was a cracking sound as layers of paint that had accumulated over the years, gluing the cupboard to the wall, submitted to Reg's efforts. After half an hour and with a bit of a squeeze, Reg had managed to drag the cupboard into the chemistry lab next to the store, without removing any doors. This was going to be a short day, he thought, as he walked back to the store slightly out of breath; things were looking up. He stood in the doorway looking at the pile of dust that had been under the cupboard, pity he hadn't brought his brush instead of his tools.

The wall where the cupboard had been was a completely different colour. Reg recognised it; the whole school had been this dark green colour when he'd been a pupil here. The ghosts from the past sent a shiver down his spine.

He wondered how many times the room had been painted since the cupboard had been put there. It was certainly there when he was at school he thought with a hint of sadness, he didn't like disturbing things that had been in place a long time.

In the centre of the patch of different coloured wall was a grill, which for the first time in years was capable of passing air. The dust encrusted cobwebs now blew gently through the grill; Reg watched it for a moment before deciding to fetch his full brush and pan set.

That's when he noticed it.

Behind the grill, as the cobwebs moved, something caught the light; something silver.

5
PROPHECY

The new Node Zero, following its programming, had spent several millennia connecting to its list of Nodes to build up a reserve of power before commencing the construction of Valheel. Then when enough energy had been accumulated, the Node had constructed one of the four rings that would eventually sit at the top of the centroid towers. Starting with a small ring the Node had added further concentric rings, each new ring absorbing the previous, until it had reached its finished diameter. The ring provided a focus for transferring the energy from Node Zero into the dimensions in which Valheel was to be constructed. Once the first ring was complete, the other three followed, now there was a means to transfer the energy. The supporting arch structures grew out from the rings terminating in the spherical shell that formed the Node Zero chamber. The four, kilometre high centroid towers, complete with the long spiral staircase that ran down each, grew out from the Node Zero chamber. With the low energy flow, progress was slow.

Each tower was closed off with a floor in the centre of which was created a clear crystal that would distribute the power to each quadrant of the city. A thin, pure white energy beam stuttered into life, traveling from Node Zero, down the centre of the spiral staircase and into the clear crystal. The primary power distribution infrastructure was now complete. In time, as energy became available, the thin beam would grow in size, but for now it was no thicker than a hair. Even as construction proceeded, Node Zero continued to connect to more Nodes, steadily increasing the power supply.

The floor from each centroid tower grew outward until the surfaces met to form the spherical shell on which the zones of Valheel would be constructed. Once the great sphere had been completed, it thickened, forming service tunnels and more power distribution structures. Then the buildings started to grow from its surface. Throughout the city lights started to shine from the windows as each building was completed. Fifty-eight years it had taken to complete the city; a single flash of light in the long night of Node Zero's construction.

The plaza's and buildings stood empty. Valheel was complete but unoccupied; there was one last process to complete before the city was activated. The contents of the buildings, the furniture, the crystals in the Great Library, the data processes of the city, the position of the Guardians, were all restored to the exact point they were in just before Amantarra destroyed the original Node Zero. Humanoid shaped green construction meshes appeared motionless in the plazas and buildings. One by one, each of the meshes was rendered into the form of a Guardian of Valheel. Then at some invisible cue, the Guardians all started moving at the same time.

The city paused on the threshold of opening it's portals to the Bruwnan.

At the top of one of the buildings in the same blue quadrant as the Great Library of Valheel; was the council chamber. The room was circular, high ceilinged and lit from the floor by lights that ran around the perimeter of the room. Two banks of empty seats formed an aisle that ran from the huge double doors to a dais which was almost twice the height of a Bruwnan. Standing motionless at either side of the door were two Guardians of Valheel. Seated behind the dais and looking down on a single figure standing on the floor in front of it, were the five Bruwnan avatars of the high council.

Seated in the centre chair and wearing a white sash was Consulus the leader of the council. He glanced to his right at the red and green sashed councillors' who nodded, and then to his left at the yellow and blue councillors' who gave a similar response. Consulus looked back down at the figure on the floor of the chamber.

'Tyrus; summarise the situation,' he said.

'The rebuilding of the city is complete. You five, as you were before, remain the only true Valheelians,' said Tyrus. 'The portals are closed and none of the Bruwnan who had not been erased by us prior to Node Zero's destruction have gained access to the city.'

'Let's keep it that way,' said Consulus. 'There is no doubt that in destroying the old Node Zero Amantarra has advanced our plan to rid the city of the Bruwnan to its conclusion. Despite the fact that they have not been erased fully, they are quite powerless while they remain locked out of the city. However, the question of why Amantarra chose this course of action remains.'

'Describe the sequence of events that led up to the destruction of the previous Node Zero,' said another of the council.

'The alarm was sounded when the avatar belonging to the Bruwnan known as Amantarra removed a data crystal from the library. Analysis has shown that the crystal contained the entire technical library, all the science and engineering of the Bruwnan. It had been collated over a long period of time by Artullus under the pretext of research so as not to arouse suspicion. Artullus left Valheel just prior to its destruction and he is not one of the Bruwnan currently attempting to re-enter the city. He is therefore untraceable. After the alarm was triggered, we attempted to disrupt the generation of Amantarra's avatar by force, but we failed in our attempt to gain control. After a brief chase Amantarra was finally cornered in the Node Zero chamber. She had acquired several of the disruption weapons from the Guardians pursuing her and used one of them to destroy Node Zero.' Tyrus stood waiting for the next question as the council considered his last statement.

'And there is no question that the act of destroying Node Zero was deliberate?' asked Consulus.

'None whatsoever,' replied Tyrus.

'Again the same question arises; why? Why take the data and why destroy the Node Zero? Would anyone care to speculate?' he asked looking to either side at the other councillors.

The red councillor to his extreme right spoke. 'The data would be of use to an intelligent corporeal species who had reached the point in their development that they may potentially seek a share of the energy that powers Valheel.'

'Such a species does not exist, it would have been detectable from the lower energy yields coming from the Node on that planet,' said the yellow councillor to Consulus' left.

'If the planet had a Node,' replied the red councillor.

'If Amantarra has created such a hidden species and the knowledge in the crystal is to be used for its advancement, then clearly this poses a threat to our plans,' said Consulus. 'The destruction of Node Zero may have been simply a means of buying development time.'

'There is also the possibility that Amantarra has created more than one species capable of utilising the knowledge,' said the green councillor to Consulus' right.

'The assumption must be made that this is the case and that there is more than one species. We must discover the nature and extent of this threat before we eliminate it.'

'Gentlemen,' said the blue councillor, 'we have another more immediate problem.' The others turned to face him. 'The Primary Key was reset to its default value during the rebuild of Valheel. I've just searched the library for a copy of it and its missing. It looks as though it was deleted some time before the destruction of the city. This means that although we have the same power that we had before, we have lost the means by which we got that power. We can no longer make major changes or repairs to Valheel. In respect of our defence, we can upgrade the guardians, but only up to the limits of their original specification and we cannot create new ones.'

'This has halted our plans,' said Consulus, 'Amantarra must have a copy of the Primary Key in the information she stole. This information is vital and must be retrieved. I assume that Amantarra is not amongst the Bruwnan currently seeking access to the city; that would be too easy.'

'That assumption is correct,' said Tyrus, 'but her Radgarc is.'

*

Every portal Elleria had tried was closed and she thought she was never going to get into the city. Elleria was patient, and although she didn't want to, she had reached the point where she thought she should give up. Just few moments more she thought, just a few minutes and then I'll have one last go. As she waited she wondered what had caused Valheel to disappear in the first place and, given the current problems she had gaining access, if it would ever be normal again.

She tried again... nothing.

Eventually she'd had enough and was about to disconnect from the portal when it suddenly opened.

Finally, she thought, but was immediately presented with another disappointment as there now seemed to be a delay; it was taking far longer to get through the portal than normal. Elleria waited assuming that there may be teething problems with the new city. Finally her patience was rewarded and her avatar materialised on one of the round portals that were set into the floor of the circular plaza at the base of the Green centroid tower.

Elleria started to walk across the plaza towards the arcade that led to Amantarra's quarters. She could see the windows to the apartment on the fourth floor of the building. The lights were on, but that didn't mean anything, the lights were always on in Valheel. She entered the arcade she'd been heading for and it suddenly struck her how quiet Valheel was, she hadn't encountered a single Bruwnan, Radgarc or Guardian. Very unusual, she thought. Perhaps the city wasn't fully restored yet and things would pick up later. Exiting the arcade she carried straight on, the entrance to Amantarra's building was on the right a short distance up ahead.

After making her way up to the fourth floor, Elleria found the door to Amantarra's quarters was open. She assumed that Amantarra was expecting her and walked straight in, but it became quickly apparent that the apartment was empty.

The main room was white walled and minimal. Four large comfortable chairs arranged around a single low table occupied the centre of the room and, apart from a desk, there was no other furniture. It was exactly as Elleria remembered it with one slight difference. On the wall facing the door there were two square windows. Hanging on the wall between and either side of the windows were three large paintings. Elleria always knew that Amantarra was interested in art; she'd often remarked that she'd suppressed her artistic tendencies for the sake of science and engineering. Elleria was therefore quite surprised to see the artwork here in the apartment, particularly as they were all signed "Amantarra". This had to be the clue that Amantarra had mentioned in her message.

All three paintings had identical matt black backgrounds. The first painting on the left had a single broad brushstroke of purple paint running from top to bottom. The stroke was unrefined and no attempt had been made to tidy it up, it was just a single line of paint with the background showing through in parts. The word "One" was written in the bottom left hand corner in the same colour. The second painting between the windows had two equally crude orange brushstrokes running from top to bottom and the word "Two" written in the bottom left hand corner. The third painting had two orange brushstrokes either side of a single purple one. These strokes were neater than the ones on the other two paintings, some effort had gone into sharpening the edges and making sure that the background did not show through. The three blocks of colour also had dark purple shadows making it look as if they were raised off the background. Written in the bottom left was the phrase "Three holds the key".

"One, Two, Three Holds the Key". Elleria recited to herself; she didn't really like abstract art, but there was something vaguely familiar about these paintings. It didn't take long for the image of the primates to pop into her head. These paintings were an abstract representation of the Ja'liem, and it would only be obvious to someone who had actually seen the Ja'liem. But what does "three holds the key" mean?

'I've never really understood the Bruwnian fascination with art.' The voice was behind her. Elleria spun round. Standing in the doorway was Tyrus. 'Especially this abstract stuff,' he continued while indicating the paintings behind Elleria. 'What do you think?'

Elleria had never liked Tyrus, in fact she couldn't think of anyone that did, he was very arrogant and seemed to consider himself a cut above The Bruwnan and their Radgarcs alike. His smug attitude always gave Elleria the impression that he had a hidden agenda. There was always the fear that she would become entwined in whatever it was that he was up to and possibly carrying the can for it. As a consequence, she just didn't like being near him. Elleria noted his attempt at trying to ingratiate himself with her and wondered what he really wanted. Still, regardless of that, some sort of reply was warranted. She considered a few choice retorts along the lines of "you can go now" but decided that perhaps she should play along. After all, it couldn't be a coincidence that he was here and Amantarra was not. Before she could speak Tyrus continued.

'The Council are trying to trace the whereabouts of Amantarra, and we have come here to ask if you can help us,' said Tyrus before Elleria could think of a civil answer.

'We?' asked Elleria.

There was movement in the corridor outside and the five members of the council entered the apartment in silence. Now this is definitely not a coincidence, thought Elleria as she watched them form a line behind Tyrus.

'Ah,' said Tyrus in mock surprise as if they'd just happened to be passing Amantarra's apartment, 'the high council.'

Elleria eyed them suspiciously. 'Right on cue,' she said with more than a little hint of sarcasm.

'As Tyrus was saying, we are trying to trace the whereabouts of Amantarra,' said Consulus ignoring the sarcasm.

'I'm sure she will be arriving in the city shortly,' replied Elleria. 'Now that it's back, I mean. What happened to the city anyway?'

This was met with silence and Elleria got the distinct impression that although unheard, a suitable reply was being discussed. She looked at them again, strange that they were so silent; it was a simple question, so surely the answer didn't need to be worked out. Tyrus seeing her studying the council offered her an explanation on their silence.

'You may have noticed that some of the cities facilities are still down. Avatar generation is a bit hit and miss at the moment,' he said.

The councillors' avatars looked fine to Elleria and his remark smelt like distraction.

'There was a fault with Node Zero,' said Consulus at last; 'but we have taken steps to protect it now. Amantarra was very close to Node Zero at the time of the fault, which is why we are concerned about her. Can you help us trace her? Do you have any information about her whereabouts?'

What was Amantarra doing way up there in the Node Zero chamber? Why would the Node need protecting if it was faulty? Elleria put all the pieces together. Amantarra's message said that she had deactivated Valheel, so she must have done something with Node Zero. Elleria didn't need Amantarra's warning not to discuss her actions; she didn't trust this lot in any shape or form.

'Well the truth is that I lost contact with Amantarra when the city disappeared and I've heard nothing from her since.' Which was the truth, but Elleria had deliberately left out the part about Amantarra's message in the Node chamber on the planet of the Ja'liem. Elleria breathed a silent sigh of relief that her Avatar was protected from the cities systems and her thoughts remained her own.

'Yes,' said Tyrus, 'we only ask because we're concerned for her.' He walked over to Elleria and placed his hand on her shoulder. 'You can understand that can't you.'

'Yes, I can. I'm concerned too,' she replied as she glanced down at Tyrus' hand where it rested on her shoulder. This mock concern was way out of character. Tyrus saw her look and removed his hand.

'I'm sure she'll be in touch soon, now that the city is back,' said Elleria.

'Well if she does, be sure to ask her to get in touch with the council.'

'Yes of course,' lied Elleria.

'And now, if you would excuse us the council have urgent matters to attend to,' said Consulus.

Elleria watched them turn and leave Amantarra's quarters. That ended suddenly, she thought. From the way the entire Council and their Enforcer turned up, Elleria thought she would be answering questions for hours. Elleria was too relieved that they'd gone to be worried about the shortness of their visit; but to avoid encountering them outside again, she studied the paintings for another five minutes before leaving the apartment. When she was sure that it was safe, she headed back down to the Green plaza and its portals so that she could leave the city. Elleria knew where she was going next and she only hoped that Amantarra was there waiting for her with an explanation.

*

Elleria materialised on top of the hill in front of the heavy metal doors of the Node chamber. She was back on the planet of the Ja'liem. She didn't need to take physical form; she could just have arrived as a phantom like Amantarra would have to. But Elleria felt that this was somehow a special occasion and she'd enjoyed her last visit here in physical form so much, that it wouldn't have needed much of an excuse to take it this time.

She looked out across the treetops in the early morning light. A small group of Ja'liem were playing a chasing game, scampering through the branches at speed; oh how Elleria wished she could be so free. She watched as the animals disappeared deeper into the forest.

But where was Amantarra?

Had she misinterpreted the message in the paintings? Was there even a message to interpret? Elleria turned to face the doors of the domed building. If there was an answer it would be in there, she thought... or not... there was something on the ground in front of the metal doors. Elleria walked towards the doors for a closer look.

Neatly placed in front of the doors was a flat console exactly like the ones on the Great Library of Valheel. Elleria picked it up and examined it. It looked old and worn; the ones in Valheel were created by the city and so always looked pristine, but this one looked as if it had been left out in the rain. Elleria turned the device over; she'd never seen a console in the real physical universe before. She supposed that at one time the consoles' did exist in the real universe, before the Bruwnan abandoned their physical existence. Tucking the device under her arm she stood close the doors of the Node chamber. The building sensed her presence and the massive metal doors silently swung open.

It was thirty two thousand years since Elleria had seen the message from Amantarra in this chamber. The Node itself was glowing brightly with the stored energy it had gathered from the life on this planet over the same time period. There was nothing else in the chamber, no further messages or paintings on the wall and no Amantarra. Elleria took the console out from under her arm and looked at it again. Finding a console on a planet was very unlikely. In fact, Elleria decided, this was probably the only console in the entire Euclidean universe. Amantarra was definitely trying to tell her something. She speculated that it was something that Amantarra did not want the High Council to know about. The paintings had led Elleria here where she would find the console. Was the console another clue? It didn't look like the thing would actually function; so did it mean her to go back to the Great Library of Valheel? Elleria didn't think that likely.

'So, what's this for?' she asked the Node because there was nothing else to address the question at. As Elleria expected, the Node remained silent. It was, she reminded herself, only a valve. Then it occurred to her... the Node instruction crystal would fit into the console. Perhaps Amantarra had left additional information on the crystal.

She quickly walked over to the Node. The instruction crystal was where she had left it over thirty-two thousand years ago. This was it...it had to be... the moment had come... what information might it hold? Elleria could hardly contain her excitement. Holding the device in the crook of her left arm she picked up the crystal and dropped it into the receptacle on the console. Elleria held her breath and prepared herself for what she hoped would be a revelation. The console flickered for a moment and then disappointingly went back to being completely inert. She tried again; taking the crystal out of the console and this time carefully placing it into the receptacle. Again there was little more than a flicker from the console. Perhaps the console was damaged, she thought, or lacked power; either way it meant the trail stopped here. Useless, she thought, as she removed the crystal and placed it back on top of the Node.

Elleria looked around the chamber, other than the Node there was nothing; and as the doors had been sealed shut after her last visit, there wasn't even a dead leaf on the floor. Elleria resigned herself to that fact that there were no answers here and turned back towards the door. Something on the ground just outside the entrance caught the morning light. Curious, Elleria walked towards it. The object sparkled in the light as she approached. Whatever it was had not been there when she entered the building. She was halfway across the floor of the chamber before she realised that it was a crystal. Elleria ran... a crystal she thought, this must be the one the console was intended for; but who had put it there?

Outside Elleria picked up the crystal and looked around. As she expected there was no one to be seen, but that didn't matter because now she was sure she held the answers to all that had been going on with Amantarra in her hand. She paused, holding the crystal just above the receptacle... teasing... savouring the moment for posterity; this would be the moment she remembered, the moment just before the truth was revealed... until finally, she dropped the crystal into the console. It made a slight ringing noise like the clinking of glasses, but otherwise nothing happened...the console didn't even flicker this time.

'I give up,' she said out loud as she resisted the temptation to hurl the console at the wall. There didn't seem to be any answers here; only frustration.

The light level in the Node chamber suddenly dropped and then went back up again. Elleria turned and looked back into the chamber. She waited... and again the light coming from the walls dimmed and then went back up again. Curious, and not quite sure what else to do, Elleria walked slowly back inside the Node chamber to see what was happening. She hadn't got very far into the chamber when behind her the double doors closed with a loud metallic sound that reverberated around the chamber. Shocked by the sound Elleria spun round. She could hear the locks clicking into place as the chamber was sealed. This should not have happened, the chamber doors should never lock when there was a physical presence in the chamber because there was no way to open them from the inside. The surfaces of the chamber flashed blue as the Node force field reactivated. Now not even a Bruwnan could enter the chamber, no matter what dimensions they existed in; or, for that matter leave the chamber.

Elleria realised she was trapped. Her mind raced, not to find a way out, because until the doors reopened there wasn't one, but to try and reason why this might be happening. This chamber was now completely isolated from absolutely everything else in Euclidian space and beyond. That meant that it was completely free from the attentions of the High Council. Perhaps Amantarra was hiding here, perhaps she was about to put in an appearance. It could be the only explanation.

'Amantarra, are you here,' said Elleria loudly, but there was only silence. 'The chamber is sealed,' she tried optimistically. Elleria waited a few moments... nothing. So what else could this mean? Why trap me here?

The console she was holding in her hands suddenly burst into life producing a complex three dimensional image of lines and colour that visually made absolutely no sense whatsoever. Elleria recognised it immediately, it was a data file. More precisely it was a data file containing the template for creating a shell. A shell like the Bruwnan one she was currently occupying.

Elleria placed the console on the floor of the chamber, sat crossed legged in front of it and watched the ever changing patterns of the data file. It was impossible to tell from what she could see what form the new shell would take. There was only one way to find out.

Elleria placed both her hands into the image that floated above the console. The image stopped changing; as Elleria suspected, the file would only be accessible by its intended recipient, which with any luck would be her. The image started to change again as the file accepted Elleria as the recipient and transferred the data into her current Bruwnian shell. Once the transfer was complete the image above the console vanished. There was the briefest of pauses and then Elleria's current shell vanished leaving the chamber empty. The force field flickered for a moment and then the light level in the chamber dropped to near darkness.

Elleria found herself sitting on a large branch of one of the trees overlooking the hill the Node chamber was on. She felt different. She looked at the black fur on the back of her hands.

She was different. She was Ja'liem. There was more; Elleria quickly realised that this was not just the hollow shell of a Ja'liem, the construct had substance. She could sense internal organs and blood pumping. Her stomach rumbled, Elleria was euphoric, was that what hunger felt like? Amantarra had provided her with some sort of Radgarc, Ja'liem hybrid.

Stretching her limbs she felt the strength in them. She tried walking along the branch, her body tingled with the unfamiliar fur, but the coordination was all there. She jumped and spun round on the spot and ran back toward the trunk of the tree. She jumped at the trunk and digging her claws into the bark climbed up and round to the left onto the next branch. Not only was the shell coordinated but all the climbing techniques were programmed in. Elleria scampered along the branch heading for the next tree and at the optimum point leapt to the right landing perfectly on the branch of the adjacent tree. Elleria had wanted this for so long. This must be a gift from Amantarra. She ran and jumped to the next tree, then another and another. Elleria had never felt so elated.

'Thank you Amantarra,' she shouted.

'Who's that... who's there,' came some unexpected replies. Off to her right a male and two female Ja'liem appeared around the trunk of a tree some distance off.

'Hello,' shouted Elleria, as she quickly moved towards them easily covering the distance in three jumps.

'Yes, hello…' replied the male a little curtly as Elleria arrived next to them, 'but who are you?'

Elleria was so caught up in the excitement of being a Ja'liem and having the freedom to run and jump through the trees; that it didn't immediately register with her that she was holding a conversation with the male. Then the realisation dawned on her.

'You can talk!'

'Of course I can talk, what a ridiculous thing to say,' replied the male grumpily. 'Now who are you? Don't you know that its bad manners to enter another territory without an invite.' The younger of the females giggled at the male's grumpy attitude and Elleria could see from the family resemblance that she was obviously his daughter. Quite how she made this distinction she didn't know; up until now all the Ja'liem had sort of looked the same.

The older of the females gasped, 'Aarlam,' she said indicating Elleria's head; 'look.'

'What, I…' a sudden look of realisation came over his face. 'Oh my gracious me; I do apologise,' he said. 'Please, please, you must come with us immediately.'

Elleria was thrilled at the almost instant acceptance; and as they started to make their way through the branches she felt a sense of belonging that she had never known. Leaping from branch to branch, occasionally jumping and grabbing a higher branch to swing up a level, they weaved their way through the dense forest; always gaining height and always moving roughly in the same direction. She would occasionally see other small groups of Ja'liem off to either side several trees away, but they paid no attention to their passing. Elleria got the impression that this was a route that was well used as the male leading them showed no hesitation in the path he was taking. She was also amazed that she had no problems in keeping up with them; this shell that Amantarra had given her was perfect.

The forest rolled by with very little variation in the types of tree; they were nearly all of the silver barked type that surrounded the Node hill. Occasionally there was a red barked tree that on average seemed a little taller than the silver barked variety. There were parasitic plants growing in the hollows formed by forking branches and creepers that enveloped the trees in a lattice work of black vines all the way up from the ground.

At one point in the journey Elleria found herself running between the male and the two females. She heard the two females talking.

'What does it mean Mother,' said the younger of them.

'I don't know. That's why we're going to see The Librarian,' replied the older female.

After twenty minutes of travelling they had steadily climbed up near the top of the canopy where the silver trees bore their small, round, orange fruit. The forest was abundant with it and the smell of it started to make Elleria hungry. She grabbed some as she passed and pushed it into her mouth. It tasted delicious.

They hadn't been travelling near the top of the canopy long when Elleria could see that they were heading for a massive red barked tree that was larger by a quarter than the surrounding trees. There were a lot of Ja'liem in the trees surrounding the giant red, and Elleria realised that as they passed, more and more of them were tagging along behind. By the time they reached the giant red tree they had quite a following.

Aarlam halted on the branch of a silver tree adjacent the large red.

'Wait here,' he said and made to go. Pausing, he turned back to Elleria and added, 'please.' He nodded to himself as if he was satisfied that that was the correct protocol and then jumped over to a branch on the giant red tree and made his way into the canopy. Soon he was lost to sight in the dense foliage.

Elleria and the two females sat in a group facing each other. The Ja'liem who had been following them as they had approached the red tree, had now formed a semi-circle in the surrounding trees around Elleria and the two females. Not one of them had attempted to join them on the tree they were on and with the exception of an occasional whispered conversation they were silent and watchful.

Elleria turned to the older female. 'What are your names?' she asked. The older female looked initially surprised at the question and then took on a look that seemed to indicate that Elleria had done her a great honour.

'Ishimaall, and this is our daughter Esamally,' replied Ishimaall proudly.

Elleria turned to Esamally and smiled. Esamally smiled back and shuffled closer to Elleria. Something moved on Esamally's back just behind her shoulder. Elleria reached out and pulled the tick from Esamally's fur. Esamally immediately moved closer to sit with her back to Elleria. The Ja'liem in the surrounding trees gasped and whispered. To Elleria it just felt natural to groom Esamally.

'You do us a great honour,' said Ishimaall, 'it is we who should groom you.'

'Nonsense, this is very relaxing… and besides, these ticks are quite tasty,' replied Elleria as she placed another one in her mouth. Amantarra had thought of everything.

'I heard you saying we were going to see The Librarian,' said Elleria while searching for another tick.

'Yes,' replied Ishimaall.

'So, is that the library?' Elleria nodded towards the large red tree.

Ishimaall looked puzzled. 'I don't know what a library is,' she said.

'It's a place where knowledge is kept.' Elleria chased a different, faster moving insect through Esamally's fur.

Ishimaall shook her head. 'I don't know of such things. This is the place of The Librarian.' Elleria decided not to ask any more questions; the place did after all just look like a big tree.

As Elleria continued to groom Esamally she became vaguely aware of a presence. It seemed to be in a slightly elevated position in the giant red tree in front of her. She stopped what she was doing and looked up; there was nothing there, just the leaves moving gently in the breeze. The presence she'd felt had gone. She checked her normal Radgarc senses… but again there was nothing. Ishimaall and Esamally seemed perfectly relaxed, indicating that they were either unaware or unconcerned about whatever it had been. Elleria went back to grooming… and there it was again. As she focused with her new Ja'liem senses of touch and sight to search Esamally's fur, in the grey area between her old and new senses there was something there, something that did not want to be seen. The sensation was illusive, like movement seen out of the corner of your eye. When she concentrated on grooming with her new senses, she could detect a slight disturbance in space time; as if whatever it was could hide from her five Ja'liem senses and hide from her Bruwnian senses but showed out in the differences between the two.

'Here's Aarlam,' said Ishimaall breaking Elleria's train of thought.

Aarlam came bounding out of the foliage of the red tree, jumped over to where they sat waiting for him.

'Is she to go in now,' asked Ishimaall.

Aarlam shook his head. 'No, The Librarian is coming out.'

Ishimaall looked surprised. 'Are you sure,' she asked.

'He's here now,' said Esamally.

Walking slowly out of the foliage of the red tree was a large male. As he drew close to the end of the branch he was on Elleria could see that he had three stripes, a single purple stripe with an orange one to either side of it. The

Librarian looked powerful and muscular, he was half as big again as Aarlam and he moved with a delicate grace that belied his size. Moments later he was sitting in front of the four of them. Aarlam, Ishimaall and Esamally all looked down and avoided looking him directly in the eye. Elleria didn't think that they feared the large male; they just seemed to be showing deference to him.

The Librarian studied Elleria closely for a moment, looking her up and down and then he stared deep into her eyes. Elleria returned the stare.

'Elleria,' he said. 'It's so nice to finally meet you. I'm The Librarian of the Ja'liem.' She was so surprised at hearing her name that she did not answer immediately.

'Yes… thank you,' she said eventually, 'but how did you know my name?'

'That was easy,' The Librarian indicated Elleria's head, 'you have three purple stripes.'

'Ah, that's what Ishimaall meant when I first met her,' realisation dawning on Elleria. 'Still doesn't explain how you know my name though.'

'It's all to do with the prophecy. I've told the story to every Ja'liem as soon as they were old enough to understand. I've embellished the story over the years, but the essence of it is that one day a Ja'liem with three purple stripes will appear. Her name will be Elleria and she is to be shown the way to The Librarian who will pass on a message.'

Elleria thought that this posed more questions than it answered. Perhaps now was the time to start getting some answers.

'Librarian.'

'Yes, Elleria.'

'I studied the Ja'liem for a very long time,' she looked down at her body, 'not in this form though; and in all the time I studied you, not once was there any clue that you had a language any more complicated than a few calls and warnings, never mind one that included words like "embellish". It was only when I took the form of a Ja'liem that this language of yours was revealed. Up to that point my impression of you, as a species, was one of a simple animal; no offense intended.'

'Perhaps that's the point. To outsiders we are animals and our language is hidden.'

'But why, why hide something like a language?'

'Let me give you some background on the Ja'liem; it may help.'

Elleria nodded.

'The philosophy I have always taught, what I have been required to teach, is one of harmonious coexistence with the forest. Things like writing, art, the worship of deities, anything that would leave physical evidence of our intelligence have all been... not supressed, but discouraged. The whole philosophy is about not attracting attention. So our society is based around the telling of stories and that is how I pass on the information I get from the dreams and visions I see. I have not however, had a vision since just before your last visit here when you activated the Node. If you remember, you drew quite an audience. And in that last vision I was given the prophecy.'

Elleria looked him up and down.

'That was a long time ago. How long do the Ja'liem live?'

'On average a Ja'liem can live up to about fifty to sixty years, barring accidents. Aarlam here is forty-two and I can remember the day he was born, as I can with everyone you see here.'

Elleria was amazed. 'But you look younger than Aarlam,' she said.

'Yes, I was one of the first of my species and was chosen to be The Librarian when I was in my prime. With the position of Librarian came a shield, and while I have changed and matured over the millennia the shield has kept me fit and well. It's also impossible to kill me, as many a predator has found to their cost. But with Amantarra's Shield came the responsibility to guide the Ja'liem and prepare them for your arrival.'

'Amantarra's Shield, you know of Amantarra?'

'Of course, she is the source of my visions. Part of the prophecy that she gave me is a message for you.'

Elleria laughed. She could see now how all the pieces fitted together and how everything had led up to this point. 'You know I once asked Amantarra about the three striped Ja'liem and how you didn't see many of them about. Now I know that the reason is that there was only ever one... you.'

'So in answer to your question "why hide a language"; it's hidden because... how did Amantarra put it... because we exceed the intelligence parameters required for the Node network. She didn't want the council to eradicate us, not after all her hard work.'

'How would they find you? You've never been connected to the Node network and it's impossible to track a Radgarc or a Bruwnian. The universe is just too big a place to play hide and seek in even for Bruwnian technology.'

'Perhaps Amantarra just likes playing games,' said The Librarian.

Elleria scratched under her arm; she suspected that she'd already picked up some sort of parasite that was more mobile than a tick. 'Don't get me wrong Librarian, but while it is pleasant to be able to converse with a species other than the Bruwnan, why create one with this much intelligence in the first place?'

'Amantarra told me that we were a stepping stone to another species, one that uses technology and therefore cannot be hidden so easily.'

'Again, why create a species that uses technology?'

Esamally reached over and removed something from Elleria's side and the tickling sensation stopped.

'Thank you,' she said to Esamally.

'Perhaps the message I have for you will help answer that,' said The Librarian.

'Perhaps it will.'

'Now,' announced The Librarian in a loud voice, 'I will fulfil the prophecy.' He leaned forward and whispered a long string of numbers into Elleria's ear; and then added, 'there's more to this than meets the eye.' Then he stood up on his hind legs. 'The prophecy is fulfilled; Amantarra Ja'liem,' he announced. All the Ja'liem who bore witness celebrated by jumping up and down and shouting "Amantarra Ja'liem" and the surrounding forest soon echoed with similar celebration as tribe after tribe responded to the call.

Elleria sat looking confused. The numbers appeared to be an encryption key; but what were they supposed to unlock? 'Was there any more to the prophecy?' she asked.

'Why, does it not mean anything to you?' The Librarian sat back down.

'Well it looks like an encryption key, but what it's for I don't know.'

'Alas I have no knowledge of what an encryption key is; remember we are a species without any understanding of technology.' The Librarian thought for a moment, recalling the vision in which he was given the prophecy. 'There is one thing; an action that goes with the final part. It's the only thing I can think of that I haven't done.'

'Show me,' said Elleria.

'Give me your right hand,' said The Librarian reaching out to take it. Holding her hand with his left he repeated the final part of the prophecy. 'There's more to this...' as he said the word "this" he patted the back of her hand with his free hand, 'than meets the eye.' The Librarian let go of her hand and sat back. 'Was that any good?' he asked.

Elleria thought about it, going over the action and the phrase in her head. 'Yes,' she said. 'There's more to this shell than meets the eye. There must be more data hidden within the file for this shell.' Elleria applied the numbers to the file. 'Yes there's a set of coordinates and another shell design. There are some instructions as well... I have to... that's unusual.'

The Librarian leaned forward and placed a hand on each of her shoulders.

'Elleria,' he said 'It's time for you to leave.'

And it was with both a sense of loss and gain that Elleria said goodbye to The Librarian of the Ja'liem and vanished.

6
THE GIFT

The shop Reg Scribbins was heading for came into view, sandwiched between a Chinese takeaway to the right and a Travel Agency to the left; it looked like something from another era. It had once been a terraced house and architecturally it hadn't changed much. Internally, the front room had been knocked through into the back room to form a long deep shop, but externally there was very little difference. The original front door, its brown paint flaked with age, opened into a small square vestibule. This door was always fastened back when the shop was open. The front room window had been decked out with shelves to display articles for sale, but was otherwise the same as it always had been. High up on the outside wall was an old sign; the words "Green and Son, Pawnbrokers" could still be made out despite the flaking paint.

As usual Reg applied the brakes early. Groaning and juddering and thanks to a slight incline in the road the bike came to a halt outside the shop. The inner half glazed door had an "Open" sign hanging in it. Reg paused, still a little undecided as to whether to proceed. The sign says "Open" he thought, what other invitation do I need? The bell above the door jangled as he opened it. Reg took a deep breath and ventured into the dark interior of the shop.

The shop was narrow and lined on either side with shelves, each crammed full of old record players, vases, dolls and other bric-a-brac. The shelves disappeared into the gloom at the back of the shop. Jack Green didn't illuminate the shop unnecessarily, he believed it gave him a negotiating advantage; there were no standard fixed prices here. At the back of the shop a small lamp shone down onto a glass counter. As Reg approached Jack looked up, the light reflecting off the glass illuminating his face from below. This gave him an Angel of Death appearance; another negotiating advantage. Somewhere in the gloom an old clock ticked slowly.

Reg hesitated. He was feeling guilty about selling this thing as it was, and now he was here, this shop was giving him the creeps. Maybe it wasn't such a good idea; after all, he'd never been any good at haggling. He remembered the last object he sold here, a German officers helmet from the First World War. The polished steel helmet with its brass detachable spike and brass badge showing the Prussian Spread Eagle with the words "Mit Gott für Koenig und Vaterland" which his father had told him meant "Made in Germany", but which Jack Green had told him meant "With God for King and Fatherland", had been the most valuable thing Reg's father had ever given him. It had been a bitter blow to sell it, but Reg's wife wouldn't have it in the house; she believed that it was haunted by the dead German officer it had belonged to, and besides, she wanted the money for a holiday. In the end, with the money he got from Jack, Reg's wife had to make do with a day trip to the seaside on the train.

'Come forward, don't be shy, I don't bite,' said Jack. 'Well not on Saturdays anyway.'

Reg thought about it, and decided to take him on trust. Removing his cap, just in case; he wasn't quite sure of the protocol for shops this old; he made his way to the counter. Jack stood resting his hands on the glass; behind him the pendulum of a large Grandfather clock swung slowly back and forth to a rhythmic clunk… clunk… clunk.

'Now, how can I help,' asked Jack with a voice like treacle.

Reg reached into his pocket, pulled out something wrapped in an oily old rag and placed it on the counter.

'How much would this be worth?' Reg indicated the cloth.

'Well, let's have a look shall we.'

Jack gingerly pulled at the cloth with his fingertips to finally reveal the object. It was impressive, all the more so for what it had arrived in, and with. Of course Jack had no intention of describing the object in glowing terms in front of Reg. Doing that would have the effect of pushing the price up. It was obviously immaculate and he could see that Reg knew it was. The only angle he could take was the "not much market for this sort of thing". That ought to hold the price down.

'Hmm,' said Jack.

Reginald looked on expectantly.

Jack retrieved it from the oily cloth and held it under the light.

'This really is a nice piece,' Jack heard himself say. Which was a bit of a shock to say the least; but then again, the more he looked at it, it really was a nice piece. Jack opened it, there was a name inscribed on the inside.

'W. Godbert,' he read. 'Where did you get it?'

Reg looked a bit sheepish; it was the question he was hoping would not be asked. His mind raced to come up with an answer.

'I… I found it up at the school; hidden behind a grill.' It wasn't quite the answer Reg was hoping for, but it was too late now; he'd been and gone and said it. This isn't going too well thought Reg. He's going to claim that I shouldn't sell it because it doesn't belong to me. And he'll probably make me give it away. Reg wondered why he never seemed to get ahead in life.

'Yes, there was a teacher of that name who taught there before the war.' It was a name Jack was familiar with and it gave him some idea of who he could sell it to; although it wouldn't be an easy sale.

'That's right; he was killed just outside the school early on in the war.'

'I wonder why he hid it behind a grill,' said Jack as he carefully closed it and placed it back on its cloth. 'Well, he won't need it now, that's for certain.'

Five minutes later Reg was standing outside the shop looking at the money in his hand. That seemed to go better than expected; he thought. Funny how he'd always thought himself as hopeless at negotiating; he remembered all the insurance salesmen he'd encountered and all the bloody useless insurance policies he'd bought. Reg counted the money, gave himself a pat on the back and considered a slick new career in insurance sales. He looked at his current company vehicle and a wave of nostalgia came over him; perhaps a career change wouldn't be such a good idea because it would mean giving up the bike. Reg looked at the money again and decided that on balance he would chalk this one up as a single victory, but perhaps this time he wouldn't tell his wife; after all, what she didn't know about, she couldn't spend.

*

The following day in the Lounge bar of the White Rose, Jack Green sat waiting for an old friend who always came in for a pint when it was quiet on Sunday lunchtime. As expected, at precisely midday, Edward made his entrance.

Edward was a short round man with bandy legs, a small nose, and thin white hair that constantly appeared to be blowing in a gentle breeze, even when there was no breeze. He always wore a white collar-less shirts and dark grey trousers, tailored to fit under his armpits, which he held up with both a belt and very short braces. Edward said "it was better to be safe than sorry", Jack preferred to think he was just pessimistic. Edward, a man who had so far managed to get through life with a minimum of financial output, was a tight fisted individual who had been raised amid the dark satanic mills of Yorkshire and used the austerity of his youth to justify his parsimonious lifestyle. Compared to Edward, Jack was extravagant with his money. Edward religiously followed the Yorkshire doctrine of the Tykes Motto he had decorating a tea mug he'd been given as a teenager:

"See all, hear all, say nowt,"
"Eat all, sup all, pay nowt,"
"And if tha does owt for nowt,"
"Allus do it for thisen."

Edward was at the bar counting out the cost of his pint in pennies and assorted small change from an old purse that his wife Maureen had thrown out and Edward had rescued from the bin. After four years, Edward still hadn't quite got the hang of the new decimal money yet and kept trying to slip in the odd thruppenny bit.

'Can't accept those any more Ed,' said the barman.

'Well you take sixpences don't you?' said Edward in his high pitched strongly accented voice.

'Sixpences were worth two and a half new pence, but not anymore. Thruppenny bits would only have been worth one and a quarter new pence, if they had been worth anything.'

'You mean a penny farthing,' said Edward digging to the bottom of his money purse. 'I've got some farthings in here somewhere.' Edward had been waiting for years to get rid of them.

'I can't accept farthings either.'

Edward gave him a reproachful look.

'What do you have to keep changing things for?' he said.

'Don't blame me; it's not me that keeps changing things. Look you're only three pence short. Take the thruppenny bit back, and give me those four new halfpennies and a penny… a new one, and then we're even.'

The barman knew that you didn't let Edward off paying the full price; no matter how difficult it was to get the money out of him; because if you did, then

Edward assumed that this was the new price, making it even harder to get the correct money out of him next time.

There was a pause while Edward converted the new money to old, did the calculation, and then converted the result back again.

The bell on the till rang out as Edward; pint in hand, purse safely in pocket, made his way to the comfy seats in the corner where Jack, his long-time drinking pal was already sat. Edward placed his glass on the table and sat back.

'Evening Jack, how's business?'

'Funny you should mention that Ed,' said Jack, 'but I have something here that you may be interested in.' Despite the expression on Edward's face Jack felt compelled to press on. He placed a white handkerchief on the table in front of Edward.

'I'm not really in the market for anything Jack.'

'I realise that,' replied Jack, thinking, when are you ever in the market for something. 'But just have a look, I think you'll find it interesting.'

Edward reached over and flicked the corners back on the handkerchief to reveal the object.

'By 'eck, where did you get that,' said Edward, thinking there was no way on Gods earth that he would be parting with the sort of money he would need to buy it.

'Open it, there's a name inside.'

Edward picked it up and opened it.

'W. Godbert,' quoted Jack. 'It was found up at the school hidden behind a grill in a storeroom. I think it must have belonged to Maureen's first husband William.'

Edward pushed his glasses down to the end of his nose and peered over them with the object almost touching his nose.

'It says J. Godbert.'

'What?'

'The name on the inside is J. Godbert not W. Godbert.'

Jack leaned over and looked.

'I could have sworn that said W. Godbert.' But there it was, plain as day, "J" not "W". Very strange he thought. Jack knew what it had said, so either he was going mad or it had changed. Well he was trying to sell the thing to Edward in the first place, so maybe he was going mad. So, he reasoned, if I succeed in selling it then I'm not mad, and if I fail, well then I'll blame the lighting in the shop; because the inscription couldn't possible have changed, could it.

'Your Maureen's Grandson John then, you should buy it for him.' Good recovery as far as naming John thought Jack, but perhaps a tad early mentioning the word "buy" so early in negotiations.

Edward closed it and turned the object over and over in his hands. His mind was switching back and forth between his years of thrift and this sudden and overpowering urge he had to buy the thing at all costs. A bead of sweat appeared on his brow. Edward tried to distract his mind by looking at his pint, something that had always worked in the past whenever his fiscal universe had been threatened. He put the object back on the table and reached for his pint.

'How much do you want for it,' Edward heard himself say, his hand just short of touching the glass.

There was silence as both men took in what had just been said.

Swallowing hard, Jack felt slightly giddy as Edward produced the often rumoured, but never seen, bank roll from his pocket. Edward didn't trust banks, and since Maureen had found his hiding place he didn't trust mattresses either, so he kept his life's savings as a roll of banknotes in his pocket. Edward started peeling notes off the roll before Jack had even given a price. Whatever price was finally agreed Jack knew that Edward would need a lie down afterwards, just for a few days, until his hands stopped shaking.

*

Monday morning, Reg's son Kevin and four teenage residents of Skutterskelfe, were playing a game of cricket on some common ground in Skutterskelfe. Skutterskelfe was an affluent; in the sense that it wasn't Penshaw Grove; suburb of Tameston. This was the last day of the holidays and they had decided to get some practice in, as the season was due to start.

Kevin Scribbins, like his father, always wore grey clothes; this was due to his mother's firm belief that all clothes should be washed in a mild bleach solution. Kevin's once black trousers had faded to grey; this blended nicely with: his grey open necked shirt, which had started out white, but was washed with his trousers; his scuffed black shoes; and grey, once dark blue, socks. His underwear however, having always been washed separately for reasons of hygiene, was brilliant white. Kevin didn't like Penshaw Grove at all, he had no friends there; but the house, like the bike came with his father's job so he was stuck there. As a result he spent more time here in Skutterskelfe then he did at home.

Kevin was currently covering the positions to the left of the batsman from square leg to mid-wicket, on the other side of John, the current batsman, was Action Gnome who was covering from point to cover. Frank, wearing a pair of gardening gloves, was the wicket keeper and the umpire; he was the only one who knew the proper rules of cricket and without him the others would not have known what positions they were playing in, they would just have been fielding. Bowling to John, was Scott.

John and Scott looked very similar, same hair colour and roughly the same build; they were often mistaken for brothers; but John Godbert and Scott Briggs were in fact completely unrelated.

The field in which they were playing had once been a training ground for Tameston Football Club, but not anymore. The ground was level and even; and with the exception of the wicket which was trampled flat, somewhat overgrown. The grass covered the feet of the players and here and there the odd bush had taken hold. There had once been two full sized football pitches marked out, but they had long since vanished under the grass. The field was surrounded on four sides by the backs of semidetached houses and it was through a gate in Action's back garden that they gained access to the field.

With only five players the rules were slightly different to normal cricket. Each one of them had taken a turn to bat, the remaining four forming the other team. Last to bat was John, who was currently on twenty six chasing Scott's score of twenty seven.

John gripped the bat, which had been made out of a plank of wood by his father, and watched Scott who was still walking back to begin his run up. This was important, one more run and he would equal Scott's score, two more runs and he would have beaten him. Scott had never lost at anything before, except when playing chess with Frank, who to John's knowledge had never lost to anyone, not even the teachers at school. John relished the thought of being the first to beat Scott and knew from old that it was usually at this point that Scott did something underhand to secure victory, but John couldn't see what Scott could possibly do. All John had to do was hit the ball and run, he should easily get two runs.

Scott had reached his start point; John tapped the ground with his bat in anticipation. Scott dropped the tennis ball they were playing with and seemed to have a problem finding it in the grass.

'He's doing this deliberately,' he said to Frank without taking his eyes off Scott.

'Of course he is; you didn't expect anything else did you?'

'No I suppose not.'

'Watch now, here he comes.'

Scott started his run, sprinting up to the far wicket. There was a glint in his eye and he wore an evil grin. This is going to be a fast one thought John and focused everything on the ball. Scott reached the far wicket and bowled. A straight ball, Scott was relying on power to get it through. John watched it as it headed for the bounce; it was only a fleeting impression, but the ball seemed redder. John pulled the bat back, ready to strike; the ball bounced at just the right height and John smacked it hard. The bat splintered in two and the ball flew over Franks head. Clinging to the remains of the bat John ran for it scoring a single run before Frank could retrieve the ball. John looked at what was left of the bat.

'What the hell was that?' he shouted at Scott.

'He's used a proper cricket ball,' shouted Frank as he ran back. Action and Kevin made their way over to look at the bat.

'I thought we agreed we weren't using a proper cricket ball on account of us not having a proper cricket bat,' said John waving the broken wood at Scott.

'Well it was getting boring, so I thought I'd spice things up.'

'You mean you were frightened of losing.'

'No I wasn't.'

'Yes you were, you always do something like this if anyone gets close enough to beat you.'

Kevin and Action were watching the argument with mild interest; they'd seen it all before, John and Scott arguing over something. They were the best of friends but they did like to bicker. In fact John was the only one that Scott argued with without using his fists. Scott did tend to fly off the handle at the slightest provocation and he didn't care how big his opponents were either.

'Anyway,' said Frank, who tended to act as mediator between them, 'Scott, you didn't lose and John, Scott didn't beat you.' That was Frank all over, always fair, always helpful. Frank had an air of authority which he himself did not promote, but which everyone seemed to respect, even Scott.

'But neither did you win,' said John, 'even if you did cheat.'

'It wasn't cheating; it was just changing the rules a bit. Anyway, that would have been a great hit if the bat hadn't broken,' said Scott.

'A six,' said Action as he picked up the cagoule he was rarely seen without.

Action had a mop of blonde curly hair and piercing blue eyes that could outstare a bird of prey. The windows to the soul; John had heard eyes described as such, and as he looked at Action's eyes now he got the distinct feeling that although he couldn't see Action's soul, Action could see his.

Action Gnome, as his nickname indicated, was a small individual who loved outdoor pursuits. Most weekends his mop of blond curly hair could be seen moving on the moors, traipsing up hills and through bogs at about chest height. It was rumoured, by Scott, that he was addicted to Kendal Mint Cake, something which he always denied, stating that; "he could quit any time he wanted to", which of course is the song of the addict. He was like a normal outdoor pursuit's enthusiast, but smaller and more concentrated; and when Action concentrated on something, there was always the danger he'd burn holes in it with his eyes.

'Looks like that's the end of the game,' said Kevin. 'I'd better be off for something to eat.'

There was a general chorus of agreement and they all started to make their way to the gate at the back of Action's house.

John fancied a girl at school called Karen, but there was the usual problem of not knowing if she fancied John and therefore if she would say yes or no when asked to the pictures. This problem had a simple solution; discuss it openly with your mates and get one of them to ask her out for you, and who better to do that than your best friend.

'Did you ask Karen?' John asked Scott.

'Yes.'

'And?'

'Well…' replied Scott, 'I couldn't persuade her to go out with you, but I did manage to convince her to show me her tits so that I could describe them to you.' That got everyone's attention.

'Really?' said Action.

'No,' said Frank, 'he's winding you up.'

'You're a bastard Scott, you know that don't you?' said John.

'I do try my best,' grinned Scott.

'I told you before,' said Frank, 'ask her out yourself.'

'She might say no,' complained John.

'She might not,' replied Frank, smiling and nodding knowingly. 'Anyway, even if she does, at least you'll know the answer.'

John thought about it. 'I suppose,' he mumbled. John knew that was the right approach, he always had; it's just that, well, you had to be brave to face possible rejection and the ridicule of her friends and worse still, she might say "yes", then what?

*

As John opened the front door to his house, a small red car pulled up in front of the removal van parked outside the house opposite. A man and a woman got out of the car. Paul Parker took the cardboard box his wife Helen had been holding and made his way to the front door.

The new neighbours had arrived.

Paul, an accountant by trade and therefore not used to technical stuff, scratched his head as he tried to work out which of the half dozen keys opened the front door. He guessed correctly... on his fourth go. He picked up the box he'd placed carefully at his feet and pushed his way through the door.

'Is the kettle on yet?' shouted one of the removal men from the back of the van.

'I thought you wanted tea after you had unloaded,' replied Paul.

'No, it was definitely before unloading,' replied the voice from the van.

'Alright, we'll compromise; you start unloading and I'll put the kettle on.' Paul ended any further debate by disappearing inside. Helen followed him in. She was looking forward to her pending supervisory role.

Although neither had mentioned it to the other, they both had the curious feeling that they were not seeing something, something that was right in front of them, but hidden. Paul made his way through to the kitchen, turned the light on with his elbow and placed the box he was carrying on the worktop. He quickly filled the kettle, plugged it in and started to organise the cups.

*

The inside of John's house was clean, but slightly worn round the edges. John's father, Tom, referred to it as "lived in". John entered the living room, stroke dining room, stroke drawing room, stroke everything else room at the back of the house.

There was another room at the front of the house; it was known reverently and unoriginally as the front room. It was never used, except for special occasions like Christmas when it was too cold to use; therefore it was never used. The best furniture was in the front room, it was all twenty years old but in immaculate condition.

Decoratively, the back room was contemporary for the time, provided you didn't try to assess it as a whole. Woodchip wallpaper, painted a sort of yellowy mustard colour, adorned the walls; clashing easily with the turquoise, green and dark blue random squares of the carpet. Pride of place went to a teak table and chairs with matching sideboard. They'd looked great in the showroom, but they were far too big for the room they were in. The three piece suite had been due for renewal about ten years ago; Tom had bought seat covers for it instead; purple seat covers, which again, had looked great in the shop. It didn't matter how often you walked into the room, the décor always took a few seconds to adjust to. John blinked twice.

Tom, who worked as an electrician at the steel works, was sat in front of the fire reading a newspaper. In front of Tom; hidden from his view behind the newspaper, sat a black dog, it stared intently up at the newspaper as if it was waiting for something.

'Uncle Edward's been round with something for you,' said Tom not looking up from his newspaper. Uncle Edward was Tom's stepfather. He'd met Maureen a year after William had been killed. Six months later, amid the austerity of war, with borrowed wedding clothes and a cardboard wedding cake, they'd married. Before the wedding, during the period when he was trying to work out why Edward always came round for breakfast every morning, Tom had called him Uncle Edward; and now John followed suit.

'Brought something for me?'

'Don't ask me what; it's all new territory to me as well. I've never got anything off him in all the years I've known him,' said Tom dropping the newspaper slightly to look over at John.

The dog took advantage of the momentary distraction and while still remaining in the sitting position, shuffled forward and put its head on Tom's knee. Tom ignored it and went back to his newspaper.

'Where is it?' asked John.

'In the front room on the settee,' replied Tom dropping the newspaper again. The dog edged further onto the chair, placing his front paws on Tom's legs. Tom continued to ignore it.

On the settee was a brown paper parcel. John took it back into the dining room, placed it on the table and started picking at the brown paper. Tearing the paper off revealed a shoebox labelled "Brogues. Size: 12. Colour: Brown". Shoes thought John; he pictured himself in a pair of brown brogues with his friends rolling around the floor laughing.

'Looks like he's got me a pair of shoes,' said John.

'I wonder who gave him those, because he certainly would not have bought them,' said Tom, looking across. The dog slipped smoothly under the newspaper, sat on Tom's lap and stared straight at him. Tom turned back to his newspaper only to find himself nose to nose with the dog.

Tom closed his eyes, sighed quietly to himself and opened them again; he had no idea why the animal insisted on doing this. The dog whined and trembled slightly as it continued to stare deep into Tom's eyes.

The doorbell rang.

'I'll get it,' said Tom, letting go of the newspaper and standing up to stop the dog hypnotising him. The dog slid off his lap finishing up on the hearth rug under the newspaper. Strangely, this seemed to be what the animal wanted. As Tom made his way to the door, a sigh emanated from the newspaper tent in front of the fire.

John reluctantly took the lid off the box to reveal… crumpled up newspapers.

Not shoes, he thought.

He dug through the newspaper until he found the clean white handkerchief that Edward had managed to include in the deal. There was something in it. John placed the handkerchief on the table and un-wrapped it

.

7
BURNSTON

Reg looked up at the thick, dust choked cobwebs above his desk in the boiler room. He watched them for a moment as they gently swayed and rippled in the convection currents. When was the last time they been cleaned away? Reg couldn't remember doing it, perhaps he never had. With the boilers rumbling and fizzing in the background, he gripped the long handle of the broom tightly with both hands and slowly advanced on the cobwebs. With a twisting motion he pushed the broom forward through the cobwebs until it found the corner. Reg continued to twist until he could see the walls and ceiling that made up the corner. Then he took the broom down and shook the contents off into a dustbin.

'There… done,' he said, and having thought for a moment added, 'sorry spiders.'

To his surprise there was an answer, or at least it seemed as though there was an answer, it was difficult to tell over the noise from the boilers especially when the person was whispering.

'Hello, who's there?'

The boilers continued to block out any reply, but there did seem to be one.

'You'll have to speak up. I can't hear you over the boilers.'

'You are the Keeper…' the voice seemed close but trailed off, and Reg didn't catch the end of the sentence; but he did work out where it was coming from. Reg went over to the door between the boilers and pulled it open, the tunnel beyond was pitch black.

'No it's Scribbins, not Keeper,' said Reg into the darkness. There was a long pause and Reg was beginning to think he had imagined the voice. Reg thought about it and an idea occurred to him. 'Were you here before... when I was a boy?'

'Before...' the voice was behind him. Reg spun round. There was nothing there; and then behind him again in the darkness of the tunnel. 'Where did you take it?'

'Take it? Do you mean the watch?'

'Watch... perhaps.'

'Well I sold it... that was alright wasn't it?' Reg was worried that he may have upset his guardian angel.

'Where is it now?' whispered the voice. It was close but seemed to be constantly moving, Reg never knew where it was going to speak from next.

'Greens, the pawnbrokers, it's in town.'

When the voice next spoke it was right next to Reg. 'You are protected, Amantarra's Shield is upon you.'

'Ama... what?' said Reg into the darkness, but there was no reply and Reg got the impression that the spirit had gone. 'Hello,' he tried optimistically, as he reached a hand round and turned the lights on in the service tunnel. There was no one there, but then, Reg wasn't really expecting that there would be.

*

Burnston was standing outside the railings that ran up the side of Penshaw grove school. On the opposite side of the road the other three members of his little clique were attempting to extort money from a small, thin boy whose ragged appearance clearly made it apparent that he had none. Haystack, the largest of the three, was gripping the top of the boy's skull with one of his enormous hands. Boxhead, a shaven headed youth whose nose had been broken so many times it was almost flush with his face, was going through the victims pockets. Holes were the only things he was finding. Clink, was the shortest of the trio. He had a large single eyebrow and a penchant for stealing books from the library. He didn't read them; they were just easy to steal. The other two thought of him as an intellectual. Clink was explaining to the unfortunate boy that it was not a good idea to come out without any money as you never know when you might need some.

Burnston leaned back on the railings and watched the others with a disinterested expression on his face. He'd seen this all before. If he'd told the others to stop, they would have, there was no dispute over leadership here; it's just that, well he just couldn't be bothered. He stifled a yawn.

Burnston had fought his way to the top and that's where he remained, unchallenged and bored. His physique reflected his journey to the top. He was the same height as Haystack, but whereas Haystack was flabby, Burnston was broad shouldered and muscular. He had a hard face, with a strong jaw line, high cheekbones and pale blue eyes. Rarely smiling, his normal expression was a scowl that made him look like he had a permanent headache. There were very few things that he was afraid of, but he did have a healthy respect of the occult and signs of evil. This was something he got from his Mother who was paranoid about such things.

There has to be something more, he thought, as he watched his peers, something more than this. Burnston had dreams of power, money and life in a world beyond Penshaw Grove. He'd glimpsed this world, it wasn't far away in Skutterskelfe, but it might as well have been a million miles away because he just couldn't reach it.

He thought he heard someone behind him in the playground. He turned quickly and looked through the railings, but there was nobody there. He shook his head; he could have sworn he'd heard someone speak. No matter. He decided to leave the other three to it, and make his way up towards the main road that separated Skutterskelfe from Penshaw Grove. He'd suddenly had the germ of an idea which he needed to dwell on, and he always did his best thinking when he walked alone.

It wasn't long before he reached the main road. He rested his arms on the guard rail that separated the pavement from the road. There, on the other side, glittering like jewels, were Skutterskelfe shops. Burnston took in the scene; his half formed idea paused by the mesmerising effect the shops had on him.

The girls in the baker's shop, all wearing the same type of overalls and how efficient and pleasant they were. There were people in conversation on the pavement, courteous people with manners. People with money. It was all so nice, so pleasant and so unobtainable for someone from Penshaw Grove.

Burnston was sick of being poor. He could see the shops, successful businesses, yes, but how did they start? How did they become so successful? It was true that he did have a way of generating money from nothing; Haystack, Boxhead and Clink were practising it now.

For years he had observed the method used by his contemporaries as they continued the time honoured tradition of wealth redistribution. Using the traditional phrase "lendus a penny", surplus cash would be extorted from anyone who came within range. The phrase "lendus a penny" a shortening of the sentence "lend us a penny" which in proper English would translate to "could I possibly borrow a penny?" You will note that the correct English is a question, and the actual phrase used is a command. This distinction between question and command is important, because it establishes the relationship between lender and borrower.

Burnston had concluded, quite correctly, that these traditional methods were inefficient and too random. He knew that there must be a better way than a load of big lads thundering around demanding money; but he was lacking the necessary social models which would have shown him what changes needed to be made.

Burnston looked along the row of shops; off licence, hardware, fish and chips, post office, bakers and a general dealer; all busy, all prosperous, but what was the first step?

'You should set your sights higher,' said a voice beside him.

'What?' said Burnston, standing up straight and turning to face…? Burnston couldn't remember his name… it was someone from school… Martin? Yes; that was it, Martin. How could he have forgotten about Martin Macadam?

'I said you should aim higher,' said Martin. 'There is nothing to compare with being your own boss, never having to kowtow to others.'

Burnston generally didn't bow to anyone's will, but it was true that people were always trying to tell him what to do, and he didn't like it. This being your own boss thing, Burnston agreed with that and always had, but where do you start?

'I can help you get started,' continued Martin.

Burnston stared at Martin, it was almost like he'd read his thoughts. Martin exhibited no signs of fear, he stared right back at Burnston. This was unusual; most people who got this close to Burnston looked terrified; there were very few who would even look him in the eye, never mind return his stare. And Martin's eyes were dark, almost black. Details about Martin were a bit woolly and he had to concentrate to recall some basic details like which classes he was in, the fact that he was a loner and things like that. Nor could he recall ever noticing how dark Martin's eyes were; they were even darker than the art master's eyes. He shuddered inwardly. A sign of evil, that's what dark eyes were. Then again, if Martin could help, then perhaps he ought to listen.

'Alright, how do we get started?'

'Let's get the other three and I'll show you.'

8

RADGARC

Tom returned from the front door.

'That was Paul Parker our new neighbour, the sockets are all off and Carol over the road told him I was an electrician.'

Tom looked over John's shoulder.

'That doesn't look like a pair of shoes,' he said.

Lying on the handkerchief was a very old silver pocket watch. Black Roman numerals marked out time on its white face.

Tom picked it up, its silver chain trailing across the table.

'That's fantastic,' he said.

Tom gathered up the chain to look at the coat of arms on the end.

'Good grief,' he remarked, 'every link on the chain is hallmarked.'

'What's a hallmark?' John asked, as he tried to see; he still hadn't managed to get his hands on the thing yet.

'It means that it's made of solid silver.'

Tom handed the watch to John so that he could see. As John took it his fingers tingled momentarily, and he thought he heard a whispered voice.

*

Paul Parker arrived back at the house and made his way through to the kitchen where Helen came up to him and gave him a peck on the cheek, a quiet moment before the real hard work started.

The real hard work had already started for the removal men, and at this moment two of them were carrying a wardrobe through the front door. Walking backwards, one of them was manoeuvring the wardrobe into the hall ready to go up the stairs, when he bumped into someone. Turning his head he saw an attractive young woman, who he swore hadn't been there a moment ago.

'Sorry love didn't see you there,' he said apologetically.

'I've arrived,' said Elleria.

'Beg pardon?'

'I've just arrived, sorry; I'll get out of your way.' Elleria smiled at the man; who went home that night feeling ten years younger.

Back in the kitchen, the feeling that something was hidden from Paul and Helen evaporated as their daughter Elleria came into the kitchen.

'I've been asked to ask you, if the kettle is on yet?' she said.

The sounds of men struggling with a wardrobe could be heard coming from the stairs. 'Left a bit... down at your end... have you got it?'

Paul smiled. 'I've organised an electrician, he should be over shortly,' he shouted through to the hall.

A strained chorus of, 'Great,' was the reply.

'I'll just go and make sure they know where they're putting that wardrobe,' said Helen, as she disappeared through the door.

'Well I suppose I'd better put some tea in the pot ready,' said Paul. He put his arm round Elleria, pulled her close and kissed her on the forehead. 'Sixteen years old, who would believe it? You know it doesn't seem like five minutes since you came into our lives.'

'Yes,' said Elleria looking a little awkward, 'five minutes.'

*

'What was that?' said John.

'What was what?' said Tom.

'Whispering, I heard whispering.'

'It was probably just the dog moving,' said Tom.

They both turned to look at the dog which was still under Tom's newspaper. There was a slight rustle as it twitched an ear.

'But it said something, I heard words.'

'What did it say?' said Tom; the hairs on the back of his neck had started to prickle.

'I couldn't quite make it out, but it sounded like; "I've arrived".'

The hairs on the back of Tom's neck stopped prickling and stood on end.

The dog rustled the paper again.

'That's what you must have heard,' said Tom with conviction. Tom didn't like strange goings on; he liked logical explanations.

'Maybe,' said John as he opened the back of the watch. 'There're more of those hallmarks inside and look it's got my name in it.'

'So it has, this gets stranger by the minute.' Tom suddenly tapped his forehead with the flat of his hand. 'I almost forgot; come across with me and meet the new neighbours.'

John slipped the watch into his pocket and followed Tom out to the shed where he kept his tools.

*

'Electrician's here,' shouted one of the removal men. There was a distant "hurrah" from upstairs.

Paul made his way through to the hall. 'Thanks for coming Tom, I'd introduce you to my wife Helen but she's upstairs supervising.'

'This is my son John,' said Tom.

'Hello,' said John as he watched a removal man carrying a heavy box marked "kitchen" upstairs.

'And this is my daughter Elleria,' said Paul.

Elleria was slim and pretty, with short light brown hair in a style that was too old for her. She had a beautiful smile and the warmest dark brown eyes John had ever seen. Usually in this type of situation John would lose all coordination and his ability to speak properly would be severely impaired; so even if he could think of anything to say, he would be normally be physically incapable of actually saying it. Therefore it came as a shock, a pleasant shock, but a shock none the less, when he said;

'Hello Elleria,' and smiled. For some reason John felt as though he had known Elleria all his life.

'So what's the emergency?' said Tom.

'Crisis,' said a man walking past with box of glasses balanced precariously on top of a small chest of draws; a disaster waiting happen.

'There's no electricity to boil the kettle,' sighed Paul.

'Oh I see, yes, well, we'll have to put that right.' said Tom putting his tool bag down and opening the cupboard under the stairs.

'That box needs to go down in the kitchen,' said Helen loudly from upstairs.

'Is the kettle on yet?' said a voice from outside.

The chaos of moving house was moving into high gear when Elleria beckoned to John.

'Come into the living room where it's quiet...' she said, adding, '...ter,' as a small man with a large tea chest struggled past her.

In the front room John and Elleria stood in the bay window out of the way. John looked out into the road. He was hoping that Scott would pass by and see him with Elleria, but he was nowhere to be seen. He's never about when there's a chance of getting one over on him, thought John.

Elleria moved closer to John. He smiled at her.

'How long have you lived here?' she asked.

'All my life, I was born in that house over there.' John became aware that the watch appeared to be getting warmer. No, the watch was actually getting hot; it was starting to burn his thigh. He tried to move the watch round without Elleria noticing.

'Where did you live before?' asked John.

'Oh everywhere and nowhere, it sometimes feels like I've never really lived anywhere.'

John's leg was really beginning to hurt; he tried shaking it without being too obvious.

'You seem distracted ' said Elleria nodding at his leg.

'Yes,' said John, 'it's this bloody watch.' He pulled the watch out of his pocket.

'It's making my leg burn.' He held the watch in his hand for her to see.

John expected a reaction from Elleria along the lines of; "Ooo" or "Wow" or "Making your leg burn?" And Elleria did react, but not in quite the way John expected.

'Ah,' she said nodding her head as if she had just seen the answer to something that had been puzzling her, 'it's a watch, a time piece; a mechanical device for the measurement of time, how original.'

John thought it was an odd thing to say almost like she was reading it from a dictionary. She also seemed to be expecting John to have the watch, or least something like it; but how could she; she didn't know anything about him. He watched her face as she looked at the watch. She really was very pretty and he decided that she could say as many odd things as she liked because nothing else mattered. Elleria looked up at him, and John, despite a flash instinct to look away, met her gaze and held it.

'It was a present,' he said.

'Oh, is it your birthday?'

'Actually... no,' said John. 'In fact I'm not sure what sort of a present it is. Uncle Edward has never given me one before.'

The watch felt cool in John's hand, he had expected it to be red hot.

'It looks quite valuable; can I hold it?' Elleria asked.

As he handed the watch over to Elleria the burning sensation in his leg disappeared.

Elleria turned the watch over in her hands.

'Hallmarks,' she remarked, 'it must be solid silver. Look they're on every link of the chain.'

John wondered if everyone but him knew about hallmarks.

'It's got my name written in the back,' he said in an effort to impress Elleria with something she didn't know.

Elleria opened the back of the watch and ran her finger across John's name. He was expecting her to say something about how it couldn't really be his name and that it must be a coincidence; but she didn't. She didn't seem surprised at all. As John watched Elleria closed the watch, turned it over and ran her fingers around its face several times.

'It's beautiful,' she said, moving to hand it back to John.

As John reached out for the watch he heard a whispered voice; "It's time", it said.

'It's time,' said Elleria.

'What...' said John.

'The watch's time, is it right?'

'I don't know.' John looked at the watch. 'It says Twelve Twenty Five; it must be somewhere near right.' As he said it, he got the strangest tingling feeling all over his body; like a mild attack of pins and needles. John shuddered and the feeling passed in a moment. Looking back at Elleria he became aware of how quiet the house was; as if the removal men had all suddenly stopped work at the exact same second.

Elleria took John's hand with her left hand, and held it as she placed the watch onto his open palm with her right; holding on with both hands slightly longer than was necessary. John didn't mind, in fact he felt quite privileged.

Elleria removed her hands leaving the watch in John's. As he looked down at it, he could have sworn that the face of the watch boiled red, just for a moment. And just for a moment, John felt as though he was moving very quickly, but going nowhere.

'It begins,' said the whisper.

John felt a little disorientated.

'It begins,' said Elleria.

John gave her a bemused look.

'The rain, it's beginning to rain.' Elleria smiled at him. John looked out the window and it was starting to rain, but the rain drops appeared to be frozen in the air and then as if he'd imagined it they started moving again and the noise from the busy house returned.

John felt that something had just happened; what it was, he didn't know. He was starting to go over the events of the last few moments when suddenly everything went black.

9

THE KEEPER

In the blackness John thought he might be unconscious, but then it occurred to him that he couldn't be because he was still thinking. Did you still think when you were unconscious? Probably not. Then, just as he was beginning to contemplate that he might have died, some writing appeared in the centre of his view.

Ref: 998-8-999-0-998-95-37
The Keeper narrative

His vision returned, but he was no longer standing next to the window in Elleria's house. She was gone, and he was somewhere else; sometime else.

The year was 1940; Reginald Scribbins was sat at the back of the music class in the same seat he had sat in for the last four years. Mr Godbert the music teacher was alright; as far as teachers went; because he never used the cane, which was a big plus as far as Reginald was concerned. And he always tried to make the lessons interesting; but unfortunately Reginald's interest in music had peaked when he was five, after discovering that he had to learn more than two verses of "This old man". Today's lesson wasn't too bad though; Mr Godbert was explaining the meaning to the lyrics of "Waltzing Matilda". Reginald looked up above the blackboard and studied the map of the world that was hanging there. There was Australia in the bottom right hand corner; Reginald stared at it as Mr Godbert talked. Australia was half a world away, half a world away from this war, this school and what was down in the basement.

Reginald had been due to go to Australia to stay with relatives until the war was over; but a few days before the ship sailed his mother had dreamt that the ship got torpedoed, and so she wouldn't let him go. In the end the ship hadn't been sunk, and the upshot of his mother's dream was that Reginald was still here. As Mr Godbert talked Reginald's thoughts meandered through the Outback to a Billabong under the shade of a coolibah tree, it was a short but welcome distraction from the pain.

The outback evaporated and Reginald blew on his hands again, but it didn't help the stinging much. What use was carrying a gas mask anyway; the German's dropped bombs that exploded, a gas mask didn't offer much protection from them. He tried rubbing his hands together; that didn't help either, so he stopped. Four strokes, two on each hand. How the headmaster expected him to remember his gas mask every day, especially when he was late, he didn't know.

The headmaster had started to use psychological methods of punishment as well as his usual array of physical ones.

'Come and see me after lunch for the cane,' he had said to Reginald after catching him without his gas mask slightly later than first thing in the morning. Reginald, who was no stranger to the cane, then had all morning to think about it. And he had thought about it, and he didn't like it; he preferred to get the cane on the spot, so he didn't have to think about it.

Reginald's brooding was interrupted abruptly when the air raid sirens started. The day just keeps getting better and better, he thought.

'Everybody stand and form a queue at the door; no talking,' said William Godbert in a clear and commanding voice.

Reginald hated air raids, he hated the air raid shelter, it wasn't the confined space he hated, it was the thought that you couldn't escape; you couldn't run, he hated being held back. And over the last few weeks he felt increasingly confined, not just in the air raid shelter, but in everything in his life. It was as if someone had planned his whole life and they were expecting him to blindly follow the path. He'd really been looking forward to going to Australia.

Air raid shelter, thought Reginald, it wasn't even a proper air raid shelter; it was just a big cellar under the science block. Someone had chalked "Air Raid Shelter" on the door; the big metal door, which they always locked. Why did they always have to lock the door, a shiver ran down his spine and Reginald's palms began to sweat.

Reginald hated air raids even more than he hated Mr Godbert's music class. Why did he need to know how to play a triangle, what use would it be? When he left school in the summer, he was going to lie about his age and join the army to fight German's, like his dad had done in the first war. His dad had lied about his age at the start of this war as well, but the sergeant had told him to go home; or something a bit more colourful that meant the same thing.

His dad had told him all about fighting Germans. He'd shown him books of propaganda posters and even given him a German officer's spiked helmet. He'd told Reginald a slightly elaborated and heroic version of how he had obtained the helmet; which omitted all the elements relating to him just finding it.

Oh yes, Reginald knew how to fight Germans.

Would he need to know how to play a triangle?

Reginald pictured himself climbing out of a trench armed with a triangle.

'Oi Fritz… Take that!'

Ting.

Fritz was so surprised he almost lost his monocle. He checked his immaculate tunic for bullet holes, and finding none, he grinned under his waxed moustache, straightened his spiked helmet and advanced with bayonet fixed.

No, that wouldn't work concluded Reginald; he definitely would have no use for a triangle.

'Come on Scribbins, join the line,' said Mr Godbert bringing Reginald back to reality; 'up to the front of the queue lad.'

The class had quickly crossed the playground to the science block cloakroom, far too quickly for Reginald. He'd dragged his feet, but all that had got him was to the back of the queue, with Mr Godbert right behind him.

Reginald could hear the distant sound of planes coming from the south. He knew he would be safer in the shelter, but his fear of the shelter had grown over the last few weeks to the point where he was willing to take the risk. Going in the shelter was a certainty, but the bombs might miss.

The coats, thought Reginald as he entered the cloak room behind the others, perhaps I could hide in the coats.

'Come on Reginald,' said Mr Godbert directly behind him, 'it's never as bad as you think it's going to be.'

That's that plan scrubbed, thought Reginald.

Reginald and Mr Godbert stood at the top of the stairs. The rest of the class had disappeared round the corner onto the second flight.

William looked at his watch and descended three steps; Reginald didn't move. He watched as William stopped and looked back. In his mind Reginald could hear the big metal door closing. Fear pulled the blood from his face; he wanted to go to the toilet; and his knees wobbled threatening to give way. He didn't want to be down there, he wanted to be out in the open air, fighting.

William climbed back up and put an arm around Reginald's shoulders. Reluctantly Reginald allowed himself to be led down the first flight to the landing.

They turned the corner and were halfway down the second flight when William paused; he seemed to be thinking about something. Reginald paused with William, it gave Reginald some hope; perhaps the "all clear" would sound before they reached the shelter; and that hope brought him round a bit.

As they joined the back of the queue just outside the door into the shelter Reginald shuddered, time was running out for that "all clear". He looked through the big door to the shelter; in the patchy lighting beyond, he could see the silent faces as they looked back towards the door. Looking to his left, the lights in the cross tunnel headed in the direction of one of the main buildings. Reginald could see the T-junction not too far away. Where does it go after the junction? He didn't care, it meant freedom. He looked back at the silent faces, once again freedom would have to wait; there was never any choice.

William moved forward to find out what the holdup was; the lights flickered once, and then went out. The chorused voices of panic broke the silence, as the shockwave hit.

'SILENCE, everybody is to be quiet,' shouted William Godbert in a voice that could not be resisted. William Godbert might only have been a music teacher, but he had incredible presence. In fact he had so much presence that even the Headmaster went quiet.

'Only the lights have gone out. Will someone be good enough to light the oil lamp please,' continued William.

Somewhere near the door a match was struck and the oil lamp lit. A sea of dust covered faces looked back towards the door as William closed it behind him.

'Will tutors please take the registers,' said the Headmaster having recovered some of his composure. He listened to the names being called out and the echoed replies of "here". He found it reassuring.

Other members of staff were lighting candles and placing them around the walls; the dust that still hung in the air blurred the light creating a halo around each one.

The roll call was quickly concluded and the headmaster surveyed the large room that they were all packed into. He wondered if they should have a sing song to keep spirits up. He turned to William to ask him to organise it, but the expression on William's face told him that his mind was elsewhere.

'What's wrong William?'

William didn't reply, he had his eyes closed. The Headmaster was just about to speak again when William opened his eyes and looked around the shelter.

'Scribbins is missing,' said William, indicating his name on the register he was holding.

The Headmaster looked around the room, to make sure. 'Can't see him,' he said, but then again, he couldn't see anything in this light.

'Did anyone see where Reginald Scribbins went,' shouted William.

Heads shook, filling the air with more dust.

'I'll go out and look for him,' William said quietly to the headmaster.

The Headmaster nodded, he knew it was dangerous, but the boy was in William's charge, he had no choice and besides, he wasn't going to go out there.

When the lights had gone out, Reginald had heard a whispered voice; "go now", it had said. And Reginald had. He slipped unseen down the dark tunnel, in the general direction of away from the air raid shelter. He'd reached the T-junction just in time to hear the steel door close behind him. The air was warm, dry, and filled with dust from the shockwave. The heating pipes clicked in the darkness, and he found the whole ambience strangely comforting.

He stood at the junction trying to decide which way to go. To his left was blackness, blacker than anything Reginald had ever known. To his right there was less darkness. There was a faint glow coming from an open door at the end of a long tunnel; and he could hear a noise, it sounded like a big kettle boiling. Reginald turned right and carefully felt his way down the dark tunnel towards the glow.

At the end of the tunnel he entered the boiler room and peeped round the boilers, there was nobody there. Shadows danced on the walls in the faint light coming from the boilers which rumbled and fizzed. He could sense the constrained power; his pulse quickened, he took a deep breath and stuck out his chest, he had never felt so elated.

Turning to face the front of one of the boilers, he observed the gas flames through the arched opening underneath; and studied the controls on the front. A square glass tube labelled "Water level", a large brass pressure gauge and two stop cocks were the boilers only instrumentation. It was the most complex thing Reginald had ever seen in his life.

Something deep within his very being stirred; it was as if a knowledge that he had always known existed, a knowledge that until now had been hidden from him, had suddenly been revealed. Overwhelming forces took control of him; he was powerless to stop them. All his previous hopes and ambitions were forgotten; they belonged to a different person, a past life. His heart raced, his thoughts switched back and forth between something he felt compelled to do, and his analysis of why he felt compelled to do it. Reg had never done anything like this in his life before, so why was the urge so strong? How did he know it was the thing to do? Was it pure instinct? He gave in, ceased all resistance, and was swept along on a tide of compulsion.

With a trembling hand Reginald reached up, paused momentarily in front of the brass pressure gauge, and then tapped it once... twice... then a third time; and although Reginald didn't know it, had just taken his first step towards becoming Captain Cardigan.

Calming himself, he turned towards the other door in the boiler room and wondered where it went. He was halfway towards it when the shockwave from a second, much closer bomb, knocked him to his knees. The only light fitting in the room gave up any pretence that it was fixed securely to the ceiling and started its journey to the floor; pausing along the way to visit the top of Reginald's head with a loud crack.

Fortunately, Reginald had inherited from his father, the Scribbins' extra thick skull; it was to turn out to be the only useful thing he got from his father.

He didn't really feel the fitting hit his head, but he did see a flash of light as it struck. This was followed by a blurring of the floor, which also seemed to be moving rapidly towards him. His nose cushioned the impact with another crack.

The flames in the boiler burned higher and higher, accompanied by the whistle of gas as the pressure built to the point where it blew the flames out with a loud pop.

Reginald couldn't move, he could smell the gas and knew he should move, but his head was ringing like a kicked football and his arms and legs just wouldn't respond. He listened to the comforting sound of the pipes clicking in the dark as they had always done, and thought about where he'd left his gas mask.

He was slipping further away from the clicking pipes, but just before he lost consciousness he could have sworn that the pipes stopped clicking.

'Scribbins… Scribbins…' said the Headmaster's voice from what appeared to be some way off… in a room down a corridor… somewhere far away. 'What's his first name?'

'Reginald sir,' said a voice that seemed a bit nearer.

'Reginald…' said the Headmaster in a concerned tone of voice that Reginald had never heard before, but it was a concerned tone of voice that was much closer now, none the less.

'Reginald, are you all right?' The Headmaster's must have flown down that corridor because his voice was right by his ear.

Reginald opened his eyes and the Headmaster sat him up.

'How did you cut your head?'

'Something fell on me,' said Reginald looking round for it. Then he realised that he wasn't in the boiler room anymore, but outside the air raid shelter.

'How did I get here, sir?'

'You tell me. We opened the door when the all clear went, and there you were. Where have you been?'

'I don't remember getting here…' said Reginald who had recovered enough to be sick on the headmaster's shoes. Revenge isn't always sweet.

'Did you see Mr Godbert? He went looking for you,' said the headmaster, standing up and alternatively shaking his shoes.

'No sir. I didn't see anybody.'

*

Then as suddenly as he'd left, John was back by the window with Elleria. The watch was still in his hand. John stared at it.

His overriding impression was that of a very vivid dream. The amount of detail was incredible, the resolution far greater than normal eyesight. He'd sensed rather than saw; the graininess of the brickwork, the individual threads on a spider's web; it was like looking close up at things that were on the other side of a room.

What about the people? He certainly knew the music teacher, he'd seen photographs of him; it was Tom's father, William; the Grandfather John had never met. Tom never talked about his father and all John knew about him was that he was dead.

John had the feeling that he knew the teenager from the boiler room; he looked like someone he'd seen around but didn't really know. He looked like... almost got it... good grief... John suddenly realised it was Captain Cardigan; when he was young.

It had been like watching a film, a film which seemed to be about Captain Cardigan, about his thoughts and opinions. Who had made the film though? John already knew the answer, if fact he knew the answer before he'd thought of the question, the question just seemed to be his mind trying to justify knowing the answer. It was the watch; the whole thing was from the watches point of view, if watches could have a point of view that is.

He put the watch back in his pocket.

'All fixed,' Tom shouted through from the hall.

'What was it?' Paul shouted back.

'Just a blown fuse,' said Tom as Paul came though from the kitchen.

'How much do I owe you?'

'Nothing, call it a welcome to the neighbourhood present.'

'Are you sure?'

'Yes of course.'

Tom had a lot of friends, but he'd never be a millionaire.

'I'd better be going,' said John. He thought about adding; "can I see you again"; but somehow he just knew that he would.

'Thanks for showing me the watch,' said Elleria as John walked out of the room backwards, smiling as he went.

10

THE RESTING ACTOR

'Wait here,' said Burnston, as they arrived outside the Chinese takeaway next to Green and Son the pawnbrokers shop. Haystack, Boxhead and Clink watched Burnston disappear into the Pawnbrokers and then leered through the window of the closed takeaway hoping to see someone they could shout "Flied Lice" at. It didn't take much to amuse them.

The bell above the door jangled as Burnston entered the dimly lit shop. Martin was waiting just inside the door hidden in the shadows which he stepped back into as the light from the open door partially lit his face.

'You know what to ask,' said Martin. Burnston nodded and made his way past the shelves of bric-a-brac towards the counter at the back of the shop where Death himself appeared to be waiting. Burnston hesitated and looked back. Martin waved him forward. When he turned back to face the counter, Death had moved to one side to see who Burnston had been looking at, and now that his face was not illuminated from below, he looked normal.

'Can I help you Sir?' asked Jack as Burnston reached the counter. Regardless of age, all potential customers were either Sir or Madam.

'Yes, hopefully; you recently bought an item from Reg Scribbins, a watch I think it was.' Burnston was using his mother's Sunday voice; but it didn't do anything to lessen his scowl.

'Yes,' replied Jack cautiously.

'Do you still have it?'

'No I'm afraid I sold it on quite quickly.'
'That's a pity. Could I ask who you sold it to?'
'I'm afraid not, it wouldn't be fair on the new owner; particularly as it was bought as a present for his Grandson.'

Ten minutes later the bell on the shop door jangled as Burnston exited the pawnbrokers.

'Come on,' he said to the other three, who were still peering into the window of the takeaway, 'we've got to visit the printers and then we need to get you a little present each.' Haystack, Boxhead and Clink looked at each other and silently fell in behind Burnston.

Charles Amadeus Rosewood; resting actor and slightly camp proprietor of "Rosewood's School Outfitters est. 1950", was more than slightly alarmed when a large vicious looking youth and three cohorts entered the premises on the last day of the Easter holidays and halfway through his afternoon coffee. He observed that the large fat one had written "Manchester United" in biro on the front of his jacket; he'd spelt it wrong, missing out the "t" in Manchester. Charles groaned inwardly; somehow he got the impression this wasn't going to be a very good day.

Charles had opened the shop twenty-five years ago with a, "close personal friend" called Rupert, another resting actor. Charles had met Rupert the previous year during a production of Cinderella at the grandly named Theatre Royal, a small flea pit on Sussex Street. Rupert had been playing Buttons alongside Charles' Ugly Sister Two. Rupert had excellent stage presence and impeccable timing; and like Charles at the time; hair. Despite Rupert's acting abilities, he did have one slight flaw. When the audience shouted; "he's behind you". Instead of the traditional reply of; "oh no he's not"; Rupert had a tendency to squeal with delight and fix his hair. The result of this was; "Rosewood's School Outfitters est. 1950" for resting actors.

Charles sighed; he'd never really wanted to work in the shop. Since his serious acting career had entered a long rest period, interrupted once a year during the pantomime season, he'd wanted to be a fireman. The attraction, he told himself, was riding around in a big red fire engine with the sirens going and everyone getting out of the way. In reality, the attraction was firemen. And as Burnston entered the shop it brought about a renewed commitment to join the fire brigade at the earliest opportunity.

Charles was a fifty something man who believed that you are only as old as the stock photograph you submitted for the pantomime programme each year. A larger autographed copy of the soft focus, black and white photograph, showing a slim young man with dark wavy hair and a distant dreamy expression, was hung behind the counter.

The young man in the photograph was never brave, but he knew how to act. Charles recalled playing a vengeful god in London just after the war; "a gripping performance" was one of the reviews of the time; he still had the clipping in a scrapbook somewhere. Curiously the vicious one was holding a book called "Best Management Practices"; Charles wondered if he'd stolen it for a bet.

He drew himself up to slightly more than full size, bowed his head slightly so that his grey eyes were partially hidden by his brow, and stared at Burnston over the top of his half-moon glasses.

'Good morning gentlemen,' he boomed, his dark wavy toupee slipping forward slightly.

Burnston hadn't been in this shop since he was five when his mother had optimistically bought him a Penshaw Grove school cap. He'd been the only boy to have started school that year wearing a cap, and it was another contributory factor in determining the path that Burnston's life took. Now he was back; and in this quiet little shop Burnston was a fish out of water. He was caught completely off guard by the loud resonant stage voice coming from a man who appeared to be possessed by Satan himself; and there was something very strange about his hair. Burnston suspected concealed horns. He stopped well back from the counter.

'It says in the window,' Burnston paused, his gaze switching between the eyes and the hair, more "signs of evil", no wonder Martin wanted him to come here, they were all in league with each other like his mother kept saying. Those eyes kept staring, putting him off his stride; it was worse than Action. His associates sensed his nervousness and herded closer together for reassurance.

Burnston recovered enough to continue; but for the first time in years, he'd lost his scowl.

'It says in the window... that you... that you have a half-price sale,' said Burnston rushing the last part of the sentence.

Charles noted the disappearance of the scowl, and the merest flicker of fear cross the young man's eyes. Charles Amadeus Rosewood, he told himself; you've still got it. Charles raised an eyebrow and was intrigued by the amount of tension it generated.

'Yes, it's our stock clearance sale. Which particular school are you interested in?' The word "in" continued to reverberate around the shop; not an easy thing to achieve in a room full of clothing.

'Penshaw Grove?' replied Burnston as a question, those eyes continued to stare and he was no longer sure of himself,

Charles's eyes flashed. Burnston flinched and his associates shifted uneasily as they tried to hide behind him. Penshaw Grove, thought Charles, he didn't sell many uniforms for Penshaw Grove, especially not in these sizes; he wondered how many years he'd had the stock. He leaned forward over the counter; and as a group, Burnston and associates leaned back and held their breath.

'And how many uniforms would sir require?' asked Charles, never taking his eyes off Burnston.

'Four?' replied Burnston, hoping that this would please the evil one.

Charles leaned back; Burnston and associates moved back to the upright position and breathed out. This would go some way towards clearing the unsellable Penshaw Grove larger sized stock thought Charles. He wanted to leap around the shop shouting "whoopee", but years of self-control and toupee retention kicked in and he managed to restrict it to; raising his eyebrows slightly and smiling without showing his teeth. Burnston felt like a mouse that had just come face to face with a cat. He began to sweat.

A thought struck Charles.

'And how is sir paying for the goods?' he said leaning forward suddenly, causing the toupee to slip a bit further.

Burnston and associates; not having enough time to lean back; nearly jumped out of their collective skins. Burnston was the first to recover and without taking his eyes off Charles's hair, he bravely took a pace forward and carefully placed a hundred pounds on the glass counter.

'Excellent!' said Charles, cradling his fingers. Perhaps this was going to be good day after all.

11
PENSHAW GROVE

Normally John hated coming back to school after the holidays; it was that feeling of impending routine and the loss of spontaneity that he hated. Normally that is, but this Tuesday morning as he descended the steps into the playground he felt different, more analytical. He was comparing the school buildings to those he had seen when he met Elleria and there was very little difference. In fact the only noticeable difference was the colour of the doors; black in the dream, and orange now. There was however another variation, less tangible than door colour, less obvious; and it took John a moment or two to work it out. It was only when he realised that instead of the usual half remembered status of dreams, the memory he had of the school was crystal clear. In fact it didn't seem like a dream at all, it was more like being there. And what was really strange was when you compared the memory to reality; it was reality that was lacking. The real world, the here and now was somehow blurred.

John looked across to the science block and saw Frank leaning against the wall, arms folded, absentmindedly watching the goings on in the playground. It was as he made his way across the playground towards Frank that something caught his attention. There was something in the science block, up on the first floor. It wasn't an object, or a shadow, it was... John struggled to pick the right words... it was a round patch of difference. It was the best description he could come up with. John had almost reached Frank when he heard it; the thing was emitting a very quiet high pitched sound. It wasn't an irritating sound, it was too quiet, but once you knew it was there it was hard to ignore. John put his fingers in his ears; it didn't make any difference, the sound was in his head. Frank raised his eyebrows at the sight of John coming towards him with his fingers in his ears.

'What're you doing?' Frank asked.

John took his fingers out of his ears.

'What?'

'I said what are you doing?'

'Can't you hear that high pitched sound?'

Frank cocked his head on one side and listened.

'Well?' John asked.

Frank held up a hand to indicate "give me a moment" and concentrated…

John waited…

Frank turned his head to the left… and then to the right. Placed a finger in his ear and twisted it several times as if the clean his ear out. 'Ah!' he said raising his hand with his index finger extended as if he'd suddenly heard something; then he cocked his head to the left again and then paused as if deep in thought.

'No,' he said eventually.

'Oh,' said John, 'are you sure?'

'Yes.'

John leaned on the wall next to Frank to contemplate the coming day.

'You know,' said Frank breaking the silence between them, 'I hate walking through Penshaw Grove to get to school.'

John forgot about the sound.

'Why?' asked John. Although he suspected that it was the same reason that he hated walking through the area himself.

'Because it's so run down and scruffy, there's always broken glass on the roads,' said Frank with a hint of sadness in his voice.

'I know what you mean, boarded up houses and untidy gardens.'

'Untidy gardens, it's more like a jungle with houses.'

'What's like a jungle with houses,' said Scott arriving halfway through a conversation.

'This place,' said John.

Scott looked around the playground and scratched his head.

'Oh,' he said.

'Not the school, the school's alright,' said John.

'Apart from the open corridors,' said Frank.

'And the unheated toilets,' added John.

Scott scratched his head again, they'd completely lost him.

'No it's the area around the school; it's just so run down.'

'I suppose it is,' said Scott. 'I hadn't really noticed.'

'It used to be so nice here,' said Frank. 'It was the first council estate in Tameston where the houses had gardens.'

'Where do you get all this stuff from?' said Scott.

'What do you mean?' said Frank.

'You're always coming up with these little titbits of information. What was that you came up with the other day?'

'I don't know,' said Frank resigning himself to another of Scott's pointless tirades.

'What was it John, you remember… it was something about Sinbad.'

'Sinbad… Sinbad… I don't remember Sinbad,' said John trying to think. 'You don't mean St John do you?'

'Yes that's it, I remember now,' blurted Scott almost tripping over his tongue in his excitement. 'You said that "the correct pronunciation of the name St John is; Sinjen".'

'Well, that's the way it is pronounced,' said Frank indignantly.

'Yes, it probably is, but that's not the point.'

'What is the point?' Frank asked.

'The point… the point is where do you get all these bits of information from? Was I asleep during the lesson when they told us all these things or something?'

Frank and John looked at each other.

'Probably,' they said.

*

Penshaw Grove had been the first council estate in Tameston to have gardens. The town council of 1923 had pictured front gardens of roses and trimmed hedges, hemmed neatly behind small picket fences; and back gardens full of vegetables; an allotment on your doorstep.

By the summer of 1927 the construction of Penshaw Grove was complete. The uptake on the houses was total. And with every house occupied, every garden tended, and every hedge trimmed, the whole place radiated civic pride.

Slowly, with each passing generation, the civic pride evaporated. Hedges were left untrimmed for longer, and vegetables were no longer grown.

Eventually fences became firewood; gardens became wild and untamed, as did the children. The privet hedges grew to the size of houses, their twisted trunks forming a maze through which compacted mud paths weaved, the boundaries between properties blurred. Nettles and weeds filled the remaining spaces between the houses.

The most recently unoccupied of the houses were boarded up; the boards usually lasting until the autumn, when they became firewood. Dotted here and there between the occupied houses were the brick shells of houses that had been robbed of everything burnable. Ivy climbed the walls and brambles grew where families once sat listening to the radio. Civic pride a memory now for only some. Only the school retained some of that original pride and had survived the decline with decorum; despite a lack of heated toilets.

*

The playground had steadily filled up. With a constant stream of arrivals, one minute the playground was almost empty and the next it was full. Clothes ranged from the latest fashion items to denim jackets and coloured shirts; but not jeans, tee shirts or red socks. The wearing of red hosiery was not allowed; for some reason the headmaster had associated these items with an imaginary gang culture within the school and banned them. Last summer, at the start of the ban, Scott had defied the headmaster by wearing red socks under some grey ones; after two days of overheating his feet had become a walking anaesthetic, which resulted in another of John and Scott's arguments.

Making his way through groups of teenagers deep in conversation and teams of first years playing football with a tennis ball, was Action. He was generally heading towards John, Frank and Scott, but his journey was punctuated with some reverse walking and several stops as he turned to look back at the entrance. He seemed oblivious to the fact that he had just reversed into a group of girls and completely ignored their complaints as he looked back again as if expecting to see someone.

He finally arrived next to John and stood silently looking back at the entrance. For a few moments this did not attract much attention from the other three, but curiosity finally got the better of them and they all followed Action's gaze back to the entrance.

'Who's that?' said Action, sensing that they were all looking at the same thing.

There was a pause.

'That's Elleria,' said John eventually.

They all turned to look at John who suddenly felt a surge of importance.

It had not occurred to John when he met Elleria the first time that she would be going to his school. And now that she was here he felt a bit stupid that he hadn't mentioned her to his friends. However, his friends didn't know all that; so in this instance just knowing her name gave John immense power.

They all turned back to look at Elleria.

Elleria was talking to a group of girls near the entrance. In fact, Elleria was laughing and joking with them as if she had known them all their lives; but surely, John thought, they couldn't have met before.

John's friends continued to be silently fascinated by Elleria, and for good reason. Elleria had a gift for communicating with people that could pierce even the noisiest environment. And as she spoke now on the other side of the playground she commanded the full attention of John and his friends despite the fact that they couldn't hear her. Elleria's gift was not oratory in nature, but more related to semaphore. John hadn't noticed before, and was convinced that last time he'd talked to her, she hadn't done it. Yet there she was communicating on multiple levels; and like his friends John was mesmerized. For Elleria had a way of moving her shoulders and twisting her torso as she talked, that made it look like she was communicating with her chest.

Twist, left shoulder forward, right shoulder back, twist, twist, right shoulder up then down, body flex, hip swing to right; Elleria was broadcasting a message. Of course it was a matter of opinion, at this distance, as to whether her chest was saying the same thing as her voice; but then again, all art forms are open to interpretation.

John's friends watched in silence as each tried to interpret the message into one that involved Elleria in one of their fantasies. Left shoulder up, thrust, twist, flex torso, shoulders back and twist; Elleria's breasts wobbled slightly. John and his friends flinched collectively and then sighed. It was hypnotic to watch and quite arousing.

'And you know her?' said Action eventually, not taking his eyes off her.

John thought about his answer, he had plenty of time Action was not in any hurry for a reply. He could be "matter of fact" about her, using a statement like; "oh she's just moved in over the road". He could improve his status by implying that she was his girlfriend, but his friends were practised cynics and they wouldn't believe him.

Action might not have been in a hurry for a reply, but the silence of John's deliberating spoke volumes to him; it implied "secret relationship". Action was impressed, and that wasn't all; the others were impressed too.

'You're not saying much,' said Frank.

John didn't need to; Elleria looked over, beamed a huge smile, and waved frantically at John, causing some more communal flinching. John's heart leapt, he suddenly felt quite privileged; but what should he do? Waving back that enthusiastically wasn't the sort of thing he did, and what would his friends think about him waving back? Should he ignore Elleria? He didn't want to. Nor did he want to leave himself open to ridicule. He decided to raise his hand in acknowledgement, in what he hoped would be a style acceptable to his peers. John needed have worried.

'She's coming over,' said Scott; whose hands had already started to sweat and had finished the sentence an octave higher than he'd started it. John's status in the group had just gone up dramatically.

Elleria made her way through the crowd towards John and his friends who were now stood in a line to get a better view.

'Hello John,' said Elleria, leaning forward, kissing him lightly on the cheek and mesmerising his friends in the process, 'aren't you going to introduce me?' John waited for his face to burn red. He was more than amazed when it didn't, a fact that did not escape his peers. John's ranking was now unassailable.

'This is Elleria everyone, and this is Frank, Scott and Action,' said John indicating to each in turn. It was strange thought John, but despite how he thought he would feel, he was quite comfortable with the situation. The usual accusations of "under the thumb" or "abandoning your mates" that would usually be thrown at you where girls were concerned did not apply when the girl was as pretty and outgoing as Elleria.

'Hello boys,' said Elleria.

John's friends smiled and considered their replies. After weighing up all possible options, they each concluded that in this instance at least, Elleria's chest had said the same thing as her voice.

'Hello,' was their considered reply, which they communicated using voice only; except for Action who puffed out his chest first, in an attempt to make himself look taller; he had after all, owing to his height advantage, received the semaphore message before the auditory.

Elleria stood in front of them like an officer inspecting troops. Her head moved from left to right, and in the case of Action down as well, as she looked each one in the eye. Only John was capable of holding the eye contact for more than a few seconds, each one of his friends, including Action, had to look down almost immediately; with the exception of Scott who never looked up in the first place.

'Action,' said Elleria.

Action's eyes lit up; a truly splendid sight.

'Yes,' he said optimistically.

'Action is an unusual name, is it short for something?'

'Yes it's certainly short for something,' said Frank.

'Thanks Frank,' said Action deflating his chest but remaining the same height.

Scott cleared his throat and Elleria turned to look at him.

'It's short for...,' Scott started, but it was no use; his voice went up through the octaves and beyond the range of human hearing. Scott's face burned red and he had to look down again.

'… Action Gnome,' finished Frank, 'it's short for Action Gnome.'

There was a clink of metal as Captain Cardigan, grey cloak fluttering behind him; appeared round the corner of the science block with his shopping bag full of tools. In his wake like a grey shadow was Kevin.

'So, can I have fifty pence then,' said Kevin to his father.

'Forty pence… what do you want thirty pence for?' This was Reg's stock answer to requests for money. Reg liked to stick with regular sayings as well as regular thoughts and he chuckled quietly to himself as he said it.

Kevin stopped next to Action and let his father continue into the science block, he knew when he was beaten.

'You'll never guess what I've just seen,' he said to the others.

12
YESTERDAY'S CROSSROADS

Reg made his way up the stairs towards the chemistry lab whistling a tune he'd heard on the radio that morning. He'd felt sure the song would have been one of Kevin's favourites and had called him into the room to listen. He was quite surprised to learn that Kevin had never heard of either the song or the artist before. The fact that it was popular twenty years ago had completely passed Reg by; as, apparently, had the last twenty years.

As he unlocked the storeroom door outside John's tutorial room, he tried to remember what he had been doing for the last twenty years. Well, he'd thought about monocles and waxed moustaches a lot, raised three kids, and worked here at the school. And there was that day trip to the seaside a few years ago, on the train with the wife and kids; with Kevin being sick on the way back. Reg paused to reflect on the simplicity of his unadventurous life; and wondered how he'd managed to fit it all in.

Reg placed his tool bag in the centre of the room, folded his arms and admired his handiwork. The new shelving he'd built yesterday only needed to be fixed back to the wall and then it was finished. There was something about this room, something about the sensation you got when you were in it. It seemed to bring back memories, not that the memories ever really went away, they just seemed more real here, closer, as if they'd happened only yesterday. Reg had noticed it when he was building the shelves; old thoughts and hopes that he hadn't dwelled on since he was a teenager; thanks to his regime of standard regular thoughts; had gently entered his mind. As the shelves neared completion the sensations had grown, until at one point he felt as though he was back in the woodwork room receiving praise for his dovetail jointed money box. Reg still had the money box; and it was still empty.

Now as he stood looking at the completed shelves, he had the strongest desire to ask Irene Todd to the pictures. When Reg was still at school Irene had caught his attention. She was dark haired and pretty, and whenever he looked in her direction she always appeared to be looking in his; she would shyly turn away and then glance back surreptitiously.

Reg pushed his cap back and scratched his forehead; which these days extended almost to the back of his head, sighed, and wondered what she was doing now. Well today was Tuesday, so she would be at home putting bleach in the washing machine. There were some opportunities that Reg hadn't let pass him by.

Click, click, click, click; Reg could hear the steel tipped shoes coming up the stairs. Click, click; the tone of the clicking changed as the wearer reached the half landing; and then changed back to the original tone for the final flight. The shoes belonged to Harry Fleming, who did not believe in unnecessary change; hence the metal on the soles of his shoes, which not only prolonged the wear of the shoes, but also informed the culpable of his approach. Harry Fleming was Penshaw Grove School's only living legend.

Harry Fleming was amongst the first intake of pupils at Penshaw Grove School in September 1927. He was the only former pupil ever to have gone on to receive a university education. Harry managed to complete his degree in industrial chemistry just in time for the outbreak of World War Two where it was of absolutely no help whatsoever. He spent the war jumping out of aeroplanes over France and Holland, eventually returning to the school to teach in September 1946. Only the Headmaster, whose subject had been history, had taught at the school longer, and that was only by two hours.

The Headmaster and Harry made a formidable team. The Headmaster having had the advantage of an education somewhere other than Penshaw Grove, a private school in York, could process paperwork and understand Board of Education directives without breaking into a sweat. Unfortunately his education put him at a serious disadvantage when it came to understanding the psychology of the indigenous Penshaw Grove populace. Mr Fleming on the other hand, had no such problems, but he hated paperwork. The Headmaster referred to Mr Fleming as his storm trooper; a term, given Harry's wartime experiences could be considered as an insult, but Harry knew what the Headmaster meant and didn't mind. The headmaster had spent his war in Stalag VII-A, southern Bavaria after being wounded in France when with the British Expeditionary Force.

Physically, Mr Fleming could be described as having a dominant presence. He was tall, broad and had the sort of craggy, lived in face you'd expect to find on a battle hardened paratrooper. His eyes were cold, grey and calculating. He commanded a great deal of respect, mainly because he didn't give anyone any other options. The thing that Harry Fleming did not look like was the very thing that he actually was, a chemistry teacher.

The long hard years of teaching at Penshaw Grove had taken their toll, but Mr Fleming loved this job and he was determined to see it through to retirement despite his medical problem. It wasn't the teaching aspect of the job that kept him going; it was the battle of wits he fought with the pupils, the little cat and mouse games that he enjoyed so much.

'Morning Reginald,' said Mr Fleming. Reg turned towards the door.

'Morning Mister Fleming, Sir.'

'I've told you before Reg, call me Harry, I've never been your teacher.'

'Sorry Mister... Harry.'

'How are the new shelves coming along?' said Harry walking towards them.

'Nearly done Sir... sorry; Harry.'

'Good,' said Harry examining the shelves. 'This really is excellent work; you should have been a carpenter.'

'A wood butcher Sir, oh I couldn't see myself as that Sir, I'm just an odd job man.'

Harry raised his eyebrows at the "Sirs'" but decided to say nothing. He turned to the tarnished brass instruments which filled the old shelves on the opposite side of the room.

'What's happening with this lot,' said Harry, indicating the instruments.

'Nothing, as far as I know,' replied Reg. He remembered that he helped put the instruments on those shelves after William Godbert was killed and he'd tried to avoid touching them ever since. He swallowed hard; the thought that the last person to touch these instruments was probably him, had just struck home. Reg was unaccustomed to new thoughts.

Reg watched Mr Fleming pick up a triangle and flinched slightly.

'I used to play one of those.' said Reg. Memories were flooding back, washing over him like a warm sea breeze. 'I suppose that meant I was hopeless at music; like everything else.'

'You weren't useless at everything; you shouldn't put yourself down so much. You've always been good at woodwork.'

'Hasn't done me that much good though, has it?'

'That's because you didn't push your abilities; you should have got an apprenticeship. I can remember having a similar conversation with William Godbert, your old music teacher, when I was fifteen. It was him that convinced me that I should grab life by the horns. It was William that inspired me to become a teacher. I am surprised he didn't have a chat with you. He always tried to talk to each of his pupils.'

'Ah well he was killed,' said Reg. 'I feel a bit guilty about it, because apparently he had gone looking for me during an air raid. I seem to remember being in the boiler room. And anyway although we didn't have a talk, I get the feeling that this is what Mr Godbert would have told me to do.'

'Speaking of dying, I was in the pub last night talking to someone who works up at the hospital and he told me that Jack Green was found dead at the pawnbrokers yesterday.'

'Dead,' said Reg, swallowing hard as he remembered the strange conversation he had in the boiler room, 'how?'

'That's what's so curious; apparently they could find no cause of death. No physical problems and there was no poison in his system. Other than the fact that he was dead, he was in good health. The safe was open but there was still a lot of money in it; the police don't know what to make of it.'

'Did you know him well?'

'Yes, I did; we were at school together, and then later we were in the parachute regiment during the war. We spent the last few months fighting with the Dutch resistance. He was a brilliant soldier, a good man to fight alongside. I always thought he'd stay on after the war, but he decided to go back to the family shop. He was my age too. Makes me feel very mortal, I can tell you.'

Harry turned to make his way towards the chemistry laboratory that had been his domain for thirty years; but paused in the storeroom doorway. He looked back at Reg. 'And by the way Reg; I used to play the triangle as well,' he said, and then disappeared into his laboratory leaving Reg with that last thought.

*

Mr Fleming stood, hands behind his back, looking down out of the window, at the scruffy, greasy haired populous of Penshaw Grove School and wondered what life had in store for them. Would any of them surpass the social status achieved by Reg Scribbins? Would any of them reach it?

His thoughts meandered back to his own youth and how inspiring William Godbert had been. He wondered if John would ever break out of his peer grouping and rise to the point of actually showing some promise; sadly there had been no indication so far that he would. Still, he thought, not exactly John's fault; you don't inherit inspiration, you have to be shown it. He recalled other people, faces and names rising out of the fog of the past and evaporating in the light of the present.

It was only the shortest of glimpses, just long enough to raise some concern, but not long enough to confirm the truth of whether he had he really seen it or not. Hands on the window ledge Harry leaned forward trying to get another look, but they'd already gone. The last time he'd seen the like, if he could believe his own eyes, was over twenty years ago. Perhaps he was hallucinating. Oh dear God, he thought, he could understand the fatigue, he just wasn't used to standing as much; but he had no idea that haemorrhoids could cause hallucinations.

*

The bell rang and the playground began to empty as pupils filed into the buildings.

Frank looked at Kevin as they entered the cloakroom at the bottom of the stairs; 'Burnston? Seriously?' he asked.

'Yes, and Haystack, Boxhead and Clink,' replied Kevin.

'And they were all the same?' said John as they started to climb the stairs.

'They were like twins.'

'There are four of them,' said Frank.

'Well you know what I mean.'

'If that's what you saw, said Action doubtfully. 'Where were you when you saw them?'

'I was down near the shed and I saw them coming in the entrance,' said Kevin.

'So you were up at the other end of the playground then,' said Scott cynically.

'Well yes, but there's no mistaking Burnston; or what they were wearing.'

As they rounded the corner in the stairs John looked at Elleria who smiled back at him. John smiled and then noticed the same quiet high pitched sound that he'd heard before. He had the impression that it hadn't really gone away at all, he'd just forgotten to listen to it, but now it seemed a bit louder and it grabbed his attention again. At the top of the stairs John saw that the door to the storeroom was open, he'd never seen inside that room before and by coincidence it also seemed to be where the sound was coming from. He paused by the door for a look.

To the left of the door there were dust covered brass instruments stacked chaotically on some old shelves. To the right, Captain Cardigan was busy working with a screwdriver fixing one side of some new shelves to the wall. The room smelt of tarnished brass and Captain Cardigan; who had a sort of oily, boiler room aroma. And there was something else in the room. At first John couldn't make anything out, he just sensed that there was something there. Then he saw, just to the left of the window against the background of the wall, a thin curved line just slightly brighter than the wall itself. John followed the curve of the line and although in places it was difficult to make out, it formed a sphere of about two metres in diameter. There was no doubt it was this sphere that was quietly emitting the high pitched tone. What on earth is it? The question John asked himself was rhetorical, and he certainly wasn't expecting an answer. So he was slightly taken aback when the following writing appeared in front of his eyes.

Ref: 334-5-749-0-172-495-34
Tunnel Technical Reference
A tunnel is a method of jumping forward in time. Owing to the frequency at which Euclidean space time operates, the jump period is fixed at fifty years to an accuracy of plus or minus twelve hours. The entrance to the tunnel remains at a fixed point in time, whilst the exit moves forward through time from its initial point of egress. In order to create a tunnel the creator needs to be in burst mode.

Reg was still brooding over lost opportunities and cursing his lack of adventure. Jack Green's death was a bit of a wakeup call. Holding the screwdriver in place, he paused his turning. 'Jack Green dead,' he said out loud. He shook his head slowly and then resumed turning, taking his frustrations out on the screw he was currently fixing; he was only talking to him the other day and now he's gone. Why hadn't he looked into broadening his horizons?

'Because you were appointed as "The Keeper" and that task outweighed all others. You are now released from that role.' The voice was whispered, like leaves in a breeze, but it was clear and it unmistakably came from behind. Reg turned around to find John standing in the doorway apparently staring into space.

'What did you say son?'

The writing in front of John's eyes vanished as Reg spoke.

'Sorry,' said John, 'I was miles away then; did you ask me a question? Something about Jack Green being dead?'

'No I was just thinking out loud. So you didn't say anything about me being appointed as "The Keeper" then?'

Ref: 998-8-999-0-998-95-36

The Keeper

Chosen by Amantarra to be the guardian of the data portion of the Node on planet earth, Reginald Scribbins is not aware of his appointed role.

This was too much, thought John; perhaps I'm going mad. He looked Reg straight in the eye.

'You're The Keeper,' stated John, immediately wishing he'd said it as a question.

This was all connected John realised; the dream he'd had when he met Elleria, this invisible sphere and these messages that keep popping up. Reg was looking at him strangely as if he were waiting for an explanation. If Captain Cardigan wasn't aware that he was The Keeper, then John had probably given the game away. How was he going to get out of this one? And who was Jack Green?

'What team?' It was Scott who'd spoke; he'd been standing quietly behind John with Frank and Elleria.

'Oh… is that what you mean, no, there's no team.' said Reg noticing Elleria for the first time. Elleria smiled at him.

'I don't even play, well not anymore, ' he said looking directly at Elleria as if it were important that he should explain this fact to her. John was relieved that Reg's question seemed to have been neatly side stepped; but he was also slightly curious, and what did it mean that Reg was "The Keeper".

Reg squatted down to get another screw out of his shopping bag and John saw the grill partially hidden behind the new shelves. Something clicked; John didn't know why, but somehow he got the impression that the grill was significant to everything that was happening. He took a step into the storeroom for a better look. Immediately the high pitched sound dropped in pitch. John turned to look at the sphere, the wall behind it had changed colour.

'Dark green?' said John involuntarily.

'Yes, that's what colour this room used to be when I was a lad,' said Reg as he stood up; 'you spotted the bit I missed near behind the old shelves, did you?'

'Old shelves,' said John slowly as he tried to work out what Reg meant. Reg pointed. It looked as if Reg had painted the wall without moving the brass instruments at all, painting round the ones that were nearest the wall leaving little splashes of paint on each instrument. 'Yes, that's right.' Reg looked more or less happy with that explanation.

John looked back at the sphere; the green wall behind it almost matched the bits Reg had missed; it differed in that the wall in the sphere looked fresh and not as faded. John stepped back to the doorway. The colour of the wall through the sphere returned to normal and the sound rose up to the pitch it was at before. John turned to Scott to see if he was showing any signs that he was seeing the same thing. He didn't appear to be. Scott rolled his eyes and mouthed "painted round them" indicating the brass instruments, 'can you believe it?'

They turned and made their way into the chemistry laboratory for tutorial.

John still had unanswered questions and once again contemplated the insanity angle. He had done it many times before when he lost a game because he hadn't seen how Scott was cheating. This time however the evidence seemed to indicate that perhaps he was losing it. Then again, having had that thought, he couldn't possibly be insane because, as Scott reasoned, people who are insane don't know that they are, therefore, if you think you're insane, then you're not. You couldn't fault the logic; not from someone as insane as Scott anyway.

Reg started work again and reflected on what Harry had said. It was strange, but in this small storeroom Reg felt as though that inspirational chat with William was not lost, that it was still to come. He touched the scar on his head where the light fitting had hit him; it seemed a bit more sensitive than normal, as if he'd only just done it. He felt the optimism and potential of his youth returning, the future still looming before him as if he were fifteen again. It took a fair amount of effort to drag his thoughts back to the here and now, was it really thirty six years ago? It felt like yesterday. Reg's feelings of guilt over William's death were stronger now than they had been for years; was that the reason why Reg didn't like change, why he always strove to keep things the same? Why he couldn't even bare to touch the brass instruments, even to move them while he was painting? He lamented the lost potential of his youth; so much opportunity, so many paths to take, all gone now, all lost to the years. A momentary flicker of resentment flashed through Reg's thoughts; he should have at least looked at those opportunities.

Reg had reached an epiphany, and although such words were beyond Reg's understanding; he was about to make a life changing decision. "Grab life by the horns", that's what William had told Harry, and that's what I should do now; no more waiting, I've put this off long enough. Reg thought about the consequences of his decision and waited for his brain to decide against it like it always did. But this time it was different; he felt changed, somehow released; and finally with a determination that was alien to him, he committed himself to a dramatic course of action. After lunch he was going to change the bulb in the boiler room.

13
CORPORATE IMAGE

The chaos of the Art room was an expression of Stefan the Art master's struggle to balance the non-conformity of his artistic ideals with the conventions of his profession. Around the room on shelves, window ledges and the tops of cupboards there were unfinished papier-mâché sculptures painted in garish colours; pencil drawings of sheep skulls and still life studies of bowls of fruit that were slightly more abstract than the students had intended. The explosion of colour and random placing of the pieces represented the non-conformist side of Stefan's existence; the other side being represented by neatly arranged jam jars full of paintbrushes sitting in the centres of the work tables, stacks of white dinner plates used as pallets and tubs of powder paint; all precisely positioned and clean. On the wall behind his desk was a charcoal drawing of the playground. Stefan had crafted in his first week at the school. He'd had it framed as an example to the pupils of what could be achieved. He touched the frame every day for inspiration. Stefan had been christened Steven, but thought that Stefan had a more artistic resonance to it.

One table tucked away in a corner, was partially isolated from the rest of the room by a makeshift washing line hung with tie-dyed cloths of blue, yellow and green concentric circles. Around the table there were six chairs with four occupants. The book "Best Management Practices" that had been specially "acquired" for him by Clink, thus reinforcing his image as the intellectual of Burnston's three associates; was resting on a brown paper parcel in front of

Burnston. Burnston had told Clink that he could pay for the book, but Clink had refused, saying that he "preferred to do things the old fashioned way". Haystack, Boxhead and Clink watched fascinated as Burnston turned a page and continued reading. It wasn't that they hadn't seen it before; it's just that they had never taken much notice before. They were only taking notice now because it was Burnston doing the reading; that, and they were curious about the contents of the brown paper parcel the book was resting on.

Burnston noticed the curiosity in their faces, closed the book and put it to one side. He spun the parcel round, carefully opened one end of it and separated three sheets from a stack of printed forms. As he pulled the sheets out of the parcel a business card came out with them; it had the word "sample" written on the back. Burnston handed a form to Haystack, Boxhead and Clink who each looked at them with bemused curiosity. Burnston turned the business card over, read it and then flipped it, holding it out so that the others could see it. Clink focused on the card.

'The Lendus,' he read out loud impressing Haystack and Boxhead.

'Seemed appropriate,' said Burnston.

Boxhead looked at Burnston, 'a... what?' he asked, unable to complete the word.

'Appropriate,' repeated Burnston. Boxhead looked at Clink, who shrugged.

'Means, suitable for the situation,' added Burnston.

'Oh,' said Clink, 'I thought it meant to steal stuff.'

'Well it can do, it depends on the context in which it's used,' continued Burnston.

Boxhead looked as though he was going to ask what "context" meant, silently mouthing the word a few times before giving up. All this thinking had left him drained.

Burnston slipped the card into the top pocket of his blazer and turned his attention to the package. He pulled another of the forms out for himself and indicated that the others should look at the forms in front of them. Haystack regarded the form with the same blank expression he used for any printed material. Boxhead made an effort by placing a finger under the first word and silently moving his lips as he moved his finger across the page. It was a valiant effort which ended when he reached the word "perpetuity". Clink was the first to comment.

'This is complicated,' he said reading the first paragraph again. 'I don't understand a word of it. What does it mean?'

'It's written in legalese, so it's not supposed to be understood. All you have to do is write their name at the top and get them to sign the bottom.' Burnston looked at Haystack and revised his instructions. 'All you have to do is get them to write their names at the top and sign the bottom.' He watched as they each picked out the places at the top and bottom of the form.

'How come,' said Boxhead as he turned the paper over repeatedly just to make sure, 'the front of the paper is white and the back is pink?'

'That's because the pink is a carbon copy. Whatever is written on the front;' Burnston wrote a small cross on the corner of the form he was holding and peeled back the corner of the white sheet; 'appears on the pink sheet. Once they've signed it you peel off the pink sheet and give it to them; the pink sheet is their copy of the agreement.'

'So,' started Haystack, 'they write their name;' there was a pause as he analysed the term signature; 'twice;' he concluded, this was actually quite good for him; 'then I give them the pink bit.'

'Yes,' replied Burnston his voice full of admiration and pride.

'So,' continued Haystack, 'what happens to the white bit?' With that question Haystack had raised his game to a new level, Burnston almost burst with joy.

'You keep the white bits and then you give them to me. Don't worry I'll show you how it's done during this morning's break. Gentlemen,' continued Burnston, 'you are now officially members of "The Lendus", or "Team Lendus" if you like.'

'Team Lendus,' said Clink, 'I like the sound of that.'

Stefan, the Art master and Burnston's tutor, made his entrance. His long black hair flowed out behind him as he breezed across the Art room towards his desk. Stefan's dark eyebrows curved up and then pointed down towards his nose mirroring his receding hairline which came to a point in the centre of his forehead. He was short, round and jolly; his chubby face sported a goatee beard and a permanent smile. Above his rosy cheeks his dark eyes gleamed and sparkled like black diamonds and he always wore black shirts. A cross between Santa Claus and Satan, it was an image that worked because everyone liked Stefan, including Burnston.

Stefan, always a master of the dramatic reached his desk. If he'd worn a cloak he would have swirled it off with great panache at this point, spinning it onto a hat stand, and then he would have stood with his arms out to the side and taken a bow. But he didn't have a cloak, or a hat stand, so he took off his fraying sleeved, leather elbowed corduroy jacket and hung it on the back of his chair with as much panache as can be achieved with a corduroy jacket.

'Morning all,' he said, waving his arms in the air. Although lacking the showmanship of the cloak thing, it had the same effect. Stefan became the centre of attention.

Stefan was one of those rare creatures that you occasionally stumble across in the course of your life; he was a teacher who never had to control a class. He never had to control it because the class wanted to know what he knew, and those eyes said that he knew everything. If you misbehaved or abused his trust, then you risked not finding out what he knew. Or, in Burnston's case you risked being; "Dammed for all eternity".

Stefan sat and started to call the register.

'Adams?'

'Here.'

'Brown?'

'Sir.'

'Burnston?'

'Sir.'

Stefan paused.

'Is that our school uniform you're wearing?'

'Yes Sir,' replied Burnston.

'Any reason why?'

Burnston pulled out a notebook from his jacket pocket; flipped back a couple of pages and ran a finger down over phrases like:

- Know your market. What sort of person is your product or service aimed at?

- The preparation of a business plan is essential.

- The business plan should incorporate a cash flow forecast, which should include all costs, including professional fees and charges.

- The representatives of a company need to project the correct corporate image.

Burnston looked up and fixed Stefan with a steady gaze that he hoped would convey professionalism, confidence and respect.

'Projecting the correct corporate image, Sir,' he replied.

'You're trying to project a corporate image?'

'Yes Sir.'

'Well it certainly projects an image, but I'm not sure that it projects the correct one, or a corporate one for that matter. Never the less you do look very smart.'

'Thank you Sir.'

'Not as smart as me in my corduroy jacket of course,' he paused to see if anyone got the joke.

But Burnston didn't get it and no one else wanted to interrupt Burnston's conversation with laughter.

The wind murmured in the following silence.

'No Sir,' said Burnston eventually breaking the silence.

Stefan sighed and carried on with the register.

Haystack, Boxhead and Clink, who at first were unsure about the school uniforms were beginning to feel quite important now. The psychology of the corporate image really does work; it was working on Stefan now. As he continued to call the rest of the register, he had the distinct feeling that he'd just witnessed an epic moment in history. He had in fact witnessed the birth of an empire.

14
THE UNBREAKABLE BOND

Mr Fleming was stood at the front of the class with his hands behind his back waiting for the room to settle down. He did a lot of that these days; standing that is; waiting for pupils to settle down didn't present him with a problem. Mr Fleming didn't consider himself a teacher, as far as he was concerned he was a "School Master" and the difference, he would tell anyone who asked, was discipline. With discipline firmly in place you had a good foundation on which to teach, without it, teaching was impossible. Mr Fleming didn't like all the contemporary free thinking self-expression ideas that were going around these days; he regularly walked past classes where the pupils were expressing themselves, and there didn't appear to be a great deal of teaching going on. Mr Flemings no nonsense approach to teaching had given him a reputation that meant he did not have to work on keeping order at all; and today he was more than thankful for that reputation because he didn't feel at all well. He felt so tired; his haemorrhoids were giving him more twinges than normal and he was convinced that he was seeing things, or at least seeing uniforms, specifically Burnston. Not that he was going to let any of those concerns show, that wouldn't do at all. He knew what would cheer him up, and it had been a while since he'd tried the trick, so memories would be faded enough for him to get away with it. This lunch time, he promised himself. Mr Fleming smiled a secret little smile. There, he thought, he was feeling better already. And as if to brighten up his day a little further, he'd just spotted the new girl Elleria arriving; she was like a ray of sunshine on a dull day.

Scott made his way between the four large benches towards his usual place on the front right bench and perched himself on one of the stools. With Elleria just behind him John hesitated between the back and the front benches. Where was Elleria going to sit? For some reason felt a responsibility for her, that he had some obligation to look after her; even though she didn't seem to need looking after; a point that was made evident when John noticed that she was attracting a great deal of interest amongst his male classmates. Wherever Elleria went it seemed, she would always have someone willing to help her, or at least leer at her. John felt a pang of jealousy; then shook his head, that was silly, she didn't belong to him, nor he to her, and it was only the second time they'd ever met, so what on earth was he thinking these stupid thoughts for. But still, she did look a bit like a damsel in distress; actually no, he thought, she looked as confident as ever. Alright, John admitted to himself, so it's me that wants her to be in distress so that I can show everybody that I know her by coming to her rescue. He turned to her.

'Do you know where you're sitting?' he asked.

'I thought I'd sit near you. If you don't mind that is.'

'Yes, I mean no; of course I don't mind,' said John indicating two spare stools near Scott. Elleria smiled at John as they sat and John noted that the leering had stopped with the exception of Action who seemed absolutely fascinated by her.

'Thanks,' she said.

Mr Fleming cleared his throat. This was his usual practice before attempting to quieten a classroom. Like the clicking of his shoes it provided that extra little bit of warning to those who perhaps thought the rules had stopped applying.

As John turned to look at Mr Fleming; thereby proving that the throat clearing did actually work; he momentarily felt his body crawl with pins and needles, it reminded him that the same thing had happened at Elleria's house. It was followed by the same deep silence. Mr Fleming's throat clearing didn't usually have that much effect, it normally only resulted in the slow winding down of the conversations; but this silence pulled at John's ears making them hurt. Even in the quietest places there is always noise; the rumble of distant traffic, the murmur of the wind through gaps in the windows, the rustle of clothes, or the click of metal pipes changing temperature; but this silence had none of that. Instinctively John yawned to try and make his ears pop; but the silence prevailed.

'I've gone deaf,' John said to Scott. In time honoured tradition, this was the cue for Scott to say "pardon", but he didn't react. Scott was frozen like a statue. John tried again, 'Scott... what's going on mate?' John nudged him in the ribs with his elbow, but it was like hitting a brick wall and it hurt. John rubbed his elbow and tried gently moving the sleeve of Scott's jacket where it hung below his wrist; it was as if it had been carved from granite.

John looked across the bench at Frank; he was frozen in the act of moving a stool so he could sit down. There was a girl behind Frank with a surprised look on her face. She'd dropped a book; it was suspended in mid-air, the pages frozen in the act of fluttering. Beyond the girl, outside the window there was a bird hanging motionless in the air. Hovering between a dripping tap and the sink was a drop of water; it sparkled as the light caught it.

What about Elleria?

The stool next to John was empty. She'd been there a moment ago; how could she have disappeared so quickly. John slid off his stool and tried to push it backwards, but the stool wouldn't move no matter how hard he pushed it. Giving up he squeezed between his and Elleria's stools and stood looking around the room. Everyone was frozen, some sitting, some standing, and some were... John couldn't work it out, but Action; who was situated on the other side of the bench to John and was staring directly at Elleria, or at least where Elleria had been; seemed unusually elevated. John looked at the girl who'd dropped the book, she was looking at Action; and had obviously noted his new vertical status. What was Action doing? It clearly wasn't anything as simple as standing on a stool, that wouldn't surprise anyone into dropping a book. Maybe, John speculated, he was stood on someone; but John couldn't imagine who.

There was something else, a sort of sensory conflict. John could see the people in the room, but he could also feel his mind touch them as if he were reaching out with his hands. He could sense some things that he couldn't see. The sphere thing in the storeroom for one, and there were mice living under the raised platform Mr Fleming was stood on. The conflict John was getting between his old and new senses was that his new sense told him that Elleria was sat down exactly where she had been and clearly she wasn't.

Or was she? John tilted his head to one side.

Like the outline of the sphere, thin and only slightly brighter than the surroundings there was an outline of Elleria. John moved closer, now that he knew it was there, it was easier to see. He touched the ghostly outline on the shoulder and silver grey ripples spread out from his finger and around Elleria's outline crisscrossing each other as they wrapped around her body. John noted her breasts just as the ripples faded and touched her shoulder again for a better look.

'THAT'S MY PLACEMARKER.'

In the silence, Elleria's voice was like a thunder clap. John nearly jumped out of his skin particularly given what he was looking at.

'Bloody hell!' he exclaimed banging his chest with the flat of his hand. John looked around, he still couldn't see her. 'Where are you?'

Elleria peeped round the mop of blonde hair under which Action resided, an act which would not normally be possible given the usual altitude of Action's hair.

'Sorry, didn't mean to make you jump,' she said.

'That's alright,' he said waiting for his heart to slow down, 'I'm just glad you're still here, you just seemed to vanish.'

'I know you've probably got a thousand questions,' said Elleria as John made his way round to other side of the bench, 'and I'll explain everything in a moment, but I need to ask you one question first.' He looked around at the frozen room; thinking, what could be more important than explaining all this? As he arrived next to her she gazed up into his eyes and smiled.

'Sorry,' she said, 'but I really need to know the answer to this question. I hope you don't mind.'

'No, of course I don't. What is it?'

'It's this,' Elleria indicated Action, "what on earth is he doing?'

'Oh,' said John expecting a different sort of question, possibly involving him and a relationship of some sort with Elleria. Oh well he thought, never mind. He took a step back and studied Action's frozen form. 'Well,' he said stroking his chin, 'it looks like he's doing a scissor jump.'

Action was at the apex of his jump; his right leg straight out in front, foot pointing in line; and his left leg behind, foot similarly positioned. His legs were almost horizontal putting a severe strain on the seat of his trousers.

'It's actually very impressive,' said Elleria. She followed Actions gaze. 'He's staring straight at where I was sitting; you don't think he was trying to impress me do you?'

John thought about the amount of leering that Elleria had invoked when she'd entered the laboratory and sighed. 'Yes, I think he probably was; but don't let him know because you'll never be rid of him. Unless that's what you want of course.'

Elleria looked at Action for a few more seconds, and then lost interest. She turned to John and looked him straight in the eyes. 'No John, that isn't what I want; the bond is between you and me.'

'Bond?'

'I'll explain it all in a moment,' said Elleria pushing her hair back out of her eyes. 'First things first, the question you're dying to know the answer to is: "Why is everything frozen?" Am I right?'

'Yes,' said John.

'Well, it's not; it only appears to be frozen. Relative to us, time is moving very slowly; I have merely pulled us outside of normal time and speeded us up.'

'Oh,' said John, but before he could ask his next question Elleria spoke.

'How?' she said.

'Yes,' replied John, 'how… or possibly why?'

'Why; that's a good question as well,' said Elleria.

'It was,' said John, 'but it doesn't sound like the sort of question I would normally think of to ask.'

'What do you mean?'

'Not sure, but it was almost as if there was something in my head that prompted me to ask the question.'

Elleria thought for a moment. 'Well this is an unusual situation; in fact not only has it never happened before, but I'm sure it's supposed to be impossible. I'm sure we'll discover all sorts of strange things as we go along.' She looked at the confusion on John's face. 'Let me try and clarify a few things first.'

John watched her as she talked; studying her face, the soft downy hair that was visible along the edge of her cheek, the fullness of her lips and the way she blinked slowly, covering and uncovering those brown eyes which seemed to glow with a warm inner light. There was something different about her as well, but he couldn't quite place what it was.

'My primary function as a Radgarc is to…' continued Elleria. As she said the word "Radgarc" the following flashed up in front of John, superimposing itself on his field of vision.

Ref: 327-2-716-1-481-002-17

Radgarc

Intelligent Avatars created to be independent from Valheel. They differ from the Guardians of Valheel in that they have the capability of functioning in corporeal space and they do not draw any energy from the city. Their primary function is Node management and they draw power from the Nodes under their control.

'Manage Nodes,' finished John. Elleria stopped talking in amazement.

'How did you know that?'

'I don't know. I keep getting these flashes of information. They just sort of pop up if front of my eyes. The first one I had was when we first met; it was like a short film set during the Second World War about Captain Cardigan and my Grandfather.'

Elleria frowned. 'Second?' she asked.

'Yes,' replied John.

'You mean you've had more than one?'

'Well… not personally.'

'Sorry, I'm just a bit surprised that the people in charge would want to have a second war.'

'My Dad says that at the time there was good reason to fight, but since the end of the war the people in charge seem to have given away everything that we fought for to the countries we were fighting.'

'The same people?'

'No, what was it he says; "Different idiots, same schools"; yes, I think that was how he summed it up. He doesn't like politicians very much; he always says "that it doesn't matter who you vote for, the government always gets in". It's best not to get him started on politics.'

'Sorry,' said Elleria, 'I've dragged you away from what you were saying about this information you're getting. Please carry on.'

'Yes, where was I?' John thought for a moment, before continuing. 'I remember. This one talked about the "Guardians of Valheel" and "Radgarcs'". And you say you're a Radgarc?'

'Yes, specifically I'm Amantarra's Radgarc; or rather I'm a Radgarc, Human hybrid. Radgarc's are usually just shells, but this form is a fully working human model. And yes, I was created by Amantarra and I manage her Nodes.'

Ref: 327-2-716-1-481-002-18

Common Node Technical Reference

Inanimate non biological regulator used to transfer biomass energy to Node Zero. The energy field generated by biological units inhibits their use as Nodes.

Nodes cannot be created directly. The process of Node creation consists of two stages:

1.   Two separate objects are created by the project Bruwnan; one is the transfer mechanism and the other the management system.

2.   The two objects are merged together to produce a Node. The merging process can only be initiated by the project Bruwnan's Radgarc. The process binds the Radgarc to the Node and the Node to the biomass.

Nodes are capable of transferring an unrestricted amount of energy and are the only means by which energy can be transferred to Node Zero. The Bruwnan cannot tap energy directly from a Common Node; they can only draw a capped amount from Node Zero.

John didn't even need to read it, as soon as the information flashed up it was already in his head. 'Whoa, that was too much information,' he said out loud without intending to. Elleria looked at him questionably. 'I just got a lot of information on Nodes and it raised more questions than it answered.' And as he explained he got the strangest sensation. 'That's weird, I feel as though something has just apologised.'

'Apologised?'

'It was just a sensation, the one you get when somebody says "sorry" and you think "thank you" and then you feel better.'

'It must be part of the management system; it obviously contains more information than I thought it would; unless, of course, this is to do with Amantarra.'

'You've mentioned Amantarra before.'

'Yes, she's the Bruwnan who created me. Look it's probably best if I just try to explain things as best I can.'

'Okay, I'll just keep quiet and listen.'

'As you said before, I am a Radgarc and I manage Nodes for Amantarra. Amantarra is a being called The Bruwnan.

Ref: 327-2-444-1-113-016-98

The Bruwnan

The Bruwnan are ethereal beings who draw sustenance from the energy field generated by the living biomass of the universe. And for the purpose of optimising that energy field, they have been instrumental in the shaping of the universe's biomass.

'The Bruwnan were once human-like in form, but they left their bodies behind and became just energy. They exist in a virtual city outside the normal dimensions of space time called Valheel. It's where Node Zero is, and the city is constructed using the energy from Node Zero. Node Zero in turn gets its energy from the Common Nodes like the ones I manage. The city is controlled by a management system that generates the buildings and creates Avatars for its defence called the Guardians of Valheel. Amantarra often questioned their purpose as there's nothing to defend the city against. And that was the way it had been for nearly half the age of the universe; but then about thirty-two thousand years ago Valheel, The Bruwnan and Amantarra all vanished.'

'What happened?'

'I don't know. I was told there was some sort of problem with Node Zero, but that's another story. Anyway, just over a hundred years ago a new Node Zero became active. The last instructions I got from Amantarra before I lost her, were to disconnect all her Nodes from Node Zero. So far, I haven't reconnected them to the new one.'

'So is Amantarra back?'

'No, I cannot detect her presence at all.'

It was an interesting story, thought John, and it did sort of tie together some of the threads in these information flashes that he'd been getting, but what had all this to do with him?

'Elleria,' said John looking deep into her eyes.

'Yes John.'

'What has all this to do with me?' he asked.

'Nothing and everything;' John cocked his head on one side like a dog waiting for a piece of cake. Elleria continued; 'as a person I don't think this has anything to do with you, but it has everything to do with what you are, what you are becoming.' John's eyes opened wider.

'What I'm becoming!'

'In a few hours John, at twelve twenty five to be precise, you will be a fully functioning Node.'

'What! But that can't be right, in that information I got about Nodes it said "The energy field generated by biological units inhibits their use as Nodes." And I'm a biological unit aren't I?'

'This information you've got is very detailed; but yes, you're right, it is supposed to be impossible. Never the less you are becoming a Node. All I can think of is that for some reason Amantarra found a way round the problem. Why she needed to; I don't know.'

'This is that bond between us, the one you mentioned earlier; the bond between a Radgarc and a Node.'

Elleria took John's hands in hers and looked up into his eyes. For all of her existence Elleria had wondered what it would be like to exist in corporeal form for more than a day at a time. Would she take on more of the aspects of the form she was in? And here with John, she felt a shiver of excitement as she held his hands, was it just the bond between them or was it something else?

'Yes that is the bond I mentioned, but I don't fully understand the implications of you not being an inanimate object. I've just got nothing to compare it with.'

John let go of one of her hands and brushed her cheek with the back of his fingers. Suddenly he remembered what it was about her that was different.

'I've noticed...' he began, and then paused. Should he pursue this? It was potentially embarrassing. He didn't know her that well and he may get a slap on the face for his question. Curiosity didn't just kill cats and he'd had his face slapped before for similar enquiries. 'I've noticed that you've stopped...' he paused to search for the right words.

'Stopped what?' said Elleria, placing her head to one side.

'Stopped doing that...' John wished he hadn't started this, but something compelled him to press on. He took a deep breath; 'I've noticed that you've stopped doing that little dance when you talk. The one where you jiggle your... move your;' John indicated her chest with his free hand.

'Breasts,' volunteered Elleria.

'Yes,' said John relieved that he hadn't been slapped yet.

'Yes, I noticed you taking an interest in them earlier.' John started to redden. 'Sorry have I said the wrong thing. I'm still getting used to the subtleties of human interaction.'

'No it's not that; it's just that I didn't think you'd noticed. And the dance thing?' said John changing the subject to a slightly less embarrassing one.

'Yes, the dance thing... I'm afraid that Elleria would have been a bit of a flirt. At least when we are outside normal time I'm more in control.'

This answer posed more questions than it answered. John let go of her hand and Elleria was surprised by the slight sense of loss it invoked.

'Would have been a flirt?' asked John.

'Yes, sorry; there's such a lot to explain.'

'You could start with: "would have been a flirt".'

Where were these thoughts coming from; it was the sort of question that John would hear someone else ask and think; yes, that's a good question; but he would never think of it himself. It was a question from a type of mind that forced other people to clarify themselves, and a week ago John's mind would not have conceived of such a question.

'Remember yesterday when we met?' said Elleria.

'Yes.'

'Well, until yesterday Elleria Parker did not exist.' She paused to let John consider his next question; it would be quicker to answer his queries than try to explain everything at once.

'What about your parents... her parents?'

'They existed; they just didn't have any children.'

'No, I mean they knew you; they thought they'd always had a daughter.'

'That's because when I came into existence I altered their minds so that they thought they did have a daughter. Amantarra left instructions on how to do it.'

'Altered their minds... do you think I'll be able to do that?'

'Probably, from the information you seem to be getting, I suspect you will be able to do anything a Bruwnan can do. But... perhaps you shouldn't try, you may finish up damaging someone. Have you noticed anything else different, anything unusual?'

John thought for a moment. Yes of course, he closed his eyes and despite the fact that she was stood in front of him, Elleria was still sitting on the stool as well. He got so used to the conflict that he'd forgotten about it.

'Yes there is,' he said opening his eyes and looking at her. 'I can see you here, in front of me now, but there is something else that's telling me that you're sat on that stool over there.'

'Inter-dimensional interference, it's what I would normally use to sense the universe and it's the reason we can hear each other, there's no sound when we are moving this fast in time, the Eraltons' that surround us are vibrating in harmony.'

'Eraltons'?'

'Sorry, I keep doing this don't I? In order to pull an object out of normal time you have to surround it in an Eralton field; like putting a letter in an envelope before you post it. They're named after the one who discovered the method. So, to answer your original question, the reason you can detect me on the stool is because in real time I'm still there. The place marker you were prodding at is actually the Eralton at its point of creation.' John felt his cheeks colouring slightly, he wished she wouldn't keep mentioning that. He ran over the other bits of information he'd been given.

'Thanks for that,' he said. 'So, what's "Burst mode"?'

'Burst mode... I don't know that one. What does it relate to?'

'That sphere thing in the storeroom.'

'What thing in the storeroom?'

'A tunnel it was called and it's a "method of jumping forward in time". It was what I was looking at when we came up the stairs.'

'I thought you were just talking to that man making those shelves.'

'Captain Cardigan; well I was, but I could also see this big sphere. It was making a noise and when I got close the walls behind it changed colour. Captain Cardigan said the colour I saw was the colour the walls were when he was at school here.'

'He could see it too?'

'No, I don't think so, he thought I'd seen the bits he'd missed when he'd painted the walls. But, the information did refer to him as "The Keeper" and that he'd now been released from that role.'

This was all new to Elleria, but then again so was a living being becoming a Node. Whatever Amantarra was up to seemed pretty big and she suspected it was all tied in with the strange meeting she'd had with Tyrus during her last visit to Valheel. She was suspicious of Tyrus' apparent concern over Amantarra's welfare; his sincerity was just plain false and the real reason was to do with discovering Amantarra's whereabouts. Elleria had half expected Tyrus to request that he accompany her as she went from planet to planet; and was relieved when he hadn't. Still, there was no need to worry about that, Tyrus and the council would not be able to trace her to this planet, it was one amongst a trillion, trillion that the Bruwnan had shaped. Elleria suddenly realised that John was looking at her waiting for an answer.

'Sorry,' she said, 'I missed that; I was miles away then.'

'Do you know what it meant by Captain Cardigan being The Keeper?'

'No... sorry I don't.' Elleria thought for a moment. 'Show me this sphere, maybe it'll provide some clues.'

John pulled at the classroom door, it didn't move. He tried again with both hands on the handle and a foot braced up against the wall.

'I can't shift it at all,' he said through gritted teeth as he heaved. 'It just won't move.'

'You've gone red,' laughed Elleria.

'Show me again,' said John giving up the struggle and moving to one side to let Elleria get to the door.

'Ready,' said Elleria with one hand on the door handle.

'How are you doing that?' asked John, as once again Elleria opened the door without any effort whatsoever.

'I told you, you have to place an Eralton field round the door to bring it into our time frame; then you can move it.'

'Yes, I know what you said; but how do you do it?'

'Well you have to picture the door, the hinges and the screws holding it to the frame and think of wrapping them in light. I can't actually show you, this is something you need to do for yourself.'

'Why do I have to picture the screws, why not just the hinges?'

'That's because you have to find a natural joint. If you just picture the hinges then you would shear the screws and the door would fall off. It's much easier to form an interface between the wood and the metal screws. You're going to have to learn how things work, how they are put together.'

'Can't I practice on something easier first? I don't want to get the blame for the door falling off.'

'Of course you can,' she said turning to look around the laboratory for an easier target. She found one. Still catching the light; because even when time has apparently stopped, light has a way of sorting itself out; was the drip that John had noticed before. Halfway between tap and sink it hovered, sparkling in the morning sun.

'Do you see that drip?'

John shifted his position slightly to see around his classmates.

'That drip, oh yes, that dripping tap has annoyed me for ages.'

'Well if you form an Eralton round it you can move it closer to the sink.'

'Okay,' said John moving behind Elleria so he could see the drip, and, he thought, a good excuse to be closer to Elleria; 'what do I do again?' he said placing his hands on her shoulders.

Elleria trembled slightly at his touch; this was very distracting, but nice. Focus Elleria, she told herself, focus, what is wrong with you.

'Picture the drip in your mind.'

John concentrated on the drip.

'Now sense the drip, rather than see it; in the same way that you can sense me still sitting on the stool.'

'Yes, I've got that.'

'Good,' this is going to be easier than I expected, she thought to herself. 'Now...' She tingled as she felt his breath on her neck. 'Now... think about wrapping it....' Oh, he was so close; she thought about shrugging his hands off her shoulders, but that's not what she wanted. What she wanted, was for this moment to last forever; which, given their current situation was almost feasible.

'Wrapping it in what?' said John, bringing her back to what currently passed for reality.

'Sorry,' she said. 'Wrap it in blue light, with your mind picture it enveloped in light; but only think of the drip; don't think of the tap or anything else.'

With his new senses John brought the drip up close almost like zooming in with a camera. Larger and larger he made it, until it filled his whole field of view. Up this close he could see that it wasn't the perfect sphere he'd expected it to be. Its surface wasn't smooth, but dimpled; each dimple catching the light in different ways. Being this close in his mind to an object on the other side of the room created a conflict between his new and old senses that made him feel slightly giddy. Like looking through a telescope and keeping your other eye open at the same time. He pulled back so that he could sense the tap as well. That was better, it wasn't a hundred per cent better, but at least he didn't feel as though he was going to fall over. There was something vaguely familiar about the shape as well, a sphere floating in the air; something he half recognised and curiously hinted that there was something missing from the inside of it.

Okay, he thought; dripping tap... drip... that tap has always dripped; no, concentrate on the drip... dripping tap... it's annoying during written tests... focus, drip, tap, drip. Eventually despite John's meandering thoughts he pictured the drip wrapped in light; it was easier than he thought it was going to be. He brought the drip up close again to view his handiwork. The surface now had a slight blue tinge to it, which was more pronounced at the edges where you could make out a very thin sliver of blue light.

'Done that,' said John.

'What?' said Elleria coming back from forever; 'oh right, okay, now think of the drip falling in slow motion.' John was surprised to find that as he pictured the drip falling in his mind the real drip followed his thoughts.

'This is easy,' said John.

'I think that all this is programmed into you, and the only thing that's missing is that you are not aware of what you can do.

'Right take a look at where the drip used to be.'

John focused, and there above the drip, in the position it had started from was its faint outline.

'Its place marker,' said John.

'Correct. Now try moving the drip back to its place marker.'

'You can do that?' John's hands moved on Elleria's shoulders and Elleria thought he was going to take them away. Without thinking she crossed her arms across her chest and placed her hands over the top of his to hold them in place. John twisted his palms up to catch hold of her hands.

'Of course you can,' said Elleria squeezing his hands in encouragement. 'Have a go. Picture the drip moving up back to its place marker.'

John tried and it was surprisingly easy too. The drip slowly moved back towards its place marker and snapped back into place as it reached it.

'Great, now think of the Eralton dissolving; imagine the light slowly fading.'

'Done that,' said John.

'Now for your next challenge; opening the door without making it fall off.' said Elleria as she shuffled round to face the door without letting go of his hands.

A few minutes later John was looking back through the door into the chemistry lab. He'd managed to form an Eralton around the door complete with hinges and screws without any real problems; it was easy when you knew what to look for. He'd even managed to open it without touching it, and more amazingly Elleria had managed to persuade herself to let go of John's hands. She was stood in front of John in the doorway to the storeroom looking in at Captain Cardigan.

'I still can't see anything except Captain Cardigan,' said Elleria. 'Why does he keep his tools in an old shopping bag?'

John quickly finished what he was doing before Elleria noticed and looked into the storeroom. In front of the new shelves Captain Cardigan was frozen in the act of putting a screwdriver back into his shopping bag. And behind him the sphere was still quietly emitting a high pitched sound.

'It's right in the centre of the room,' said John.

'And it's a sphere?'

'Yes, it's about two metres in diameter. I'll show you the edge of it with my hand.' John walked forward and the tone fell through the octaves again, but to a much lower level, presumably, John thought, because he was closer this time. He stood to the side of it and placed his hand on the surface. There was a slight resistance, so it was easy to hold it in the right place.

'See anything now?' he asked.

From the doorway, Elleria shook her head.

'No,' she said.

'Come a bit closer, the sound changes when I get closer, maybe you'll be able to see it then.'

Elleria took a pace forward.

'I can't hear it either; does anything else change when you get closer?'

'Yes, the walls change colour; they turn dark green.'

'What about Captain Cardigan, does he turn dark green?'

John looked through the sphere towards Captain Cardigan; leaned forward to look around the sphere to check that he was still there and then leaned back.

'Actually, he's not there, neither are the new shelves, there's just a cupboard. Captain Cardigan told me that this room was painted dark green when he was young. So that's where, sorry when, the other end of this link must be; back when Captain Cardigan was a lad.'

John walked slowly round the sphere looking through it.

'It's like looking through a lens to a different time; it's the same room, but the colours and the things in it are different. I wonder if the door is open, I might be able to see down the stairs.' John moved round the sphere to the back of the room.

'Is it?' said Elleria.

'Yes it is, but there's something else there as well, between the sphere and the door;' John rocked gently from side to side.

'What is it?' said Elleria.

'It looks like a place marker.'

A place marker; thought Elleria, it could only be Amantarra. 'Can you see who it is?'

John did some more rocking and bobbed up and down a few times.

'It's a man, and...'

John stood with his mouth open; he just couldn't believe what he saw.

'And what?' said Elleria impatiently.

'And it's my Grandfather.'

'It's your Grandfather!' exclaimed Elleria. So Amantarra was disguised as John's Grandfather, there was a chance that she could make contact. 'Where's your Grandfather now? Is he still alive?'

'No, he died during the war, but I don't know how; my Dad's never talked about it.'

Elleria was puzzled, how could Amantarra become a parent, how was it even possible? Unless... William Godbert's body was a hybrid, like this one. As to the question of why Amantarra would want to become a parent? Well the answer to that was standing right in front of her, but how Amantarra had achieved the impossible and created a Node called John, was a complete mystery.

'I think he must have frozen time and travelled through this tunnel to the future,' said John.

'You mean, to now?'

'No, this end of the tunnel moves forward through time; so it could be any time in the future from the fixed end I can see through the sphere.

'I wish I could see it,' said Elleria. She moved towards John stopping dead as she encountered the invisible sphere. 'I might not be able to see it but I can certainly feel it.'

Elleria moved round the sphere like a mime artist trapped outside a box. She reached the back of the room and stood next to John.

'I've got an idea,' said John. 'Take my hand.'

Elleria's heart gave a little jump. She'd stopped asking herself why these things were happening, it just seemed easier to accept them. So she took his hand and two things happened. One, her heart rate went up. Two, right in front of her appeared a two metre diameter sphere, and the walls of the room they were in, when seen through the sphere, were green, exactly as John had described them. Looking directly at her, across time and space, was the place marker of their creator in the guise of William Godbert.

15

THE CONTRACT

John and Elleria were sat back in the chemistry lab. Elleria, her head turned away from John was looking back towards the door. John watched her for a moment, watched the way the light caught her hair as she moved her head slightly down. Her reaction to seeing William had been one of sadness which was something John had not been expecting. He too felt a sense of loss for the Grandfather he never knew but not to the extent that it seemed to have affected Elleria. He reached out and touched her shoulder.

'Sorry,' he said. Elleria turned to face him. Her eyes were welling over with tears and as she turned a single tear ran down her cheek which she quickly wiped with the back of her hand.

'It's not your fault, I'm just being silly.' Elleria took a deep breath and sighed. 'I've never felt sadness before, but when I saw Amantarra… it just suddenly hit me how much I've missed her.'

'Her? Are you sure?' said John raising his eyebrows and looking surprised.

'Oh… I see what you mean, that must seem very strange to you.' Elleria half smiled, her melancholy fractured by the thought of John's confusion. She wiped both her eyes with both hands, smearing the tears that had formed to either side of her eyes. John reached into his pocket and offered her a handkerchief.

'It's clean,' he lied; 'well… mostly,' he added thoughtfully.

'Thank you,' she said as she dried her eyes and started to explain. 'When Amantarra was corporeal, flesh and blood, she was female. And when she lived in Valheel after she'd left her physical body behind, she retained that same form, most of the Bruwnan did, even though it was completely irrelevant to what they'd become. The place marker we saw through the tunnel is… was… just a vessel for the consciousness.'

'Is that what you are? What your body is, just a vessel?'

'Yes, but this is different to the ones I normally occupy, this is a sort of hybrid, somewhere between a Radgarc and a Human. It has internal organs, a digestive system and blood, but it is still a construct.'

'What about me? Am I the same?'

'No, you're different, more human, but not quite all human. You've been enhanced.'

'Your construct seems very human to me, tears and sadness; is that normal?' John brushed away a strand of hair that had stuck to her damp cheek.

'No, it's not. Maybe it's because I'm spending a lot of time around humans. I often wondered if the constructs would start to become more like the creatures they represented; or maybe it's because this shell is a hybrid and it's designed that way.' Elleria finished drying her eyes and handed the handkerchief back to John.

'Ready?' she said.

'Ready? For what?'

'We need to re-join the real world.'

John nodded, even though he'd rather not re-join the real world.

'Oh, I almost forgot just one more thing for future reference; when you are outside normal time try not to interact with any objects because they'll catch up with your actions once the Eraltons' are dissolved.'

'Well I…' started John, but it was too late Elleria brought them back into normal time.

The noise of the world returned with a bang as the frozen forms of John's classmates re-animated. Several things happened if not simultaneously, then in very quick succession. The stool John was sitting on flew backwards from under him clattering into the sink behind him; and as he started his journey to the floor Scott made an involuntary noise as the wind was knocked out of him because John had nudged him in the ribs with his elbow, the force of a slight nudge speeded up immeasurably was enough to push Scott sideways off his stool and he too was heading for the floor. Action, on his way down from his impressive scissor jump, discovered to his horror that two stools, which had not been there on the way up, had somehow got themselves under his feet for the descent. The result was that as his body continued to move down, his feet remained at the same height pushing the tolerance of the seat of his trousers beyond its limit. The subsequent ripping noise was even more impressive than the jump. Behind John, the tap that he had inadvertently placed an Eralton around which Elleria had inadvertently failed to notice, sheared off from its pipe landing in the sink with a clatter. A jet of water shot over John's head and across the top of the bench to strike, not only the only person who couldn't get out of the way, but the only person wearing a waterproof cagoule. Action, suspended as he was between two stools further demonstrated his athletic prowess by springing up and over the jet of water on the rebound from his stalled descent. The room descended into chaos.

There was a time when no one would have dared, or perhaps that was just looking at the past through rose tinted spectacles.

There was a time when they would have dared, but they would have shown more respect for authority, well perhaps not, but they would have been a bit quieter.

There was a time when Mr Fleming would have taken all this with a pinch of salt.

There was a time when Mr Fleming could sit down.

Those days seemed a long time ago. Mr Fleming felt as though he was losing his grip. The day had started to slide downhill when he'd started seeing uniforms. And now all this chaos; and it really seemed like such an effort to take control again.

'QUIET!!!!' he shouted, with far more vigour than was good for his haemorrhoids.

It had no effect.

Time to use the secret weapon, he thought; and he produced from his pocket a school whistle. Taking a deep breath he gave a long piercing blast, emptying his lungs completely. This had the desired effect; the only sound he could hear now was the throbbing of his piles, or was it blood rushing through his ears? Either way, he made a mental note not to tense his buttocks the next time he did that.

'Scribbins put your finger over the hole in that pipe.'

'Yes Sir.'

'Atkinson, do something about your trousers.'

'Yes Sir.'

This was more like it, there was nothing quite like being in control.

Kevin, who had tried his finger in the pipe and found that the only thing it achieved was to thoroughly soak Kevin, was now experimenting with his thumb while standing out of the line of fire. He quite quickly discovered that he could aim a jet of water with some degree of accuracy. Frank and Scott were his first two victims; unfortunately his third, was Mr Fleming.

'SCRIBBINS STOP THAT,' screamed Mr Fleming taking his blood pressure to dizzy new heights and his haemorrhoids to new dimensions.

'My thumb slipped Sir,' said Kevin sporting a demonic grin.

Reg, who had heard the unusual chaos followed by Mr Fleming shouting his name; stuck his head round the door to find out what was going on.

'Reg,' said Mr Fleming, 'could you turn the water off please.'

Reg walked to the window, reached down and turned the stopcock. With the water off he left quickly to go and get his mop and bucket.

Fifteen minutes later after calling the register and with Scott still rubbing his ribs, the bell rang for first lesson. As everyone stood to leave, Mr Fleming, without the usual throat clearing preamble, made an announcement.

'Before you go,' he said. 'For those of you who managed to get yourselves a soaking; if any of the other teachers question you about why you are wet, just say that Mr Fleming knows about it already, that there is no action to take and that I'll confirm it at break time.' John and Scott both looked at Frank who shrugged his shoulders.

'Don't ask me,' he said.

*

The end of Burnston's first lesson was rapidly approaching. Up until today he hadn't really seen the point of taking Business Studies as a subject, other than he thought that it would be easier than History. This morning's lesson however had been an eye opener; he could see how the theory and practice all tied together and the relevance of what Mrs MacDonald had been trying to teach him for the last year.

The last hour had just flown by, and Burnston put it all down to Best Management Practices. The book he now realised could quite possibly change his life. This was in contrast to Mrs MacDonald's last hour which had been one of the longest in her life. She had predicted a certain type of future for Burnston, one which consisted of heat, dirt, hard labour, poverty and beer. Today's lesson, in contrast to Burnston's normal silent brooding at the back of the class, had revealed a previously hidden personality. It had also revealed that perhaps the future held something different for Burnston, something involving money and power. She'd found the whole lesson an endurance beyond the call of duty. She knew something was amiss when Burnston and his usual entourage had entered wearing the official Penshaw Grove School uniform. He'd sat in his usual place in the back corner of the class but somehow he seemed less isolated than normal. The brooding was absent, or perhaps more diluted, as if he had projected it out from his corner and across the rest of the classroom. The first question she'd asked had been rewarded with a sea of hands... including Burnston's. Her initial reaction was one of curiosity, after all this had never happened before and she did for an instant consider choosing Burnston for the answer. But before she had made her mind up, Burnston cleared his throat; and everyone else put their hands down. This pattern of; question, hands up, throat clear, hands down and Burnston answers the question, ran throughout the lesson. It wasn't so much the fact that he was answering all the questions that had worried her, it was when he gave an answer that she didn't agree with that was the problem. On those occasions there would be a short debate which had in five instances resulted in her conceding the point just to avoid the brooding menace that seemed to grow during the deliberation. As the bell rang for the end of the lesson; Mrs MacDonald searched her handbag for a Valium.

The Lendus stood at the top of the steps that led down into the packed playground. They gazed across the sea of heads. Martin was leaning against a pillar at the side of the steps.

'Behold Mr Burnston,' said Martin, 'your customers.'

Burnston nodded sagely as he scanned the playground. 'Gentlemen,' he said drawing the gaze of his associates; 'we've got work to do.'

*

At the far end of the playground Action adjusted the knot in the sleeves of his cagoule, which he had tied around his waist. With the body of the cagoule strategically placed behind him, he twisted round first this way, and then the other, in an attempt to see if the split in his trousers was properly covered.

'Can you see anything?' he asked John giving up the attempt.

John glanced at Elleria, but looked back at Action quickly to avoid her accusing look.

'No,' replied John.

As Action moved away with Frank, Scott and Kevin; Elleria and John followed but at a slower pace.

'You shouldn't have done that; you can't afford to give yourself away,' she said. John noted that Elleria was communicating with her chest again, but decided to spare himself any further embarrassment by pretending not to notice.

'It was only a joke,' replied John. 'And anyway, it wasn't me who missed the tap; I thought you were supposed to be checking what I was doing.'

'Yes, you're right I should have been paying attention. Did you see the look on Action's face, it was a picture.' She couldn't stay angry with John for long, not when he was looking at her with those gorgeous eyes of his.

'I know, and his leap over the water was very impressive as...' John paused because Elleria had stopped walking placing a hand on John's arm to stop him. 'What's wrong?'

It was just as she was looking at John's eyes that she got the same feeling she got on the jungle planet; in the grey area between her old and new senses there was something there. She deliberately didn't try to focus on it with either set of senses, trying to gather more information about it. Could it be Amantarra? Elleria knew she must be on this planet somewhere; but why observe from hiding? Unless, as Elleria suspected, she was afraid of the high council finding her. Standing in the playground with John, Elleria knew that she was surrounded by the reasons why the High Council would want to find her, and why she would want to remain hidden. To Elleria, Amantarra was being overly cautious; there was no way that the council could trace her to this planet, there were billions in this galaxy alone and there were billions more galaxies in the universe as a whole; it was just completely impossible. The sensation of being watched vanished; whether it knew Elleria could sense it, or whether it just came and went randomly, she didn't know.

John looked at Elleria; she looked distant for a moment, as if she was concentrating on something.

'There's something I need to tell you about,' she said looking quite serious.

'Didn't you see the stools when you jumped?' asked Kevin who was walking next to Action.

'Well no, I didn't.' Action adjusted his cagoule, the wind was whistling round the teddy bears on his underwear; which in contrast to Action did not appreciate being outdoors. 'I could have sworn that there weren't any stools there when I jumped.'

'There must have been,' said Scott, 'the stools couldn't have moved by themselves.'

'Was there anyone watching when you jumped, maybe they saw what happened?' said Frank.

'Elleria was… and John… probably.'

'Let's ask them then,' said Kevin and they all turned, but John and Elleria were some distance back through the crowd.

What happened next could be compared to a magician's sleight of hand, the art of distraction; where despite everything you do, the magician gets you to pick the card he wants you to pick. You know he's manipulating the cards, you know he's using distraction to hide what he's doing, but, try as you might, you just can't see how it's being done. Those that possess the magicians' art are in the minority; sadly for most people, like John, experience of the art is always from the wrong side. Very few people possess the ability to initiate the circumstances that put them on the other side. It seems to be something that you are either born with, or not; and it is best illustrated with an example.

Take for instance a situation where Scott, your best friend, is trying to stab you in the leg with the point of a compass, just for fun you understand, and in the best interests of peer bonding. After a number of attempts, you get sick of trying to stop him by grabbing his compass hand, and decide to terminate Scott's attempts at bonding, by elbowing him in the ribs. Now this is the mysterious bit, during all the attempts Scott had to stab you, the teacher saw nothing; but as soon as you retaliate it's; "Godbert, behave yourself". Now granted, this was a one off and by no means indicates that Scott possessed the gift himself, but it illustrates what happened next quite nicely.

'Gentlemen,' said Burnston appearing as if by magic behind Action, Kevin, Scott and Frank two seconds after they'd turned to look at John and Elleria. When it came to utilising the magicians' art, Burnston had almost God like powers. Despite his bulk and the size of his entourage, not one of them had seen him coming. With an inner groan, they turned back slowly to face him.

With Burnston and Haystack at the front, and the two smaller associates, Boxhead and Clink to either side but stood slightly back; the grouping had a strong and united feel to it. All four were smartly dressed with trousers neatly pressed and white shirts ironed, complete with finishing touches which included school badges, and ties correctly fastened.

'Thank you for seeing me at such short notice,' boomed Burnston.

'Is that our school uniform?' asked Scott.

'See, I told you,' said Kevin, 'they're all like twins.'

'You are correct Mr Briggs,' said Burnston giving Kevin a funny look, 'Allow me to take the opportunity to introduce you to my new company.' And like a magician doing card tricks, Burnston flipped a business card into his fingers with a snap. Frank took it and read out loud;

B. Burnston
Managing Director and Sales Executive
The Lendus
(Financial services)

'And we are here today to discuss your financial requirements,' continued Burnston.

'What financial requirements?' asked Kevin before he could stop himself, and before Frank's slap on the back had registered. As a general rule, regardless of the subject, you didn't enter into a debate with Burnston, you just agreed with him.

'Insurance and other associated products,' said Burnston.

Much to everyone's alarm Scott decided that a debate should indeed be entered into.

'Insurance against what?' he asked.

'Well accidents happen all the time,' said Burnston. 'Why only the other day Haystack here was involved in an incident that resulted in a black eye, a split lip, and two loose teeth.' Haystack grinned.

'His eye looks fine to me,' said Scott.

'Oh, it wasn't Haystack's eye that was involved.'

'So, if the person involved had had insurance, you would have paid out compensation,' enquired Frank.

'No, we wouldn't have needed to, because the incident wouldn't have happened in the first place.'

Burnston paused to let that one sink in.

'Now, to business… my associates,' Burnston indicated Boxhead and Clink; 'will help you fill in the forms. They're quite simple.' Action had to bite his tongue, he'd almost added "and the forms as well" which would not have been a good move. As Boxhead and Clink handed the sheets out, Burnston explained the forms to them; 'name at the top and signature at the bottom.' It was the abridged explanation; there's no need to confuse the customers with unnecessary detail.

The newest prospects of The Lendus started to read the contracts.

'I think you'll find them in order,' said Burnston. Haystack cracked his knuckles to emphasise the point. 'Name at the top, signature at the bottom; these are standard contracts, everybody gets the same one, so there's absolutely no need to read them. Come along gentlemen we have a lot of clients to see and not much time to do it in.'

Reluctantly they all signed and Boxhead and Clink collected the forms, handing them the pink carbon copies before they could change their minds.

'Could I take the business card back as I only have the one,' said Burnston, as he reached over and took it from Frank. Team Lendus turned to go.

'Hang on, you haven't told us how much,' stated Frank.

'Only ten pence a day; and I'm sure you'll all agree that it's not much to pay for the peace of mind it brings.' And with that Team Lendus disappeared into the crowd.

Scott, whose face had turned red with anger, clenched his fists and made to pursue them. Frank and Kevin, seeing the look on Scott's face stood in front of him to prevent him from committing suicide.

'Can't let you do it mate,' said Frank, 'there's always another way.'

'What did all that mean?' asked Action.

'Not sure,' said Kevin.

'It means Burnston has started a company,' said Frank.

'It means Burnston has started a protection racket,' said Scott.

'What's a protection racket?' Kevin asked.

'It's where if you don't pay Burnston every week you have an accident involving your teeth and Haystack's knuckles,' said Frank.

'So now we've got to pay protection money,' said Action.

'Ten pence a day,' said Kevin, 'that's fifty pence a week, same as the lunch money. I can't afford that.'

Frank scratched his head. 'What I want to know is; who's put these ideas into his head. This is too well organised for Burnston. The name; "The Lendus", from the phrase "Lendus a penny", that's very clever, far too clever for him and the image with the school uniforms, you can't tell me that this is all his work.'

'So what are we going to do about it?' said Action. 'Whether it's Burnston's idea or not we've all signed contracts to say that we're going to pay him.'

'Don't let that fool you; the contracts aren't legally binding because none of us are eighteen, so he can't enforce them,' said Frank.

'No, that's wrong; they don't have to be legally binding because it's Burnston that'll be doing the enforcing,' Scott pointed out. 'Remember the card; the "B" in "B. Burnston", that "B" probably stands for "Bastard". So I don't think he'll be letting a little thing like legal or not stop him.' Scott was red faced again and was clenching and unclenching his fists. He was thinking about his collection of military weapon magazines and which one contained the most appropriate item to exact his revenge.

'So we're stuffed then,' said Action.

'Maybe we could steal the money back,' suggested Kevin without much conviction.

'How would we do that?' asked Action, amazed that Kevin would even suggest it.

'I don't know. I was just thinking out loud. Forget I said…' started Kevin but he was interrupted.

'Would be difficult,' said Scott looking thoughtful. 'Let me think about it.' The other three looked at each other and then at Scott. Thinking about things, generally that wasn't what Scott did.

John looked at the seriousness in Elleria's face. 'What could be that serious?' he asked.

'I think Amantarra is still here, but she's in hiding.'

'Hiding; from what?'

'The High Council, her own people and I think it's because of humans.' Elleria indicated the occupants of the playground with a sweep of her hand.

'Why, what have humans done?'

'It's not what they've done; I suspect it's what the Bruwnan think they may do. Humans are the most advanced species I've ever encountered and I don't think the Bruwnan welcome the competition.'

'I don't understand.'

'The Bruwnan will be worried that once human's reach a certain level of development they'll start using some of the energy the Bruwnan currently have a monopoly on.' John watched a couple of fourth years who were having a competition to see who could mess the others hair up the most, and wondered what the current level of human development was.

'So what would they do about it?' asked John turning to look at Elleria.

'I don't know, but whatever it is, it wouldn't be good for humans.'

John looked out over a sea of heads as they moved around the playground like a Brownian motion experiment. The loss of the human race, in the grand universal scheme of things, might not amount to much, but he was sort of attached to them. He might not be totally human, but he was here with them, and he suspected that he would be the initial target of any attack on them.

'Good morning Mr Godbert,' boomed a confident voice behind him. 'Could we have a quick word about your financial requirements?'

16
THE NEW NODE

Ref: 998-1-001-0-002-08-26
The William Godbert narrative
Start sequence in Laon, Picardy 1918

It was dark and the ground was cold; too cold for bare feet. The air was near freezing but fortunately there was no wind, just a penetrating cold that pulled at the man's naked form. The stars were out, sharp in the cloudless night; and there was silence. Thoughts were being gathered and bearings taken. John could see some of the thoughts but by no means all; it was as if he was being given the highlights. John's thoughts remained just that, his own; and he concluded that he was an observer in someone else's head. He could feel the cold on the skin but it was as if he was wearing the body like an overcoat, it was part of him but detached. A "shell", the vessel he occupied was known as a "shell" he remembered, but not a hybrid like Elleria's. This shell was solid, like a lump of plasticine. Although John could sense the beginnings of internal organs they had only just started to form. Perhaps it was in a state of transition.

John had no control over the shell, if he had, he'd have put some clothes on because the cold was beginning to get to him. The shell looked down at its naked feet. The ground was churned mud that had been frozen into sharp ridges, and then covered in a heavy frost.

The brief moment of tranquil calm was shattered as shouts interrupted the still night. This was followed by a repetitive series of loud bangs which John recognised as machine gun fire. The shell didn't recognise the noise at all. The stars overhead swept by as the shell toppled over backwards. An overwhelming amount of information as if a thousand people were all talking at once flowed into the mind of the vessel.

Then there was blackness and silence.

As John continued to observe, there was another burst of information which slowed to reveal a single whispered voice… French it appeared to be. John was amazed, he understood every word. The man was saying a prayer… no, he wasn't… he was giving the last rights. Then the blackness ended abruptly and he was looking at the shocked faces of two soldiers and a priest. The names came instantly to mind, like a commentary added to a film; the officer was Captain Robert Fortesque, his Sergeant Billy Fairweather and the priest was Father Benoît.

The shell lifted its head and in the dim light from two oil lamps John saw a partially covered torso. The body he found himself in was the focus of attention for the other three and he got the impression that they had not been expecting any signs of life. Father Benoît took a step back as the corpse propped itself up on its elbows.

'Hello,' said the corpse; 'my name is…' there was a pause as if a long list of possibilities was being considered, 'William Godbert.' William looked around. 'What am I doing here in the cathedral?'

The officer pointed at William. 'Your chest,' he said.

William looked down at his chest.

'Oh dear,' he said as he saw the gaping holes.

The collective jaws of the Captain, Sergeant and the Priest fell open as William closed the bullet holes before their very eyes, leaving only some nasty but fixable wounds.

William looked up, Billy and Robert flinched, but they were too frightened to speak. Benoît, eyes tightly closed, had started to say a prayer about deliverance from evil. William turned to the priest, whose hands were clamped so tightly together in desperate prayer that his knuckles had turned white, and spoke to him in a reassuring voice.

'Père, vous avez attendu votre vie entière pour observer un miracle, et quand il vous arrive ne le reconnaît pas.' Father, you've waited your whole life to witness a miracle, and when it happens you fail to recognise it.

William spoke far too quickly for Robert's basic French to interpret what was said, but he saw the old priest visibly relax. Benoît opened his eyes and lessened the tension in his hands. The colour returned to his knuckles and wave of calm swept over him. It was true; he had waited his whole life to witness a miracle. And it was also true that the list of people who knew of Benoît's only ambition was very short and it did not include William. Therefore, given what William had said, coupled with what they had just witnessed, there could only be one conclusion: and that was divine intervention. Benoît felt an overwhelming sense of fulfilment. A single tear ran down his cheek.

William turned his attention to the soldiers. They were far too cynical to accept the reassurance of witnessing a miracle for too long; William would need something longer term.

'Who would believe you?' William asked Robert.

The question initially provoked no reaction. Robert was looking at Benoît, trying to work out what William had said that could make him weep; and Billy was trying to check the shadows above William without taking his eyes off him.

Eventually Robert responded; he was the officer after all.

'Sorry... what did you say?'

'Who would believe you? I mean, if you told anyone what you've just seen?'

Robert's thoughts turned to how his family would explain why he'd been committed to an asylum. That would not go down at all well in society, Aunt Gertrude would never forgive him, and in fact it was a fate worse than death. The stranger did have a point. He turned to look at his sergeant who risked a quick look directly into the shadows.

'He... he... just,' said Billy struggling to state the obvious, once he'd decided that he couldn't see anything in the blackness.

'I know Sergeant, I saw it,' said Robert, wondering how he was going to stop the sergeant from starting any unhealthy rumours that would upset Aunt Gertrude.

'Sergeant...' said Robert. Billy ignored him; he was staring at William again.

'Sergeant...' Robert tried again louder this time.

'Yes Sir, sorry Sir.'

'You're to speak of this to no one. Do you understand?'

Billy didn't answer.

'Do you understand sergeant? That's a direct order,' said the Captain sharply, indicating that he meant business.

'Yes Sir, I understand,' replied Billy as years of military conditioning responded to the tone of his officer's voice.

'And Sergeant,' said Robert, 'bandage his chest, I don't want anyone else treating him, only you; do you understand?'

'Yes Sir,' said Billy.

'And Sergeant… put him in the north transept.'

'Yes Sir, right away Sir.'

The north transept was where they put the dying, the ones that weren't expected to last, the Captain thought it helped the morale of those in the Nave. Billy knew that the Captain wanted to keep William separate from the rest of the wounded.

The last images John saw were of a badly wounded soldier as he lay on the floor of the north transept. He looked bloody awful thought John.

William placed a hand on the soldier's forehead.

'Just hang on; it will be alright in the morning,' said William.

Then the images abruptly stopped.

*

'You can wake up now Mr Godbert, the bell has gone,' said Mrs Porter over a background of scraping chairs and general chatter as students stood to leave. John came back to reality with a start. He looked up at his friends who were already standing.

'Was I asleep?' he asked Scott, as he stood up.

'Difficult to tell with that normal blank expression you have,' replied Scott. John stood and mouthed a sarcastic "thank you" back. He could remember the whole of the history lesson he'd just had; he looked at the clock on the wall, it said twelve fifteen; it was only in the last few minutes that his mind seemed to have wandered off on another of those indexed historical episodes. He started to make his way towards the door with Elleria at his side.

'I've just seen my Grandfather again,' he whispered to her.

'At the school again?' Elleria asked.

'No he was younger than last time. I would guess from the uniforms that it was during the First World War.' They paused in their conversation as they joined the queue to exit the classroom.

'So your Grandfather was in uniform?' asked Elleria once they were on the north corridor and heading towards the stairs.

John pulled a face. 'Actually no, everyone else was in uniform; my Grandfather was naked,' said John slightly louder than he'd intended.

'Who was naked?' asked Frank. It was the first time he'd spoken since before the lesson; which for Frank was very unusual, particularly in history where he seemed to have an opinion on everything. Fortunately for John he didn't have to answer, as Scott suddenly became very excited and animated.

'I've got it; I've got it,' he said in a loud conspiratorial whisper. He waved Action over and they both joined John, Elleria and Frank. 'I've just had the most brilliant idea for getting back at Burnston and this Lendus rubbish.'

'Thank God for that,' said Action. 'Leaping about like that, I thought you were having an attack of the heebie-jeebies.'

'What is it?' asked John.

'What's what?' said Scott, who was so excited he'd forgotten that only he knew what the idea was.

'The brilliant idea,' asked Frank, 'what is it?'

'Yes, yes, it's brilliant; you're going to love it,' said Scott grabbing Frank by the shoulders. 'I've got to organise a few things, so I'll catch up with you all later.' And with that he turned and made his way down the corridor in the opposite direction to the one they'd been going in.

'I thought he was going to kiss you then,' said Action.

'I think it was a pretty close run thing,' replied Frank.

They looked at each other for answers as to what Scott was planning, but there weren't any to be found; so they watched him as he flitted down the corridor. Scott paused several times on his journey to wave his arms about and tap himself on the head before continuing. Just before the northwest stairwell he met Kevin as he was coming out of another classroom. There was a short animated conversation between them and then they both disappeared into the stairwell leaving the rest of them staring open mouthed down the now empty corridor.

Click, click, click, click; heard from behind, it was a sound that struck fear into anyone who was currently engaged in anything illicit and guilt into those that weren't. Moments later, Mr Fleming walked passed them heading in the same direction as Scott; he turned his head and in a single glance noted every face and the current activity of its owner. Satisfied, and without breaking the rhythm of his clicking shoes Mr Fleming continued his journey down the corridor. They watched him go both relieved and puzzled. Relieved that they hadn't been doing anything illicit and puzzled as to why Mr Fleming was carrying a bucket of water.

'That's something you don't see every day,' said Frank once Mr Fleming was out of earshot. They watched him make his way down the corridor; the red plastic bucket distorting under the weight of the water and spilling slightly with each step.

'Some days are just full of weird stuff; have you noticed that?' said Action. 'Nothing happens for weeks and then all of sudden you get a day that's just not normal.' He adjusted his cagoule to limit the amount of draught he was getting through the split in his trousers.

John looked at Elleria. 'Tell me about it,' he said. They watched until the teacher had turned the corner into the northwest stairwell. 'But none of those things matter at the moment, because I'm hungry; let's go and eat.'

*

Mr Fleming smiled to himself as he made way down the corridor with his bucket. He was trying to remember the last time he had done this; he thought it must be six years at least. So with no prior knowledge of what was about to happen amongst the current intake of pupils, the success rate should be quite high. He turned into the northwest stairwell, made his way to the window at the far left corner and placed the bucket on the floor. Reg painted the metal windows every couple of years, but he didn't oil the hinges, as far as Reg was concerned there was no point, the windows in the stairwell were never opened. Trying to make as little noise as possible Mr Fleming used both hands to slowly open the two catches on the window. They hadn't been used for years and offered some resistance, each one jolting open with a dull creak. With some strength and a great deal of control he pushed at the window to open it slightly and crack the rust on the hinges. The rust appeared as a thin brown line of powder on the white paint of each hinge. Picking up the bucket, he rested it on the window sill and prepared himself; the next action had to be smooth and quick, and he knew from experience that the window would make a noise as he opened it.

With a loud creak Mr Fleming pushed the window open wide, leaned out with the bucket, took aim at the upturned faces and tipped the water over them. There were seven of them; a slightly disappointing number, but not bad. Mr Fleming felt his spirits rise; this was by far his favourite ruse.

Since he'd given up smoking twenty years ago Mr Fleming had waged war on pupils who insisted on starting the habit; on the premise that if he couldn't have a fag, then neither could they. It was pure Penshaw Grove vindictiveness. The bucket and window scheme was a cunning stratagem based on the fact that there were limited places around the school where smokers could congregate.

Sooner or later; when new pupils reached the age where either hormones or peer pressure urged them to buy ten cigarettes and a box of matches from the corner shop; they would get round to discovering the bushes at the north end of the rear yard. The bushes occupied a narrow strip of land between the end of the north building and the boundary fence. Secluded and sheltered from the wind it was an ideal place to light up. The location had that "no one will ever find us here" feel to it. It was the very same place that in 1930 Mr Fleming had started smoking.

With stage one of the scheme complete, now all Mr Fleming had to do was wait in the dining hall entrance and pick out anyone who was wet. He had noted all the upturned faces and allocated names to them as the water descended, he probably could just pick them out from that information alone. If they were wet however, there could be no possibility of denying that they were there. There was the added bonus that dousing the flames made a far stronger point, but the primary reason was that Mr Fleming just plain enjoyed doing it. There was an extra zing to the clicking of his shoes as he made his way down the stairs. As he crossed the playground Mr Fleming whistled a tune and swung the empty bucket back and forth. None of the pupils heading for the lunch queue had ever seen him this happy before.

*

'There he is again with that bucket,' said Action as they entered the playground from the opposite end to Mr Fleming.

'Bucket looks empty now,' said Elleria, 'I wonder what he's done with the water.'

It was a question that they all considered as they joined the back of the queue for lunch. Further up the queue in front of them they could hear a phrase that was almost becoming a mantra.

'Name at the top and sign at the bottom,' it went.

'Name at the top and sign at the bottom,' and again with a different voice.

'Name at the top and sign at the bottom.' It was a very abridged version of the sales pitch that John's friends had received; as all four members of The Lendus worked their way along the lunch line. In order to speed things up they'd dropped persuasion in favour of intimidation. The Lendus continued to work the queue outside the dining hall as John, Frank, Elleria and Action moved with the queue into the dining hall entrance area.

The distance across the entrance area to the dining hall was short and soon they were stood inside the gloomy unlit hall looking at the queue as it made its way along the wall to the serving hatch at the far end. Mr Fleming was stood behind the open door so that he couldn't be seen until you were actually in the hall; the empty bucket was by his feet. He looked at the four of them knowing that they wouldn't be wet as he had passed them on the corridor before the event.

'Sir,' said John who was behind the other three, 'what's the bucket for?' Elleria, Frank and Action turned to hear the answer.

'Let's just say Mr Godbert that it would not have been in your best interests to have been wet when you came in here.'

'Oh,' said John looking puzzled.

'Smokers, Mr Godbert, I douse them after they've lit up and then pick out anyone who's wet when they come for lunch.' Mr Fleming knew he would not be giving anything away by telling John this, the deed was done and it would probably be the last time he performed the trick.

'That's clever Sir,' said Frank.

'Of course it is, I thought of it,' replied Mr Fleming.

Frank smiled and then he and Action turned back to face forward in the queue. Elleria turned the other way to face John and placed her hands on his upper arms.

'John,' she said looking deep into his eyes, 'it's time.' Mr Fleming raised his eyebrows, what a curious thing to say, he thought. And then, as he continued to watch them, for an instant they both seemed to glow with an inner light. The glow lingered in John's eyes for a full two seconds before it was gone and then Elleria turned to face the right way in the queue as if nothing had happened. Perhaps it hadn't happened. Mr Fleming no longer felt as elated as he had done before, he felt quite shocked and unsure; he looked out of the window at the clouds, anywhere to take his mind off these hallucinations he seemed to be having.

*

The council chamber in the city of Valheel was empty. The lighting level was low; a perimeter of lights set into the floor where it met the walls formed alternating light and dark shafts on the walls. The dais was silhouetted against the lighting pattern on the wall that ran behind it. A green humanoid shaped grid appeared in front of the dais which immediately rendered itself into the form of Tyrus. As the lighting levels rose, five more grids appeared behind the dais rendering into the council members. Tyrus stood before them waiting for them to respond to his presence.

Consulus addressed Tyrus. 'What progress have you made?'

'I was able to track the Radgarc Elleria first to a planet which did not yield anything of interest to us. It was here that Elleria, for reasons unknown, took the form of a small primate for a short period; I suspect that this may have been for entertainment purposes. The next planet she visited proved to be more significant. As we suspected Amantarra has indeed created a species that has the potential to rival the Bruwnan. The species call themselves "human" and I would place their evolutionary status at approximately seventy five percent of that required by Bruwnian standards prior to ascension. Given the short development period, this species has obviously had significant help. The planet is enveloped in a dampening field making it difficult to detect any Bruwnian technology or presence.

I was however able to locate an individual who had been exposed to Amantarra's shield for a long period of time and was therefore resistant to the dampening field. Residual traces on the shield indicated that he had been allotted the task of Keeper to a Node segment; a position normally held by a Radgarc. I do not believe he was aware of his status, as when asked, he revealed where he had delivered the segment.

The next human refused to reveal the location of the segment and I had to copy his thoughts so they could be properly analysed. His resistance to the process was high, giving an indication of the advanced development of the species, and resulting in the termination of the human's brain function.

The information retrieved led to the human known as John Godbert. Radgarc Elleria, who had taken human form, was in close association with John Godbert. Her tracking device could be detected when in close proximity. John Godbert is also protected by Amantarra's shield and I suspected at first that he was Amantarra in human form; one, because of the close relationship between Elleria and him, and two, he was now in possession of the Node segment. On closer inspection this assumption proved unfounded and I was curious as to why John was shielded and in possession of the Node segment. I continued my observations waiting for evidence of the whereabouts of the other Node segment when there was a surprising development. It would seem that the human John Godbert was the other segment. This fact was not apparent until the Node became fully functional a few moments ago. Given that Node technology cannot be applied to living organisms this was a development that I failed to anticipate. How the incorporation of a living organism into a Node segment has been achieved, I do not know.

It is my belief that Amantarra is present on the planet and presumably close to John Godbert. I have detected one other who bears Amantarra's shield, but I have no evidence that this is Amantarra. Past evidence seems to indicate that Amantarra will attempt to defend against injustice; and to this end I have instigated a stratagem that may succeed in flushing Amantarra out into the open.

That concludes my report.'

The council sat in silence as they considered the report. After a few moments Consulus spoke.

'This new factor of a living Node is of concern to us, and again we must assume that this is not the only occurrence. It is therefore imperative that Amantarra is brought back to Valheel for questioning so that we can determine the best method of eradication as well as retrieving the Primary Key. Continue in your attempts to flush Amantarra out of hiding and if possible assess any means that may be available to us to achieve the removal of this species.'

Tyrus nodded to the council and vanished.

17
THE VISIT

Scott's Grandparents lived in the same road as Scott, in the same type of semi-detached house that all of Scott's friends lived in except of course Kevin, who lived in a mid-terraced house near the school. The round bay windowed front looked out onto a small garden which was separated from the pavement by a low wall and a neatly trimmed yellow privet hedge. Black wrought iron gates led onto a paved driveway that ran up the side of the house. Elleria, John and Frank arrived at the gates, and stood waiting for Kevin and Action who were making their way towards them. John was looking at the rainwater pipe which ran down between the bay windows, marking the boundary between the two houses; the half on Scott's grandparent's side was painted blue to match the windows, the other half was painted dark red to match their neighbours windows. John was mystified as to why they didn't just agree to paint it black. He gave up trying to work it out and turned to face Action and Kevin as they arrived.

'Any idea why we're here,' asked Action.

Frank looked at the others who were shaking their heads. 'No,' he replied. 'Scott just flashed past us at the end of lessons saying; "meet me at my Granddad's house at six o'clock; all will be revealed", and then he was gone.'

'Pretty much the same for me,' said Action.

'He did ask me to get my Dad's keys and then meet here,' revealed Kevin.

'Your Dad's school keys?' asked John.

'Yes, and it wasn't easy; he normally doesn't let them out of his sight, but for some reason he's bought a new set of darts and gone to the pub to play. Mam's being trying to work out where he got the money from.'

'So you've got them here, now?' Kevin nodded and jingled his coat pocket.

'We could go there now and have a nosey around,' said Action, looking all excited.

'Aren't we there often enough for you?' scoffed Frank.

'I suppose… it just seemed like an opportunity not to be missed.' Frank rolled his eyes.

At the end of the driveway was a small brick garage with a corrugated iron roof and blue double doors. One of the doors opened with a creak attracting their attention.

'In here,' shouted Scott, poking his head round the door. Frank opened the gate and they all made their way down the drive and into the garage. At the side of the garage facing onto the back garden was a single door with a grimy glass panel, and across the back was another equally grimy window. It looked out onto a small square of land between the garage and the back fence where Scott's Grandfather accumulated rubbish. The dirty windows made the interior gloomy; there was no other lighting, there wasn't even electricity. On the wall opposite the side door were shelves full of rusty old paint tins. They hadn't been touched for years. The garage had a musty smell from lack of use. Across the back, under the window, was a lawnmower, some large step ladders and an old bicycle. Apart from that the garage was fairly empty. Scott was sitting on an upturned bucket facing the double doors. In front of him was a table made up of a square sheet of plywood resting on four kitchen stools. On the table there were six piles of different coloured buttons and opposite each pile, arranged around the makeshift table were five more seats consisting of; two deckchairs, another bucket, a short three legged stool and a small set of stepladders.

'Grab a seat,' said Scott.

Mystified, they all settled into place and then looked at Scott, waiting for it all to be revealed.

'I thought we'd play a game of pontoon,' said Scott producing a pack of cards from his pocket. They all looked at each other.

'Scott,' said John. 'Why are we in your Granddad's garage?' The others nodded their approval at the question. Scott looked at a bit of a loss for words, as if he hadn't anticipated the question at all.

'To play cards?' he replied more as a question than an answer.

'Yes, but you said you were going to reveal your grand plan for getting back at Burnston and this Lendus rubbish,' said Action.

'Humour me,' replied Scott. And then, as if he'd just remembered; 'did you get the keys Kev?'

'Yes,' said Kevin placing the large bunch of keys on the table.

'Great,' said Scott picking up the bunch and flipping through each unlabelled key until he eventually seemed to settle on one and took it off the metal loop. He handed the rest of them back to Kevin. 'Thanks, I'll give you this one back tomorrow.'

'Okay,' said Kevin with a certain amount of uncertainty in his voice. 'What does that key open?'

'I'll show you tomorrow. Don't worry; your dad won't miss this one.' Scott looked round at the others. 'Shall we play then?'

Realising that they weren't going to get any answers they all nodded in agreement and Scott began to deal the cards. 'They call this game "Blackjack" in America,' he informed them.

'Why?' asked Action.

'Don't know,' said Scott.

'Why do they call it pontoon?' asked Elleria.

'Don't know that either.'

Elleria looked at the cards in front of her. 'How do you play it then?' she asked.

'You've never played before?' Scott looked surprised.

'No.'

'Okay, so you get two cards and the idea is to get as close to twenty-one as you can by getting more cards without going over, picture cards are worth ten and aces are worth either one or eleven. You'll soon pick it up.'

'And the buttons, what are they for?' she asked.

'Each person puts a button in the middle, the one that wins the round gets the buttons, and the overall winner is the one with the most buttons at the end.'

John picked up his cards. 'These cards look ancient, how old are they?'

'They belong to my Granddad,' replied Scott nodding at the side door where right on cue Samuel Briggs passed dragging a large cardboard box towards the back of the garage. Elderly, Samuel struggled with the box which his new television had arrived in last week. He proceeded slowly, taking a step backwards and then dragging the box towards him as he progressed past the door. Samuel coughed, his chest rattling with years of accumulated nicotine; drawing some sympathetic looks from Scott's friends.

Seeing their faces Scott said; 'just ignore him and let him get on with it.' Their looks changed from one of sympathy to surprise. 'Look if we help him he'll have us working all night. He wouldn't even be doing this if my Grandma was in.'

'Are you sure?' asked Elleria.

'Yes, he just likes to have people to boss around; and he'll give up in about ten minutes. Now shall we play?'

Half an hour and two more cardboard boxes later, Scott was doing better than everyone else by a big margin. Samuel wasn't going to give up that easily, not with Mary out and this much untapped labour sitting in his garage.

John looked at the pile of buttons Scott had accumulated, and compared it to his own and everyone else's diminishing pile. Elleria and Kevin had already lost all their buttons. Frank, who was now the dealer, was shuffling the cards when John was distracted by the appearance of Samuel at the back window of the garage. Samuel glanced in the window and John felt a pang of guilt that they hadn't lifted a finger to help him.

Samuel turned away from the window to face the boxes he'd piled one on top of the other near the fence, and paused for a good lung clearing, window rattling, and heart stopping retch of a cough. Just what the Doctor ordered after all that exercise he thought.

In his youth, Samuel Briggs had been a brash and over confident young man who was going to take on the world and win. In 1914 he got his opportunity and enlisted in the Durham Light Infantry. After four years in the trenches having lost his youth but gained a couple of serious wounds and a lance corporals stripe, Samuel felt that he had gone some way towards achieving his ambition. He returned to "Blighty" full of confidence and married the girl of his dreams.

Mary, the object of his dreams had taken his brash confidence and beaten it into submission. After 56 years, what was left of the confident young man Samuel once was, had learnt to live with it. Samuel took solace in his pipe; and in secret, in case Mary found out, passed his pearls of wisdom on to his Grandson Scott.

Today, after a sudden resurgence of brashness, he had decided against Mary's wishes to burn some cardboard boxes behind his garage. Though strictly speaking, it would only have been against Mary's wishes if she had known, and as she was out at the bingo, that was practically the same as having permission.

Now after an epic struggle to get the boxes round the back of the garage; a struggle that he'd hoped Scott and his friends would have helped with; he felt justified in lighting the boxes before Mary came back.

Samuel took out his cigarette lighter and stooped to light a corner of one of the dry boxes. He straightened up; pleased to see how quickly the box had caught. He took a step back, feeling the warmth on his face as the other boxes took light. It was with a little less satisfaction that he noticed the flames licking the back fence.

Things just seemed to happen quicker these days, he thought, as the heart of the fire transferred itself to the fence. He recalled that the brash confident young man he once was would have been able to do far more than beat the flames feebly with his cap. Finally he concluded; as he abandoned it to the flames; that he needed a new cap anyway.

John watched Samuel through the grimy window as he bent down and then straightened up again. The yellow orange glow that lit Samuel from below, indicated that he'd set the boxes on fire, threw flickering yellow patterns on the garage ceiling giving the place a warm and cosy feeling. As the flames grew Samuel became silhouetted against a brightening more intense yellow background. The interior of the garage was bathed in a golden yellow light which caught everyone's attention, except Scott's, who seemed determined to ignore his Grandfather. It was when the silhouette of Samuel took his cap off and started beating at the flames, that John realised that perhaps it was time to lift that finger to help.

John stood and moved towards the door. 'Scott,' he said, 'you might want to go and get some water.'

Scott turned on his bucket, and then fell off it as he was greeted with the scene of a solid wall of flame, with the silhouette of Samuel waving his cap about in an ineffectual manner.

'Bloody hell!' he exclaimed, leaping to his feet and almost falling over backwards again as his body tried to keep up with his legs.

'Let's get some water,' John heard Frank say from inside the garage as he made his way quickly up the side of it, with Elleria close behind. Without really having to think about it, John froze time, continued to the back of the garage and stood next to Samuel.

'That was very smooth,' said Elleria who was automatically included in any Eralton field that John created. 'What are you going to do now?'

'I don't know; I just needed some time to think.' They both stood and looked at the flames which were higher than the garage. The fence was well alight, and there was smoke rising from the shed in the garden on the other side of the fence, indicating that it too would soon take to flame. Samuel was staring at the ground near his feet; the final resting place of his cap. Although the frozen flames consuming the cap were minor, the look on Samuel's face told John that the cap was a far greater loss to him than the fence.

'Can you feel that?' said John.

'What?'

This close to the flames John had expected to feel the heat radiating, but there was none; there was however a harmonious ringing coming from them. The harmonies changed constantly, forming new chord sequences and rhythms. John reached out to the flames and as his hand came close the tones and rhythms changed. The flame nearest his hand bulged out towards him. John felt physically stronger and his senses sharpened, both old and new.

'Harmonies, it's a bit like music but its random and changing all the time.'

'Careful,' said Elleria as John placed his fingers in the flame.

There was still no sensation of heat or burning.

'It's not hot,' said John, 'but there is something else.' John concentrated for a moment. 'There's a structure in there. I can't tell if the harmonies form the structure or the structure makes the music. There's definitely more going on with fire than just heat and combustion.'

John rotated his hand slightly and the structures seemed to change. There was nothing in the changes to indicate what the structures were, and John couldn't explain where the knowledge came from, it wasn't like the reference flashes he kept getting, it was more like he was being fed an entire concept. He suddenly understood that what he was sensing wasn't just happening in three dimensions, it went back further than that, expanding into new dimensions where the structures made more sense. And like Reginald Scribbins all those years ago in the boiler room when he saw the boiler for the first time; it was the most complex thing John had ever seen in his life. He suspected that the flames held the key to something else but he didn't know what, until he saw the following:

Ref: 327-2-716-1-481-002-19

Node Regulator Technical Reference

Energy flow through the Node is controlled using minimal energy applied directly to the physical exterior of the Node.

The larger the amount of energy applied the greater the flow.
Burst sequences of maximum energy flow can be achieved by applying large amounts of energy, for example by immersing the Node in fire for a short period.

'Elleria, this is the key to burst mode, which is something to do with that tunnel in the storeroom at school,' John explained as he pushed his hand further into the flame. 'The structures are changing; they seem to be responding to my presence.' John watched as the harmonics altered, realigning themselves into new patterns. John almost, but not quite, felt as though he understood the process; the key to the knowledge was tantalisingly just out of reach. The structures surrounding his hand had stopped changing now, they felt solid, real, or had his hand become like the structures? His head buzzed, he felt more alive than he had ever done. John felt the gentle pull on his hand; he was being invited into the flames. He stepped forward immersing his whole body in them.

'John, no,' exclaimed Elleria her voice full of concern.

As John stepped into the flames he crawled with blue light, he could see it all over his hands and arms. And as the yellow colour of the flame began to fade, John began to feel stronger; much stronger. After a few moments the flames were pale, ghosts of their former radiance, and then they were nothing. The structures that had formed around John's hand remained. Resembling pictures in a gallery they floated in front of John; but they portrayed more than just images, as John held his hand near each of them in turn he got the sense of the concepts behind each choice, and an in-depth explanation of what each did.

'Can you see this?' he asked.

Elleria was still fascinated by the fact that the flames had vanished.

'See what?'

'These picture things in front of us.'

'No, look this is making me nervous; we should stop until we know what's happening.'

'Take my hand,' he said to Elleria.

The images flashed into view as soon as she held his hand. Elleria's eyes opened wide. 'What do they do?' she asked forgetting about her apprehension.

'This one,' said John indicating one of the images, 'creates a tunnel through time to the future like the one we saw in the storeroom.' John indicated another, 'and this one… this is the one I want to try.'

'Try? No John we shouldn't,' but it was too late.

John touched the image and they were instantly plunged into blackness. There was no real sense of time; the blackness could have lasted seconds or hours, John simply couldn't tell. Then a field of blue stars replaced the blackness. Only they're not stars, thought John, this is not real space. Here, time and scale are not related to real or Euclidian space. What I'm looking at, are the shadows of stars as they cross the dimension boundaries of Euclidian space. Where were these thoughts coming from? He could sense Elleria close to him but he wasn't holding her hand any more, they were both without physical form.

Floating in front of them was a green sphere that reminded John of the drip in the chemistry lab, but this one had an internal structure. Against the backdrop of blue stars it was impossible to get any idea of scale, but from their position it was about the size of a golf ball, and increasing in size with each moment.

'What is that?' he said.

'It looks like Valheel; but I've never seen it from the outside before,' replied Elleria.

The sphere was now about the size of a football and was slowly rotating. Its outer shell was a semi-transparent green and through it could be seen the internal structure. John could see four coloured towers linking the centre of the sphere to four separate circular collections of roads and buildings on its inner surface.

The sphere had continued to grow in size and it now stood before them about the size of a house as viewed by someone stood two paces back. As the zones moved slowly round, the other side of the sphere could be seen between the buildings moving in the opposite direction, which was a little disorientating.

'What's the green sphere?'

'It's the force field that binds Valheel together,' replied Elleria as the yellow zone moved in front of them.

'It looks fascinating. Let's go and visit.' The sphere expanded suddenly to fill their entire field of view.

'No John I don't think…' objected Elleria, but it was too late.

The base of the yellow centroid tower expanded so rapidly towards them that it looked as though it was exploding. In a fraction of a second they were through the outer shell. There was a blinding blue flash and a crack of arcing electricity as they passed through the base of the yellow tower. They veered off to the left and slowed down rapidly. They were now floating above the blue zone.

'What was that?' shouted Elleria.

'Sorry, I overshot that yellow bit; but still, I was right on target, did you see? I took us right through the bull's eye. Let's try landing on the blue one, it's the closest,' said John before Elleria could speak.

*

Jack Green had been trying to wake from a dream. He'd had similar dreams in the past, where he couldn't see properly, and he had hated them. In the dream he couldn't decide whether it was his eyes that were at fault or if he was in a fog. He could sense what was around him, he just couldn't tell how. The closest way he could describe it, was a memory. It was as if he'd been here before, like a familiar room in the dark; but from what he'd sensed as he explored, he knew he'd never been here before. He found the loss of sight very frustrating. If he could see the buildings instead of just imagining their outlines he might be able to pick out something familiar. He supposed that was the nature of dreams, they never quite did what you wanted them to.

Normally in his dreams there was something happening, the events may be disjointed and chaotic, but they were at least action. This dream was strange; it seemed to consist entirely of a long period where nothing had happened at all. Jack was bored. He'd never been bored in a dream before. To regain his eyesight he'd been rubbing his eyes, but although he could feel his hands on his face, he couldn't see them. It must therefore, he concluded, be his eyes that were at fault.

He could hear things though, unpleasant things off in the distance. The forlorn cries of people pleading for help. Anger, there was anger in their voices. Sometimes there was just one or two and sometimes there seemed to be thousands. Jack would have helped if he hadn't had his own problems. Damn it, if only he could wake up. He moved out of the room he was in and down a short corridor towards the building entrance. To the left of the entrance there was a door to another room; Jack felt the closeness of the door frame as he entered. It was the same as the others he'd been in; empty.

His fingers tingled with a pins and needles sensation. Normally Jack would not have welcomed this, he hated pins and needles, but his fingers suddenly felt warm and he realised just how cold his hands must have been despite the fact that he had felt nothing. The warmth spread up his arms and the rest of his body tingled with returning sensation.

There were voices close by, different to the angry ones from before. They were coming from outside, and on the grounds that it was the only interesting thing to have happened since he fell asleep, he decided to investigate. As Jack made his way outside he heard a female voice say; "this is not a good idea John". Jack could sense them clearly now as he made his way out onto the large circular plaza that surrounded one of the tall towers in this strange place.

There were two of them, and the male, appeared to be made from shadow; a silhouette against the background as if he didn't really exist here. The female looked like an infrared photograph that Jack had seen once, but her shoulder shone with a brightness that hurt. Despite the pain he wasn't going to just ignore them, this was far too interesting. As Jack approached them, the darkness from the male seemed to vacuum the fog away from his eyes making this unseen place visible. He could feel strength returning to his body and limbs, his hands became visible and with a flash, his eyesight retuned.

Jack stood blinking at the now normal looking newcomers as they turned to face him with surprised looks on their faces, as if he'd just appeared out of thin air. The girl was pretty but looked concerned. It took a moment or two, but Jack recognised the male.

'John Godbert... Tom's son,' stated Jack. And after a moment's thought asked, 'did you get that present off your Uncle Edward... the pocket watch?'

'How did you know that?'

'I sold it to Edward... it had your name in it.'

'Yes I did thanks,' said John. He thought he half recognised the old man, like he'd seen him around, but he couldn't put a name to the face. 'Sorry for asking,' he continued; 'but, what was your name again?'

'Jack Green, I own the pawnbrokers.'

'Of course, I've heard my dad talk about you and I'm sure I heard your name mentioned recently as well,' added John thoughtfully. 'But... what are you doing here?'

'"What am I doing here?" Well, it is my dream.'

'But this isn't a dream,' said Elleria, 'this is Valheel.' Elleria indicated the city as it arced overhead. Jack looked up at the city following the sweep of Elleria's arm. It was true that since these two had arrived he'd felt more awake, but this place was impossible so he must still be dreaming.

'Valheel,' repeated Jack thoughtfully, 'I've never heard of anywhere called Valheel; and this place,' Jack looked up at the city, 'it's like the world turned inside out.' As Jack looked at the yellow zone, the power there seemed to switch off and back on again. 'Should that yellow bit be doing that?'

John and Elleria both watched as the power in the entire yellow zone went off and came back on again moments later.

'No,' said Elleria, looking at John accusingly, 'it shouldn't be doing that at all. I can't imagine what might have caused it to do that.' John was going to defend his honour with a "how is that my fault" when he was beaten by Jack.

'This place can't be real, can it?' Jack asked.

'Well it's a different kind of reality to the one you are used to,' answered Elleria, 'but it is a reality none the less.'

Jack tapped his foot on the ground. 'So I'm not dreaming then?'

'No,' said John.

'So if I'm not dreaming, what am I doing here? And how did I get here?'

John suddenly remembered where he'd heard Jack's name, it was Reg Scribbins saying something about him being dead, and Reg had seemed a bit put out by it. John looked at Elleria.

'Didn't Reg Scribbins say something about Jack Green when we saw him in the storeroom?'

Elleria nodded.

'Storeroom,' said Jack, 'that's where Reg said he found the watch. It was behind a grill.'

'I knew there was something special about that grill,' said John. 'As soon as I saw it, something just clicked. So, Reg found the watch behind the grill, sold it to you and you sold it to Uncle Edward, who gave it to me.'

'Yes, I would say that probably sums it up,' said Jack. 'Did you say that Reg said something about me?'

John looked at Elleria again. He'd remembered what he'd heard.

'You'll have to tell him,' she said.

'Tell me what?'

John considered his reply, how do you tell someone that they're dead. In the past John had thought about how horrible it would be to have to tell someone that one of their relatives is dead, the way the police have to sometimes; but he'd never thought about having to tell someone that they were actually dead. You would have thought most people would have noticed.

'Reg said you were dead,' replied John. Thinking that the easiest way to say it; would be to just tell him outright.

'Dead,' repeated Jack, 'but how can I be when I'm here?' Jack looked up at the impossible city. 'You did say Valheel and not Valhalla didn't you?'

Elleria pulled a face; 'Valhalla?'

'In Scandinavian mythology it means "Hall of the Slain" it's a sort of Viking heaven,' said John; adding, 'I have no idea how I know that.'

'No it's definitely Valheel and it's certainly not heaven,' said Elleria turning to Jack. 'Actually this is worrying. If you're here, it means that I must have been tracked to earth, but I can't see how.'

'I think I can,' said John. 'Remember Mr Fleming's bucket trick. Where he soaks the smokers and then picks out anybody who's wet.' He indicated Elleria's shoulder. 'Your shoulder is wet. I think you've been tagged the same way.' Elleria looked at her shoulder and noticed it for the first time. Although it didn't feel wet, it looked wet.

'Yes, I see what you mean, but if anyone had poured water over my shoulder the last time I was here, I'd have noticed.' Elleria thought for a moment. 'On the other hand, Tyrus did touch me there on that shoulder; perhaps that was how he tagged me. And last time, I was in Bruwnan form not human, so having a wet shoulder must be some sort of human interpretation of the tag.'

'Who's Tyrus?'

'He's the council's Enforcer and he's rather unpleasant,' said Elleria pulling a face.

'So if Tyrus followed you; how come we haven't seen him?'

'I don't know, obviously he must be in disguise.'

'Before I could see you properly, your shoulder shone very brightly if that's any help,' said Jack wanting to contribute to the conversation.

'Before you could see us properly?' queried John.

'Well, before you arrived, everything was sort of… foggy. I thought I was having a dream. I don't suppose you've got any idea how I got here, or perhaps… how I get back?'

'What was the last thing you remember before you were here?' asked Elleria.

'Good question… let me think now,' Jack rubbed his chin in a thoughtful manner. 'I was in the shop; although there was nothing unusual about that because I'm always in the shop. Then a big lad came in; you probably know him he's P.C. Burnston's son… Bob I think he's called.'

'Yes, we call him something else,' said John.' So then what happened?'

'Well now, let me think… oh yes, that was it; he was asking about that watch of yours, who I'd sold it to; but I wouldn't tell him, client confidentiality and all that. Then I seem to recall thinking about the past, a bit like the phrase "my life flashed before my eyes", and then I was here dreaming in the fog.'

Elleria wrung her hands together. 'So how could Burnston know about the watch?' And why would he be interested in where it went? It could only mean that he's Tyrus, or that Tyrus is controlling him somehow.'

'So… how did I get here then?' asked Jack.

'You've been copied,' said John. 'You wouldn't tell Burnston or Tyrus what he wanted so he copied your mind. I think the process must have killed you. I don't know how I know that either.'

'So I am dead then.'

'Your human body is, but obviously your mind isn't. It does make going back a bit tricky though,' said Elleria.

'But I have a body at the moment,' said Jack patting his chest.

'No you don't, what you're seeing is an avatar. Why it's in human form, or for that matter, why John and I are in human form when the city doesn't know what a human looks like, I don't know. Perhaps...'

'DOWN!' shouted John. They all hit the deck as a pulse of energy zinged over them and hit a wall next to them.

'What the hell was that?' yelled Jack.

'I don't know but it didn't seem friendly,' said John. Looking across the plaza he could see six figures running towards them.

'Guardians'! They're trying to disable our avatars so that they can take control of us,' said Elleria. 'DO NOT GET SHOT.'

'Keep low and follow me!' Jack shouted as he started to make his way back to the room he was in.

The figures stopped running and took up a kneeling position so they could aim better. The volley of shots that followed was close; far too close for comfort. The wall next to them crackled as each pulse struck, offering a brief glimpse of the underlying green construction grid. Jack reached the doorway, went inside and turned immediately right into the room he'd been in, Elleria followed him as several shots flew through the outer door and into the building itself. Still framed in the doorway John stood up straight as he entered the building. He was struck right in the middle of his back, the force knocking him forward and leaving him sprawled face down. John's prone form became a silhouette.

'JOHN, NO!' Elleria cried, she turned to go to him, but Jack held her back, grabbing her around the waist.

'They'll get you too missy,' he said. Elleria reached for his arm to try and remove it so she could go to John, but the arm was no longer there.

'Damn,' said Jack, 'that fog's back.'

18

WILLIAM

'Bloody hell son; that was quick!' exclaimed Samuel.

It took a moment for John to realise that he was back behind Samuel's garage and standing in the remains of the fire. He took a couple of steps back to look down the side of the garage; Kevin and Action were just coming out of the side door. There was no one else around.

'I've never seen anyone stamp out a fire that quick!' Samuel looked at the damage the fire had done to the fence. 'Then again, everything seems to happen quickly these days.' John turned to look at the charred fence as Samuel continued with his praise. 'I didn't even see you arrive and the next thing I know the fire is out.'

Kevin arrived at the back of the garage. 'Fence is a bit of a mess,' he said.

Samuel looked worried. 'Aye, it is that; but with a bit of luck Mary won't see it for a while,' he said.

Some of the planks making up the fence were almost burnt through, their blackened tops tapering to uneven points. Lower down, the fence was lined with charred grooves and cracks that broke the surface up into charcoaled blocks and squares. The air was heavy with the smell of wood smoke. They stood in silence watching the wisps of smoke that still rose from the fence. It didn't look like it had been the sort of fire you could just stamp out, but nobody had said anything; after all the fire was out and that was all that mattered.

There was a sloshing sound as Scott appeared. He was carrying a washing up bowl half-full of water. The bowl had been full when he'd set off from the kitchen, but now a large amount of it was down his clothes.

'You're too late,' said Samuel indicating the fence, 'the fire's already out.'

'Well, almost,' said Action. He pointed at Samuel's cap. A ring of small flames burned around a hole in the top of it.

Scott tipped what was left of the water over the cap and then looked down at his soaking clothes.

'Great,' he said without any enthusiasm. Frank arrived a few seconds later with a kettle full of water. He looked at charred fence, the steaming cap and then at the kettle.

'Cup of tea anyone?' he asked.

Samuel picked up his charred cap and shook the water off it and examined the hole burnt through the cloth. 'Yes son, that would be nice,' he said.

'I'll go and plug it in then,' said Frank. He turned and made his way back to the kitchen.

John followed Frank as far as the side door of the garage and stepped inside. The garage was empty.

As Action, Kevin and Scott were passing the door they noticed John.

'Lost something?' asked Action.

'Yeah, did you see where Elleria went?'

Action looked puzzled. 'Who's Elleria?'

Kevin looked at Scott. 'Do you know?'

Scott shrugged.

They looked at John for the answer, but he didn't have one. Normally he would suspect that his friends were winding him up, but in this case he didn't think that they were. It was a gut feeling, almost instinctive, but John was absolutely positive that they genuinely did not know who Elleria was. John felt cut off. It wasn't just that Elleria wasn't here in Samuel's garden, she wasn't anywhere. He hadn't really noticed his connection to her until it had gone.

'Doesn't matter,' he said. The other three lost interest and continued towards the kitchen.

John had assumed that Elleria would have arrived back here with him; but she must be still in Valheel. Why? John looked around the garage and thought about all the things that had happened in the city. His mind rattled back and forth between each event; the view from outside the sphere, Jack Green, the Guardian's, arriving back here and finally why did no one seemed to remember her but him. There were too many thoughts all at the same time; it was not helping at all.

'The answer is there. Think about one thing at a time.' The whispered voice came from behind. John turned, the garage was still empty. Perhaps he'd only imagined it; but the advice did seem good. John went over the events again, slowly this time.

Getting shot by one of those weapons didn't do much damage; all it did to me was send me back here. Elleria, as far as he knew, didn't get shot at all. Perhaps that was it; they shot you to get you out of the city. That can't be right, that wasn't what Elleria said they were doing. "They're trying to disable our avatars so that they can take control of us". So what had become of her? Had she been taken over? What would happen to her? John felt anxious. He must try and get back there; he couldn't just abandon Elleria to these Guardians'. He needed her. Actions he had previously thought were his had in fact been guided and influenced; by Elleria. When it came down to it, he didn't really know what he was doing at all. Who would help him get her back? Who could help? Nobody here remember her.

John looked around the garage for evidence of her existence. There were four piles of buttons, Elleria and Kevin already having lost theirs; Frank hadn't even started to deal the cards which sat in a single pile, so there was no evidence that there had been six players; and the two buckets making up the seating were rolling around on the floor well away from the makeshift table, they looked as though they could have been discarded at any time. What would it achieve if he could prove that Elleria had existed? It wouldn't get her back; none of his friends possessed the means, even if he did manage to convince them. There was only one way to get her back, thought John, and he turned to leave the garage and go back to where the fire had been. John stopped and looked at his hand. In the gloom of the garage it glowed with some inner light as if he were shining a torch through it.

'You must learn to take control.' Again, the voice came from behind. John didn't bother to turn round this time. He knew what the voice meant; with Elleria gone, he was a Node without a Radgarc to control it; another reason to get Elleria back. He willed his hand to stop glowing and was surprised when the light faded slightly. He tried again, and the glow faded to the point where it was hardly noticeable.

John left the garage and walked back to the charred fence. He looked at the blackened seat of the fire and asked himself where he going to find a fire that big without creating one himself.

'Damn,' he said in his frustration. He didn't want to go around starting fires. John became aware that Samuel was looking at him and turned to face him.

'Thanks son, you got me out of a lot of trouble there,' said Samuel. 'I don't think I could have done anything about that fire. Your Grandfather William would have been proud.'

Samuel had known John since he was three years old, but they'd never actually spoken beyond saying "hello", or Samuel asking "can you keep the noise down boys". Previously, Samuel just didn't have anything to say that a small child would understand, but now that John was older… well things were different now.

Tom had never really talked to John about his father; the subject seemed to upset him. Consequently nobody else talked about him; so apart from the fact that he was dead, John knew very little about his Grandfather. Now it turns out that Samuel Briggs knew him, probably better than Tom.

'You knew my Grandfather?'

'Yes, I met him in a field hospital during the First World War. He was laid next to me.'

'He was actually in the next bed to you,' said John.

'Bed… not exactly. I was lucky, I had a straw filled mattress, but that cathedral floor was still cold, you could feel it pulling the heat out of you. William only had a blanket, I don't know how he could stand it, but he never complained.

'Did you say cathedral?'

'In Laon, in northern France; it was a creepy old place, not to mention bloody freezing, but it was better than being outside. I remember the Medical Officer and his Sergeant were very skittish around William. They seemed frightened of their own shadows sometimes. The Sergeant stank of garlic; he used to have pockets full of it, Captain Fortesque was forever complaining about it.'

'Why did the Sergeant carry garlic?'

Samuel paused to gather his thoughts; it had been a long time ago. 'One of the medics told me that he'd scared himself silly reading Dracula.' Samuel had run out of steam; he stood with a faraway look in his eyes as he relived his few days in Laon cathedral with William.

'The only thing my dad has ever told me about him was that he died during the war,' said John, filling the silence and interrupting Samuel's train of thought. 'I take it, that it wasn't this war?'

'Nay lad, he died in an air raid during the Second War. No, he was in the cathedral with chest wounds, bloody lucky to have survived too.'

'Why, were the wounds bad?' John asked.

'Well, I suppose they must have been because they'd put him in with those not expected to live. Mind you I never saw his wounds; in fact I can't recall them ever changing his dressings. I do remember there were a lot of strange rumours about how he got the wounds though. I didn't take much notice of them myself; we had other things to do, your Grandfather and me. And besides, he saved my life.

'Really, how did he do that?' asked John, as he wondered what the strange rumours were.

'It was the night William was brought into the cathedral. I'd been caught by a shell the day before. The wounds to my legs and lower back were terrible. The Medical Officer thought that amputation would not do any good; so he decided not to put me through the trauma of it. I don't think they expected me to survive the night and to be honest the pain was so bad I didn't want to survive the night. They'd put me in a quiet part of the cathedral with the rest of the dying… the north transept…' Samuel swallowed. 'The name still gives me goose bumps. When they brought William in I could see the saints in the stonework looking down on me. They looked real as the lantern light swung back and forth. I could feel myself going to them, anything to get away from the pain. They laid William down and left. There was one candle burning in a large candle holder. William, despite his wounds; leaned across, put his hand on my forehead and said; "just hang on; it will be alright in the morning". The candle was directly behind his head, it made him look as though he had a halo. Then I must have blacked out, because the next thing I remember was that it was morning and the pain had gone.'

Samuel paused, there was something else he just remembered, and it was something he'd never told anybody before. He looked at John; well he was William's Grandson, so perhaps he should tell him. Perhaps John may know the answer to a question that had plagued Samuel for years.

'There was a frail old priest we called Father Ben, who used to comfort the soldiers in the cathedral. He made a point of visiting William every day. They would talk quietly in French for hours. It was him who remarked how well I was doing after they didn't think I was going to survive. Father Ben was always smiling and he always looked happy. On the third day though, he collapsed whilst talking to William. He was desperate to see another priest for his last confession and they sent one of the orderlies to go and get one. William said to him, "Benoît, you don't need a priest, like me, you have nothing to confess." Father Ben looked at him strangely, "Pierre?" he asked. "Oui Père," replied William and then added "I told you once that the journey of my life was not written on my face." And Father Ben replied; "you were right." And then the old priest closed his eyes and he was gone. I never could quite work out what that was all about, but I got the impression that they knew each other from before the war. Your Dad has never mentioned anything has he? Only, I've often wondered.'

'No, my Dad has rarely mentioned my Grandfather.'

'That's a shame,' said Samuel sadly, as John confirmed what he had always believed. This was a question he was never going to get an answer to.

'But what were the rumours?' John asked. 'You said there were strange rumours about how he got his wounds.'

Samuel cast his mind back… he got as far as five o'clock when Mary left for bingo, and then switched back onto his original more comfortable train of thought. 'I can't remember son; all I can remember is that there were strange rumours.' The conversation had taken Samuel to a subject very close to his heart, but not actually onto it; and as he seemed to have an audience that was actually interested in his anecdotes, he decided that perhaps he ought to steer the conversation directly towards the topic.

'Anyway me and your Granddad, we got shipped back to a hospital in England; and while we were there we used to play cards a lot. We managed to clean out all the lads on the ward; we never lost, except when we wanted to.' Glory days thought Samuel realising that although the subject was very close to his heart there was actually very little to say about it unless you recounted every single game, which even he thought may prove boring.

'Shall we get a cup of tea?' said John sensing that the conversation had run dry. He stood to one side and indicating that Samuel should make his way past. Samuel nodded. As he passed, John noted Samuel's bowed legs; "couldn't stop a pig in an alley" was the expression that Scott had used to describe them.

What did my Granddad do after the war?' asked John as the made their way slowly past the garage.

'He used to teach music, up at your school.'

'And he was killed in an air raid?' John asked.

'Aye that's right; he was out looking for a lost pupil during an air raid. One bomb hit a gas main just down from the school. I'm afraid the only thing they found of poor William was a shoe, and it wasn't even scorched 'The gas pipe produced a huge flame for days. The air raid wardens nearly wet themselves.'

Samuel laughed, his chest rattling in unison, triggering another coughing fit. 'Lucky there wasn't another raid,' he concluded quickly in order to complete the coughing without interruption.

'That explains why my Dad won't talk about it.' They walked in silence at Samuel's slow shuffling pace, until they were outside the kitchen door.

'What did you mean when you said "Never lost except when you wanted to"?' asked John as they made their way through the door and into the kitchen. The others were stood waiting for the kettle to boil as Frank put milk in cups.

'We played with marked cards,' said Samuel, his face split into broad grin; 'we used to let the other lads win occasionally, so that they wouldn't suspect.'

'Marked cards, they wouldn't be the ones you gave to Scott by any chance would they?' asked John.

'Aye, they will be.'

'Well no wonder he was winning,' complained Kevin.

'It's just the bit about letting the others win occasionally that he hasn't mastered yet,' said Frank.

'I'd just like to remind everyone that we were only playing for buttons,' defended Scott.

'It's not so much about letting others win; it's more about forcing yourself to lose if you think about it. It's making that decision that's the hardest part of cheating,' said Samuel.

'Anyway, don't you see… that's the plan!' exclaimed Scott. 'We play The Lendus at cards and win the money back. And as I've just proved; it works like a dream.'

'But won't they notice that you're winning all the time Scott?' said Action. 'I mean Burnston isn't that stupid… the others are, but he isn't.'

'No, not if we all play as individuals and make sure that Burnston and Co win often enough not to be suspicious. The big difference is that we pool our winnings, so overall we are going to come out on top.'

'You've thought this through haven't you?' said Action.

'Or your Granddad has,' retorted Frank. Samuel nodded, although he couldn't remember telling Scott about pooling the winnings.

The conversation revolved around the cards for a while, with Scott showing everyone how they were marked. Frank then went on to decide the rules on how often one of their team should win. John had lost interest, he was thinking of Elleria, Valheel and what Samuel had just told him about Father Benoît. John remembered the old priest from the vision he'd had in History that morning.

All these things were connected in some way and John wished he knew how. If only Elleria was still here, she might be able to make the connection.

19

GHOSTS

Elleria moved back through the door into the entrance hall where John had fallen. He was no longer there. Her vision had been replaced with a swirling mist. She could sense the room, but it was more memory than reality. Where John had fallen the mist was slightly thinner, but already the boundaries of John's outline were being eaten away as the fog took back possession. Moments later she could not tell where he had been.

She held her hands up in front of her face and could see nothing, she was mist; but that couldn't be right. She had lost her human form, true, but she still had the sense of it; she could still feel her limbs and move them. They just didn't seem to be there. Elleria clasped her hands together; and yes, she could feel each hand with the other. If she was in a non-physical form then why did she still have the sense of a body; normally this would not happen.

Elleria soon found it best not to try and use her senses, it was just frustrating. Valheel seemed to exist as a model in her head, just as her body was, and she found that it was easier to navigate using the model. She could imagine Valheel all around her and she knew that Jack was here with her, she could picture him in her mind standing in the doorway of the room they'd been in. It was workable, but it lacked the clarity of sight. Jack had mentioned before about not being able to see properly until she arrived with John. Perhaps that was it, they were trapped in the system without avatars; she searched the city with her mind, John wasn't anywhere in it, but why not? He was shot, but that should have placed his avatar under the city's control, not expel him. She sensed Jack as he arrived at her side.

'He's gone missy. And I don't suppose this fog will lift until he's back,' said Jack almost as if he'd been reading her thoughts. Elleria felt it must be true; somehow John's presence caused the creation of the avatars that were necessary in order to sense the city properly. She was convinced that it had been John who had created the avatars not Valheel, because they had been human and not Bruwnian. And now, like Jack, she was here in Valheel but outside the main system... ghosts.

She reached out and touched his arm, more out of curiosity to see if she could, than any desire for comfort; but the sense security it gave her made her realise how much she missed John. Jack placed a reassuring hand over hers. And then she heard the voices, angry voices all shouting at once.

'Do you hear that,' she said, 'all those angry voices?'

'Nearly all the time,' replied Jack. 'They sort of come and go, as if they were walking past your house in the dead of night.'

'You can hear them nearly all the time! That's strange because I...' Elleria lifted her hand from his arm and replaced it. 'I can only hear them when I'm touching you.'

'Ah,' said Jack knowledgably, creating the impression that he was about to reveal to Elleria why she could only hear the voices when she was touching him and raising her expectations. 'So what does it mean?' he finished, dashing her anticipation to the floor.

'I don't know,' she replied with an air of slight disappointment.

'Do you know who they are?' Because they're very persistent,'

'I'm not sure,' she replied thoughtfully, 'but, I...'

Her train of thought was interrupted when four of the six guardians entered the room they were in. They appeared as shadows in the fog, but they were unmistakable. They were followed by the last two who waited in the entrance. The four guards who had entered the entrance area Jack and Elleria were in, split up and started to search the adjoining rooms.

'They can't see us,' stated Jack, removing his hand from hers, 'these shadow men I mean. I spent ages avoiding them before I found that out.'

'Or hear us,' replied Elleria, as she noticed that Jack's voice had caused no reaction at all.

Elleria removed her hand from the comfort of Jack's arm and moved closer to one of the guardians standing by the door. She positioned herself immediately in front of him. There was still no reaction. She reached out to touch the guard but there was no substance to him and her hand passed straight into his chest. Immediately the fog vanished and was replaced by the view the guardian had of the entrance area he was guarding. Elleria quickly pulled her hand back and the fog returned. The guardian showed no sign that he had detected Elleria's brief occupation of his avatar.

'Jack, come over here a moment,' she said, 'and stand next to the other guard.' As Jack arrived beside the guard, Elleria continued. 'When I count to three; place your hand on his chest.'

'Right you are missy, ready when you are,' replied Jack.

'One... two... three,' counted Elleria.

The view the guard had of the entrance returned to Elleria. Movement on her right caught the guard's eye and Elleria instinctively turned towards it. Through the doorway Elleria could see one of the other guards noisily search an adjoining room. It took a moment for her to realise that the guard she occupied had turned his head in response to her impulse. Not only could she see and hear what the guard could, but she could also control him as well. This revelation was proved beyond all doubt when a few moments later the smooth featureless metal face of the guard Jack was occupying appeared in front of her and spoke to her.

'You can wear them like a suit of armour,' he said.

Elleria raised a finger to where the guard's lips would have been, to tell him to stop talking and then indicated that Jack should take the guard back to the other side of the door. She checked the other guards; fortunately they didn't seem to have heard him. Removing her hand from the one she was controlling, she reached into the other guard, grabbed Jack and dragged him out of the avatar.

'I wish I'd thought of doing that earlier,' said Jack excitedly. 'Can we do it again?'

Elleria's first reaction was to say no, it would be very risky to have Jack running amok, and what would happen when he realised that the guard had a weapon. But when she thought about it, this was too good a gift to pass up lightly.

'Yes, but not here. We need to find two unaccompanied guards, we can't risk being detected.' Elleria thought for a moment longer. 'And there is something else we can do as well.'

'What's that?'

'Well I think it's time we found out what's really going on, don't you? Are you with me?'

'Are you kidding? This is the most exciting thing that has happened to me since the war; of course I'm with you.'

'Good,' said Elleria, 'follow me.'

*

Back in Penshaw Grove Burnston was having a conversation with Martin Macadam. The streetlight under which Burnston stood flickered off and on, as it struggled to cope with the air gun pellet damage inflicted on it by a nocturnal resident who didn't like the intrusion of light. Martin was stood in the shadows under an over-grown privet hedge that was now half the height of a house, so that even when the streetlight was on he was hidden by the darkness.

'How do you think the business is going?' asked Martin as the streetlight went out.

'I think it's going very well. Now that it's up and running I can see how it all fits together,' replied Burnston. 'And thanks for pointing me in the right direction.'

'In a week's time I want you to double the amount you collect.'

'Double the amount of contracts we've sold in a week?'

'No, you misunderstand; I want you to double the amount you charge,' said Martin. The streetlight flickered and came back on.

'No problem, but can I ask why?'

'Well it will increase the profits and I want to turn the heat up a little, to see what sort of a reaction we get.'

Burnston thought about it. Martin had been right so far, so why not; it would be interesting to see this reaction when it happened. 'Okay,' he said.

Movement to his right caught his eye, and Burnston turned to see the unmistakable forms of Haystack and Clink silhouetted against the light from a lamp further down the road. As he waited for them to approach, the lamp he was stood under suddenly glowed brighter and brighter and then with a terminal pop, went out.

'Now that's interesting,' said Martin, as Burnston watched the glow in the bulb fade to nothing.

'Who're you talking to mate?' asked Haystack as he arrived next to Burnston.

'Martin,' replied Burnston, indicating the shadows under the bush. 'Oh, he's gone.'

Clink and Haystack gave each other a puzzled look as Burnston peered deeper into the shadows to see where Martin had gone. Clink mouthed "who's Martin?" Haystack shrugged, but they said nothing; it was Burnston after all.

20
THE CHALLENGE

The bell on the wall just outside the mathematics room was ringing. On the corridor the trill sound marked the start of morning break. Inside the room it sounded as though the bell was trying to hammer its way through the wall. The sound echoed around the inside of Ted Crawford's head as his pupils stood to leave.

'Don't forget to hand your homework in!' He shouted above the noise as he massaged his temples.

He couldn't say he hadn't been warned. Liz MacDonald had told him. "Watch out for Burnston," she'd said, "he's suddenly started… taking an interest." Not in mathematics, surely, Ted had thought.

Mathematics was the only subject that Burnston took at a higher level. It had been a surprise for all, including Burnston, when two years ago, when the aptitude tests had shown that he had the ability. Since then, he'd only ever done enough work to remain at the higher level. Always sitting at the back of the class, he wasn't what you would call interactive, but he was never any trouble; until today. Liz had been right; the best way to describe it was that he was "taking an interest".

The bell had stopped now, but the memory of it continued to hammer in Ted's head. He pinched the bridge of his nose between finger and thumb as Burnston placed his homework book on top of John's and turned towards the door.

Ted felt he needed a quiet moment. He looked up. Burnston, the last to leave was framed in the doorway.

'Burnston,' he called. Burnston turned to face him, his grim expression never changing. 'As you're the last out, can you make sure the door is closed properly.' Burnston looked at Martin who was still sitting in the seat next to Burnston's. Martin looked at Ted, then back at Burnston and shrugged.

'You go on I'll catch you up,' said Martin.

'Okay,' replied Burnston.'

'Thank you,' said Ted.

Burnston gave Ted a funny look, irritated by the fact that Ted was completely ignoring Martin and had assumed the reply had been directed at him. He turned and closed the door behind him.

The south corridor was crowded and Burnston was in a hurry, he had a meeting to attend. According to "Best Management Practices", chapter seven states, "a weekly sales meeting is of benefit to management and staff alike, as it lets everyone know the current status of the business". Burnston didn't fully understand the statement, but the idea of a meeting appealed to him and he didn't want to be late. Although technically he couldn't be late; the others would just be early; setting the right example was important to Burnston; a subject covered in chapter five. The crowds parted before him as Burnston ploughed on up the corridor. Those approaching him would drag aside those moving in the same direction who were about to be mown down by the large motivated youth. Burnston looked around to see if Martin had left the classroom, veering slightly to one side and causing chaos as the crowd tried to react to his change in direction. Unable to see Martin, Burnston resumed his original course, completely oblivious to the problems he was causing.

Just outside the main hall, at the opposite end to the stage, was a cloakroom. A single door to the left side of the room was the only entrance. The décor consisted of plain brown tiles to the bottom half of the walls and cream paint to the upper. A dozen sinks ran under the windows at the far end. South facing, the sun shone through the glass at a steep angle, striking one end of the orange post and rail coat pegs that split the room into four narrow coat lined walkways. By contrast, the back of the room was dark.

Haystack was the first to arrive and he set about transforming the cloakroom into a conference room in preparation for the meeting. This consisted of grabbing the nearest occupant, hurling him through the door, and then glaring at the other occupants until they hurled themselves through the door. Although the method was less enjoyable than hurling each one through the door in turn, it did require less effort, and was faster. All this book reading and business knowledge that Burnston was immersed in was rubbing off; even Haystack was learning.

Clink and Boxhead, fresh from the woodwork room, were the next to arrive. They made their way down to the sinks at the far end where Haystack was waiting. Clink raised his eyebrow in greeting, dislodging a small cloud of sawdust which floated slowly down in front of his face causing him to sneeze and dislodge the rest. Boxhead, who was busying himself turning all the taps on full, paused in his endeavours.

'Gesundheit!' he said, it was a word that he'd heard in a film.

'Thanks,' replied Clink sneezing again.

'Gesundheit!' interjected Haystack, so that Boxhead could get on with his water project. Haystack was really getting into this "learning new stuff" thing.

With the front of his jacket looking like it had been out in the snow, Clink was brushing the remaining sawdust from his eyebrow when, precisely on time, Burnston arrived.

'Can we have these taps turned off, I can't hear myself think,' he said nodding at Boxhead.

'How did you know it was me?' Boxhead knew better than to deny it to Burnston.

'Burnston sighed, 'because you've done it every day for the last five years. Now, if you wouldn't mind,' said Burnston indicating the taps.

Boxhead and Clink started to turn the taps off.

*

John, Frank, Kevin and Action were standing in the playground near the wall of the North Building. The playground was full and noisy as usual.

'Seen Scott, anybody?' asked Frank.

'He's gone to see Burnston about the card game,' replied Action.

Frank laughed. 'We should have wished him luck. Still, we'll soon know if the invite doesn't go down well because we'll be able to hear him screaming.'

'I'll bet,' laughed Action.

John was listening to the conversation but not really taking much notice. He spent most of the morning thinking about Elleria and worrying as to what might have happened to her when she didn't return from Valheel. He was frustrated by the fact that because nobody remembered her, he couldn't talk about her. He didn't think it was strange that nobody remembered her. After everything he'd seen recently, having no memory of someone was quite tame, when compared to say, Valheel. In the past any problems could be talked over with his friends; Action and Kevin would always show empathy, Frank would offer helpful advice and Scott would be dismissive, or obstructive, or confrontational; which was sort of helpful in its own way, as Scott tended to show the problem in perspective to everything else, thus diminishing its impact. But this option was not available for this problem, and John missed it.

For the last hour John had been distracted from the Elleria problem by having some very strange notions on the nature of matter and energy. Ideas made all the more disconcerting by the complex mathematics that kept flashing up in front of his eyes. It wasn't the appearance of the equations that bothered him; it was the fact that he understood them. The thoughts were not like the flashes of information he had been getting in response to learning new concepts like Nodes and Radgarc's, they were more of a steady stream of information. He got the distinct feeling that somebody was trying to tell him something.

'That was a joke,' said Frank, when John didn't react to his humour.

'Sorry' said John, coming out of his reverie slightly. He'd been trying to construct some metaphors to explain some of the theories he been receiving; although he wasn't quite sure why. His thoughts had been so deep, that when Frank had spoken to him he felt like he was waking up from a sleep. John shook his head to try and bring himself back into the real world. He reached out to steady himself against a drainpipe running up the side of the school. As John's hand neared the pipe there was a blue flash as a bolt of electricity leapt from his hand discharging into the metal pipe. It made a sound like a gunshot.

'What the hell was that!' exclaimed Action, followed by 'lookout!' A crow which had been perched on the gutter high above fell to the ground stone dead.

'I think someone has just shot that crow,' said Kevin pointing at the unfortunate creature as it lay on the floor smoking slightly. There was a smell of singed feathers.

'And one of the pellets just missed us! Look, the drainpipe is smoking by John's hand where it hit,' said Action. They all leaned forward to look. There was a circle of exposed metal where the paint had burnt off and right in the centre a small hole from which little wisps of smoke escaped. Quite why Kevin would think that someone would be running around the playground with a shotgun taking pot shots at crows is unknown, but it was generally how his mind worked. Action bought into the theory big time.

Kevin and Action disappeared into the crowd looking for the owner of the shotgun and some adventure. Frank watched them go, slowly shaking his head. And John continued to stare at the drainpipe. Had he really done that?

*

'I'll need someone to take minutes,' said Burnston as the sound of running water and gurgling sinks receded. He was met with blank faces. 'Write down what we say in the meeting,' he explained.

Haystack nodded. 'I'll do it.'

'Do you have any paper?' asked Burnston.

Haystack thought about it. 'No,' he eventually replied, saying the word slowly as if he was still thinking about it. The length of time the answer took made Burnston suspect that Haystack was working out what paper was. He surmised that it was probably the first honest answer Haystack had ever given in his life.

Burnston tore three pages from his notebook. As he was handing them to Haystack they were interrupted by two unsuspecting first years.

The boys had wandered into the cloakroom and suddenly realised why it was empty. They had learnt quickly that at Penshaw Grove there were certain people whose attention you avoided at all costs; and now, after a moment's inattention, they found themselves in the regrettable position of being the sole focus of four of them. And as if that wasn't bad enough, they had obviously witnessed some sort of illicit transaction possibly involving drugs or soap or whatever it was the large people did with their time. These four had an air of guilt around them at all times, and always looked like they were contemplating some sort of crime. For a moment the first years were mesmerized by the attention, but quickly regained their senses and immediately turned to leave.

'Wait!' boomed Haystack. The first years froze in the act of turning and awaited certain death. Haystack was next to them in an instant. 'Turn out your pockets,' he commanded.

Burnston rolled his eyes, this was exactly what The Lendus was meant to replace. He noticed Martin in the shadows at the back, away from the door; he hadn't seen him come in.

Martin shook his head slowly, resigned to that fact that old habits die hard. 'Let him get on with it,' he said. Burnston nodded.

Haystack was inspecting the contents of their upturned palms. Collectively, the boys had; twenty seven pence, a packet of mints, two elastic bands, one broken six inch ruler and an assortment of pencils, pens and coloured crayons. It was, for Penshaw Grove, all the academic equipment you would need to surpass the highest standards currently attainable at the school. Haystack studied the offerings whilst stroking his chin thoughtfully; then with a sudden movement of his hand, that made the boys flinch, snatched a purple crayon. Haystack examined the point of the crayon and found it to be adequate. Focusing his attention back on the unfortunate lads he leaned in close.

'Go away,' he said.

They'd managed to retain not only their lives but also the money and mints. The boys couldn't believe their luck and left quickly stuffing the items back in their pockets. Haystack returned to the meeting holding up the crayon. 'I needed something to write with,' he informed Burnston.

'I would have lent you a pen,' said Burnston, 'but full marks for initiative. Now, shall we make a start?'

Haystack beamed at the other two. 'I've got a nish... a... tive,' he said. The other two smiled back at him, they didn't know what it meant either.

Burnston felt as though he had gained some respect with the formation of The Lendus. The teachers liked the uniform and his customers seemed to appreciate the predictability of the arrangement. Customers of The Lendus, he felt, no longer had the worry of an unexpected encounter with Haystack. This, of course, was an interpretation born out of the narrow view Burnston was getting of the situation. His customers still had the worry of an expected visit from Haystack. Customer empathy was covered in chapter seventeen, and Burnston hadn't got that far yet.

'Thank you for attending gentlemen,' said Burnston as if they had a choice. 'As this is our first meeting and there are no previous minutes to go through, I will proceed straight to the sales report.' His voice was clear and confident, almost as though he'd done this all his life.

Haystack raised his hand and Burnston turned to look at him; but Haystack said nothing and continued to hold his hand aloft twirling the crayon in the air.

'Yes,' said Burnston eventually.

Haystack dropped his hand and held the paper and crayon at chest height. 'What do I write?' He waved the paper about a bit to indicate where he was supposed to be doing the writing.

'Well, said Burnston calmly, 'write the date on the left, then the title "Meeting", then all our names, and then you write down any important points or decisions that we arrive at.'

'Okay, got it,' said Haystack. Leaning over a sink and resting the paper on the window sill. He started to write, his tongue mirroring the movement of the crayon as he worked.

'I'll just give you a brief summary of the sales while Haystack catches up. Yesterday as you know was our first day of trading; and after your initial training during morning break I'm pleased to say that you all did very well.' Boxhead and Clink nudged each other. 'You two did well with your sales technique,' continued Burnston as he indicated Boxhead and Clink, 'closely matching that which we used during training. You both managed to close seventeen deals each; well done.' Burnston paused to shake both their hands and then continued.

'I myself closed twenty-five, not including the ones during the first morning break.' Boxhead and Clink nodded their approval at the figures. 'But even my efforts pale into insignificance when compared to our salesman of the week Haystack, with forty-seven closures.' There was a snap as Haystack, in his excitement at winning something, broke the point off his purple crayon. He'd got as far as:

MEATIN
Tooday
Me
Burnsten
Box Ed
Clinc
~~sa Sell~~ Salekz

Which to be fair was a lot to remember for Haystack and he'd surpassed his own standards by a long way. Haystack stood up straight and turned to show the broken crayon. Burnston was already holding a pen out for him to take.

'Congratulations on becoming salesman of the week and you can keep the pen,' said Burnston as he shook Haystack's hand. Haystack beamed and leaned back over the sink. 'So, with the five sales we made during training that makes a total of one hundred and eleven; in cash flow terms that equates to £55.50 a week and as you are all on one hundred percent commission you will each receive ten percent which is £5.55.'

Haystack stood up straight at this news and looked at the other two who were silent and thoughtful.

'Er,' said Clink from somewhere under his eyebrow, which he'd lowered during his thought process completely hiding his eyes. 'And we get this every week?'

'Yes, until next week when you'll be getting £11.10 each.'

There was a stunned silence as they each reflected on the fact that it was more money than any of them had seen in their lives.

'Why's it going up?'

'Because, starting next week we're doubling the fees,' answered Burnston before he realised that the question hadn't come from one of the other three. He turned to face Scott who was standing halfway down the centre aisle of coats.

'This is a private meeting for members of The Lendus only,' said Burnston sharply as all four turned to face Scott.

'Good,' said Scott curbing his anger at the doubling of the fees, 'because what I have to say is for the members of The Lendus only.' He stopped just out of Haystack's range, just in case.

'Let him continue,' said Martin from the shadows.

Burnston looked passed Scott and into the corner where Martin was stood. Scott turned to see what he was looking at and the other three, noticing Burnston, looked into the dark corner as well.

'Continue,' said Burnston bringing everyone's focus back to him.

'We have noted the change in your circumstances…' started Scott.

'We?'

'Let's just say, like minded associates. And it has been decided to invite The Lendus into our card school.'

'I've not heard of this card school before,' said Burnston.

'No, you wouldn't have. Given the illicit nature of what we are doing, we meet in secret. As you can imagine, membership is very exclusive.' Scott was a convincing liar; he almost believed it himself; although he wasn't sure where the phrase "illicit nature" had come from.

Burnston thought about it. This had a plausible feeling to it; he had long suspected that people from the Skutterskelfe area were members of one secret society or another, and this confirmed it. This invitation may lead to other things, memberships of other secret societies, further advancement; a way into that world he'd glimpsed at Skutterskelfe shops… money. He looked back at Martin.

'What do you think?' he asked.

Scott was unsure if Burnston was asking him because he was looking right past him. 'Who, me?' he asked.

'No, I'm asking Martin,' replied Burnston; adding, 'my business advisor,' by way of explanation.

The others gazed into the shadows as Martin replied. 'This one also carries Amantarra's shield. Yes, accept the invitation. I think this is the reaction I've been waiting for. It looks as though we don't need to double the fees after all.'

Burnston looked back at Scott, who was bobbing up and down trying to see Martin, and wondered where this shield was. 'Yes,' he said, 'we accept. Now, if you wouldn't mind we would like to finish our meeting in peace.'

Scott gave up trying to catch a glimpse of Martin and turned back to Burnston. 'We'll meet up in the dining hall this lunch time;' then he tuned and left the cloakroom.

Boxhead walked to the aisle furthest from the door and looked into the darkness at the other end of it. There was no one there. 'Who's Martin again?' he asked looking back at Burnston.

'Our business advisor,' replied Burnston. 'He likes to stay in the background so he can get an overall view of the business.'

Boxhead walked back to the group. 'Oh,' he said, 'do we get to meet him?'

Burnston looked into the corner where Martin had been. 'Doesn't look like it,' he replied.

21
ARTULLUS

'I'm sure we've been down here before,' said Elleria. In the fog, the thoroughfare they were on curved away to the right as it circled one of the centroid towers. Jack looked back the way they had come; it looked the same as the way they were going. The shadowy outlines of buildings loomed up on either side like a misty scene from a half remembered horror film.

'How can you tell?'

'That's the problem; I can't.' Elleria had led Jack on a complex tour of Valheel as she tried to find her way without the normal visual cues. She'd had to try and remember her way, and now she had to admit that they were hopelessly lost.

'So what do we do now?' asked Jack.

'I don't know.'

'Well, we could always ask a policeman.'

'Ask a policeman? What do you mean?'

'My old Mam, God rest her soul, used to say that whenever you're lost, you should ask a policeman or was it if you wanted to know the time.' Jack pondered the question. 'Anyway, the point I'm trying to make is that there's one of those guardian chaps coming round the corner now. If you have a look through his eyes, you might be able to work out where we are.'

'That's a brilliant idea.'

'Thank you, said Jack, 'I do occasionally have my moments.'

The guard was obviously on some sort of patrol and was walking quite slowly so Elleria had plenty of time to prepare her interception. As he passed them, she stuck out an arm and the guardian walked right into it. Elleria caught a brief glimpse of the city and then lost it again as the guard continued walking passing right through her outstretched arm.

'Damn,' she said, 'I didn't get a good enough look to tell where we are.'

'You'll have to jump right into him, and then you might be able to see more,' said Jack helpfully.

Elleria caught up with the guard and jumped into the shadow, but the image of the city flashed on and off as again the guard continued walking. She tried again and the same thing happened.

'This is hopeless,' she said; 'we'll have to chase him halfway round the city. By the time we find out where we are; we won't be here.'

'Let me try,' said Jack.

Elleria watched from the back as Jack positioned himself alongside the guard and matched his pace. Then when he was completely in step, like two marching soldiers, he slowly moved sideways towards the guard until he was completely enveloped by him. The guard halted and Elleria walked around to the front of it.

That went well, she thought. What next though? If Jack left the guard it would just resume walking and she didn't think she would be able to do what Jack had just done. Even seeing through the guardians eyes Jack would not know where he was. Perhaps he could describe it to her… or perhaps not. On reflection that probably wasn't such a good idea; Elleria didn't think she would be able to understand what he was describing.

'I don't think this is going to work,' she said and then realised that Jack wouldn't be able to hear her. She reached into the guard intending to pull Jack out but found herself being pulled in.

'Hello missy,' said Jack's voice by her ear once she had been fully enveloped by the avatar.

She was surprised when she found herself inside the guardian, wearing him, as Jack had said, like a suit of armour. She was surprised because it actually worked; it had never occurred to her that they could share a guardian.

'How did you know that this would work,' she asked.

'Never occurred to me that it wouldn't,' replied Jack. 'Can you tell…?' Jack stopped because the angry voices had returned; the crescendo increasing and then falling again.

'How do you put up with that?' asked Elleria as the voices died away.

'Well it doesn't last long. They sort of give up when they don't get a response.' Jack tried asking the question again. 'Can you tell where we are?'

Elleria tried to look around but the guardians head would not move, nor would the rest of him.

'I can't move,' she said.

'Looks like I'm driving then,' said Jack with some enthusiasm as he turned the guard through one hundred and eighty degrees.

'Head for that junction,' said Elleria, 'I'll see if I can work it out from there.'

After a stuttering start Jack got the hang of moving the guard forward but he lacked control and the guard tended to swing his upper torso from side to side as he walked. Elleria was worried that the strange lurching gait would attract attention. Still, she told herself, it could be worse; he could have raised the guard's arms out to the side to emphasise the lurch. It was with some relief when they arrived at the junction and Jack halted.

'They're harder to control with two of us on board,' said Jack, 'they just don't respond in the same way.'

'And the guard doesn't talk when you speak either,' commented Elleria.

'An added bonus,' replied Jack.

It didn't take long for Elleria to establish where they were.

'We need to be back towards the centroid tower one junction,' she said. Then we need to turn left.'

'Okay,' said Jack turning the guard round. The radial road they were on gave them a clear uninterrupted view of the blue centroid tower. Jack followed the line of the tower up until it met the Node Zero chamber and then the lines of the other towers; red, green and yellow until they met the plazas where they terminated.

'This is beautiful,' he said, 'don't you think?'

'I've never really stopped to look at it before, but you're right, it is beautiful.'

The yellow quadrant flickered off and then back on again.

'That yellow bit still looks faulty; looks like they've got a bad connection. They should give Tom Godbert a ring; he doesn't charge much.'

'Yes,' said Elleria distractedly; she was trying to work out what damage John had done to the yellow zone when they had first entered Valheel, but couldn't. The mechanics of the city were beyond her. 'I think we should get out of this avatar now.'

'That's a pity I was enjoying this,' said Jack.

'Yes, but I don't want to attract any more attention than we have to.' A thought occurred to Elleria. 'I wonder if the guard will remember this little detour; or if he'll just suddenly find himself in a different place and carry on regardless.'

'I don't know,' said Jack absentmindedly as he took in a final view of the vista before him.

Elleria tried to leave the avatar, but she had the same problem as before, she just couldn't move.

'I can't get out,' she said. 'I can't move.'

'It can't be that hard. How did I get out last time?' asked Jack.

'I pulled you out,' Elleria recalled.

'Ah!'

'See if you can get out?'

Jack tried, but this only resulted in the guardian striking some rather strange poses that were guaranteed to attract attention.

'Stop, stop,' said Elleria, 'let's think about this. I can't move, so there's no solution there. You can move, but when you do all that happens is that the guard moves, so that's no good. You got in by walking in and I got in by being pulled in by you.'

'That's about the top and bottom of it,' said Jack. 'So, what's the solution?'

'Let's reverse what we did. Try pushing me out.'

'How? I can't actually feel where you are, all I can do is hear your voice.'

'Yes, but you know where I am, so you must be sensing me at some level. Just imagine that you are pushing me out of the guard and see what happens,' said Elleria, thinking that if this didn't work she really did not know what she was going to do next.

Jack recalled the image of Elleria from when John was here and then imagined pushing her away from him. Had it worked? It seemed very quiet in here. The next thing he knew was he was being pulled from the guard. He was back in the mist. The guard looked around, confused at the sudden change in surroundings, but he seemed to get his bearings quite quickly and resumed his patrol. Elleria breathed a sigh of relief.

'I think we got away with that, they seem to be a little disorientated when you leave them,' she said. 'Now, follow me.'

It was a little difficult in the fog, but Elleria managed to guide them both into the building, down a wide corridor and into a large room. She stopped just inside the door.

'Where are we?' asked Jack.

'This is the council chamber. If there are any answers to be found, this is where we will find them.

There were two guards stood inside the chamber on either side of the entrance. Opposite the entrance in a slightly higher position there were five other figures; but these figures were different to the guards. While the guards appeared as shadows in the mist the five figures glowed with power, each one had a slightly different hint of colour; red, green, yellow, blue, with the one in the centre glowing white. It occurred to Elleria that the colours matched those of the city's quadrants; and that, she told herself cannot be a coincidence. The yellow figure flickered.

'Did you see that,' she said.

'Like that dodgy connection in the city and he's the same colour, yellow.'

'They must each be linked to a quadrant of the city.'

'What about the white one?'

'Maybe he's linked to the other four,' replied Elleria. It seemed a plausible explanation; but who were they? Elleria did not think that they were Bruwnan avatars despite the council seats they occupied. Time to find out, she thought.

'You occupy the guard on the right and I'll take the other,' said Elleria. 'And Jack,' she continued with a warning edge to her voice, 'don't talk or move or attempt to occupy any of those glowing ones up there.'

'Well that's not going to be much fun,' replied Jack.

'It's not supposed to be fun; we're trying to find out what's going on. Look as soon as we find something out we'll occupy two more guards outside and go exploring. Would that be alright? Can we agree on this?'

'Agreed,' said Jack.

'Remember, no talking or moving about. We don't want to give our presence away, especially in front of those five up there.' Elleria thought about it. 'On second thoughts, I'm going to go into the same guard as you. Then we'll able to talk to each other. At least we know how to get out when we have to.'

Elleria let Jack go in first and then she stepped into the guard after him. Elleria just caught the tail end of the angry voices as they moved on and hoped that they wouldn't come back to drown out any useful information she might hear.

Four of the councillors were turned towards the yellow quadrant councillor. The white councillor spoke. 'Is there some sort of problem?

'Yes Consulus,' said the yellow councillor. 'There are some problems with the energy flow levels in the distribution crystal. I have guardians working on it now, but it is difficult without full access to the system. Please accept my apologies in advance should I temporarily vanish from this meeting.'

'They don't look human, what on Earth are they?' Jack asked, regretting his use of the word "Earth".

'They're Bruwnan,' replied Elleria, 'or at least they're supposed to be. Consulus must be the leader.' A green humanoid shaped grid appeared in front of the dais and rendered itself into the form of Tyrus. 'That one is called Tyrus. Keep quiet now, we need to listen.'

'Report,' said Consulus.

'The stratagem to flush Amantarra appears to be working and I believe I have identified Amantarra's human disguise,' said Tyrus.

Elleria's attention was brought into sharp focus.

'There is some work required to draw her out, but another significant element may play a part in that,' continued Tyrus.

Elleria was in agony, but who is it? She cursed Tyrus for not revealing the name.

'What is this significant element?' asked the green councillor.

'The living Node John Godbert has somehow lost his controller, Elleria, and he is having substantial problems in regulating his power flow. I suspect that as the level of energy increases he will quite soon suffer a catastrophic failure. This will, without doubt, lead to the complete destruction of the stellar system.'

'What does he mean missy?'

'He's saying that because I'm not with John he'll probably accidently destroy the entire solar system.' Elleria felt helpless and frustrated, John was about to destroy himself, she was powerless to prevent it, and she still didn't know who Amantarra was disguised as.

'That's not good news,' said Jack.

'No, and I'm stuck here. At least we know where John went after he was shot, which is sort of a relief.'

'It looks as though the eradication of the human species will take care of itself,' said Consulus, 'but it is still vital that we retrieve the Primary Key from Amantarra.'

'What's the Primary Key?' asked Jack.

'I don't know, but it sounds like something important that Amantarra has and they don't. I suspect that this key is at the centre of everything that's happened.'

'I'm sure you know what to do Tyrus,' said Consulus.

'Yes, Consulus; it's already been done.'

'For the record,' said Consulus, 'who is Amantarra's human disguise?'

'Listen,' said Elleria to Jack just in case he was thinking of talking.

'I believe that Amantarra is in the guise of Scott Briggs,' said Tyrus, putting Elleria out of her torment. 'Although I have yet to prove this; Scott Briggs has, nevertheless, been the first to respond to the trap I set and is one of only two humans who bare Amantarra's shield, the other being the Keeper, Reg Scribbins.'

'Scott Briggs?' said Jack, 'Samuel Briggs' Grandson?'

'I would never have guessed that,' replied Elleria.

'Very good,' said Consulus. 'Proceed with your plan.'

'Yes Consulus.' Tyrus vanished from the chamber followed closely by the disappearance of the council. The light level in the chamber began to drop.

'Well at least we know a bit more about what's going on,' said Jack, 'but what do we do now?' He said the last part quickly because the angry voices were returning.

'I think it's time we found out who this lot are,' said Elleria as the volume increased.

'Good idea,' replied Jack.

Elleria concentrated. 'Hello, I'm Elleria. Who are you?' The sound of the voices stopped abruptly at their loudest point. 'That seemed to get their attention,' she commented.

The voices all started up again. They were all trying to get different points across at the same time. It was chaos.

'One at a time please!' shouted Jack, and the voices stopped again.

'Impressive,' said Elleria.

Then a single voice spoke. 'Did you say your name was Elleria?'

'Yes.'

'Do you also happen to be Amantarra's Radgarc?'

'Yes, that's right,' replied Elleria, surprised that she was known. 'Who are you?'

'I'm Artullus, and although such titles are meaningless now, I am... was, Amantarra's father.'

22
THE SCIENTIST

After morning break the weather had deteriorated. The sky darkened, and the air became charged with the static electricity of an impending storm. In the still, windless air ink black clouds formed over the town, turning day into near night. Lights went on in classrooms all over the school. The warm yellow light shone from the windows casting light out onto the playground. It was almost lunchtime when John saw the first drop of rain hit the window and slowly start to make its way down the grimy glass. The first drop was followed moments later by another. John watched as they raced each other down the glass. Within seconds the drops were landing in twos and threes, and then with such a frequency that individual drops could not be made out. A flash of lighting lit the clouds from above, followed almost immediately by a long rumble of thunder. The storm was directly overhead. The drumming of the rain on windows and roofs grew louder; breaking concentration and disrupting lessons.

'You've all seen rain before,' said Stefan. 'I bet none of you have ever tried to draw it.'

Soon the rain was falling too fast for even the slope of the playground to carry it away, and a layer of churning water built up. Shallow waves rippled across the surface of the playground, moving down the slope. Water poured over the sides of the gutters; the rainwater pipes unable to carry it away fast enough. It was true, everyone in that classroom had seen rain before; but nobody there had seen rain like this.

Almost drowned out by the sound of the rain the lunchtime bell rang. Scott turned to John.

'We're going to get wet,' he said.

Action looked out of the window, 'really?' he said sarcastically.

As the class filed out of the art room Stefan looked at the drawings as they placed them onto his desk. His charges had improved over the years but none of them possessed the gift… until now. He couldn't believe his eyes.

'John,' he said, 'this is brilliant. Where is it?'

'They're of a city built on the inside of a sphere.'

'They?' Stefan lifted the top sheet. There were five drawings in total each one showing a different view of the city. 'This is excellent work, truly excellent.' Stefan sat down to study the drawings as John left for his lunch.

The dining hall was located in the block in the centre of the playground directly under the chemistry lab. It had its own entrance. South facing solid double doors from the playground opened into a small vestibule. Facing the doors, on the back wall, were two glass cabinets containing various cups and shields for sporting achievement. John and his friends had studied the trophies when they were in their first year and the latest date on any of them was 1956, twenty years ago. It was a representation of the school's past glory.

To the left of the entrance was a set of double doors which were never opened, and opposite them was the entrance to the dining hall. High quality food served in a relaxed and friendly atmosphere amid beautiful artwork and contemporary décor, the charm and character of the dining hall had none of these qualities. Eight rows of inspirational; that is to say heavy on the graffiti; Formica topped tables were set out amid the relaxed, grey walled ambience of a Siberian prison. The slightly grubby, orange plastic chairs were the only cosy objects in the room.

It was dark in the hall as John and his friends entered.

'Did you know that Burnston has an invisible friend?' asked Scott. The others gave him a disbelieving look; it was after all the sort of thing you'd grown out of by the time you'd reached four years old. 'It's true. He's called Martin.'

'If I had an imaginary friend it would be a girl,' Kevin inputted.

'Well none of us want to know about your imaginary girlfriend,' said Frank firmly, effectively closing the subject.

The hall was briefly lit by lightning, the blue white-flash casting shadows from the windows that ran down either side; it was immediately followed by a loud clap of thunder.

'That was right above us,' said Action.

They joined the back of the queue that snaked round the right side of the hall to the serving hatch at the far end. Serving lunch today, serving lunch every day, was Carol, a disinterested middle aged lady who could hurl food onto plates at an incredible rate. She kept the line moving by wearing an expression that did not encourage lingering. It did not take long to get to the front of the queue. Today's menu consisted of sausage and mash, with optional mushy peas for the more adventurous or constipated diner. Carol's arms moved rapidly as she delivered three sausages, a dollop of mash and a ladle of peas onto each plate. Whether the peas were intended to be mushy or whether that's just the way they turned out, John didn't know, but he risked life and limb by whisking his plate away from Carol's green coated ladle as it rapidly zeroed in. Carol growled under her breath and while still glaring at John, delivered the thick, green, lumpy liquid onto Frank's plate before he could object.

John, Frank, Scott, Kevin and Action sat at the end of row one, facing the entrance. They hadn't been there long when The Lendus entered the hall and joined the back of the queue. Looking round the hall, The Lendus noted that there were no teachers present and so immediately made their way to the front of the queue, where the next person to be served had been keeping their place for them. They took seats three rows over facing John and his friends.

Click, click, click, click; glad to be out of the rain Mr Fleming paused in the dark entrance to the dining hall and was silhouetted in the doorway by a flash of lightning. He shook his umbrella to get the worst of the rain off it. As he folded the umbrella to make it easier to carry, he noted how dark and gloomy it was in the dining hall. Moving to the side of the doorway he ran his hand down the switches on the wall. Eight, large, egg shaped, white glass lamps hanging dustily from the ceiling on greasy chains, glowed into action; their yellow warming light improving the ambience of the room, but not by much. The advantage of the lights was that everyone could now see what they were eating; this of course was also the disadvantage.

Completely ignoring the queue Mr Fleming went straight to the serving hatch to collect his lunch. A twinkle appeared in Carol's eye; it was the closest Carol ever got to being "all of a flutter". Carol smiled, not only with her mouth but with her body as well. Her whole demeanour changed; like a little girl excited about going to the park, if she could have jumped up and down she would have. It was like watching the dawn on a spring morning. Carol's eyes; except for a momentary flash to the left as a small boy looked as though he might get in the way; were fixed permanently on Mr Fleming's as he took a plate from her.

Unfortunately for Mr Fleming, the attraction Carol felt for him, manifested itself in the form of larger potions; which she delivered to his plate with a slow deliberate panache reserved only for him, and all without ever taking her eyes from his. As soon as Mr Fleming turned to find a seat; plate in one hand, umbrella in the other and knife and fork in the top pocket of his jacket; Carol's face dropped and darkness returned once more to the queue. She glared at the small boy standing at the front of the queue; motivating him into action with a growl that coincided with a rumble of thunder.

The drumming of the rain outside obscured the general chatter in the dining hall, and John and his friends ate in their own preoccupied silence. Kevin was reading the latest instalment of an interesting narrative about Haystack's parentage, which had been written on the table by someone who'd been adding to the piece for weeks. The anonymous writer was probably fortunate that Haystack, who was mindful of his manners as well as being semi-illiterate, tended not to read at the table. Scott prepared himself for the forthcoming game by clearing his mind with repetition; cut sausage, add mash, dip in peas, eat, which he repeated to a slow precise rhythm. Frank was trying to keep his sausages and peas apart by building a dam out of mashed potatoes; he'd sort out the contaminated mash later. John chewed slowly; he'd formulated a theory of sorts about the nature of matter and energy and was going over the key points in his head. It was Action who broke the silence with a profound observation.

'Why does the room smell of overcooked cabbage?' The statement hung in the air as the others turned to look at him.

'It does, you're right,' replied Kevin waving his knife in the air to indicate where the smell was. 'I've never really noticed before, but it definitely smells of cabbage.'

'I don't know what you mean,' said Frank who just taken a forkful of mash and was now trying to close a breach in the dam with his knife.

'It's sausage and mash today; we haven't had cabbage for days, but it still smells of it in here,' clarified Action.

'I see what you mean,' said Frank sniffing the air.

Scott stopped his rhythmic eating and added, 'come to think of it; it always smells of cabbage.'

Mr Fleming sat; albeit rather gingerly on the uncompromising plastic chair at the end of the row adjacent John, and hung his umbrella on the edge of the table. From this position he could observe the entire dining hall. As he retrieved his knife and fork from his top pocket he looked despairingly at the five sausages, extra mash and peas piled on his plate.

'But why does it smell of cabbage?' repeated Action.

'Perhaps its magic,' offered Kevin.

'A gifted cook,' chimed in Scott, turning to look at Carol, who glared back without breaking the rhythm of her serving.

Mr Fleming thought it would be due to poor hygiene, but he'd heard many fatuous teenage conversations before and made a point of not getting involved.

'Or a design feature,' said Frank. 'Jeremiah Ramsden Priestly did have a flare for the quirky.'

Frank always was the clever one thought Mr Fleming. He wondered where Frank would lead the conversation; somewhere interesting perhaps.

'There you go again,' said Scott. 'Who's Jeremiah Ramsden Priestly?'

'He was the Architect who built the school,' replied Frank. Scott looked flabbergasted.

'How do you know these things? How could anyone possibly know that the Architect was called Jeremiah Ramsden Priestly? I mean I've never even heard of him.' Scott turned to Kevin. 'Have you ever heard of this Jeremiah bloke?' Kevin shook his head. 'Where do you get this stuff from?'

So much for an interesting conversation thought Mr Fleming; trust Briggs to bring it down a notch.

'I don't know,' said Frank, 'I just remember stuff.' Scott shook his head and inserted an entire sausage into his mouth; seemingly ending the conversation.

John had been silent throughout the great cabbage debate, preferring to concentrate on his theory. There had been a deliberation of his own going on in his head, part of him wanted to dwell on Elleria's plight, but that train of thought seemed to be drowned out by the theories and equations that continued to flash in front of his eyes. It was something he'd been working on for days, but now something seemed to have decided that the theory should be finalised. With only the sausages remaining on his plate he looked up and noticed Mr Fleming for the first time. John had always respected Mr Fleming's point of view, he was rock solid in his opinions on any subject you would care to choose. John realised that here was an opportunity to get a scientist's point of view on his theory.

'Sir,' said John. 'Can I ask you a question? I'd like your opinion as a scientist.'

This might be interesting; thought Mr Fleming. 'By all means Godbert; Fire away.' And although flattered by the term "scientist", he thought he ought to correct the boy nonetheless. 'And it's Chemistry Teacher, not scientist.'

John looked as though he was contemplating a change to the proposed question due to the change of Mr Fleming's title. Finally he seemed to reach a decision and asked the question.

'What is the relationship between energy and matter?'

Mr Fleming froze; a forkful of mash about to enter his open mouth. If he'd had to guess what sort of question John was going to ask, this wouldn't have been it.

'That's an interesting question,' Mr Fleming replied lowering his fork. 'What makes you ask?'

'It's something I've been thinking about, and I just wanted to get your perspective on the subject.'

Was this John Godbert? Was this the same John Godbert that was always arguing with Scott Briggs? Mr Fleming found it difficult to relate the question to the boy, never mind the use of the word "perspective".

'Well now let me see, what is the relationship between energy and matter?' Using his training and years of experience as a chemistry teacher, Mr Fleming recalled a program he'd seen on the television two weeks ago about this very subject. 'Matter has been described and defined by scientists' as a form of energy,' he quoted in his best authoritative voice.

John digested the answer for a few seconds while he chewed.

'But that's not really an accurate description of the true relationship between the two,' said John, surprising Mr Fleming again, who hadn't expected a counter argument. 'A truer description would be; that energy and matter are different aspects of the same thing. And that "same thing" is not energy, well not in the classic definition of energy.'

Mr Fleming's mouth was open again but his fork was still on the plate. He recovered beautifully with another question.

'So what is it then, in your opinion?' Not a brilliant question, but Mr Fleming was in shock.

'I'm not sure I can explain it,' said John, scratching his head with the handle of his knife.

Mr Fleming felt a sense of relief, he'd been worried for a moment there, but it looked like he wasn't losing his grip after all. Unfortunately John continued.

'The true nature is too complex to understand in three dimensions. The relationship between energy and matter is probably therefore best described with a metaphor,' said John spraying a bit of sausage onto the table.

'A metaphor… yes,' said Mr Fleming. He'd had more than enough shocks this week, and John's sudden use of the word "metaphor"; a word he never expected to hear spoken in the hallowed surroundings of Penshaw Grove School; didn't help. Mr Fleming felt as though the world was racing away from him and he started to consider retirement.

'Imagine that this sausage is energy,' continued John waving the bit of sausage on his fork from side to side, 'and the plate is matter. But, what is the common denominator? What links them together?'

'Mashed potatoes?' asked Mr Fleming, who still hadn't recovered from the word "metaphor".

'No, that's more energy.'

Mr Fleming thought for a moment, he'd been clutching straws when he'd suggested mashed potatoes. 'I give up,' he said finally, 'what is it?'

'Money, the common denominator is money. You can sell a plate and buy a sausage or vice versa. Therefore the common factor that is not one thing or the other, energy or matter, is money.'

'I see what you mean now by saying energy and matter are different aspects of the same thing. And that "same thing" is not energy. That's very well thought out, well done.' Mr Fleming thought that he should comment further but he was still trying to reconcile the new John. Perhaps a little humour might help. 'Yes, and hasn't it always been said, that sooner or later it all boils down to money?' It was delivery like this that ensured that Mr Fleming would always be a chemistry teacher and not a stand-up comedian. Mr Fleming paused to see if John got his little joke, but John was preoccupied with something else.

Images and formulae flashed rapidly across John's field of vision. The metaphor hadn't helped Mr Fleming, but it had helped John, and whatever was feeding him this information seemed to know it. John had quickly written some equations down the other day, but until this moment he hadn't fully understood them.

'The second law,' said John, totally confusing Mr Fleming because he thought it was a response to his joke.

'The second what?'

'The second law of thermodynamics, it wouldn't apply... you could create perpetual motion machines, or stockpile energy, and ... and it would explain how you can slow time for specific objects,' said John. 'Do you see?'

'Slow time for specific objects... no I'm afraid I don't see, not really, but you should write this all down because it sounds like you're on to something there,' said Mr Fleming.

John didn't respond to Mr Fleming, he was trying to remember where he'd left the equations. He remembered writing them down just after he'd done his maths homework; which for the first time in his life he'd found easy; but what he'd done with the sheets of paper after that, he couldn't recall. He noticed the silence to his left and turned to see his friends looking at him with open mouths.

'What?' he asked.

'There was a lot of long words there mate,' said Scott. 'Look you've confused Frank into eating his peas.'

'Oh God no!' exclaimed Frank, as he suddenly realised and put his knife and fork down in disgust.

'Yes Godbert, there were a lot of long words there, but don't let that worry you, it does you good to exercise your mind. And now I have a question for you,' said Mr Fleming, who felt he should bring the conversation back into a world that he understood.

'What is it Sir?'

Mr Fleming pointed at the remains of John's meal. 'Why have you left the ends of your sausages?' John's friends smiled, they all knew the answer to this one.

'I never eat the ends of sausages Sir.'

Mr Fleming looked curious.

'Why?'

'Ah,' said John, 'I'm glad you asked me that, just wait a few minutes and the answer will present itself.'

Mr Fleming was fascinated, he looked at John's friends but they were giving nothing away. This was another aspect of John's behaviour he had never observed before; the boy was far more intelligent and confident than he'd thought; and now he was presenting a mysterious and intriguing side to his nature. The boy was maturing nicely. He seemed full of the zest of life, in contrast to the tired apathy that Mr Fleming felt these days. In fact, Mr Fleming could almost swear that the boy was positively glowing. There was a triple flash of lightning and for an instant John's skin seemed to crawl blue with electricity in harmony with the lightning. Mr Fleming put it down to fatigue; his, not John's.

John looked round the dining hall and then leaned forward to speak. Mr Fleming leaned forward to listen and wished he hadn't, this fascinating conversation had made him forget about his haemorrhoids.

'Observe,' said John and leaned back.

There are many examples of symbiotic relationships in the animal kingdom; the crocodile bird, "Pluvianus Aegyptius" and its association with the Nile crocodile, actually getting into the crocodiles mouth to remove parasites and the fleshy remains of the last meal; and Remoras, fish that perform a similar service for sharks. Predators which in return for the cleaning services of other animals, automatically offer protection to that animal from other lesser predators.

Mr Fleming watched in quiet fascination as he observed the closest thing to a symbiotic relationship Penshaw Grove had to offer. Haystack appeared at John's side, and as he stood there Mr Fleming noted that the school uniform seemed to significantly increase his IQ, at least in appearance anyway, possibly putting it into double figures. Placing a two pence coin on the table, Haystack proceeded to eat the ends of John's sausages and then left. Not a word had been exchanged between them.

'That was fascinating Godbert. And he never spoke a word.'

'No Sir, we said all that needed to be said a long time ago; "do you want the ends of your sausages?" "No." "How much do you want?" "Two pence." "Okay." And that was that.'

'And he always pays? Only he doesn't strike me as the sort of person who would normally ask to take something, let alone actually pay for it.'

'Yes Sir, he always pays, the trick is not to let him mug you and steal it back later.'

Symbiosis in action; although John didn't actually receive any obvious benefit from Haystack in the form of protection, he got paid, and at the time of the transaction he didn't need any protection from Haystack. And of course in return Haystack got his bits of sausage. This example of symbiosis only occurred within the confines of the dining hall, once outside it was business as usual.

Haystack had made his way back across the dining hall where he re-joined the rest of Team Lendus who were having a "power lunch"; part of chapter seven just after "weekly sales meetings". The author of "Best Management Practices" proposes that the lunch break can be profitably used to bandy ideas back and forth in the hope of creating new directions, or clarifying old ones. Team Lendus hadn't quite got the hang of it yet and had spent their time closely observing Scott with the attentiveness that a cat reserves for a mouse; a fact that had not escaped Mr Fleming, despite his conversation with John.

Scott stood up and the others followed suit, following him to the dirty plate stack to the left of the serving hatch. John placed his plate on the stack and turned to follow Scott. The room seemed to ripple as if he was looking at a reflection of it in a pond. Time slowed and John felt a tingling sensation in his fingers. John's finger tips were glowing blue white. As he watched, small arcs of electricity grew slowly out of the ends of each finger. The arcs seemed attracted to each other and although they zigzagged randomly, two joined together to form a larger arc. The pattern was repeated for his other fingers until there were just two brilliant arcs of electricity extending up towards the ceiling. The two arcs became one just above John's head and were joined by a third, which he realised had emanated from the top of his head. The single bolt made its way up towards the ceiling, and John realised that it was heading for the tunnel in the storeroom upstairs. He felt no sensation of pain or heat from the discharge, and although he couldn't explain how, he suddenly knew that he was the source of the storm that was attempting to wash the school away.

As the bolt of lightning started to fade, John's attention was drawn to a noise like stone grinding against stone, coming from the far side of the dining hall over near the entrance. A black sphere formed in the air. It was roughly the same size as the tunnel upstairs and John wondered if the two were connected.

One moment the sphere was empty and the next, standing inside it and looking directly at John, was a small black furred, bear like creature. It beckoned to John and then turned and walked seemingly receding into the black sphere without getting any further away. Down its back ran a single purple stripe and two orange ones. John started to move towards the sphere but abruptly, time returned to normal, the black sphere vanished and the lights went out.

The thunderclap that followed John's bolt of lightning was deafening, rattling windows, cutlery and pupils alike. After a couple of seconds the lights came back on with the exception of two bulbs above John's head which had not survived the strike.

'What the hell was that?' exclaimed John, referring to the creature he'd just seen.

'That was close,' said Kevin, 'almost like lightning struck inside the room.'

'And we've got to go out in this,' said Frank, indicating the view out of the window.

'A bit of rain won't hurt you,' replied Action.

'It's not the rain I'm worried about,' said Frank.

'Well we can't stay in here; we've got business to attend to,' said Scott with finality.

As they moved away from the serving hatch Mr Fleming's eye was drawn to the floor where John had been standing when the lightning struck; it was smoking. He watched John as he moved towards the exit, looking to see if he was alright. It was then that he saw Scott nod slightly to Burnston. Team Lendus immediately stood up triggering an alarm bell in Mr Fleming's head.

Years of teaching had honed Mr Fleming's radar, and although the years had taken their toll, the barely perceptible nod by Scott followed by the instant reaction by The Lendus shone like a beacon across the dining hall. Mr Fleming suspected an arranged fight. Given his recent conversation with John, he felt a slight pang of disappointment. He was puzzled though. Where were they going to have it? It was absolutely throwing it down outside; so the traditional place, the yard at the back of the school didn't seem likely; or at least he hoped it wasn't, as he didn't want to get soaked trying to break it up. So where was this fight going to take place? It didn't really matter, there were only so many places it could be, and Mr Fleming knew them all.

Five minutes later with his lunch finished, Mr Fleming stood in the entrance looking at the short walk across the playground to the South corridor. As the rain fell it caught the light shining from the windows opposite causing the drops to glitter. The standing water on the playground danced and sparkled in the same light, its surface in a constant state of change. He stood for a while reflecting on the beauty of the scene and wondering if there was going to be a pause in the deluge. The drumming increased indicating that the deluge had just got started. Mr Fleming cursed silently under his breath; but being a seasoned veteran of the lunchtime patrol, was undaunted. He positioned his umbrella outside the door and pressed the button to unfold it. The rain pattered heavily on the black cloth, causing the umbrella to twitch in his hand and without any further hesitation he launched himself into the storm.

The standing water on the playground reached just far enough up the side of Mr Fleming's shoes to find the leaks between the soles and the uppers. The rain was driving down almost vertically, bouncing up to knee height and coming back down again. Dignity forbid him to run and so by the time he'd reached the corridor he was soaked from the knees down.

He shook each leg in turn then turned right and made his way to the end of the corridor. The end of the south building ground floor corridor terminated with a T-junction. To the left was the stairwell leading up to the first floor. To the right, projecting into the playground was a square portico with a pyramid shaped roof. Sandwiched between the corridor and the covered area known to all as "the shed" the portico had another two entrances; one led straight back into the playground; and the other, an archway in the back wall, descended six steps into the yard. The shed was deserted today; there were warmer places to be.

Once in the portico, Mr Fleming stood looking through the arch into the rear yard. This was the lowest point on the whole school site, a fact borne out by the depth of the water. Mr Fleming breathed a sigh of relief; the only thing moving in the yard was the surface of the water. Breaking up a fight here would have resulted in him getting very wet indeed. But, if the fight wasn't here, then where was it? Perhaps he'd been mistaken and read the signs wrong. The thought sapped his strength and made him feel old. He paused to reflect and reanalyse his thoughts. He still couldn't lose the feeling that something was going on. No, something just kept nagging, he couldn't be wrong. Being wrong was something that just didn't happen and no matter how tired he felt, he couldn't be that far out of touch. He stood for a moment watching the patterns the rain made on the surface of the flooded yard.

23
THE GAME

Like the ground floor, the first floor corridor of the South building was open to the elements. Floor to ceiling openings ran the entire length of the corridor, and in what looked like an afterthought, Red painted railings extended halfway up the openings to block the long drop into the playground. The rain reached in through the openings forming semi-circular damp patches on the floor.

To avoid a soaking, John, his friends and The Lendus walked on the side of the corridor away from the railings. The darkness caused by the storm was barely countered by the poor lighting. The light fittings were too far apart and the bulbs of too low a wattage to make much of a difference.

They were approaching the main hall from the opposite end to the cloakroom where The Lendus had held their meeting. Scott halted next to a blue door set back slightly in the brickwork. The paint on the door lacked the wear and tear of the other doors in the school, indicating that it wasn't used much. The others gathered around Scott, with John stood slightly back from the group halfway between them and the railings.

'I don't think I've ever noticed this door before,' said Action. 'What's inside?'

'Somewhere we'll never be found,' replied Scott as he produced the key he got from Kevin the night before. He slid the key into the lock, it was a little difficult to turn and he had a couple of failed attempts before Burnston intervened.

'Let me try,' he said.

Scott stood aside looking nervously up and down the corridor. Burnston turned the key without any apparent effort and pushed the door open. He indicated that Scott should be the first to enter. Scott stepped over the threshold and then hesitated unsure of his footing. The room was in total darkness. The dim lights on the corridor formed a pale rectangle of light on the floor, which indicated the bottom of some steps that climbed up to the left. Scott peered into the gloom trying to make out any details. For an instant a flash of lightning lit the area beyond the stairs in a cold blue white light. The illumination faded, leaving it to memory to interpret the briefly glimpsed image. The impression of the room was cavernous, with six steps climbing to a raised floor. To the right, up on the raised floor, stacked ten high along the back wall were three rows of old chairs. Beyond the chairs leaning against the far wall, although it was difficult to make out in the single flash, were what appeared to be large works of abstract art.

The following thunder was raw and palpable and each of them felt the resonance in his chest. Scott decided that it would be better to be inside in the pitch black, than on the open corridor. He pulled his shoulders back and stepped fully into the room. The others watched from the door as Scott paused at the foot of the steps waiting for his eyes to adjust to the darkness. Holding onto the handrail he tentatively climbed two steps and then looked back at the door. There was an old brass light switch just to his left; it glinted in the low light. He reached across to it. With a heavy metallic click, two lights which hung from the high ceiling on long twisted cloth covered cables, lit up. The lights were of such low wattage that all they did was make the room less dark, but it was better than nothing.

'Inside quick, before someone sees us,' ordered Scott as he continued his climb to the top of the steps.

As the others quickly piled into the room another bolt of lightning jumped from John's right hand and discharged itself onto the railings opposite the door.

'I swear this lightning is getting closer,' said Kevin, who was just in front of John. 'I could feel that one on the back of my neck.'

These thunderbolts were becoming an embarrassment, John wondered how long it would be before someone noticed it was him that was causing them. The railing was still glowing dark red as John closed the door behind him, the hot metal hissing as the rain struck it.

Back inside the dimly lit room the others looked around in wonder. Now that there was some light, it was now apparent that the artwork, leaning against the far wall, was in fact stage scenery. There were representations of houses and castles, trees, barrels, and a view across a lake. Above them hanging from suspended steel bars, was an assortment of various sized spotlights. Occupying almost the entire left wall was a large cream rectangle with the words "Safety Curtain" printed across it in large black letters. To the left of the safety curtain was an ancient control panel full of Bakelite switches, knobs and levers. Just below the control panel was a large crank handle for opening and closing the blue velvet curtains visible from the hall.

'Where are we?' Kevin asked.

'This is the stage off the main hall,' said Frank.

'I didn't know there was anything behind the platform in the hall,' said Clink. 'I thought it was just curtains with a wall behind.' This was the first non-menacing communication John's friends had ever received from any of Burnston's henchmen, and each of them felt as if some sort of bridge had been formed. The feeling was to be short lived however. 'I looked behind the curtains once and it was just solid.' Clink wasn't being conversational; he was issuing a challenge as to whether the school had a stage at all, despite their location adjacent to the hall and the evidence all around them.

'The solid wall behind the curtains is the safety curtain,' said Burnston pointing at it and ending any argument before it could start.

Clink looked at the large cream rectangle and read the words "Safety Curtain" his lips moving as he silently formed each word in his mind. 'Good hiding place,' he acknowledged.

The architect, Jeremiah Ramsden Priestly, had lavished a great deal of time and money on equipping the school with "proper" stage paraphernalia; proper in the sense that the school couldn't possibly afford to maintain it. A prime example of this was the safety curtain. Located immediately behind the proscenium arch, the safety curtain was an expensive and unnecessary accessory for the school. It was constructed of steel and asbestos, weighed nearly two tons, and had been jammed in the down position since 1957.

Thanks to the safety curtain the stage was almost hermetically sealed. The air inside was warm and stuffy. A thick layer of dust covered the floor and everything else. Nobody had been in there for years.

Frank made his way over to the ancient control panel and studied it for a moment. Extending out from the top of the panel was a short piece of brass pipe which ended in a brass clamshell shaped light. Immediately below the bracket there was a round brass light switch. The switch made the same heavy clunking sound as the one on the stairs as Frank turned the clamshell light on. A pool of warm yellow light illuminated the control panel and the floor in front of it.

'We could use some of that scenery to make a table under this light,' said Frank. 'Bring some chairs over and I'll get that scenery of a bush with a cat in it.

A few minutes later, under Frank's supervision, they had constructed a makeshift card table and positioned nine chairs around it arranged in a horseshoe. Kevin, being the son of a caretaker, had dutifully cleaned each one with his sleeves. Both his sleeves were now black with twenty years of crud. He studied them with a pained expression on his face knowing that he was going to have to endure another of his mother's lectures.

Their occupation of the stage had kicked up a great deal of dust which hung in the warm stale air, obscuring the lights hanging from the ceiling which resembled two suns on a foggy day. The large volume of noise coming from the hall was reduced to a dull murmur by the safety curtain. Preparations complete, they stood back and admired the scene. The makeshift card table was illuminated by a hazy cone of yellow light, the dust in the air showing the path of the light from the control panel. The subdued noise from the hall, the hazy light, and the conspirative atmosphere; the scene resembled a backroom gambling club from a gangster movie. The comparatively bright area around the control panel threw the rest of the stage into deep shadow, with vague shapes being picked out through the dust by the ceiling lights.

'Shall we get started,' said Scott, indicating that everyone should take a seat.

The Lendus positioned themselves together on one side of the horseshoe; with Action, Frank, John and Kevin; aka team Briggs; on the other. Scott occupied the centre seat between the two groups. As Scott shuffled the cards The Lendus removed their jackets and draped them over the backs of their chairs. Haystack found it easier to hang his jacket on one of the large levers sticking out of the control panel. He grinned at his own genius.

Scott began to deal.

*

Mr Fleming let his mind meander as he watched the rain in the flooded yard from the portico. Holding his umbrella to the front it drummed as the rain hit it. The patterns on the surface of the water and the drumming were hypnotic. A flash of lightning brought him back from his reverie. Taking a step back from the archway he put his umbrella down. He was convinced that he couldn't be wrong about the fight. Although he hadn't really expected to find the fight in the yard, not finding it knocked him back slightly. Doubt was ever present, lurking in the background. He felt weary with the world and that seemed to be sapping his resolve.

What now?

The main hall! They must have gone up to the main hall. Come on Harry; get a grip. That's where you should have gone in the first place.

He turned and climbed the stairs, intending to deposit his wet umbrella in the staffroom, before grabbing a cup of coffee. Coffee that's what he needed, it always perked him up.

The staffroom was adjacent to the cloakroom at the opposite end of the hall to the stage. Mr Fleming opened the door and entered the smoke filled atmosphere. Located below the headmasters study, the nicotine stained ceiling was low enough to touch and Mr Fleming often had the urge to stoop when entering the room. Mirroring the colour of the ceiling the floor was covered in brown lino. There was a square of faded beige and blue patterned carpet in the centre. The white walls, mostly hidden behind notice boards, shelves and a few prints of classic paintings, were yellow with years of carcinogenic, academic comforters. The lights were on and the rain rattled against the single, long low window. The window faced south across Penshaw Grove, but today the sky was so black with the storm that you couldn't see out. A collection of variously coloured easy chairs were clustered loosely around five round coffee tables. On each table there was an interesting collection of coffee cup rings and a full ashtray.

All the teachers were there, some marking exercise books, some dozing in the large comfy chairs. Cigarettes rested on ashtrays burning like incense sticks. You didn't need to buy any cigarettes to get your nicotine fix; Mr Fleming reflected. All you needed was ten minutes in the staffroom. He made his way through the clouds towards the coffee.

'What happens to the unpleasant ones when they leave us?' Mr Fleming asked the staffroom in general as he entered. 'I ask only because we never seem to see them again once they've gone.'

'Thank God,' replied Ted Crawford looking up from marking the hilarious attempts at algebra John's class had handed in on Tuesday. He was saving Frank's book until last as it always cheered him up. Next in the pile was John's. He flicked through the pages to find the completed exercise and five loose pages fell out.

Next to a sink in the corner of the room was a work surface. Stacked upside down along the back were a set of clean coffee cups. Mr Fleming put his umbrella down and switched the electric kettle on. It boiled almost instantly. He was stirring his coffee when he noticed the expression on Ted's face. He seemed to be mesmerised by some sheets of paper. The expression he wore was one of awe and wonder, with an occasional nervous tick. Mr Fleming had never seen anything like it.

'You look a bit put out; everything alright?'

Mr Crawford didn't reply. He quickly compared the writing on the sheets to John's book.

'It's John Godbert's work; it's his hand writing.' First Burnston shows an interest and now Godbert, thought Ted; what on earth is going on?

'Godbert, I've just had an interesting conversation with him, about the relationship between energy and matter.'

Mr Crawford held up a sheet of paper.

'This is a mathematical representation of the relationship between energy and matter.'

'Does it involve mashed potatoes?'

Mr Crawford looked bemused. 'Sorry?' he said.

'Don't mind me, just a little joke. I mean, is it correct?'

'I don't know it's beyond the limit of my understanding.'

Mr Fleming raised his eyebrows.

'I recognise some of the mathematical phrasing and that's correct,' continued Mr Crawford; 'but the context in which it's used is beyond me.'

'Now that is interesting.'

'And that's not all.'

Mr Crawford held up another sheet.

'This one is titled "Three dimensional representations of variable dimensional energy flow and containment". There are two pages of it. The theory is way beyond me, but from what I do understand, it seems to work. There's a nice little proof at the end.'

The rest of the teachers in the staffroom had now started to take an interest.

'So you're saying that Godbert's mathematical skills have suddenly improved?' queried Mr Fleming.

'No, I'm saying that Godbert is pushing at the boundaries of human understanding.'

'What a strange week,' said Stefan the art master. 'First Burnston is wearing our school uniform "to project the correct corporate image", so he tells me.' He reached down the side of his chair as he spoke and produced a large folder. 'And as well as Godbert apparently being a mathematical genius, he produced these drawings last lesson.' The art master slid a number of highly detailed pencil drawings from the folder. 'They're of a city built on the inside of a sphere, so he tells me.' Stefan paused to let the others get a look at the drawings. 'What I find amazing is that for all the detail that's in them, Godbert produced all of them in less than an hour.'

'They are truly amazing,' said Mr Fleming, who was momentarily distracted from his mission. 'The proportions of the buildings are excellent, there's some skill there. What an imagination Godbert has.'

'Yes Harry,' agreed Stefan, 'and if you notice, the buildings match from one drawing to another, it's almost as if he'd been there.'

Harry remembered that he was on a mission. 'I'm going to have a wander up to the main hall to see what Burnston might be up to.' He turned and left the staffroom. As he left, the other teachers gathered around Ted and Stefan.

There were two entrances to the hall, one at the stage end and one at the end nearest the staffroom. Mr Fleming entered the hall using the nearest entrance. The main hall was packed and the noise level deafening. The six large circular lights were switched on; six hundred, forty watt bulbs lighting the hall to almost migraine levels; Mr Fleming imagined the electricity meter in reception screaming with over consumption. He made his way through the crowd towards the stage with his cup of coffee balanced on a saucer, and thanks to years of practice, didn't spill a single drop. Two short flights of stairs ran up either side of the stage, Mr Fleming and climbed up one of them, crossed over to the centrally placed lectern in front of the curtains, and placed his cup and saucer on it. From here he had a commanding view of the hall, and everyone in the hall had a commanding view of him. With his appearance on stage the noise level in the hall dropped measurably. Mr Fleming's spirits rose, he felt satisfied in the fact that his presence still commanded that sort of power.

From his position behind the lectern Mr Fleming scanned the occupants. Most were just standing talking, but a few of the smaller ones were playing chasing games in and out of the crowd. It was still noisy, but at least the levels were tolerable. He scanned the crowd again… not a uniform in sight.

There were times when Mr Fleming enjoyed this job the way he used to when he first started; but the gaps between those times seemed to have increased. He thought about it, analysing why that might be. He was happiest when he had a goal, some target to aim for, like the bucket trick. Years ago he always had some scheme or other on the go, but nowadays he just couldn't be bothered with all the time it required to set them up. These days the kids seemed wise to his tricks; often not falling for them at all. Suspicious, untrusting lot, he thought. Taking this lunch time as an example; he thought he had an easy target in Burnston and his cronies, he was sure something was going on. Perhaps he'd been wrong. Perhaps his radar really was failing, or perhaps it wasn't; maybe the hall wasn't the best location to look for that arranged fight. Years ago, a setback like losing the target would have spurred him on to enthusiastically meet the challenge with fresh ideas. Now, he just felt tired and drained.

He took a sip of coffee, it was too hot. Holding the cup to his lips he blew gently across the surface of the liquid. Taking a deeper breath he blew with more vigour… the light level seemed to drop. That's quite worrying. His wife had been saying for weeks that if he didn't slow down he'd have a stroke and now it looked as though she might be right. He sagged, as doubt once again crept into his thoughts and a wave of fatigue engulfed him. He was fed up of being on his feet. He was sick of being up and down, one minute all fired up; the next deflated and target-less. The light level dropped ever so slightly again and Mr Fleming placed his cup and saucer back on the lectern; he didn't want to drop it and make a fool of himself.

Placing both hands on the lectern for support, he closed his eyes, took a deep breath and let it out slowly. Only five more years to retirement; could he wait that long? If he had lost his teachers radar, his finely honed ability to detect "trouble brewing", the gift that was the envy of the other staff; did he want to wait five years? And if he was having a stroke, he'd have to give up teaching anyway. What could he do without his health? He hadn't spent any time thinking about what he was going to do after retirement; he'd only ever pictured himself doing this. If he didn't have his health… well… the thought was depressing. The loss of power and control, a slow decline into the twilight of old age; perhaps they were the good points, he could be dying right here on this stage. His health couldn't be that bad; could it? Opening his eyes he was dismayed to note that his eyesight had grown even dimmer. He closed them again and waited, hoping the problem would go away.

*

Scott dealt the cards again. After five quick games the Briggs party were up four games to one, Haystack being the only winner on The Lendus side. Frank, John, Scott and Kevin had each won a game, but as they were all pooling their winnings, unlike The Lendus, the individual wins didn't matter. So as long as The Lendus believed that the game was about individuals and not us and them everything should run smoothly.

'What does that lever do?' asked Kevin as Scott finished dealing.

Frank looked at the control panel. 'Which lever?'

'That one with the jacket hung on it,' replied Kevin.

'I don't know; why?'

'Because it keeps moving,' said Kevin, 'watch.' They all turned to look at the lever which after a few seconds slipped down slightly under the weight of the jacket. 'See, I told you so.'

Haystack immediately lost interest and turned back to the cards. He couldn't see what the problem was and he certainly wasn't going to volunteer to move his jacket, not without a fight anyway. All he wanted to do was win another hand.

'Probably doesn't do anything. Nothing in this place works. Now,' said Scott turning to Action and showing him the top of the pack of cards, 'twist or stick?'

Action looked at his cards; he had a nine and a six, fifteen; not enough to win. Scott was holding the cards in one hand poised to deal with the other. Action looked at the top card searching for the position of the faint mark that would indicate its value. After a moment he spotted it, the card was a ten. 'Stick,' he said, reflecting on the fact that being able to read what the next card was gave you a serious advantage.

John's enthusiasm for the game wasn't very high. He was thinking of Elleria. He missed her. Not just her presence and her company, but her advice. She always had answers to his questions. John looked at his hands where he held them under the table. They were glowing in the dark, slowly pulsating with an inner light. Elleria would know why. Each time the light reached its brightest point John had fought to lower it. He had the feeling that if he didn't control the light, he would cause another lightning strike and he didn't want to have to explain that to his fellow players.

The light from his hands was gaining in brightness again. John concentrated on slowing the rate of increase, but with each pulse it was getting more and more difficult. This one continued to increase in intensity, passing the point at which John had stopped the last one and threatening to overwhelm him. John tried harder, but it was like trying to stop a bus by running in front of it. The power pushed him back, forcing him to loosen his control, which allowed the power to increase at a greater rate. John realised that he'd held the power back too long, when he lost control this time it would produce more than just a lightning strike.

A mathematical formula flashed in front of his eyes. In an instant John understood, this would give him the equivalent of a lever to control the power, but how would he apply it to his situation? The intensity of the power dropped back down and John realised that just thinking about the formula applied it. But how long would it work for? Although the level had dropped, it hadn't dropped as low as it had been last time. This was building up to something and John did not think that it would be a good thing at all.

*

'Sir... Sir... Mr Fleming, Sir.'

Mr Fleming opened his eyes and looked down. A small boy with a cheeky grin was looking up at him.

'Yes Adams, what is it?'

'What's wrong with the lights, Sir? They keep getting dimmer.'

And right on cue, the lights dutifully dimmed again.

'See, Sir.'

'Ah,' said Mr Fleming.

Man and boy, teacher and pupil, Mr Fleming had spent most of his life in these buildings; he knew every nook and cranny. He didn't know why he hadn't thought of it before. He turned and looked at the stage curtains all thoughts of premature death forgotten.

'Gotcha,' he said.

*

John stood up and stepped away from the card table.

'Are you alright?' asked Frank.

John could feel another power surge building and had begun to sweat. Even with the new formula he was finding it difficult to control. 'I'm too hot,' he said.

'It is hot in...' started Kevin, but he was interrupted when the stage door opened. Lightning flickered outside, silhouetting the unmistakeable form of Mr Fleming as he stood framed in the doorway.

The surprise was total, nobody had been expecting this. John's concentration was broken and in an instant he lost all control.

Time froze.

John was thrown backwards out of his place marker landing heavily on his back. Dazed and winded, he felt like he'd been hit by a car. He ached all over. He kept his eyes closed and tried to gather his thoughts. Slowly, the pain subsided and he started to gather his wits. There was absolute silence, but what had just happened?

He opened his eyes and blinked a couple of times. He found himself looking up at the spotlights. They were casting stark shadows on the ceiling from a harsh blue white light. John propped himself up on his elbows to see where the light was coming from. What he saw took his breath away. His place marker was enveloped with arcs of electricity. They coiled around his body and his limbs, and several of them were starting to make their way out from the ends of his hands and the top of his head to various points on the stage. It was spectacular and looked very painful, no wonder he ached.

Standing up, John looked closer at his place marker. The lightning was bright, but there was something else there which hurt his eyes. The pain drilled into the back of his head making it difficult to look at his place marker for long. It was hard to pick out, but eventually he saw it. Inside the chest of his place marker there was a dark violet sphere about the size of a fist. It was dull, almost black, but John could sense that it was emitting a huge amount of radiation. It was that which was causing his pain. He went over the formulae he'd been shown, they didn't explain the sphere or what was happening.

John's thoughts turned to Elleria. What would she do now? He was sure she would have an answer.

"What if she didn't have an answer? Where would she go for one?"

The questions seemed irrelevant because she wasn't here, she was stuck in Valheel. Elleria, sighed John… how he missed her. He thought of the last time they were together closing his eyes and reliving the moment. When he was with her it felt so right, as if the world aligned itself to fall into place alongside them; and now the world just didn't make sense. John felt alone and isolated. He shivered involuntarily.

The question came again. "Where would Elleria go for an answer?"

Elleria would have just known the answer, thought John.

"But, supposing she didn't know the answer, what would she have done to find it?"

I don't know, thought John, but it's a silly question, she would have just known what to do.

"I can guarantee that Elleria would definitely not have known the answer to this question. Remember that until you managed to get to Valheel, Elleria had no idea that burst mode existed."

Was he thinking these questions, or was there someone else there? There was a noise behind him like stone grinding against stone.

'I can appear visible, if that's any help,' said a distant voice behind John.

John turned. There was a black sphere about two metres in diameter floating in the air in front of him and standing inside it was the same bear like creature he had seen in the dining hall.

'Who are you?' asked John.

'I'm the one who has been feeding you all the information you've been receiving in response to the new situations you have found yourself in. I am The Librarian. And I have been a part of you since you got the watch, so even after you managed to lose Elleria, you haven't been alone.'

'You look like a bear or an ape or something.'

'True, I'm not human; but then again, neither are you.'

'Fair point,' said John.

'There are things I need to show you. Things that may help you contain this situation, and maybe some background to what's going on. The trick is that you need to be where I am.'

To John this was good news, because he definitely felt that this was the moment when perhaps he needed some help. Since he'd lost Elleria everything seemed to have gone completely pear shaped; but now, just as things looked as if they were as bad as they could get, this strange creature appears offering to help. The creature looked so strange that it must know the answers. John felt relief that finally he may get some control back.

'No problem,' said John walking towards the sphere. Based on the grinding stone sound that it had made when it appeared, he assumed that it would be solid, but it was no more substantial than vapour and he stumbled slightly when he didn't find the expected resistance. John faced The Librarian with a questioning look on his face.

'Unfortunately that isn't the way in. And the problem I have is that I can't tell you how you do get in, you have to work it out for yourself,' said The Librarian.

'Why?'

'Because it's the realisation of where I am that is the key to getting there.'

'Oh,' said John, 'can you give me a clue?'

'Where would Elleria go to find answers?'

John looked at his place marker; the dark violate sphere in his chest had grown; it was now twice the size it was.

'Remember that time has not stopped, it's just moving very slowly. If time had not been slowed your solar system would be history now,' said The Librarian.

'What, the whole solar system?' asked John, believing The Librarian's statement to be an exaggeration.

'Yes, but now is not the time to be distracted. You need to be where I am, where time doesn't exist. Now think, who am I? Where would Elleria go to find answers? Where would I be?'

How could he have been so stupid? He was thinking of too complex an answer. He blamed all those equations. 'A library,' he answered.

'Finally,' replied The Librarian.

Then, without any apparent transition from one to the other, John was no longer standing on the stage he was somewhere else.

24

THE LIBRARIAN

The place felt real. It had the same look as Valheel, it was made of the same material in the same style; but there was something else, and the only way John could describe it was that it felt like Penshaw Grove School. There were references all over the school to the past; the old trophies in the dining hall entrance. Old photographs on the wall of the woodwork room with the pupils sporting strange hairstyles. The older teachers would often recall glorious past events involving pupils who had left long ago; taking their strange hairstyles with them. To John and his friends these references were ancient history; only the here and now mattered. And the here and now was always dull; there was the general feeling that nothing they did would ever be recalled with fondness in future years by teachers reminiscing. Within the confines of the school, the past was always pushed by the teachers as being more important, more glorious and more interesting than the here and now. From John's first days at the school he had sensed this, he could feel the history of the school all around him, it emanated from the walls, it hung in the air, it reached out from the past to influence the present. Perhaps it was that invisible stimulus which prompted the teachers to keep ancient photographs on the walls and wax lyrical about the past.

John looked around the place he was in now. There were no photographs on the walls or old trophies, the place was clinical and pristine, but it had that same feeling as Penshaw Grove, the sensation that there was a weight of history embedded in the walls.

John was standing near the centre of a large octagonal chamber. Glowing with some inner light, the floor and walls were made of what looked like white marble. To his right floating, just above the floor, was a brightly glowing, constantly changing shape. The object didn't seem to hold its form; it seemed to be a cube, a sphere, everything in between and none of them, all at the same time. All the colours imaginable appeared fleetingly in patches across its surface, constantly fading and merging into new colours. It was hypnotic and it felt... John found it difficult to describe how it felt, but it felt close, not physically, it was more like the feeling you get with your parents... bonded. Yes, bonded; that was probably the best word to describe it, but more than that John felt that it was somehow very important.

Directly in front of him was an arched corridor about the height of a two storey building, it too was constructed in white marble. The corridor was broken into regular sections by piers that ran up to the bases of arches that spanned the corridor. Lining the walls of the corridor, between the piers and all the way up to the arched ceiling, were shelves filled with neat, identically sized books. The white shelves were of equal height and perfectly symmetrical on both sides of the corridor, the receding parallel lines they formed met at a vanishing point a long way off. It was a perfect example of perspective, and John wondered how long the corridor was.

In black marble, set into the floor in front of the corridor, was the number three. John turned himself round on the spot; two, one, eight, seven, six, five, four and back to three again. Like the spokes of a giant wheel there were eight identical corridors leading off the room. On the wall between each corridor was a large black zero. John wondered if the far ends of the corridors were linked by a circular corridor. He felt the answer must be "yes". He didn't know how he knew, but he had an overwhelming feeling that he was right. He also had the notion that if this was a library, then the space between the spoke corridors would be wasted if there weren't more circular corridors within the outer one. And again he was utterly convinced that that was the case, in fact so much so that he came up with a figure of nine hundred and ninety nine concentric corridors.

John was trying to comprehend the vastness of the library when he looked up. The room he was in had no ceiling; he was stood at the bottom of a shaft. Running around the shaft above the arched corridors was another identical set of spoke corridors. Above that, another, and another, on and on to a vanishing point. The corridors opened straight onto the shaft, there were no railings to prevent anyone from falling. Between the corridors the numbering sequence continued for each level, one... two... and on up to... up to... nine hundred and ninety nine.

How, thought John, could I possibly know that?

'Because you are creating it,' said a voice behind John.

John spun round. Emerging from corridor number seven into the central chamber was The Librarian. The black furred creature had long muscular arms and walked upright on short legs. As it drew closer John noticed it had a bear like snout and large teeth. A single purple and two orange stripes ran over the top of its head and down its back. The overall impression John had, was that it looked like a cross between a primate and a bear and although John didn't actually feel threatened, the large black claws were of particular note. There was a slight waddle to its walk and John thought that the creature seemed to have been designed to climb trees or walk on all fours not on two legs.

'You're quite right of course,' said The Librarian, 'the Ja'liem are tree dwellers.'

'You can read my mind?' asked John.

'Well technically it's actually our mind.' The Librarian stood in front of John and bowed its head slightly to acknowledge John. John felt as though he should do likewise and nodded in return.

'Let me explain. I am the other half of the Node, the watch you received as a gift, so technically I'm you and you are me. Please sit.' John did without thinking and was pleased to note that there was a chair behind him that hadn't been there a moment ago. He was now at eye level with the librarian who had remained standing.

'The Ja'liem?' asked John.

'That was the name given to us by Amantarra, our creator.' The Librarian's voice was deep and soothing and all the better for hearing it up close; on the stage his voice had sounded distant. 'And I am a copy of a very ancient Ja'liem known as The Librarian.'

John scratched his head, 'a copy, like Jack.'

'Amantarra took a copy of the real Librarian before the destruction of Valheel. I imagine he's still out there somewhere.'

'So, what is this place... this library? And how did I manage to get here?' John asked.

'This place is a fabrication, there's nothing here from the space you would call real. Don't get me wrong, it's still a reality, it just exists in a different set of dimensions and its rules were fabricated.'

'Fabricated? You mean made? Made by whom; Amantarra?'

'Partially; this is all the technical knowledge of the Bruwnan, Amantarra's race; plus a lot of Amantarra's own research. The knowledge of the Bruwnan exists in more than three dimensions; but like me, you are incapable of understanding it in that format. The solution, is for you to construct a three dimensional interpretation of that knowledge; in other words, a library. This place exists outside normal space time and its form came from your subconscious. The entrance had to come from you. This is why you had to have the idea for yourself and why I couldn't tell you.'

'So you're saying that the entrance is in my head.'

'That's probably a close enough analogy,' replied The Librarian. 'Now that you are fully merged with the watch you will slowly absorb the knowledge in this library and then we will speak with one voice. Until then I will act as your guide to this knowledge.'

John looked up at the balconies at each level as they disappeared into the distance. 'Technical knowledge,' he said, 'so all those messages that kept flashing up in front of my eyes, all that technical stuff; it all came from here?'

'The oldest knowledge is here at the bottom and the top level, the newest, was added by Amantarra after she left Valheel. All complete with references in my index,' said The Librarian proudly, adding, 'to help you,' when he saw the puzzled expression on John's face.

'Those were the numbers at the top of each reference?'

'Yes… did they help? '

'Well they might have done if I'd understood them.'

Ref: 998-1-003-0-532-08-26
The indexing system
Ref: level – segment – lun – face – stack – shelf – volume
Where:
Level: floor level (0-999)
Segment: Radial corridor plus area to the right between radial corridors (1-8)
Lun: concentric corridor (1-999), (0) if on radial corridor.
Face: left (0) or right (1) on radial corridors; inner (0) or outer (1) face of concentric corridors.

Stack: stack number – each face is split into a varying number of stacks of shelves (3-999)

Shelf: shelf number in the stack.

Volume: Book number on the shelf.

The glowing blue text was huge and floated in the air behind The Librarian. 'Does that help?'

John read it several times. 'Well it makes the index understandable, I can see how it relates to this place; but I'm not sure that it would be of any help. It's the information that's useful, not where it is in the library.'

'I'm sorry, but the Ja'liem were created as an intelligent but none technical race. And although my mind is disciplined and well organised, to any observer we appear to be nothing more than simple tree dwelling creatures.

Behind The Librarian, as he spoke, there appeared an image of the Ja'liem in their natural habitat. John watched as the image followed a group Ja'liem making their way through the treetops, pausing occasionally to eat and groom. It looked peaceful and idyllic.

'We have a social structure and a language which can only be understood if you happen to be a Ja'liem,' continued The Librarian, 'This hidden intelligence and lack of technology was deliberate and designed to keep us hidden from the Bruwnan. We were the stepping stone to your species in more ways than one. But please understand that it is very difficult for me to know what is useful and what is not when it comes to anything technical; and while the way my mind is structured makes me the perfect keeper of this knowledge, it's impossible for me to interpret or apply it to any problems. I will show you things that I think may be useful, please feel free to tell me if they are not.'

The image of the Ja'liem vanished as The Librarian paused to let John reflect on what he'd told him.

'Why… why hide your species?'

'There's something going on with the Bruwnan, some sort of power struggle over control of Valheel. From what I've been able to surmise, your species has been created with one purpose… to rival the Bruwnan. One of the key components of the plan was the creation of an intelligent Node and it was the task of the Ja'liem to secretly send Elleria to your world in order to enable the creation of that Node. That part at least worked, because here you are.'

'But I'm hopelessly out of my depth,' said John, 'I have no idea of what's going on and since I lost Elleria I seem to have no control.'

'Yes, according to Amantarra's library records her plan was to turn herself into a Node, but something went wrong.'

'So if I had never got the watch, none of this would be happening?'

'Not exactly, one way or another you would have finished up with the watch. We were both created to be joined together. What I'm saying is that you should have been Amantarra. As for the lack of control, that's down to the small matter of losing your Radgarc. It was Elleria that was controlling the power flow through you and now that she's no longer here, there is, as you've noticed, no control. I showed you the relevant calculations earlier, but I'm afraid that I have no understanding of them.'

John recalled the complex formulae and they appeared in the air behind The Librarian.

'Yes that's the one,' said The Librarian.

John studied the calculations again in more detail this time. 'Feedback,' he announced. 'All the biomass energy is being fed directly into me and as I'm part of the biomass I'm looping all that energy back into myself.'

'Yes that makes sense,' said The Librarian. 'I knew that the result of what was happening would be catastrophic but not the cause of it. Once again I apologise for not being technical. Still with my help, you have at least worked out what the problem is.'

'But not the solution,' said John.

'I think the solution is Elleria. You need to get her back.'

'And the question is; how? She's in Valheel and to get there I need to be in burst mode. I only know one way to do that, but I don't have time to build a fire.'

'Yes, the moment you unfreeze time you will destroy your solar system.'

'What about Amantarra? She would know what to do,' said John.

'Yes I believe she would.'

'I don't suppose that you have any idea where she is?'

'I currently have no answer to that question,' said The Librarian. 'The last identity I have for Amantarra was William Godbert, your Grandfather.'

'Yes, that's as much as I know.'

'I do know that the last thing Amantarra did as your Grandfather was irreversible. She totally committed all her remaining energy to this one action and it was only partially successful; in the sense that a Node was created, but she wasn't it.'

'What was her last action?'

'I'll show you. This entry contains Amantarra's memories up to the last moment that she was in the guise of William Godbert and some of Reginald Scribbins thoughts, whose mind seems to read like a comic book.'

As the image appeared behind The Librarian, he moved towards John and climbed up onto a seat that had just appeared next to John's. All we need now is popcorn, thought John.

Ref: 998-1-001-0-532-08-29
William Godbert narrative – closing sequence

The library seemed to dissolve around him and John became part of the image. He could feel the size and shape of the William Godbert shell and remembered it from the images he'd been shown in the history class. Those had been of William Godbert's first moments and now John was about to witness William's last. There was something a little different this time thought John, or was it that he just hadn't noticed it before; but he could sense other minds; and as the librarian had pointed out, chief amongst them was Reginald Scribbins.

William stood at the front of the class. The walls were mostly bare but there were a few posters from a number of musical shows that had done the rounds before the war. Above the blackboard there was a map of the world; since their first days at school all the pupils had been told that "all the pink bits are ours" and from the tiny British Isles to India, Canada, South Africa, New Zealand and Australia; there was a lot of pink. For the last few weeks, to aid the war effort, the general school theme had been the British Empire and the map had been borrowed from the geography room to emphasis just what that entailed.

William had been teaching the class to sing "Waltzing Matilda" the only popular colonial song he could think of and it was during a pause between verses that a hand shot up.

'Denise,' said William,' you have a question for me.'

'Yes Sir, please Sir but who's Matilda?'

'Does anyone know who Matilda is?' William asked the class in general. A number of hands went up in response. William picked one.

'Was it his wife, Sir?'

'No it's not his wife.' William picked another hand.

'I know Sir; was it his dog?'

'No, not his dog either. Let me give you a clue; it's not a person.' There were some murmurs as possibilities were discussed quietly, but no more hands went up. 'Do you give in? Would you like me to tell you?'

'Yes Sir,' chorused the class as one voice. The pupils here were rough, but discipline was absolute.

'A Matilda is a bag strapped to your back, similar to a backpack, and waltzing Matilda means hiking with your backpack on.' William watched the realisation dawn on their faces. 'And the first line talks of a "swagman camped by a billabong," a swagman was a drifter, who wrapped a few belongings in a cloth attached to a stick, called swag, and carried it over his shoulder. So the song is not about a man looking forward to dancing with his wife, it's about a traveller sitting by a pond wondering who will come walking with him and his backpack. Just remember, sometimes there's hidden meaning in Music and Art. It's something for you to think about.' William looked at the back of the class where Reginald Scribbins was sitting. It was with a certain amount of satisfaction that he noted that even Reginald, the most unimaginative human William had yet encountered, was thinking about it.

William enjoyed teaching, but time was short and this would be the last lesson he would ever teach. The end game had started and the pieces were already in motion. William Godbert had prepared for this moment for more years than most humans live. Although he hadn't chosen the target or strength of the Luftwaffe's raid, he had influenced its planning; forcing a time for it, and subduing the questions and fears of the pilots who were to carry it out in daylight. Such was the power of Amantarra.

For months now he had been developing Reginald's natural fear of being locked in, to a level where he knew Reginald wouldn't let him down. Reginald, like most humans, was open to suggestion. But unlike most humans, where the suggested influence was very short term, the influence over Reginald lasted long term.

William liked Reginald, and he didn't particularly want to do this to him, but William was short of options; Reginald was the only person in the school who was capable of providing him with a plausible explanation. And for the greater good of William's grand scheme, he was willing to give Reginald a bit more of a phobia than he already had. And of course William needed someone he could trust, someone open to suggestion that he could use later. William needed a Keeper for the watch, someone who would eventually play his part in getting it to the other half of the Node.

Long before the air raid sirens had sounded, he had sensed the first of two waves of bombers as they approached across the North Sea. Their planned route to the steelworks brought them in from the south, directly over Penshaw Grove.

And now the sirens were sounding and Reginald was hesitating at the back of the class his head full of images from the First World War propaganda posters his father had shown him. Waxed moustaches, monocles, duelling scars and spiked helmets; all these things were calling to Reginald, "Come and join the fight, don't go to the air raid shelter". Good man, thought William.

'Come on Scribbins, join the back of the line,' said William.

After crossing the playground to the science block, they were the last class to start the journey down the steps that led from the cloakroom to the shelter. William watched Reginald eyeing the coats, looking for somewhere to hide.

The first wave of twenty four bombers was very close; William was running out of time, he must get Reginald underground.

'Come on Reginald,' said William gently, 'it's never as bad as you think it's going to be.'

How long does it take to descend two flights of stairs? How long does it take to descend two flights of stairs without actually pushing Reginald down them?

The bombers were closing rapidly. The plane that would pass almost directly over William's first target was twenty five seconds from optimum position.

It took ten seconds to get Reginald down the first flight.

Fifteen seconds to optimum position.

Reginald paused halfway down the second flight, mainly because William had paused; he appeared to be thinking about something, Reginald wondered what it was.

Ten seconds to optimum position.

William focused his mind on the bomb aimer.

Five seconds to optimum position.

At a point in space, some one thousand nine hundred and sixty six metres above, and two thousand, one hundred and fourteen metres almost due south of Penshaw Grove School, in the nose of a Dornier 217; a nervous former "librarian" from Düsseldorf pressed the "Bomb Release" button.

Or from the point of view of Fritz Schwarzkopf, a former "bibliothekar" from Düsseldorf, he pressed the "Bombe Freigabe" button; which achieved the same thing, but from a different ideological perspective. Despite having the correct name, Fritz had neither a monocle nor a waxed moustache; Reginald would have been very disappointed if he'd known that his closest encounter yet did not resemble in any way the pictures in his father's book.

Twenty seconds to impact.

William and Reginald arrived at the bottom of the stairs and joined the back of the queue into the shelter.

Fifteen seconds to impact.

William who was directly behind Reginald watched him. Reginald was staring into the shelter with occasional glances down the cross corridor. Freedom!

Ten seconds to impact.

William moved forward to see what the holdup was, and give Reginald the opportunity he was waiting for.

Five seconds to impact.

The bomb struck the electricity substation that fed Penshaw Grove. The lights flickered once, and then went out.

Inside the shelter, after the initial panic had been contained, the registers were being called by the flickering light of an oil lamp and the "crump..."; "crump; crump..."; "crump..." beat of bombs landing further into town. The smoke rising from the first bomb was acting as a beacon for the other planes and as a result the planes were releasing their loads short of the steelworks.

William closed his eyes and sensed that the second wave of bombers was fast approaching; time to put his plausible disappearance plan into action; time for the second target. The Headmaster asked him what was wrong. William looked around the shelter, more for effect than anything else, and then turned to the Headmaster. 'Where's Scribbins?' he said.

The door to the shelter closed behind William and the candle he was holding flickered in the draught from it. Where was Scribbins? William blew out the candle; he didn't need it, he could sense far more without using these eyes. He searched the school. Every corridor, classroom, desk and chair appeared in his head as a three dimensional model, there was no detail that escaped William's scrutiny. There you are, thought William, as he detected Reginald entering the boiler room. Now, let's see if we can keep you there. William focused his mind on Reginald instilling in him a lifelong passion for the boilers he seemed so fascinated by.

In the boiler room Reginald stood in front of one of the boilers staring at the brass pressure gauge; with a trembling hand he reached up, paused momentarily in front of the gauge, and then tapped it once… twice… then a third time. That should hold you there for a while, thought William.

The second wave of bombers was approaching. Karl Steigerwald was concentrating on the approaching target his mind cleared of everything else, when for some unknown reason his thoughts suddenly switched to his Uncle Gerhard.

Gerhard not only sported a monocle, but had a waxed moustache with the edges twisted up into spikes, a square jaw and a duelling scar down his right cheek. His family considered him a little eccentric, the general opinion being that he'd never been quite right since the last war. Despite all efforts to convince him otherwise Gerhard insisted that during the first war the British occasionally sent their troops into battle naked and that he had shot one himself outside Laon in France during the last days.

Gerhard, thought William, so that was his name. William considered the image of the man that Karl had recalled; Reginald would have been impressed; Gerhard looked exactly like the pictures in the book his father had shown him. In fact the only thing that spoilt the image was that Gerhard had no teeth, so his face looked as though it was folded in two. But still, Gerhard had looked impressive in his youth.

Back to business, thought William. In the nose of the plane Karl saw the smoke rising from the bomb that had hit the substation and instantly thought he had overshot the target. His mind racing Karl pressed the button. Perhaps it was the adrenalin, but Karl could have sworn that although he thought he'd pressed the button, his thumb had delayed the action for a split second.

Like the previous plane, of the four bombs released by Karl only the last one reached the steelworks; and while William regretted the damage they caused, it was all for the greater good. The first bomb struck William's intended target; the centre of the crossroads three hundred yards from the school and the gas main that lay under it.

The bomb travelled through the surface of the road and into the clay beneath it before detonating very close to the gas main and severing it. Most debris was blown up, but enough was blown outwards to shatter all the nearby windows including those on the north east corner of the school. The shockwave took out more windows at a greater distance; detached the light fitting from the boiler room ceiling sending it on a collision course with Reginald's head; and travelled up the gas pipe blowing out the flames in the boilers, flooding the boiler room with the remaining gas.

Dust and other small pieces of debris fell from the ceiling of the corridor and William could hear the fearful cries from the inside of the shelter. He scanned the crossroads, excellent, he thought as he ran quickly up the stairs through the cloakroom and on up to the storeroom outside the chemistry lab. William turned the key in the lock, entered and went straight over to the cupboard. Gripping both sides of it dragged it one side at a time away from the wall. Taking out a small penknife he removed three of the four screws. Slackening the fourth he let the grill slide away from the vent. Without hesitating he took out his silver pocket watch he held it tightly in his right hand and concentrated. The watch faded until it appeared to be no more substantial than mist. It stayed like that for a moment and then slowly reformed, returning to its former solidity, but not its former function. The watch was now one half of a Node. William laid the watch inside the vent and replaced the grill. Pushing the cupboard back into position was hard work. After converting the watch William felt drained, creating a Node segment had used up a great deal of his energy.

With the cupboard back in place William walked to the door and turned to look out of the window, resting a moment while he summoned the last of his energy reserves. This was to be a one way trip. William froze time; only a few steps left now, he thought. William walked down the stairs and out across the playground towards the school gates. As he turned left onto the road he could see the flame from the ruptured gas main up ahead.

Standing beside the crater William looked up at the frozen sheet of flame, it was nearly as high as the surrounding houses, which William considered had survived the blast quite well despite their lack of roofs. He jumped down into the crater, slipped off a shoe without undoing the laces and threw it back down the road towards the school. Plausibility; "the only thing they found was a shoe", they would say, "and it wasn't even scorched".

Turning, he placed both hands into the frozen flame. The surface of his hands crawled with a blue light. He took a step forward, immersing himself in the flame. Slowly the flame began to diminish, its bright yellow colour losing some of its intensity, fading through pale yellow to a thin, white mist and eventually nothing.

William tingled with the energy he had just absorbed as he made his way back through the gates and into the playground. He found that he was noticing things for the first time, details in the brickwork, the way the clouds looked and other trivial things. Perhaps it was just a consequence of his heightened state, or perhaps it was his human side desperately trying to find a reason to stay. Stop and look at this, it was saying. It was by no means certain that what William was about to attempt would work, the human aspect of his mind knew this and it was starting to panic. William shook his head to refocus his mind; for better or worse, this action must be completed.

Re-entering the storeroom William took a last look at the cupboard to check it was back in place properly. He focused all of the energy he had absorbed from the fire into the centre of the room. About a metre off the floor there appeared a tiny point of light which expanded to form a sphere two metres in diameter. This was the entrance to a tunnel which linked this single fixed moment in time to the future. William moved the other end of the tunnel through time; he was searching for two things. Eventually, he found what he was looking for, some nineteen years, seven months, four days, eleven hours and twenty seven minutes into the future. William concentrated, the first part was relatively easy and now it was done. The second part was tricky and more than a little experimental. He pulled the other end back five minutes. That should give him enough time. In order to use the tunnel he would have to tie the far end into the normal time frame; which meant, it would only move forward in time. All the pieces were in place, the half of the Node that contained the control and management systems including all the technical knowledge of the Bruwnan, was safely behind the grill, the Keeper had been designated, and the plausibility of William's death affirmed.

William fixed the other end of the tunnel. He was now committed, he would only get one chance at this. In the future, he knew that the watch would find the other half; which should, if everything went to plan, be William in another form. The Keeper would find the watch and start it on its way to find its other half; and the Keeper was at this very moment in the boiler room studying the boilers…no he wasn't, he was in the boiler room being gassed.

William could have kicked himself for not checking before. Just when he thought he had a few spare minutes for a last look around, he now had another important task to perform. He ran down the stairs and through the tunnels, to the gas filled boiler room, where Reginald lay unconscious on the floor. Placing a time envelope around Reginald he brought him into the same time frame. Then he picked him up and carried him to the air raid shelter where he placed him on the floor outside the door. He couldn't let Reginald die, Reginald Scribbins still had an important role to play, too important to leave to chance. William laid his hand on Reginald's forehead and enclosed him in Amantarra's shield. That should ensure his survival until the big day, he thought.

Time was now working against William. Even though time was standing still here, it wasn't at the other end of the tunnel. William ran back up the stairs to the storeroom, and without pausing ran into the sphere and vanished forever.

Like an image forming out of a mist, the library rematerialized around him. John turned to The Librarian who was still sitting next to him.

'Did that help?' asked The Librarian looking up at John.

John shuddered; part of what he'd just witnessed wasn't something he'd expected. 'Not really,' he said. 'All it showed me was what I already knew; the trail ends with my Grandfather and points to me. It's as you said earlier, it was Amantarra who was supposed to be the Node and not me.'

They both sat in silence their intertwined thoughts meandering in different directions looking for a solution, occasionally crossing on the only common ground, the thought that John needed to do something.

'I need to go back,' said John. 'I can't think here, it's too…'

'Safe,' completed The Librarian.

'Yes, there's no incentive to find a solution. I need to go back to the stage and look around.' John stood and took a last look at the library.

'There is something that I've discovered about humans that may be relevant.'

'What is it?'

'There is a reference to another planet where Amantarra's sister was carrying out a similar exercise to this one on Earth. It looks older than Earth and seems to have been abandoned for some reason.'

'Abandoned? Why?'

'The entry wasn't specific, but there are references to fighting a battle on two fronts and the loss of her sister. It may not be relevant to our situation, but I thought I'd mention it. In the meantime I'll observe what you're doing now and feed you any information I find.'

'Thank you,' replied John, and then after a moment's thought added; 'how do I get out of here?'

'Picture yourself not in the library; back on the stage for instance.'

John thought of himself back on the stage and suddenly that's where he was. The Librarian was useful, but did not hold any solutions, thought John; which was a little disappointing. John felt as though he was back at square one. What I need to do now is analyse the situation and try to find a way forward. He looked again at his place marker. The dark sphere still hurt to look at, but at least it hadn't grown while he was in the library. Looking away from the sphere, John studied the card players. With one exception, they all wore expressions of surprise as they looked towards Mr Fleming framed in the doorway. The exception was Burnston, he was looking at John's place marker and he was doing something John had never seen him do before, he was grinning. Despite Burnston's unusual behaviour, there was nothing really remarkable about the scene, no clues as to what his next move should be.

John turned his attention to the door. Walking round his place marker he descended the short flight of steps, brought his face close to Mr Flemings and stared into his eyes. He would never have dared do that in real time, and despite the fact that Mr Fleming could not see him it was quite scary. John considered the fact that once again Mr Fleming had come out the victor. It was the same with the bucket of water and the smokers; he always had some knack of knowing what was going on. Mr Fleming was someone you always wanted on your side. It was just unfortunate that on this occasion John was the opposition. That thought made John's heart race, he'd never been on the wrong side of Mr Fleming before. John shuddered. It was more the embarrassment and the ruination of his reputation he was afraid of.

Like something out of a ghost story, a hand rested gently on his shoulder. John nearly jumped out of his skin.

'Sorry mate, I just couldn't resist it,' said a familiar voice behind him.

25

JACK

'Artullus… yes, Amantarra has mentioned you in the past although we've never met,' said Elleria.

'We've never met, that's true, but I am more than aware of your existence and the role you are playing in the current situation,' said Artullus.

'Where are you Artullus?' asked Elleria.

'We are nowhere. The minds of those of us that remain have been expelled from Valheel. We wait to re-occupy it. How is it that you can communicate with me? Can I ask where you currently are?'

'We are occupying a Guardian of Valheel inside the council chamber.'

'Occupying a Guardian… in Valheel, so you're not on Earth?'

'It's a long story,' said Elleria.

'I don't doubt that it is, but I'm concerned that you're not on earth where you should be,' replied Artullus. 'Why are you here?'

'Apparently I was copied,' said Jack.

'And I came here with John… the Node,' said Elleria. 'Somehow he found a way here and when he was shot he vanished and I was stuck here.'

'If he's been shot by one of the Guardians then he'll be under the control of the city; so that must mean that the council will have the Primary Key,' said Artullus.

'Yes, they mentioned that,' said Elleria, 'but they don't have it.'

'No that's right, they are still trying to retrieve it,' said Jack.

'And from what they were saying, John is back on Earth and about to go critical because I'm here.'

'I don't understand how, but it's a relief that the Node went back to Earth it's very important that the council do not get the primary key. And it's equally important that we get you back to Earth as soon as possible. The thing I don't understand is why Amantarra came here in the first place,' said Artullus. 'She knew the plan and it did not involve turning up in Valheel.'

'When was this?' asked Elleria. 'When was Amantarra here?'

'You said that you came here with her.'

'No, I came here with John. I don't know where Amantarra is. Tyrus seems to think that it's Scott Briggs...' said Elleria, adding, '... another human,' for Artullus' benefit.

'Are you telling me that Amantarra is not the Node?'

'Yes, the Node is definitely not Amantarra.'

'Something has gone very badly wrong,' said Artullus.

'Welcome to my world. I'm Jack by the way.' said Jack.

'Jack... yes, I do apologise for being abrupt; and thank you for allowing me to communicate through you; but how did you manage to breach the security? You seem to be half in and half out of the system.'

'Just natural talent I expect,' replied Jack.

'He doesn't know,' corrected Elleria. 'Jack was copied here by Tyrus and now we both seem to be ghosts in the system. When John and I arrived, Jack was re-activated and somehow formed a bridge between the system and us. It must be to do with John being a Node.'

'I wish I was there in the city with you; it would be so much easier to find out what was happening,' said Artullus.

'If we understood how we came to be in the situation we might be able to work something out, but I simply don't understand how we can be part of the city's system but separate from it,' commented Elleria.

'It's an interesting problem and if we could solve it, it may give us an advantage and enable us to find some way of getting you back to Earth,' said Artullus.

As Artullus and Elleria talked an idea was forming in Jack's mind. He kept recalling an event he thought he'd forgotten. In fact, the more he thought about the memory, the more he realised that until now, he had forgotten it. Over and over he played the event in his mind's eye. Initially he was blinded by the nostalgia he felt for a situation that almost cost him his life, but a single aspect of the event played repeatedly. Jack instinctively felt that the memory was somehow related to their current situation, but he couldn't see the connection. For his own benefit Jack summarised the state of affairs. He and Elleria were occupying a guard in a place that didn't exist, talking by… by radio, that was probably as good an explanation as any, to Artullus, someone who used to live here in the place that doesn't exist but now wasn't anywhere, and if they left the guard, then they wouldn't be able to see this non-existent place except as fog and shadows. John should have been someone else and Amantarra should have been John. Jack wasn't sure how he knew these things; but it all seemed to make sense, providing you didn't try to label some of the things, like the term "radio" which Jack didn't think really applied. And now he was thinking of a television and the event from his past... the event from his past on the television; but why? Then it suddenly occurred to him.

'I think I may have an explanation,' said Jack, 'but I'm not sure because I can't quite make the dots connect.' Jack thought for a moment, maybe these people didn't know what a dot to dot was. 'There's just too much that's weird,' he added by way of clarification.

'Tell us what you have and maybe we can make the connection,' said Elleria.

'I think I can do better than that, I think I can show you.' Jack imagined them all sat in front of a television watching his memory. 'Can you both see that?'

'I can see some moving images,' said Artullus. 'Once again you surprise me.'

'Elleria?'

'Yes I can see it too,' she replied, 'but how are you doing it?'

Jack didn't answer; he was recalling, with a clarity that amazed him, Tuesday the 19th September 1944. The place was Arnhem in the Netherlands and it was day three of "Operation Market Garden", the Allies massive airborne attempt to shorten the war by capturing strategic bridges to allow heavy armour into Germany. The Second Battalion of the First Parachute Brigade held the approach ramp at the north end of the bridge. Heavily outnumbered, they were waiting for the arrival of the armoured column approaching from the south, unaware that it had been halted at Nijmegen. With ammunition and supplies running low, the situation was becoming desperate.

Privates Harry Fleming and Jack Green had been ordered to make their way west of Arnhem towards Oosterbeek and link up with any units available and bring them back to the bridge along with any spare ammunition and supplies. The area immediately to the north and west of the bridge was overrun with German units, so Harry and Jack were making their way east in the hope of heading north out of Arnhem and then to the west once they'd left the town.

It was late morning and Jack and Harry were in a narrow lane called Kastanjelaan. The houses were three storeys high with half a dozen steps leading up to the front doors. From his hiding place, on the steps that led down to the basement to the right of the main door, Jack looked up at the houses opposite. Compared to those in Tameston, these houses were beautiful.

Harry was laid flat at the top of the steps. He crawled forward on his belly to look out onto the street around the bottom of the low wall that separated their hiding place from the lane. The wall stank of dog pee, Harry tried to ignore it.

Jack continued to look at the houses opposite, despite their beauty Jack wasn't interested in the architecture; he was looking for snipers. He spotted a boy of about ten years old looking out of one of the upper windows at him and held a finger up to his lips to encourage his silence. The boy nodded and then pointed up the lane, did a Nazi salute, pointed again and then finished off his mime by holding up six fingers. Jack nodded and gave him the thumbs up.

Harry shuffled his body back and down the steps and then sat up to face Jack who handed him his Sten gun back.

'SS, at the end of the lane,' said Harry, ' and they're heading this way.'

'Yes I know; six of them.'

'Now how did you know that?'

Jack pointed up at the boy. 'I have my sources,' he said.

Harry looked up at the boy and saluted. The boy returned the salute and then looked up as if he'd seen something else. He held up two fingers in a "V" for victory sign and then pointed at Jack and Harry. For one terrible moment Harry thought the boy had given away their position, but then the boy was pushing his hands, palms facing out, away from him, indicating that they should move back down the steps. Jack and Harry could hear the SS moving furtively up the street. Keeping low and close to the walls there were three SS on either side of the lane; the two in front crouching in gateways as the third made his way to the front. Like Jack and Harry these soldiers were professional and battle hardened. If Jack and Harry chose to fight, they may get two on the opposite side of the lane; if they were lucky; but they certainly would not get any more than that. Although the two paratroopers had surprise on their side the SS were prepared for any surprises. Harry judged that they would have about ten seconds at most before the grenades arrived at their location.

Jack and Harry moved down the steps towards the basement entrance and pressed their backs against the wall. They were under the steps that led up to the front door but there was no shadow to hide in, the covered area faced south and the sun shone directly into it. They could hear the footfalls of the SS and the slight clinking of their equipment as they made their way cautiously up the lane. They were very close now. Perhaps they would keep on going, missing the paratroopers, but they both doubted it; the Germans' did tend to be thorough. They couldn't attack, that would be suicide, and they couldn't surrender, the Germans were too close. Not that surrendering was an option they would consider; there were too many people relying on them.

The door into the basement was in front of them. Harry took a pace forward and tried the handle... it was locked. The SS were too close to kick it in; the noise would definitely attract attention. Harry went back to his position next to Jack, turned to him and shook his head.

The sound of a key being turned in the lock made them both look at the door. It opened and middle aged man beckoned then inside. They didn't need asking twice. Once inside the man closed the door silently and turned the key.

'English men,' he said, 'Diederik pointed to you... you are safer... here. I am Arne.' His English was good but he lacked practice and it was certainly better that Jack or Harry's Dutch. 'Please move to the back of the room away from the window.'

'Thank you,' replied Harry as they moved into a shadowy corridor at the back of the room, 'and please thank...' he couldn't think how to pronounce the boy's name.

'Diederik,' finished Arne.

'Yes, Diederik; please thank him for me,' said Harry.

'How can I help you?' asked Arne.

Harry and Jack looked at each other; they both knew that each was thinking what the other was. Could Arne be trusted? He'd just rescued them, so he probably could be trusted, but trusted enough to risk your life? Harry was staring long and hard into Arne's eyes looking for any sign of potential betrayal. Jack had known Harry a long time and he'd never got used to that stare, but Arne never flinched.

'Anything,' said Arne, completely unperturbed by Harry's steely gaze, 'we wait for four years for this,' indicating Jack and Harry. 'To make Duits... German... go home, this is our best chance. So how can I help?'

'Alright,' said Harry, resigning himself to the fact that they had no choice. 'We need to get back to the landing zone in the west near Oosterbeek.'

Arne nodded. 'I understand,' he said. He looked at Jack who was about the same height and then looked Harry, who was a head taller than Jack, up and down. 'You are very...' he indicated Harry's height with his hand.

'Tall,' said Harry.

'Tall,' repeated Arne, 'yes… we must go and see my friend, he is also tall. But first… please wait.' Arne disappeared into another room. Harry and Jack looked at each other. Harry shrugged his shoulders.

'Don't ask me,' he said.

The sound of artillery could be heard coming from the direction of the bridge and both men turned towards the window. At the top of the steps outside the window the last of the SS infantry stood up from his crouching position just inside the gate, stepped back into the lane and moved off.

'That was a bit close,' said Harry. Jack nodded as he listened to the heavy guns.

'They must be shelling our positions near the bridge,' he said, wondering if there would be anyone left to bring any acquired supplies back to.

Moments later Arne reappeared carrying a pair of grey trousers and a dark blue polo necked jumper. He handed the clothing to Jack. 'Please, put them on… over your uniform.'

Harry suddenly twigged. 'We can get some clothes from your tall friend for me?'

'Yes.'

Jack placed his gun on the floor and quickly donned the clothes. 'What about the Sten,' he asked as he picked the weapon back up. The civilian clothes were a good idea, but carrying a sub machine gun was a bit of a giveaway.

Arne thought for a moment. 'Follow please,' he said. Arne left the room and climbed some stairs up into the main part of the house. At the top he led them towards the rear of the house and into the kitchen where a woman and two teenagers were sat at a central table. Arne said something in Dutch to one of the teenagers who immediately left the room and went upstairs. As Arne busied himself opening cupboards and draws, the woman smiled at Jack and Harry.

'Thank you,' said Harry. Jack nodded to her, not knowing what else to say and being all too aware of the danger that these strangers had put themselves in to help them.

'You are more than welcome.' The woman's English was flawless and it made Jack feel guilty about his lack of linguistic skills.

A few minutes later Arne finished what he was doing. 'Please hold out your gun,' he said to Jack. 'Handle up please.' With the gun pointing at the floor Jack held the weapon for Arne who passed some thick string through the open framework of the gun butt and looped it over Jack's shoulder.

Arne's son came back into the kitchen carrying a long overcoat which Arne indicated that Jack should put on. After some adjustment of the string length the gun could be hidden under the coat but brought quickly into the firing position. Arne worked quickly and soon had Harry's Sten gun fitted out the same way.

'Now we see my friend for your clothes.' Walking a few paces towards a door that led out into a rear garden Arne turned and said, 'this way please.' He led Jack and Harry down to the bottom of the garden and over a low fence which they climbed easily. Turning right they climbed two more fences and then knocked on the door at the rear of a house on Prins Hendrikstraat. The door was answered by a tall man who was obviously the friend that Arne had talked about. Seeing Harry's uniform he quickly ushered them into the corridor and closed the door.

'Be very quiet,' whispered the tall man without any hint of a Dutch accent. Walking backwards he beckoned them into a gloomy basement room with both hands and an air of the melodramatic.

'This is Kaarl,' whispered Arne once they were inside the room. 'Kaarl, we need some of your clothes.' He indicated Harry's height and the fact that Jack was already disguised.

Kaarl nodded. 'I'll get some shortly,' he said quietly dropping the whisper. Jack thought he sounded like one of their officers. 'But at the moment we have a slight problem. There's a Panzer out front… right outside, with a least twenty SS infantry in support.' Now that Kaarl had pointed it out, they could hear the idling engine of the stationary tank. 'I'm really worried that they're going to come in here.'

'They'll be waiting for orders to move forward,' said Jack reassuringly while wondering why Kaarl thought that they might want to enter his house. 'They won't come in here unless you give them cause to.'

'That's right,' said Harry, 'they'll only be interested in what's going on at the bridge. Listen!' The sound of artillery had intensified.

Kaarl looked at Harry's steel grey eyes and the weapons that both men held with well-practised hands and decided that they probably knew what they were talking about. 'Yes, you're probably right, I'm just being paranoid. It goes with the job.'

Jack wondered what sort of a job Kaarl did, which would make him so fearful. 'We must get out of Arnhem and towards Oosterbeek as soon as possible,' he said, throwing Harry's previous caution to the wind.

Reassured that his house was not about to be stormed Kaarl focused his attention on Harry and Jack's plight. 'I'll get you some clothes and an overcoat. There are also two bikes you can use to get out of Arnhem. The only problem is…' Arne stopped speaking because the Panzer's engine had started to rev up. This was followed by the familiar squeaking of the tracks as it moved off. They could hear shouted commands as the infantry followed. They all listened intently.

'What's the only problem?' asked Jack as the sound of the Panzer faded.

'I was going to say that the bikes are outside at the front; but it doesn't seem to matter now,' answered Kaarl.

'Does everyone in Holland speak perfect English?' said Harry asking the question that Jack had been thinking about.

'No not at all,' said Arne, 'my English is terrible.'

'That's true,' retorted Kaarl, 'and I did study at Oxford, which helped a fair amount.' That explains him sounding like an officer thought Jack, they probably all went to the same college.

Ten minutes later Harry was suitably disguised in some of Kaarl's clothes. Kaarl paused at the front door with his hand on the handle. He turned to Jack and Harry. 'If for some reason you cannot complete your mission, make your way back here. I'm sure the resistance will find a use for your skills.'

'You're in contact with the resistance?' Harry asked.

Arne and Kaarl looked at each other. 'I am the local resistance leader,' said Kaarl.

'You're taking a risk by telling us that,' said Jack, seeing now the cause of Kaarl's earlier paranoia. 'We could be German spies.'

'Riskier than jumping out of an aeroplane into enemy held territory? I think not; besides your northern accents tell me that you are not German.'

'Northern accents?' said Jack, who until now was unaware that he had one.'

'Fair play,' said Harry who'd always known.

Kaarl opened the front door.

'What about the bikes?' Jack asked.

'Don't worry about the bikes,' he said. 'Leave them by the side of the road, they have my name and address on them and someone will bring them back to me.'

'Really,' said Jack incredulously. 'In England you'd never see them again.'

Kaarl and Arne both laughed; they thought Jack was joking.

'Turn left out of the gate and then left again at the end of the road,' said Kaarl who was still chuckling to himself.

'And be careful,' said Arne.

'Once again thank you,' said Harry as Kaarl opened the front door.

A few minutes later as they turned left onto Spijkerstraat Jack turned to Harry.

'I don't think they believed me,' he said quietly, 'when I said that in England they would never see the bikes again.'

'That's because they haven't had the benefits of our upbringing,' replied Harry.

At the end of Spijkerstraat they came to the main road that led south to the bridge. They turned north, away from the bridge. The road started to curve to the northwest towards Oosterbeek and almost immediately they found themselves heading straight for a dozen or more stationary Panzers. There were two lines of SS infantry either side of the road probably around two hundred in total. Standing in a group talking at the head of the column of tanks were six officers. Harry cursed under his breath but carried on pedalling towards them. What else could they do thought Jack; they were a little short of options. As they neared the officers' a nearby sergeant held up a hand and positioned himself to block their path.

'Halt!'

Here we go thought Jack. He knew what would follow if they couldn't bluff their way out of this situation; and given their linguistic skills the chances were slight. He fixed the group of officers with a steady gaze weighing up how many they could kill before they were cut down. He knew from experience that Harry Fleming had no idea how to lose gracefully, and when faced with absolute and total defeat he would always choose complete defiance. Harry had once admitted to Jack that he had never knowingly allowed anyone to savour a victory over him in his life.

'The officers?' whispered Jack.

Harry nodded once as they slowed their bicycles.

'Nein,' shouted one of the officers and waved them through before the bikes had come to a halt. The SS sergeant moved to one side and waved them on as well. Half the British army had fallen from the skies and the last thing the officer wanted was a couple of Dutch men on bicycles getting in the way.

'Oh it's stopped,' said Elleria as the images ended abruptly and she found herself back in the Council Chamber still occupying the guard with Jack. 'I want to know what happened next. Did you get out of Arnhem?'

'Yes we did, but we finished up back there; but that's not what I was showing you,' said Jack. 'Are you still connected Artullus?'

'Yes,' said the voice of Artullus. 'Humans are very adversarial; you've almost turned confrontation into an art form.'

'It's in our nature; but that isn't what I was showing you either.'

'What then?' Elleria asked.

'I know it was a bit long winded; that was just me working it out, getting it straight in my head; but what I was trying to do was highlight the connection between the situation in Arnhem and this one,' said Jack.

'I don't understand,' said Elleria.

'The point I'm trying to make is that we got out of Arnhem by disguising ourselves. The Germans' didn't see us for what we were. Here I'm in the city, but I'm human, and I don't think the city recognises human; so I'm here, but invisible, except when John turned up.'

'This is why you are half in and half out of the city,' said Artullus. 'The same must be true for Elleria who arrived in human form. You both must have drawn power from John and formed Avatars.'

'Yes, that's it,' said Jack, 'and I'll tell you something else, my memory has improved dramatically. My ability to work things out is much better than before; I can see problems much more clearly.'

'Yes,' said Artullus, 'the copy of your human self exists in a much more efficient environment than your biological self.'

'That's not all. Like the images I've just shown you by imagining them on a television, I'm sure I can do other things by imagining them in a context that I understand.'

'What sort of things?' Artullus asked.

'I think I can get you into the city.'

'How?'

'By lending you some clothes.'

26
AMANTARRA

John turned and the hand fell from his shoulder.

'Bloody Hell Frank, you nearly scared me to death,' said John, forgetting for a moment his current situation. A quick glance up onto the stage reminded him. The surprised card players, the arcs of electricity and the dark sphere in John's place marker. John stared at Frank for a moment; gathering his thoughts.

'Amantarra?'

'Nobody has called me that for a long time,' said Frank, 'but yes, I'm Amantarra.'

'You're also my Grandfather.'

'Yes, I was also William Godbert and a million other people besides.'

John couldn't believe it, from what Elleria had told him, everyone had been looking for Amantarra and she'd been here all the time.

'What do I call you?' John asked.

'Why don't you call me Frank? After all that's who you've always known me as.'

'Okay... but why aren't you hiding anymore?'

John followed Frank as he climbed up the short flight of stairs and back onto the stage.

'There's no point,' said Frank indicating the dark sphere in John's place marker. 'You're in the process of destroying the solar system... and all my thousands of years of hard work.'

'Feedback,' said John.

'Yes, your unplanned trip to Valheel with Elleria certainly caused a few problems.'

'Sorry about that,' said John.

'Oh it's not your fault. I was close enough to stop you, but didn't. Tyrus was too close.' Frank thought for a moment. 'That was another unexpected turn of events; I didn't predict that the council would track Elleria to this planet. Not after the effort I put in to prevent it.' Frank turned to Burnston. 'Still, at least Burnston is free of Tyrus now, but I suspect that he will remain, at least in part, the ruthless businessman he has become.'

'Tyrus, yes Elleria mentioned him when we were in Valheel. She didn't seem to like him.'

'Yes… he's not the most pleasant of individuals. But he's gone now, probably gloating to the Council about his victory.' Frank spoke as if destroying the solar system was an everyday occurrence, like spilling a cup of tea, he didn't seem in the slightest put out.

'We met Jack Green in Valheel, he sort of appeared just after we arrived,' said John.

'Jack Green the pawnbroker, I used to teach him you know. And Harry there,' said Frank indicting Mr Fleming. 'They grew up together and they were both in the same parachute regiment during the war. They spent the last part of the war fighting with the Dutch resistance. Did you talk to Jack?'

'Yes, I told him he was dead and that he'd been copied. I found that more than a bit weird.'

'I'll bet you did.'

'There was something else as well. When we left for Valheel time was frozen, and when I came back, it was still frozen, but in Valheel time was normal. And I'm curious…'

'To know why,' finished Frank. 'Valheel exists in a different set of dimensions and there are more than four of them, if you count time as the fourth. These dimensions are completely independent from the ones you occupy now. That is why time can be stopped here but appears normal in Valheel. When you were there you would have experienced only the four dimensions you are used to, but the city's systems exist in other dimensions that are not normally evident. Does that help?'

'Sort of,' said John, 'I remember Jack saying that before we arrived everything was foggy, he thought he was dreaming, but he must have been in those other dimensions.'

'Or halfway between the two; a sort of ghost in the machine,' said Frank. 'Tell me, when you were in Valheel did you all appear in human form?'

'Yes we were; Elleria was wondering how, when the city doesn't know what human looks like. But we never talked about it anymore because she realised that she must have been tracked to Earth. Her shoulder was wet and we reckoned that it was some sort of tag.'

'Her shoulder was wet,' repeated Frank. 'How do you get that to be a tag?'

'Like Mr Fleming's bucket trick, where he picks out the wet smokers during the next lesson. Elleria thought that that was the way we interpreted the tag.'

'Now that is really interesting.'

'What is?'

'It's something I hadn't really considered, but it looks like you're assigning human values and attributes to Bruwnan technology.'

John nodded. 'Yes, that's what I thought it might be. I've been thinking about it and it's a bit like algebra, where you assign values to tokens; for example you could say that "a = 10"; but suppose you had no understanding of numbers, then you might see the "10" as an "a", in other words see the token, not the value. So because I don't know about the technology behind the tag, I saw a wet shoulder.'

Frank smiled. 'Your mind has certainly improved since you got the watch.'

'You're telling me. I wonder what would have happened if we'd dried Elleria's shoulder with a towel or a hair dryer. Do you think the tag would have been erased?'

'It's a good question, and I'm willing to bet that it would. You can see what I mean about it being interesting?'

'Here's another question for you; why did Elleria and Jack see the shoulder as being wet?' John asked.

'Because you're a Node and they were there,' said Frank. 'In other words they were linked to you.'

'The Librarian cannot find any reference to tagging,' said John.

'I was going to ask you about him. Has the library survived intact?'

'Yes, The Librarian says it has.'

'Good,' said Frank. 'I've never heard of this tagging technology either, which probably explains why it's not in the library; it must be something new that the city has come up with.'

'The Librarian says "welcome back" by the way.'

'Thank you, I have missed our conversations.' Frank was looking closely at the dark sphere in the chest of John's place marker which had grown slightly during their conversation. 'Then what happened?'

'Then, we were attacked. I got shot and finished up back behind Scott's Granddad's garage.'

'I was wondering why you arrived back without Elleria.' Frank tapped his chin with his forefinger as he studied the sphere.

'Why did nobody remember her? I realise that you couldn't say anything, but nobody else remembered her.'

Frank replied without looking up from the sphere which had now grown so that it was now just outside the front of John's place marker. 'That's because she exerts an influence on humans that makes them believe they know her; but it has to be constantly applied. Once the influence has been withdrawn the most you could expect would be a vague recollection.' He reached out and held his hand just above the surface of the sphere

'Frank…'

When John didn't continue Frank looked up from the sphere and looked at him. 'Yes, John?'

'Frank, why am I a Node?'

'Ah,' said Frank, 'that, is a very long story.'

John indicated their surroundings with a sweep of his hand. 'Well, we appear to have a lot of time.'

'Not quite as long as you think,' replied Frank nodding at the sphere. 'Remember, as Elleria told you that time hasn't stopped, it's just moving very slowly. What you are looking at here is a very slow explosion.'

'So give me the quick version, but I would like to know what's going on. The Librarian seems to think that there is some sort of power struggle going on in Valheel.'

Frank stood up straight and gazed up into one of the far corners of the ceiling. John got the impression that he was looking much further away than the ceiling, as he recalled past events. John waited patiently, and eventually Frank spoke, but his voiced tinged with sadness.

'No, it's not a power struggle. The Bruwnan had already lost before we realised that anything was going on. A better description would be annihilation; we've almost been wiped out. When Valheel was first occupied, when we first left our physical bodies behind, there were ten million Bruwnan. Now there's only a few thousand left. Although biologically we are already extinct, the essence of what we were, what we are now, has slowly and secretly been erased by our own creation. Humans were our last hope and as you are aware it hasn't exactly gone to plan.'

'Sorry,' said John, 'I didn't realise things were so bad for you.'

'The good news is that at least no more of us can be eliminated. The bad news is that there are no Bruwnan in Valheel and so at the moment we're pretty powerless.'

'You said you were being erased by your own creation. What creation?'

'It was Valheel; or at least the controlling intelligence of the city.'

'Like the software in a computer?'

'Sort of,' Frank considered his reply and decided that it probably didn't come close to the truth. 'No, not really; software is too simple an explanation. It's a set of rules that define a reality. The city's control mechanism is sentient; it's a being in its own right and it exists in its own set of dimensions. You are partly right in that it had a set of instructions to maintain the city, but it could make decisions of its own. We think it developed some sort of multiple personality disorder quite soon after its creation. Exactly when it started to remove the Bruwnan I can't say, but I certainly think that shortly after Artullus, my father, stood down as the leader of the council, all the councillors were replaced by replicas.'

'Your father?'

'I know it's silly that we still cling to these titles. Artullus was my father when we were biological but after we had left our physical forms behind there weren't any replacement titles, so the old ones remained.' Frank paused for a moment and then reverted to his original subject.

'Artullus noticed changes in the remaining council members, small things, but he'd known them all when we were still biological and the city hadn't, so it was noticeable to him that they were different. For a long time he said nothing, putting it down to the normal changes that people go through. After all he had nothing to be suspicious about. Then he noticed a pattern; as relationships and occupations change over time, occasionally a Bruwnian would be isolated for a period, perhaps researching some large project. It was during these periods, which could last centuries, that the changes would occur. On many occasions Artullus documented instances where a Bruwnan had left Valheel to carry out long term projects in Euclidean space never to return.

The problem with the "disappeared" is that you didn't know if they were just not in the city or actually disappeared; it was impossible to tell. After we realised what was happening we always made sure we kept in contact, returning to the city and meeting up regularly. Frustratingly we couldn't warn anyone for fear that the city would target us next; and so slowly over time the city continued to eliminate its inhabitants one by one. The sad part is that instead of just kicking them out, it erased them completely.'

'So what did you do?' John asked.

'You mean, what was plan A?'

'There was a plan!'

'Of course there was a plan; it just didn't work that's all.' Frank paused and John thought the explanation complete, but Frank was obviously being eaten by feelings of guilt. 'Alright it went horribly wrong… and yes, it probably was my fault, before you ask.'

'Your right about that,' said John.

Frank was slightly irritated; although it was his fault and he freely admitted it, he didn't like the implied accusation in John's voice. 'About what?' he asked.

'I was going to ask,' said John with a laugh in his voice. He was pleased that Frank had risen to the bait. 'Tell me about the plan.'

'Hmm,' grumbled Frank as his irritation subsided. John had been winding him up. He would miss this banter between friends. He took a deep breath and sighed. 'There were a number of stages to the plan and most of them worked quite well. Stage one was to stop any more Bruwnan from being erased. I did that by destroying the city.'

'Wasn't that a bit extreme?'

'It was the only way to get all the Bruwnan out of the city safely. I knew they would all be okay, they wouldn't be very happy but at least they would be safe in the void.'

'But the city is still there, I saw it.'

'Yes, Artullus designed the city to rebuild itself and restore its last state. It was a process that took thousands of years and it bought me some time.

The next stage was to progress human evolution to the point where a Node could be activated on Earth. Humans wouldn't go un-noticed forever and in order to complete the evolutionary process, which is some way off, they would need the power of the Node to remain hidden.

Stage three was to raise an army of humans and take back Valheel. There are too few Bruwnan left to do this now. Did you never wonder why the human race is so adversarial?'

'No, I've never considered it. Is that what you meant when you said that humans were your last hope?'

'Yes, I've been coaching them to fight a battle in dimensions that they are not even aware of yet,' replied Frank.

'The final stage, with the city back under Bruwnan control, would be to charge humans with the task of encouraging intelligent life on other worlds. This has been something which was discouraged and I think that was a mistake. And, as you are aware, it has almost all gone beautifully to plan... apart from the last bits.'

'But where did it all start to go wrong? I mean I know I'm not supposed to be the Node, but how did that happen?' John asked.

'My fault I'm afraid. I was all set up to transfer myself into the egg that would become you, moments before conception; an egg that I had already converted into one half of a Node. Nodes can't be constructed of anything actually living because of the energy field they generate, unfertilised eggs don't generate the field so they can be made into Nodes, and they are close enough to life that I could transfer into it and survive long enough for the few moments until it became life. The result would be a sentient living Node. I'm pleased to see that it worked.' Frank indicated John with a magnificent bow. 'Unfortunately while I was saving Reginald Scribbins I missed my chance and finished up in the wrong egg.'

John laughed. 'Now there's something you don't hear every day.'

'You're not wrong there,' said Frank. 'The first years were a nightmare. I did manage to influence my parents to move round the corner from you so I could keep an eye on you; although they weren't very happy about me going to Penshaw Grove School.'

'So what next, there must be something you can do?' asked John.

'Yes, we can stabilise you by getting Elleria back, but after that I'm a bit stumped. There's no chance that I can hide humans now, the city knows where you are. But let's get Elleria back first and then take it from there.'

'I've thought of doing that, but the only way I know is to walk into a fire, and how are we going to get a fire going here?'

'We don't need to; it's not fire that you need, it's energy,' said Frank nodding at the lightning coming from John's place marker, 'and there's more than enough energy there to put you into burst mode.'

'Oh,' said John, 'I hadn't thought of that.'

'And I think we should take Harry with us. I have a feeling that when he's reunited with Jack the pair of them may prove useful.'

'Frank, why was the council looking for you?' Was it just a revenge thing?'

'No it wasn't revenge; I've got something they need... I've got the Primary Key. Without it they can't progress their plans.'

'Wouldn't going back be dangerous?'

'Only if I got shot and they gained control of my avatar and besides,' again Frank indicated the growing dark sphere, 'it's less dangerous than here. Once this detonation is complete Tyrus will get me anyway; I'll survive, but the shockwave will prevent me from hiding in any dimensions.'

*

Harry Fleming turned the key to the stage door and entered in one smooth silent movement. He was rewarded with the wide eyed, surprised looks that he treasured so much. Some of them turned in their chairs to face him, others stood, knocking their chairs over backwards in their panic. Excellent, he thought; now who have we got? He picked out Burnston, Haystack and Briggs, which was not unexpected given what he'd seen in the dining hall. Suddenly there was a bright light, somebody must have switched the spotlights on, he thought; still it wouldn't do them any good I'm blocking the only exit. He shielded his eyes from the source and continued to scan the stage in the presence of the new light. Cards, he thought, not a fight after all, but I was still right about something going on.

'What are you boys doing in here?' He wasn't expecting an answer; in these situations nobody would ever volunteer to be the spokesman for fear of carrying all the blame. Keeping quiet meant collective responsibility. And they were all keeping very quiet, even the ones in the hall had suddenly gone quiet… which was odd, because it didn't usually work that way. Normally, when Mr Fleming left a room the noise level went up. Then he noticed that in addition to the silence, they were all keeping very still… so still in fact that there was a chair frozen in the act of tipping over backwards.

He took a step forward and noticed something even stranger; now that his eyes had adjusted to it, the source of the bright light was a figure standing in the centre of the stage that appeared to be made out of lightning. Mr Fleming's jaw dropped. He closed his eyes and reopened them; just make sure he wasn't imagining it.

'Excuse me Sir,' said a voice behind him.

Mr Fleming hesitated, unable to take his eyes off the bright figure on the stage. Eventually he turned. It was Godbert and Carter.

'Yes boys?' he said turning back to look at the stage.

It had been a bit of squeeze getting past Mr Fleming but Frank and John wanted to be on the right side of him when they brought him into the same time frame. In other words, they wanted to be behind him.

'Would you help us with a little problem?' asked John.

Harry half turned. 'Well I'm a little busy at the moment boys,' he said with his eyes glued to the most interesting thing that had ever happened on the stage in its entire history. His head was full of partially formed questions; "how…", "what…" was about as far as each question got before his mind lost its focus. He just stared. Eventually he realised that there had been no reply from the boys and he finally relented to giving them his full attention and turned to face them. Then he noticed that the rain was frozen in the air behind Frank and John. 'What…' he began, but he somehow couldn't think of what to ask.

Frank answered the question anyway. 'Time is frozen, Sir.'

Harry moved his torso from side to side watching the patterns in the raindrops change. The effect was hypnotic and Frank's words didn't initially register. 'Time is frozen,' repeated Harry, to confirm the statement. He stopped moving from side to side. That was the only explanation, time was frozen. This wasn't some clever practical joke or a trick. Time was actually frozen. Once you accepted that fact and lost the incredulous feelings it became possible to think straight. 'How is time frozen?'

'I did it sir,' said John.

'Well done Godbert.' It was a standard teachers' response usually reserved for subjects in which the teacher was an expert, but in this case was used because he didn't know what else to say. 'But why did you freeze time?'

'I thought you might like to see how time can be slowed for specific objects.'

Harry recalled the conversation he'd had with John earlier. 'I know I said you were on to something Godbert, but I didn't know you could actually do it.' He looked at Frank. 'And can you… do you freeze time as well?'

'I used to all the time Sir,' replied Frank.

'And now you don't,' said Harry. It occurred to him that this was the sort of conversation you have with someone who'd given up riding his bike to work or stopped smoking. 'When did you stop?'

'I had to limit myself about thirty two thousand years ago, to conserve energy,' replied Frank.

'Thirty two thousand years ago,' laughed Harry and then realised that Frank wasn't smiling; 'you're not joking are you?'

'I'm afraid not.'

'So you're telling me that you are thirty two thousand years old?'

'No, I'm much older than that; approximately half the age of the universe, give or take a few thousand years,' replied Frank.

Harry turned to John, 'and what about you? Are you as old?' Harry always found it a comfort to be as normal as possible in alien situations; somehow it made them less strange. It was a trick he'd learnt in the army from the officers, where no situation was too dire to ignore the requirement for polished boots.

'No, I'm sixteen; I only found out about all this a few days ago,' said John.

'That's a relief; I'd hate to have been the youngest here. So, then...' Harry thought for a moment about nouns and how they might relate to Franks age, but couldn't come up with a better one than, '... boys... what's all this about?'

Frank indicated that they should go onto the stage. At the top of the steps he turned and led them over to John's place marker. 'What you are looking at is the end of a story that started thirty two thousand years ago, and that is only one chapter in a much older story. We, that is John and I, would like the story to continue, and we would like your help in order to do that.'

'How could I possibly help? I have no idea what's going on.'

'You do have a particular set of skills that I think would be invaluable to what we are about to do,' said Frank.

'Teaching chemistry?' Harry asked with more than a hint of exclamation in the question.

'No,' replied Frank.

'We're going to try and rescue Elleria,' said John.

'Who's Elleria?' asked Harry.

John cursed under his breath; he'd thought that she'd be remembered in these circumstances. 'My girlfriend,' he said.

'Your girlfriend!' exclaimed Harry; 'that doesn't sound like the sort of thing I should be getting involved young Mister Godbert. Pleased though I am that you have one, it may not go down well should I be seen to be getting embroiled in the sex lives of teenagers.'

'There's a little more to it than that,' said Frank. He indicated the dark sphere in the chest of John's place marker. 'This object is a release of energy that marks the end of this solar system. Elleria is the key to stopping it.'

Harry put his reading glasses on and studied the dark sphere. 'It's a bit painful to look at,' he said standing up straight and placing his glasses back in the top pocket of his jacket.

'You'd be saving the planet,' said Frank.

27
THE RETURN

'I can see the logic behind your thinking,' said Artullus, 'but do you really think that lending me some imaginary clothes will get me into the city?'

'Well, you remember the images about Arnhem that I showed you?' Jack asked.

'Yes, they were most interesting,' said Artullus.

'I got you to see them by imagining seeing my memories on a television.'

'You mentioned that before, what's a television?'

'It's that box I showed the images on,' said Jack with a little uncertain edge to his voice.

'I saw images, but I didn't see them on a box.'

'Oh,' said Jack, feeling a little put out, 'that's how I pictured us; sitting in front of a television. I thought it would work.'

'Well it did,' said Elleria, 'I saw the images on a television and Artullus just saw the images, but he doesn't know what a television is, so that's why he didn't see one.'

'So my idea might work then?' said Jack feeling pleased that his assumptions may well be correct after all.

'Yes I think it might,' said Elleria, 'but only if John were here. He was the power source for the avatars when we first arrived. As long as you choose some common ground, some clothes and a form that you would both recognise, then I'm sure it would work.

'Like the people and uniforms in the images you showed us,' said Artullus optimistically, he quite fancied the idea of a uniform.

The light level in the council chamber rose signalling the imminent arrival of the council and within moments four of the councillors appeared sitting behind the dais.

'Back already!' remarked Jack. 'Are we never to get any peace?'

The seat normally occupied by the yellow councillor was empty and the other councillors turned to look at it. They waited a few seconds to see if he was going to appear.

'The problems with the yellow zone seem to be getting worse,' said Consulus when he failed to materialise. 'We may have to carry on and hope that he can attend at some point.'

Elleria relayed the events to Artullus.

'I said they should have given Tom Godbert a ring; looks like they've blown a fuse completely now,' commented Jack.

The yellow councillor appeared, flickered a little and then seemed to stabilise. 'Apologies,' he said. 'I have established that there is some damage to the power distribution crystal which is affecting its function.'

'What sort of damage?' asked the green councillor.

'Another set of dimensions has been added to its structure and the power flow is alternating between the system dimensions and the new ones.'

'How did this happen?' asked Consulus.

'I have not been able to establish that Consulus,' replied the yellow councillor.

'Hmm,' said Artullus after Elleria had relayed the information. 'Would I be correct in assuming that John has been in contact with the crystal?'

'Yes, when we first arrived he managed to collide with it,' said Elleria.

'Thought so,' said Artullus.

Elleria was going to ask for an explanation but Tyrus appeared in front of the council.

'Report,' said Consulus.

'John Godbert has gone critical and there is now very little chance that he can be stabilised before the detonation sequence is complete,' said Tyrus.

'Good,' said Consulus, 'and the acquisition of the Primary Key?'

'Scott Briggs has been duplicated and is currently being held in the system awaiting analysis,' said Tyrus.

The yellow councillor flickered in and out of existence rapidly for a few seconds and then vanished. At the same time Jack fingers tingled with pins and needles. He knew instantly what it meant.

'Brace your-self missy,' said Jack, 'I think John is returning.

Elleria felt a moment of excruciating pain as if she was being crushed from all directions at once. There was a flash of light and the pain stopped. She was dazed, but it quickly dawned on her that she had left the guardian and was now face down on the floor of the council chamber.

*

John, Frank and Harry appeared in the blue plaza. They were holding hands in a circle, which was not something Harry had been very happy about.

'Can I let go now?' he asked.

'Yes,' said John dropping Frank and Harry's hands, 'we're here.'

Harry turned slowly looking at the buildings surrounding the plaza. When he was facing the structure at the base of the blue centroid tower, he stopped. Frank and John watched as Harry followed the line of the tower from its base all the way up to the Node Zero chamber, some nine hundred and fifty metres above them and then beyond it to the other zones.

'Are those buildings up there on the ceiling?'

'Yes,' replied Frank, 'but it's not the ceiling; Valheel is constructed on the inside of a sphere.'

'I've seen this before. Godbert, didn't you do some drawings?' Harry took in the whole scene for a few seconds. 'Why does the yellow area switch off and on like that? Look you can see blue stars when it goes off.'

'I don't know,' said Frank. John kept quiet; he didn't want to be accepting the blame for anything until it was obvious that it was his fault. Despite what Elleria had implied during his last visit.

'So where is it again?' Harry asked.

'Well it isn't really anywhere. Valheel exists in its own set of dimensions which are completely isolated from the four you are used to,' said Frank.

'Four dimensions?'

'If you count time as the fourth,' said John. 'Valheel has seven dimensions; one time and two sets of length breadth and depth.'

Harry pinched the bridge of his nose. He had always had a great capacity for the acceptance of new ideas and the adaptability to pass himself off as an authority on those ideas even when, as was the case now, his grasp of the concept was non-existent. But, seven dimensions; he wouldn't even know where to start to pass himself off as an expert. Stick to what you know Harry, he told himself, there are always questions that can be asked, keep things simple. 'Why do you need two sets of ordinary dimensions?'

'There's the three we are in now and there's an additional three where the system that generates this place operates.' John smiled as he said it; he could visualise the whole thing and understand every aspect of the city. The knowledge gave him a feeling of elation he had never known before.

'Useful chap, The Librarian, isn't he?' said Frank.

'The Librarian, who…?' Harry thought about the fact that this was yet another question to which he probably would not understand the answer. 'Never mind, it's probably something I don't need to know. You know boys; I fail to see what it is that I can do for you. I stand here in this incredible place.' Harry indicated Valheel by raising his arms in the air. 'With two boys who can not only manipulate time, but can move at will between dimensions, who know more about the workings of this place than I will ever understand; and I wonder what possible contribution I can make.'

'The enemy we face knows far more about this place than we do,' said Frank, 'because it is this place. The city is sentient and highly intelligent, but it lacks the same thing that John and I lack.'

'What's that?'

'Combat experience.' Frank indicated that they should enter one of the buildings. 'Before we're seen,' he explained. Once inside Frank continued. 'You and Jack Green fought in Arnhem with the Dutch resistance for six months until its liberation in April 1945. During that time you made a serious contribution towards arming the resistance from the Germans own supplies as well as many operations designed to interrupt German supply lines.'

'And generally annoy them,' completed Harry. 'Yes, that's true; but how did you know? Is mind reading another of your skills?'

'While I can exercise a certain level of mind control, to the extent that I can influence humans', mind reading itself is difficult because people constantly change them. Their minds are in a constant state of flux, which incidentally, is also the reason why it's so easy to influence them. But that's beside the point and I'm afraid that the truth is much more mundane. Jack Green told Scott's Granddad and then he told me.'

'Oh,' said Harry, 'yes, compared to everything else you can do that's positively boring.'

'Anyway, John tells me that Jack Green is here in Valheel,' said Frank; 'and I thought if we could get you two together again it would give us a serious advantage over the city.'

'Sorry to spoil your plans, but Jack can't be here because he's dead,' said Harry.

'His human body is, but without going into too much detail, the process that killed him created a copy of him here. All we have to do is find him.'

'Oh that should be easy,' said Harry sarcastically.

'I think I've found Elleria,' said John.

Frank looked at John. 'Excellent,' he said, 'where is she?'

'Hang on... The Librarian is getting a map.'

*

Elleria pushed herself up into the kneeling position. The guard not occupied by Jack, moved forward, but Tyrus held up a hand to stop him. Tyrus drew his weapon and pointed it at Elleria. Jack felt helpless as he struggled to maintain control over the guard.

'What manner of creature is this?' asked Consulus standing and leaning forward to get a better view.

'This is Elleria,' replied Tyrus,' in human form.'

'Elleria,' repeated Consulus. 'Tell me Elleria, how did you get here in this form?'

Elleria gave no answer, but simply looked at him.

'And why do you not show up on the system's scans?' continued Consulus. The Red, Blue and Green councillors leaned forward in anticipation of an answer.

Elleria remained silent.

The guard and Jack's avatars were locked in a battle not to occupy the same space, it was like trying to push the north poles of two magnets together as each avatar tried to push the other away. Jack fought to retain his tenancy of the guard and as he struggled the guard fluctuated back to its green construction grid for a few seconds, drawing the attention of the council.

'Another fault you seem to have caused Elleria,' said Consulus as he indicated the flickering guard. 'First the Yellow councillor and now you've started to damage the guards. How are you doing this?'

Elleria looked blankly at him.

'You will tell us what we want to know. One way or another we will find out how you have done this,' said Consulus.

'Elleria, you do not register on the power grid,' said the Red councillor, 'from where are you drawing your power?'

'Answer the councillor,' shouted Tyrus when she did not answer.

Elleria looked at Tyrus and smirked at him. She felt quite smug about it.

'I see you have the same attitude as Amantarra.' Tyrus seemed to be very annoyed. It gave Elleria a deep feeling of satisfaction.

Jack was managing to hold the two avatars together, it wasn't easy but if he concentrated he could balance the forces trying to push them apart. The scene in front of him was disturbing; Elleria, a pretty young woman was on her knees in front of Tyrus who held some sort of a gun to her head. What could he do? If he attempted to rescue her at this moment in time he would finish up in the same situation, and what use would he be then. He would have to bide his time and wait for a better opportunity.

'Very well,' said Consulus, 'if you won't tell us what we want to know, then we will have to take control of your avatar and extract the information that way. Tyrus, if you please.'

There was no hesitation, no ceremony, and no gloating little speech. With a coldness that chilled Jack to the core, Tyrus shot Elleria in the head. Her lifeless body fell backwards into an awkward position with her legs bent under her. Jack nearly lost it and the guard began flickering again. He couldn't believe how callous the action was. Jack fought to regain control as his thoughts darted between disbelief, horror and revenge. He'd seen this sort of thing before during the war and it wasn't something you ever got used to. Then Elleria changed, one second she was a pretty young woman and the next she was a creature like the ones looking down on her now. Then, just as Jack was trying to work that one out, she vanished.

'Guard, go back to command and see if you can be repaired,' said Consulus; and addressing the rest of the council, said, 'We can't afford to be losing guards if we have no means of creating new ones.' The rest of the council nodded in agreement. Tyrus and the council vanished from the chamber and the light levels began to fall.

'What's happened?' Artullus asked.

Jack didn't want to risk speaking out loud so he thought the answer. They've shot Elleria.

Artullus made no reply.

There's nothing more I can do here, thought Jack. He was feeling very guilty about not helping Elleria, but at least he now had an excuse to leave the chamber. He attempted to turn the guard towards the door, but it was difficult, every time he moved he was in danger of being pushed out. Slowly he developed a technique of moving a leg just far enough back to feel the magnetic like resistance, and then using it to push the guard's leg forward. Three stuttering steps later and Jack was facing the door. Then he was through the door and making his way down a corridor. By the time he'd reached the outer door at the end of the corridor he'd almost got the hang of controlling the guard. A thought had occurred to Jack; how was he going to get out of the guard? He assumed that he would be solid, like he was the last time John was here. If he was solid then the guard would shoot him as soon as it saw him, and he'd be in the same boat as Elleria. Jack left the council buildings and entered the wide walkway outside. Which way? He asked himself. The dominant feature of the blue centroid tower caught his eye and he decided to head for that.

*

Harry stood on the edge of the blue road looking down through the misty green shell at the stars below.

'It's difficult to tell where the green bit starts,' he said. 'I can't tell if it's level with the road, a hundred feet below it or even if it's there at all.'

They had just left the arcade that led up from the plaza. Frank and John were already stood on the green and Harry looked up from the stars to their feet and then back down at the stars again. They appeared to be standing on nothing. To Harry it defied all logic.

'Oh what the hell,' he said stepping onto the green transparency that filled the gaps between the roads and the buildings. Despite his fears the green was solid and in fact felt no different to the road.

'We can't stay out here long,' said Frank, 'we'll have to make our way to Elleria staying inside as many buildings as we can.'

They ran across the green to the nearest building and ducked inside. About halfway down a corridor that led through to the other side John stopped. The others halted.

'What's wrong?' Frank asked.

'Elleria's vanished.'

Harry placed a hand on John's shoulder. 'Are you sure?'

'Yes, just seconds ago she was in the council chamber and then she just vanished.'

Harry looked at Frank. 'What now? Do we still go to the council chamber?'

'Well, I don't think we have any other choice; we'll have to make our way there and see if we can figure out what happened,' said Frank.

'Okay, we continue to the chambers.' said Harry, who had taken command of their journey through Valheel.

The corridor ended with another door that led out onto more of the misty green surface. Harry studied the buildings opposite and then pointed at a door. 'That door there, the next one is too far away. Ready?'

'Wait… I can hear something,' said John. 'Something is coming; it's around the corner of the building to the right.'

'Yes, I can hear it,' said Frank, 'but what the hell is it?'

The sound wasn't right, not for Valheel; Frank knew it for a fact, and The Librarian had just told John, but it was Harry that recognised it.

'It sounds like swearing,' he said.

'You're right, it does, doesn't it,' replied Frank.

The swearing got closer and Harry stepped out of the doorway.

'What are you doing?' Frank whispered urgently.

'It's alright,' said Harry, 'I recognise the voice.'

The guard came round the corner and stopped dead as it saw Harry. From the doorway John and Frank held their breath as they watched the standoff between a shiny metal robot and an old teacher in a tweed jacket with leather patches on the elbows. For what seemed like an age, they just stared at each other; and then the guard broke the silence.

'Bloody hell… Harry, as I live and breathe,' said the guard. 'It's me, Jack.'

'Jack! They told me you were here, and I thought I recognised the grumbling,' said Harry as the guard started towards him again.

'Quick you two, in here,' said Frank.

Once they were inside the building Frank closed the door.

'They didn't mention that you looked like that,' said Harry.

'I don't,' said Jack, 'I'm on the inside of this tin thing.' And he told them about how he and Elleria had suddenly got avatars when John had returned, and how Elleria had been executed after she'd been thrown out of the guard they were occupying. 'When they shot Elleria it was the most callous thing I've ever seen.'

'She's not dead,' said Frank. 'She's under the control of the city. At least it explains why she suddenly vanished.'

'Nothing is ever straightforward is it,' said John. 'This was supposed to be a quick rescue.'

'So…' said Harry, 'what now?'

'First thing is to get Jack out of the guard without alerting the city to our presence,' said Frank.

'Getting out isn't going to be a problem,' said Jack. 'It's all I can do to stay inside the thing. It's what happens when I'm out and it sees us.'

'We could always just shoot it with its own gun,' said Harry with a glint in his eye.

'That would alert the city that something was wrong,' said Frank.

'Here's an idea,' said John after a moment's thought. 'Jack stands outside with his back to the door, then he steps out of the guard backwards and we close the door before the guard knows what's happening.'

'Will that work?' Harry asked.

'It might, the last time I left a guard it just sort of carried on from where it left off and didn't seem to remember what had happened,' replied Jack.

'Has anyone got any other ideas?' asked Frank. And when he didn't receive an answer, 'I'll take that as a no then.'

A few minutes later Jack was standing with his back to the open door. Harry went to take the guard's gun.

'Can't do that,' said Frank, 'he'll notice the missing gun and report it.'

'Damn,' said Harry.

'Right, so, is everyone ready?' asked Frank, holding the door open. 'Now Jack.'

The guard flickered back to its green construction grid as a figure started to emerge from its back. The emerging figure was halfway out when it was thrown with some force into the room landing on its back with a thump. Frank closed the door immediately and held a finger to his lips. After a few seconds they could hear the guard moving off in the direction of the council chambers.

'Looks like he's heading back to where I found him,' whispered Jack.

John, Frank and Harry all turned to look at the newest member of the team as he stood and dusted himself down. Harry couldn't believe his eyes. Standing before him was the young fit paratrooper that he'd known as a young man. He was wearing the same uniform he wore when he fought in Arnhem.

'Why do you look so young and I'm still an old man?' Harry asked.

'It's certainly an improvement over the last time I saw you,' said John.

Jack looked down at his uniform and then felt his face with his hands. 'Brilliant,' he said. 'It was something I was thinking about just before John came back.' He nodded to John in recognition. 'That reminds me, now that you're here, there's something I need to try.'

'You mean you were thinking about being young and in the army and when you got your avatar that's what you were?' Frank asked, but Jack wasn't listening. He had his eyes closed and seemed to be concentrating very hard.

'Are you alright?' Harry asked, leaning forward to study Jack's face. His eyebrows were twitching randomly, first the left, then the right, and then a double twitch from the left as the right remained raised. It was fascinating to watch and they all leaned in closer to see what his eyebrows would do next. Then abruptly, the twitching stopped and Jack opened his eyes and flinched when he saw they were all looking closely at him.

'Excellent; it worked,' said a loud voice behind them. Now it was Frank, John and Harry's turn to flinch. They spun round to find a tall man standing there. He was dressed in the same uniform as Jack and was currently admiring the way the tunic fitted.

'I don't believe it,' said Harry, 'Kaarl, is that really you?'

'No, my name is Artullus. I borrowed the images of the human and the uniform from Jack.'

'Artullus,' said Frank moving forward and gripping the tall man's upper arms. 'It's me, Amantarra.'

Both Jack and Artullus looked surprised. Artullus was the first to speak.

'Amantarra,' he said, 'I thought you'd been captured. I can't tell you what a relief it is to see that you haven't been.'

John thought they were going to embrace, but they merely smiled at each other. 'The Bruwnan don't go in for shows of emotion,' The Librarian informed John.

Jack tried to speak but Artullus continued.

'You realise that it's very dangerous for you to be here.'

'Yes, but not as dangerous as being on Earth; things there aren't exactly going to plan.'

'So I understand,' said Artullus.

'Can I interrupt,' said Jack, who thought he'd been polite for long enough, 'you say you're Amantarra?'

'Yes,' said Frank.

'Only the one that shot Elleria, he seemed to think that your friend Scott Briggs was Amantarra.'

'Yes, that's true,' said Artullus.

'And just before you all arrived back here, I heard Tyrus saying that Scott had been duplicated,' said Jack.

'So Scott is here as well,' said John. For some reason this information made him feel more confident.

'Amantarra,' said Artullus, who seemed to relish saying the name, 'what now?'

'This is going to get confusing; everyone else here knows me as Frank, perhaps it would be best if you call me that.'

'Okay…Frank. What now?'

'We rescue Elleria,' said Frank, glancing back at John. 'If we can't do that then the Earth is finished.'

'And Scott,' said John. 'He's another one we've got to rescue now.'

'Yes, and Scott,' replied Frank, 'but knowing Scott, I think he will cause the system a few problems.'

John thought that would probably be true. 'Even here?'

'Even here,' confirmed Frank. 'We might finish up rescuing the system from him.

'Let's not forget that Elleria has disappeared and we don't know where Scott is,' said Harry. 'We can't rescue them if we don't know where they are.'

'If they're under the control of the city then they will both be in the system dimensions,' said Artullus.

'And how do we get into the system dimensions?' Harry asked.

'We don't.' said Artullus, 'John does.'

'Me?' John asked. 'How do I do that?'

'First, we would have had to get you close to one of the city's power distribution crystals, but from what Elleria tells me, you've already been in contact with one,' said Artullus.

'I have? How do you know?'

'You'll have noticed that the yellow zone is flickering,' said Artullus. 'That's because when you arrived here the first time you came into contact with it before you'd formed an avatar. That contact attached your system dimensions to it.'

'My system dimensions?'

'Yes John. A Node Zero is just a standard Node with some intelligence bolted on, and I suppose you could be described as some intelligence with a Node bolted on, which amounts to the same thing,' said Artullus.

'So I'm a Node Zero, not just a Node?'

'Yes, and your collision with the distribution crystal formed a bridge between you and the system. That's our way in, but first we've got to get to the yellow zone. Without getting caught!'

'I knew it was a good idea to bring these two together,' said Frank, turning and indicating Harry and Jack. 'Evading capture is something...' His voice trailed off as he, Artullus and John turned to look at Harry who was doing press-ups.

Harry looked up at them and sprang to his feet. His physique was transformed; young, fit and broad shouldered. You couldn't describe his face as youthful; it had the same hard, lived in appearance that John had always known, but it was younger. His cold grey calculating eyes seemed even more intimidating than before, now that there was the physique behind them to back up their menace. He was wearing the same paratroopers' uniform as Artullus and Jack, and he looked good in it. 'This is great,' he said, squatting and then jumping up again. 'My piles are gone.'

'That's a little bit more than we needed to know,' said John.

'How did you manage this?' Frank asked.

'That was me,' replied Jack who was beaming from ear to ear at his own accomplishment.

'Jack seems to possess the ability to interpret Bruwnian technology into a human context. It's probably a combination of being human, copying by Tyrus and John's link to the system dimensions,' stated Artullus.

'And I can do much more than change things.' As he spoke five Sten guns appeared on the floor in front of him. 'My interpretation of the weapons those guards carry,' he said.

Harry's eyes lit up as he picked up one of the weapons. With hands that had lost none of their expertise with the weapon he removed the cartridge, checked the bullets and then replaced it. 'Welcome back,' he said as he caressed the barrel.

'You won't need to check the ammo either,' said Jack picking up a weapon, 'because it will never run out.'

Frank picked up two of the guns and passed one to John. 'I've got mixed feelings about these. Yes, I think that they're a good idea, but remember, as soon as we use them our cover will be blown.'

'So we only use them as a last resort,' said Harry, who was now holding his sub machine gun close to his chest with both arms. The barrel was sticking up above his left shoulder and John thought Harry was going to kiss it. He noticed that they were all looking at him and lowered the weapon.

'He was like that with the last one he had,' said Jack. 'What was it you used to call it?'

'Betty,' replied Harry without any hesitation.

Artullus stopped examining the gun he'd picked up and turned to Frank. 'You've done an excellent job Amantarra... sorry... Frank; humans have turned war into an art form.'

'Okay Harry,' said Frank, 'over to you. Get us to the Yellow Zone.'

'At last,' said Harry, 'some action.'

28

THE SYSTEM

Elleria's hearing was the first sense to return followed by sensation. She could sense her old Bruwnian body; it was so familiar to her that there was no mistaking it. The intense darkness before her eyes melted into a grey light without definition. It was as if her eyes were registering the fact that there was light without actually seeing it. Then, with a sudden flash of intense colour, her eyesight returned.

She was stood in a clear tube lit from below with white light. The tube was on a low plinth of the same diameter. It was one of fifty identical tubes arranged around the wall of a large circular chamber. To Elleria's right there was a larger gap between two of the tubes which was occupied by something that looked like a church spire attached to the wall. In the centre of the chamber was a circular plinth about the height of a table and arranged around its perimeter were twenty spheres the same diameter as the tube Elleria was stood in. One of the spheres was glowing orange, the rest were dark.

Elleria tried to raise a hand up to the glass of the tube, but it became increasingly harder to move and before she had got half way she gave up. She wondered what was going to happen next and stared out at the chamber, waiting.

Then she sensed it.

It was very subtle. What it was, she couldn't really tell, and she was even less certain that it was even there at all. It was the primal sensation you get on the back of your neck, when you think something is waiting and watching close by in the dark. The sensation was elusive, but the more she focused on it the more obvious it became. Then Elleria realised that the sensation wasn't on the back of her head at all, it was on the inside of it. She got the distinct feeling that it was looking for something, something specific in her mind. There was structure and intelligence to the intruder as it scanned her memories. Most memories it discarded hardly bothering to study them beyond their starting point, but some it pulled up and ran them in full. One such memory was when Elleria and John had first visited Valheel and John had collided with the yellow distribution crystal. After that, it searched for evidence that John had returned to Valheel. She got the impression that whatever it was that was doing the searching had concluded that he hadn't returned. Elleria controlled her thoughts, she didn't want to reveal Jack's opinion that John had returned. It pulled up Elleria's experiences when she occupied the guard, but they seemed of little interest and those thoughts were discarded as well. This meant that Jack's part in all that had passed had remained undiscovered. Finally it reached the point where she was shot by Tyrus. Now that it had stopped searching it became aware of her, but its interest was fleeting and intruder melted away.

To Elleria's relief, her ability to move returned and she looked around the rest of the chamber. There was no entrance, at least none that she could see. There wasn't even an opening in the domed roof. She tested the strength of her prison by pushing against it, but the clear tube did not move in the slightest. She threw her weight, shoulder first against the tube, and again there was no movement.

A flash of light from one of the tubes to her right caught her attention. The tube was now occupied by one of the guardians. A hoop of blue light passed down the length of the tube seemingly scanning the guard. The white lights in the tube dimmed and the guards outline changed to a green construction grid before reverting back to normal. There was another flash of light which left the tube empty. Maintenance, thought Elleria, the guards must come here for maintenance; and it looks like the only way in and out is through these tubes.

Elleria knew why she was here; it was the reason why you never wanted to be shot by one of the guardians weapons. It put you under the control of the city. Once the city had you under its control, it could read your normally protected thoughts; which was exactly what had just happened. She had expected the system to be more thorough, more than just the quick browse through her mind that she had experienced; and she felt lucky that she had retained at least some secrets.

One after another over a period of thirty seconds all the remaining tubes flashed into action and the guards now occupying them were at various stages of being scanned. As each guard reformed, the tube flashed releasing the previous guard and replacing it with another which again was scanned. As Elleria watched the process she noticed there was a difference between the old and new guards. The new ones carried rifles. They were clearly of the same design as the handguns the guards' had always carried, but looked significantly more powerful. She watched the process for a bit longer just to confirm that they were all being upgraded. Perhaps, Elleria thought, she hadn't managed to retain her secrets after all. It looked like the city was preparing for an attack.

The lights in the tube she occupied turned red. Elleria looked down at them wondering what was going to happen next. Initially nothing seemed to be going on, but then she felt it. Starting with a slight tingle in her fingertips, the sensation quickly spread up her arms to cover the rest of her. The tingling grew, turning into a loss of sensation followed by complete numbness. Then the horrible truth dawned on her. She was being erased.

*

The journey to the outskirts of the Blue Zone had been relatively uneventful. Following Harry's lead they'd flitted from one building to the next undetected. Finally they found themselves on the upper floor of a building on the outer edge of the blue zone. They were in a room which looked like it had once been used as a study. There was a large desk close to the window and two big comfy chairs either side of it. John and Frank sat down while they decided on their next move. Artullus was stood behind the chair Frank was sat in, looking out of the window. The ceiling was glass and through it the yellow zone was clearly visible.

'We'd be spotted straight away if tried to cross that,' said Harry indicating the semi-translucent expanse between them and the yellow zone. He was stood to one side of a window with his back to the wall with his head turned sideways so he could see out. He focused his attention to the walkway that circled the zone, looking along it for any signs of movement.

Jack was positioned on the opposite side of the window so he could watch the other direction, but he was looking at the blue stars through outer shell of Valheel. 'I still can't believe that you wouldn't just float away if you tried to cross that,' he said.

'We've crossed it several times between buildings,' said Frank.

'Yes, I know,' replied Jack, 'but that big expanse of stars just doesn't look safe.'

'I know what you mean,' agreed Harry glancing back up at the stars.

The nature of the light outside changed as the yellow zone flickered off and then back on again. Since John had been watching, this was the third time it had done it. It confirmed to John what he had noticed last time; that it wasn't just the lights that were going out. If it were just the lights going out then the buildings would be lit by the light of the other zones, but that wasn't the case. The whole zone was disappearing, the buildings and everything. They were being replaced by the blue star shadows of the void. John felt stronger every time the zone went off and it set him to thinking.

'There's a single guard coming along the road,' said Jack, 'no… wait…'

John thought that Jack was going to say that the guard was about to enter the building. They all waited with baited breath for him to finish. After a moment or two it became obvious that he was going to leave the sentence hanging in the air.

Finally, Harry couldn't stand the suspense. 'What?' he said in a loud whisper.

'He just vanished,' replied Jack.

'Vanished?' asked Artullus.

'Yes, he just disappeared into thin air… hang on… he's back, and there's something different about him…' Jack risked moving his head closer to the edge of the window for a better look and then quickly moved it back. 'He's carrying a bigger weapon.'

'The guards are being upgraded,' said Frank turning to Artullus, 'I thought that was impossible without the Primary Key, what's going on?'

Artullus edged forward towards the window until he could see the guard as he passed below. 'It's within the initial parameters,' he said dismissing Frank's unease; 'but what you should be concerned about is why the guard has been upgraded. I would speculate that the city knows John is here.'

'No, that isn't our main concern,' said Harry. 'Whether they know we're here now or not is irrelevant, because at some point they will know, and our main concern then, will be how many guards there are. Up to now I've only seen two, and one of them turned out to be Jack.'

'Point taken,' said Artullus. 'There are one thousand guards per zone, so that's four thousand in total. That number cannot be increased without the Primary Key.'

'That's a relief,' said Jack sarcastically, 'only four thousand. How come you know so much about this place?'

It was Frank who answered him. 'Artullus designed Valheel. There is nothing he doesn't know about it.'

Jack looked out of the window again. 'Wow,' he said without looking back into the room, 'that should give us a serious advantage.' Harry shook his head; he'd forgotten how cynical Jack could be.

'You would think that,' said Artullus missing the sarcasm in Jack's retort, 'but unfortunately I designed the system to evolve. So quite what it is now, I don't know.'

John had been quiet for a while. 'We don't need to go to the yellow zone,' he said, surprising them all. 'In fact, I think going there would be fatal; at least for you four.'

'Why?' Frank asked.

John held up his hand to hold off any further questions. The Librarian was showing John some equations. 'Because,' he said eventually, the yellow zone is flashing in and out of existence. Its power is switching momentarily over to me. If we were there when it switches, and I can't see that we wouldn't be, I don't know what would happen to you.'

The others looked at each other in dismay.

'That was the only plan we had,' said Frank.

'Don't worry;' said John, 'there is another way.'

*

The thought of the erasure procedure frightened Elleria. She didn't think it would be painful, she'd lost all sensation in her Bruwnian Avatar; but that wasn't what frightened her. The thing she feared most was the loss of her mind. Would she feel the memories slipping away until she couldn't remember what it was she was missing? Or would she lose her cognitive ability first, reducing her mind to a random collection of orphan thoughts, unable to tie them together? Thought was all she was. The shells she occupied came and went; Bruwnan, Ja'liem and Human, each had its merits but in the end they were all transitory. For most of her existence Elleria had, like Amantarra been nothing but pure thought; continuous thought that never paused, not even for a moment, not even to sleep. The end result didn't worry her, if she was nothing then it would be over, but the process of getting there, the slow dissolving of her mind terrified her. Elleria hoped the process would be quick, so she didn't have to feel herself slipping away.

As it started there was, as she suspected, no pain; but like snow melts from the land in the spring her Bruwnian avatar started to erode around her. At this stage the process wasn't affecting her mind. Perhaps her mind would go last; a deliberate and cruel arrangement that she could well believe of Tyrus and the council, everything about them had a vindictive tinge to it.

Her vision started to go. As Elleria looked out at the chamber the colours slowly drained away to a grey blur. She cursed Tyrus and the Council for leaving her the ability to witness it. Through the blur, the tubes continued to show as flashing bright patches, like lightning seen through grey cloud, as the guardians continued to be processed.

Elleria strengthened her resolve to hang on to her memories as long as possible. John, her thoughts about him seemed the strongest, how she missed him. Elleria wanted to close her eyes and concentrate only on him, but that was no longer an option. Strange though, since Tyrus had shot her in the council chamber she hadn't really thought about John; in fact, she hadn't thought about him at all and now that her avatar was gone, melted to nothing, John's image filled her thoughts.

The erasing of her mind must start soon she thought. Elleria waited… Any moment now… She focused her mind on John; she wanted her last thoughts to be about him. John waved to her across the playground on that first day. Then she pictured John looking at the frozen form of Action doing a scissor jump. Her mind was still intact, or at least it seemed to be. Or had the process started and she had already lost her ability to recognise it. That scary thought represented her worst nightmare.

It wasn't what she would describe as sensation, but she was getting a returning sense of, not an avatar, but of the boundaries of one. Was it real or imagined? It seemed real, it was definitely getting stronger, and it felt… it felt human; the shape of it was definitely human. And, she realised, her thoughts were human too. She pictured John in the chemistry lab sitting on his stool and felt a wave of emotion, human emotion.

All aspects of her Bruwnian avatar were gone; including the thought processes, but in its place her human state of mind had re-emerged. The system didn't know how to erase humans. Both she and Jack had been through the erasure process and survived.

All her fears evaporated, she felt invincible and a new resolve took hold. In the fog Elleria could sense that she was still in the tube. She reached out to touch it and her hand passed straight through. She didn't waste any time and quickly moved out of her prison and into the chamber. There was no way she was going to get trapped in there again if John turned up, and she was sure he would. Then another thought occurred to her; if John turns up now she would be trapped in this chamber without doors. She had to leave the chamber.

If, she speculated, she could move through the tube she'd been held captive in; then she should be able to walk through the walls of this chamber and into the next one where there might be an exit. Pick a direction Elleria, she said to herself. The curved wall behind the tube she'd been in was closest and it seemed as good place as any, so Elleria turned and without hesitation passed straight through the wall.

The other side of the wall was not at all what she was expecting. Instead of another foggy chamber the view was crystal clear. Set against a general background of black, Elleria found herself surrounded by hundreds if not thousands of linked geometric shapes. Elleria still had no substance, but she found she could move just by thinking about it.

As she drifted slowly away from the chamber she had just left Elleria spun round to look at it. It was circular with a domed roof as she had expected, but it also had a domed base making it look like a stretched sphere. She tried to make a note of the positioning of the unit in amongst all the other shapes, in case she needed to find her way back there. The Upgrade Unit, that's what I'll call it, she thought.

The unit was made of a glowing green translucent material. Along the edges of the unit the colour of material was more intense. The tubes could be seen clearly through the wall of the unit and they were still in constant use as yet more guards were being upgraded. Strange how you can see into the unit but not out of it, she thought.

From the top and bottom of the unit, broad twisting streams of plasma slowly writhed their way over several hundred metres to spherical structures. The colour of the plasma fluctuated from white to the blue green of an electrical arc. The spheres were constructed of the same glowing green material as the upgrade unit and were linked to other structures by tubes of the same material. There was a myriad of ever changing coloured lights inside the spheres. The Upgrade Unit was connected to a cube of similar size by one of the glowing green tubes and the cube in turn was connected to five other shapes, one from each face.

Elleria spun round slowly. There were other shapes; cubes, pyramids, flat square planes that intersected with the other objects. They were all interconnected by straight tubes and had either an inner glow or changing lights like the spheres. The whole thing was immensely complex and had no discernible pattern to it. This was the true structure of the system and it bore no relationship to the spherical ordered construction of Valheel.

Why was the view here crystal clear? And where was here? Beyond the structures was blackness. Where were the blue star shadows? For her own satisfaction Elleria needed to work this out. The structures, well they must be the system speculated Elleria. Currently she was outside the system… but in the same dimensions, therefore her normal senses would apply and she could see the structures that made up the system. When she was in one of the structures with an avatar, the system creating the avatar would supply the visual information. So, in order to be in one of the structures without an avatar and be able to see, she would need to tap into the sensory feeds. She thought about John. When she was in the same dimensions as him she must be taking her sensory feeds from him, but that must mean that John was a Node Zero. The thought was intriguing and she wondered why she hadn't thought of it before. Not that the thought helped her, she still had no idea how to tap into the sensory feeds. Still, that didn't matter at the moment because her vision was perfect.

As she started to move through the complexity of the system dimensions, it became apparent that there was one central structure that had more connections to it than any of the others. It was a huge, long, square sided object, like an office block; she immediately named it the tower. The other objects were more numerous and densely packed around the tower, seemingly emphasising its importance. It was also the only structure that she could not see into. Elleria decided to pay the tower a visit and moved towards it. Every few seconds a green pulse of light would travel down one of the thousands of local link tubes from one object to another. Elleria watched the never ending light show as she journeyed towards the tower. The whole place seemed alive.

Arriving at the centre of one of the tower's faces she stopped some ten metres back from it. This was the only section which did not have any link tubes. Above and below her the tubes filled all the available space of the remainder of the face, but here in the mid-section it was empty. It had been difficult to judge the scale of the tower as she had approached it, but now she was here it was obvious that the tower was immense. Looking to her left and right she estimated that the width of the tower was at least a hundred metres and the nearest tubes thirty metres above and below her. The total height, if height was the right word, must be near enough a thousand metres. This has to be the centre of the system, Elleria told herself. It had to be worth a peek inside.

*

'Jack, come over here a minute,' said John.

Jack slid down the wall until he was below the window level and then keeping low made his way over to John. 'How can I help?'

John indicated that Jack should look at the wall running along the back of the room. 'You remember what Elleria looked like don't you?' John asked him.

'Missy, oh yes, I remember,' replied Jack with a lustful glint in his eye.

Frank noticed the glint. 'Jack! You're old enough to be her Grandfather.'

Jack had the good grace to go red in the face. 'Sorry,' he said, 'it's this body. I've been thinking about things that I haven't thought about for years.'

John waited until Jack's focus returned and then continued. 'Picture a door in that wall that leads to her,' said John.

'But I don't know where she is.'

'Do you remember her wet shoulder?'

'Yes,' said Jack.

'Think of that, picture Elleria's wet shoulder on the other side of the door, with Elleria attached to it of course, and it will lead to her wherever she is.'

'Very clever,' said Frank, 'I like the idea of using the tag, using their technology against them.'

Jack didn't look convinced. 'Are you sure?' he asked. John nodded.

As the others watched, Jack closed his eyes; there was a brief twitching of his left eyebrow and a black door sized oblong appeared on the surface of the wall.

'Everyone else wait here, I'll go and get her,' said John.

'Are you sure you don't want us with you?' said Harry.

'Certain,' John replied to Harry. 'I'll be as quick as I can. Oh, and you're going to lose your avatars as soon as I go through, so don't wander about, stay in this room.' Without waiting for any replies John hefted the Sten gun he was carrying and stepped into the blackness. As he did so, the others dissolved into nothing.

'I hate this bloody fog,' said Jack.

*

Elleria moved forward and through the wall of the tower. Inside, the entire structure was hollow. From the inside the walls were translucent and she could see the complex of structures outside.

Above, halfway between Elleria and the top of the tower was a large sphere, its diameter more than half the width of the tower. The sphere was connected to multiple spire objects, identical to the one she had seen in the upgrade chamber, by constantly twisting streams of blue green plasma. She realised that the spires must be the termination points of the tubes on the outside of the tower. She watched as the plasma connections danced around each other on the surface of the sphere always moving but never colliding. Below her, the structure was mirrored at the other end of the tower.

Occupying the centre of the tower, directly in front of her was another stretched sphere. It was smaller than the Upgrade Unit and opaque. Plasma streams from the spheres above and below were the unit's only links. This is the centre of everything. Elleria wasted no more time and made her way forward and through the curved wall. From the inside the walls were translucent, and the rest of the tower could be clearly seen.

Floating in the centre of the chamber, arranged as if attached to the sides of an invisible cube, were six small silver spheres. The object that floated within the boundaries set by the spheres defied description. It was made up of constantly changing shapes in ever changing colours that faded and bloomed. If Elleria put her mind to it she could pick out individual shapes. As she watched, a red pyramid and a blue cube merged into a yellow sphere which became a purple blob. That could only be the core she thought.

Standing in a group next to the core were the five councillors.

'What did we learn from the Radgarc?' Consulus asked. The Yellow Councillor flickered and vanished, only to appear a moment later.

'Elleria believed that the Node, John Godbert, is here in Valheel,' said the Green Councillor.

To Elleria this confirmed that she hadn't managed to retain any secrets after all, despite her initial optimism. It was strange being talked about in the past tense. The Green Councillor continued.

'This is borne out by her appearing before us in human form. It was noted that her form changed to Bruwnian when she was brought under the control of the city. This would seem to indicate differing power sources for her avatar.'

'Have we begun the interrogation of Amantarra yet?'

Interrogate Amantarra, Elleria was shocked. It hadn't occurred to her that they might actually have succeeded in capturing Amantarra. Tyrus must have copied Scott the same way that he copied Jack. Elleria's spirit dropped like a stone, this was very bad news indeed.

'Not yet Consulus, we have only just finished interrogating her Radgarc Elleria,' said the red Councillor.

'Then proceed immediately.'

'Yes Consulus,' said the Red Councillor. An arc of energy reached out from the core to the councillor and he vanished. The core turned red momentarily, the colour transferring to the plasma link outside the chamber that went up to the top sphere and then onto one of the links to the spires on the wall of the tower.

Elleria realised that must be how they moved around the system and wondered if she could do the same and follow the Red Councillor to where they were holding Amantarra. She didn't know what she would be able to do once she got there; but, she decided, that even if all she could do was watch, it was better than not knowing.

Elleria turned; ready to rise up to the spire, when a black oblong appeared in front of her. The shape had height and width but no depth, it was impossibly thin. She stopped dead, and was trying to work out what it was when John stepped out of the blackness. Elleria tingled all over and suddenly found herself occupying her human avatar again.

'Elleria,' said John enveloping her in a huge embrace, 'I came back for you.'

'I thought you might,' she replied kissing him on the lips.

John looked past her at the four councillors who were stood staring at them both. 'You've got company,' he said slightly embarrassed that he'd kissed Elleria in front of them. He wondered what manner of creature they were.

'They're Bruwnan,' The Librarian informed him.

'I'm sure I've got one of those in the library,' said John as he noticed the core for the first time.

'That's the core,' said The Librarian.

John didn't really have time to think about it, his first instinct was to protect Elleria. He manoeuvred himself in front of her. There was now nothing between him and the councillors. John started to bring the Sten gun he was carrying into a firing position. Suddenly a brilliant blue arc of energy passed from John's chest into the Yellow Councillor where it changed direction and headed up through the ceiling of the chamber and onto one of the spires in the tower wall. Elleria, despite being shocked by what was happening, noted that it was the same spire that the Red Councillor had travelled down. The burst of energy lasted several seconds its light casting stark shadows from the councillors along the walls which had momentarily lost some of their translucency. When it had stopped, the chamber was dark by comparison. The councillors stood immobile. At first John thought he'd just stunned them into inaction, but then he realised that they had stopped completely.

'Sorry,' shouted John, as the chamber brightened and the walls became translucent again. The councillors remained immobile. John looked from Consulus to the green councillor and then blue as he tried to work out why he had apologised. It was strange, but as John looked around the chamber he got the impression that there was someone missing.

'Where's the Yellow Councillor gone,' said Elleria as she peeped around John at the place where he had been. That must be it, thought John, it was the councillor that was missing, but there was another part of him that wasn't convinced.

The three remaining councillors started moving again. After no more than a brief glance at John and Elleria they turned to face the core. Around the perimeter of the chamber green outlines started to appear.

'Guardians,' exclaimed Elleria.

'I think it time we weren't here,' said John. He turned, and placing an arm around Elleria's shoulder, guided her through the black doorway.

29

THE PRIMARY KEY

The red councillor was stood near the centre of the upgrade chamber next to the circular plinth supporting the spheres. Ignoring the dark spheres he placed his hands on the plinth in front of the sphere glowing orange.

'And now Amantarra,' he said to the glowing sphere, 'we shall see what your master plan was.'

A number of images appeared in the air above the plinth. The councillor studied them as he tried to determine the best method of interrogation. He gestured upward with his hand and another set of images appeared, replacing the original ones. He highlighted two of the new images by touching them and then brought the fingertips of both hands together in a gesture that created a third larger image above the others. The councillor studied the new image briefly before replacing the smaller images with another set. He highlighted another image and added it to the larger one which grew in size slightly and became three dimensional. The tool was almost ready and he paused to consider further refinements, changing the smaller images several times before selecting another. He brought his fingertips together adding the image to the tool. Placing his index finger on the large image he spun it so he could study every aspect of it.

The image was still spinning slowly when a colossal arc of yellow energy erupted from the spire on the wall. The two upgrade tubes either side of the spire exploded, their fragments scattering across the floor of the chamber. The arc discharged itself into the plinth in the centre of the room. In turn the plinth produced a myriad of smaller blue white arcs which filled the chamber discharging into the walls, the ceiling, and the upgrade tubes. For a moment the air was full of lightning and flying glass. The councillor didn't flinch, even as pieces of debris struck him creating patches of green construction lines which were quickly rendered back to normal. With the discharge of energy over, the final pieces of debris rolled to halt on the chamber floor. The images he had been working on had vanished and the sphere that had been glowing orange was now dark like the rest. He turned to look at the destroyed upgrade tubes. There was no emotion on his face as he stood taking in the damage. Finally, when he'd seen enough, a less intense arc of energy reached out from the spire to transfer him back to the core.

Unseen by the councillor on the floor to the other side of the plinth from where he'd been standing, was the green grid outline of a figure. As the councillor vanished from the chamber the figure began to render itself and take form.

*

'Jack,' shouted Harry, 'where are you?' In the fog Harry turned to Frank who was stood next to him. 'I know what Jack means now about this bloody fog, once you are more than a few paces apart you can't sense each other.'

'Well he can't be far away,' said Frank.

'I'm not.' Jack's voice sounded quite distant, off to Harry's right somewhere.

'Get back over here;' shouted Harry, 'you out of all of us know what's going to happen when John comes back through. We need to be all together.'

'All right, all right, keep your hair on,' said Jack loudly, his voice starting to get closer. 'I only wanted to see if I could walk through walls. When I first got here I kept using the doors. Proper daft I feel now.'

Jack was almost back to the others, when his fingers tingled with pins and needles. He found himself looking at the wrong side of the wall he'd walked through. 'Blast it,' he said. He looked to either side along the length of the wall. There were no doors. 'Damn!'

Jack could hear voices coming from the other side of the wall. It was John. 'Where's Jack?' he heard him say, followed by; 'the city knows we're here now.' Then it went silent. Jack placed his ear on the wall to listen. He could hear Harry talking quietly and quickly but he couldn't make out any of the words. Jack pressed his ear harder against the wall and strained to hear more. He thought he heard a couple of clicks and then he was almost deafened by gunfire.

'Oh bloody hell,' Jack said out loud as sound of three Sten guns resonated around the room he was in. Then the gun fire stopped abruptly only to start again a few seconds later. Jack stood back from the wall a couple of paces. The firing seemed to be coming from the left, which presumably meant that what they were firing at was on the right. It sounded intense and he had no doubt that they needed him, but how was he going to get to the other side of the wall to help? Jack was so frustrated that he couldn't think straight. Perhaps he could find a way round. He looked around, the only door was behind him, in the completely the wrong direction, not a good option. Then it struck him.

'Oh you bloody idiot Green,' he told himself, 'create a bloody door.' Then another thought occurred to him, he slapped himself on the head, how could he be so stupid. 'No, not a door…'

*

Harry was knelt, waiting, gun pointed at the black doorway and as another guardian came through he opened fire again. It made Elleria jump. The others instantly dropped to their knees. The guard's chest flashed green, the construction grid clearly visible as the bullets ripped into his avatar. The guard fell forward onto the floor next to the first one that had come through the portal from the system dimensions.

'We've haven't got much cover,' shouted Harry, 'keep down everyone.'

Elleria kept low behind one of the large chairs. There was something familiar about this soldier and she couldn't work out what it was. He was very confident, almost comfortable with the situation they found themselves in. The others seemed to accept what he was saying without question and there didn't seem to be any doubt that he was in charge.

John was kneeling next to the soldier behind a desk. The desk was open at the bottom and didn't offer that much cover. 'Be careful John,' she said.

'Elleria,' said Frank. He was waving to her from his position next to Artullus behind another chair on the other side of the desk. 'Elleria; give me a hand to turn this desk on its side.' Elleria nodded.

The desk was heavy and they struggled to start turning it from their kneeling positions on either side. 'Push,' shouted Frank red faced from the effort.

'I'm trying,' replied Elleria, as Harry and Artullus opened fire again.

John stood up, grabbed the back of the desk and lifted. As the guard fell to the floor, the desk started to tip over. Another guard appeared. He got off one shot which John had to twist sideways to avoid letting go of the desk in the process. As the desk fell back into its starting position, Elleria stood. She had some compulsion to protect John, but he grabbed her arm and pulled her to him.

'Careful,' he said, as he dragged them both down behind the desk.

'Me? You need talk,' Elleria couldn't believe he'd come out with something like that, not after he'd just stood up right in front of that guard. She looked at his face, it was just so good to be with him again and it made her feel all warm inside.

Frank made his way over behind the desk next to Harry. He placed his hands on the edge of the desktop ready to push up and turned to look at the other two. 'Ready,' he said. John and Elleria followed suit. As Harry opened up again; they all pushed from a kneeling position. Slowly the desk reached its tipping point and went over with a thud. Frank and John held on to the legs on either side to stop it going all the way over. Then Frank closed the slight gap between the chair and the desk by pulling the chair close, John did the same on his side. Now they had a defensible line. Frank made his way round to the chair Elleria had been behind and made ready his Sten gun.

'We used to play this sort of a game round your house,' John said to Frank, 'do you remember?'

Frank smiled. 'Defend the settee,' he said, 'I remember; although I've been doing similar things for a lot longer.'

'Will those weapons penetrate this?' Harry asked knocking on the desk with his gun.

'The old ones wouldn't; I don't know about the new ones.' said Frank.

Two guards came through at the same time with the head of a third appearing between them. As Harry, Artullus and Frank opened fire the third guard disappeared back through the portal.

'Did you get the third one?' asked Frank.

'No,' replied Harry.

'That means they now know our strength,' said Frank.

'Brace yourselves; they'll be coming through in numbers now,' said Harry.

John picked up his Sten gun. 'I think it's about time I used this,' he said to Elleria. She leaned in close and John thought she was going to kiss him, but she whispered in his ear instead.

'John,' she said, 'who are the soldiers?'

'Sorry, of course... you don't know. This is Harry Fleming, or Mr Fleming as you would know him,' replied John.

'What, our Mr Fleming? Mr Fleming the chemistry teacher?'

'Yes.'

'I thought his voice sounded familiar. Why does he look so young?'

'That was Jack's doing; he looks just as young by the way.' John indicated Artullus. 'And that's Artullus.'

'So Jack was right then, he got him into the city by lending him some clothes... and a body as well, Kaarl's body by the looks of it.'

'How did you know he was called Kaarl?' John asked.

'Jack showed us both a film of his time in Holland. He really is quite skilled at manipulating Bruwnian technology.'

Three guards entered firing indiscriminately as they came through. The upgraded weapons they carried fired more rapidly than their previous ones. The energy pulses struck the walls, the ceiling and the furniture, but did not penetrate. Fire was returned from four Sten guns and the guards fell to the floor to join the others. They were immediately replaced by another three, then another three, until there was a steady stream of guards coming through the portal. The fire from the Sten guns was stopping them. Jack's never ending ammo was a success. After this had gone on for a few minutes, Harry realised that they had a different problem. A wall of fallen guards was building up; it was already four guards high. Some of the guards had come in low behind the corpse wall but the majority of guards were still entering in an upright position, fully exposed to the fire from the Sten guns. Harry's initial thoughts were that the guards where stupid, if they came in low they would avoid getting shot. Then he realised that the guards behind the wall were guiding the corpses to the top of the wall as they fell. Soon the wall was six high and the guards were firing indiscriminately over the top of it.

'Artullus... Frank,' shouted Harry above the noise, 'move as far out to the sides as you can. Try to fire round the end of that wall they're building.'

With Harry and John providing cover, Artullus and Frank went left and right respectively. They both opened fire taking out some of the guards at the ends of the wall and initially it seemed like it was working, but it quickly became obvious that all they were doing was simply extending the wall to protect the flanks.

'This is not working,' shouted Frank, as more and more guards poured through the portal. 'We're just doing what they want us to do.'

'I can't believe they would plan to sacrifice this many,' shouted Harry.

'They can afford the resources and these corpses will regenerate later; so they haven't sacrificed anything,' shouted Artullus.

Harry looked horrified, he shook his head as he fired.

'What we need is Jack to close the portal,' said John. 'Where the hell is he?'

The guards' return fire was getting more difficult to anticipate, they were pushing their arms through the pile of the fallen and firing, you couldn't tell the deactivated avatars from the active ones.

'John, fire at any movement in the corpse wall,' shouted Harry as a pulse struck the desk just below his head.

John started firing at the wall, but after a while it seemed to him that the whole wall was moving and not just arms.

'They're pushing the wall forward to give themselves more room,' shouted Artullus. And slowly but surely, bit by bit, the corpse wall was moving towards them.

'We can't hold them, there's too many of them,' shouted Harry. He knew that when they had enough guards in position they would rush them and there wasn't a thing they could do to stop it.

Suddenly over the top of the Sten gun fire there was a much louder noise, it sounded like a chainsaw. There were two long bursts of sound followed by a series of shorter ones. Harry, John, Artullus and Frank stopped firing.

'What the…' John started to ask, but the last part of the question was drowned out by another burst of sound.

Harry leaned in close to John and shouted between bursts. 'That's an MG34… a machine gun. I'd recognise the sound anywhere… They were very popular… with the German's when… I was in Holland.'

The guards had stopped firing. Harry cautiously looked over the top of the upturned desk. Through a slit in the wall that enclosed the right side of the room poked the barrel of a machine gun. It was now being fired in controlled one second bursts at new guards that were appearing through the portal. The initial firing had obviously made short work of the guards who had been behind the corpse wall.

'Jack… Jack… is that you?' shouted Harry between bursts of fire.

'Of course… it is,' replied Jack.

'Jack…' shouted John.

'What?'

'Close… the door.'

'Just… a few… more,' said Jack as he continued to fire controlled bursts of machine fire at the guards who were still coming through.

Harry rolled his eyes. 'He always wanted one of those when we were in Holland, but he never managed to get one,' he told John.

'We need to leave; the city knows where we are now,' said John. 'There'll be guards heading our way through the streets.'

'Now, Jack,' shouted Harry, 'we need to go.'

'Yes, yes,' shouted Jack indignantly. The black doorway vanished leaving only the faintest of outlines to show where it had been. 'There, it's closed.'

'Is everyone okay,' said Harry standing up and walking over to the slit.

'I'm fine,' replied Jack who was grinning like an idiot through the slit in the wall. Everyone else confirmed that they were okay.

'We need to get out of this room,' said John loudly and with some urgency.

'Jack,' said Harry putting his face close to the slit Jack had been firing through, 'a door through here would be good about now.'

'No problem,' replied Jack.

The wall surrounding the slit melted into an opening and they made their way quickly through it. Once on the other side it seemed to Elleria that the fire fight had lasted hours, a lifetime maybe, but in reality it had only lasted five minutes. Harry was the last to come through the opening and as he passed Jack, who was stood looking at the fallen guards, he slapped him on the shoulder.

'Cheers Jack,' he said.

'How many do you reckon?' asked Jack.

'Over a hundred,' replied Harry.

'One hundred and thirty one to be precise,' said Frank.

'You were counting?' asked Jack.

'Can't help it; it's automatic,' Frank replied.

'Seal this opening Jack,' said John. 'That should buy us a few minutes.'

Jack sealed the opening and then looked down admiringly at the MG34 that was on the floor at his feet. The machine gun looked ready to fire with the stock resting on the floor and the barrel propped up on two legs. Jack squatted down and looked up at John. 'They look the business don't they,' he said picking up the weapon and standing.

'They do,' John agreed.

'It's beautifully designed,' continued Jack, 'watch this.' Jack pulled the two legs on the barrel back so that they ran parallel with the barrel and the squeezed them together to lock them into position. 'See, the bipod just folds away, it's part of the gun, which means you don't have to carry around a separate stand; and you see how close to the end of the barrel it is, that makes it more accurate when you're pivoting around it.'

Harry rolled his eyes.

John leaned back, took in the weapons design and nodded approvingly; it was, as Jack had said, "the business".

'I've always wanted one of these,' said Jack as he placed the leather carrying sling over his shoulder. 'I had a name picked out and everything.'

'I know, Harry told me,' commented John. 'What was the name?'

'Marlena,' replied Jack all misty eyed.

'That figures,' said Harry, who didn't seem to like the name.

'Better than Betty,' retorted Jack.

'What's wrong with Betty?'

Elleria watched the two younger versions of the old men she had known arguing like children over what they had named their weapons. Perhaps they had been like this when they were in Holland together, she could only guess as to the answer. What was obvious was that currently they were taking on the traits of younger men. It was as if the bodies they occupied were dictating their whole personality.

'Now, now boys,' she said, 'we can't have you arguing about whose gun has got the best name can we?' To ensure their full attention; as she spoke Elleria twisted her torso and moved her shoulders in that way that John hadn't seen since the playground. It was a moment or two before Jack and Harry could drag their gaze away from her chest, but it had the desired effect.

'No missy,' said Jack. Both Jack and Harry looked abashed.

'Besides, I've got something important to say,' she continued. 'I overheard the council talking and Amantarra's been captured. They copied Scott.' The others looked at each other with slightly confused looks on their faces, but they didn't seem overly concerned. 'One of the councillors has gone to interrogate her.' This still didn't produce the concerned reaction she was expecting. 'That means they'll get the Primary Key,' she summarised addressing Artullus, who had emphasised how important it was that the council should not get it.

'No, they won't get the Primary Key,' said Frank, 'because I'm Amantarra.'

Elleria looked stunned. 'Amantarra,' she whispered hardly able to believe that Amantarra was standing in front of her. How long had she waited? And each time she thought Amantarra was going to appear, she didn't. All this time, all the expectation, the waiting; and Amantarra had been with her ever since she had arrived on Earth. Tears began to well in her eyes. 'Do you know how long I've waited for you to reappear?'

Frank nodded.

'And you didn't think to tell me?' Elleria felt aggrieved and her voice broke before the end of the sentence. The first tear rolled down her cheek.

John put his arms around Elleria and cuddled her. 'I didn't know either,' he said softly. 'Amantarra couldn't tell you, she couldn't tell anyone, it was just too risky.'

Elleria gave a great shuddering sigh. 'I know... it's just... upsetting. I looked forward to the reunion for such a long time and then it turns out to have happened without my knowing.' Elleria felt silly, it would seem that now it was she who was being dictated to by the body she occupied.

'Well it's happened now,' said Frank placing a hand on her shoulder. 'It wasn't something I liked doing, but it had to be done.'

'In copying Scott I think that the council have opened up a bit of a wasps nest,' said John. 'You know what Scott is like.'

Frank looked thoughtful. 'A Trojan,' he said quietly to himself, as if he'd forgotten the others were there.

'What did you say?' John asked, but Frank seemed deep in thought and didn't answer.

'Trojan,' replied Elleria, 'he said Trojan. What does that mean?'

'It's a story from ancient history where the Greeks were laying siege to the city of Troy. They weren't getting anywhere with the battle so they withdrew their army, leaving a large wooden horse as a parting gift. When the Greeks had gone, the Trojan's pulled the horse inside the city walls and celebrated their victory. But the Greeks had hidden soldiers inside the horse. When it was dark and the Trojans were still celebrating, the soldiers left the horse and opened the city gates. The rest of the Greek army then took the city,' answered John.

'That was very clever of the Greeks,' said Elleria.

'Well, I'm impressed,' said Harry. 'I didn't know that history was one of your strong points.'

'That was an "in a nutshell" explanation from The Librarian,' said John.

'Alright, so it's this Librarian chap I'm impressed with,' said Harry.

'Frank, are you saying that we can use Scott as our man on the inside?' John asked.

'Not exactly,' said Frank. 'Scott being Scott, I'm sure he will cause them a few problems; but he has no weapons so his effectiveness will be minimal. No, I'm thinking of the distraction he could create.'

'How,' asked John, 'if he was copied like Jack then he'd just be a ghost wouldn't he?'

'Well initially he wouldn't even be that. His memories would be held in storage until they interrogated him. But tell me, when you rescued Elleria did anything happen, did you get sense of him?'

John thought about it. 'I got a sense that there should be someone there who wasn't. Right after I zapped the Yellow Councillor.'

'Are you saying that Scott may already have an avatar?' Elleria asked.

'I think John's visit to the system may have changed things; so yes, Scott may well have an avatar,' replied Frank.

'We need to be moving,' said Harry, cutting short any further discussion. 'John, you've got access to the maps; which way do we need to be going?'

'Are we going to rescue Scott?' John asked.

'I don't know,' replied Harry, 'but we've been here too long, we need to be as far away from here as possible.'

'Scott will have to take care of himself for the moment,' said Frank. 'I'm sure he'll be alright.'

'Okay,' said John, 'The Librarian says there is a service tunnel at the end of the corridor on the other side of the back wall.' John indicated a place on the wall. 'Jack, would you do the honours.'

Harry watched Jack's eyebrows dance as the others watched the opening form in the back wall. Artullus was first through, followed by John and Elleria. The new opening came out just before the end of a corridor which ran off to the right. It was dark and Artullus started to move down the corridor, Sten gun at the ready.

With John behind her, Elleria had gone two paces when Jack's MG34 opened up. John turned quickly bringing his weapon up into a firing position. Frank was stood in the opening effectively blocking it. John looked over Frank's shoulder, behind him, near the entrance; a single guard was falling to the floor. John raised the gun ready to fire past Frank at any more guards that may come through the door.

'This isn't as bad as it looks,' said Frank.

'What isn't?' asked John, taking his eyes off the entrance to look at Frank. Harry turned and as he and John watched, Frank's body transformed into the form of Amantarra.

'This,' said Amantarra, and vanished.

As John stood open mouthed, Harry never lost his cool. He stepped through the opening placed a hand on John's arm, turned him and started to guide him down the corridor. 'Jack,' said Harry, 'get through and seal the opening.'

'What did he mean by "this isn't as bad as it looks"?' said John as Harry ushered him down the corridor. 'How bad does it have to get?'

Artullus was reversing back up the corridor to meet them. 'What's happened?'

'Frank's been hit,' replied Harry.

'Ah,' said Artullus, 'this is going to make things difficult.'

Jack caught them up. 'What now?'

'It won't be long before they work out where we've gone; so it's the same as before,' said Harry, 'get to the service corridor and get away from here. Once we're safe we can plan what to do next.'

Elleria looked at John with sad eyes. 'I know,' he said, 'it was a short reunion; but remember, we got you back, so we can get Frank back.' Yet another distraction, John was thinking, but these things happen.

'Service tunnel entrance?' asked Harry.

'We need an opening through the wall at the end of the corridor,' said John.

'Come on,' urged Harry, 'we don't want to hang around here.'

The corridor ran for about fifty paces and then turned sharp left to run towards the front of the building and the centroid tower. The light at the far end had a blue tint to it and was bright by comparison to the corridor, it reflected off the walls and the floor making it difficult to see down the corridor clearly. Both Harry and Jack didn't like it; the potential threat level had just gone up a notch as far as they were concerned.

John indicated a place on the wall. 'Here Jack,' he said.

'Before you do that Jack,' said Harry, 'create another three MG34's.' The weapons appeared instantly on the floor in front of Harry. 'John, give your Sten to Elleria and grab one of those; the other one is for you Artullus.' Harry placed his Sten on the floor and picked up the third machine gun. 'Get rid of the two spares Jack.' The surplus Sten guns dissolved into nothing.

With the weaponry sorted, Jack created the opening and they stepped into a small square room with a door opposite the opening they'd just come through. A flight of steps led down into darkness and Artullus descended three steps and bent to look into the gloom weapon at the ready.

The opening filled with a slightly glowing mist as, eyes closed, Jack started to seal it. The mist began to solidify, losing some of its translucency and taking on the colour and texture of the wall. Suddenly the process stopped. Jack opened his eyes; the corridor on the other side of the wall could still be seen. It was like looking through a dirty window.

'It's stopped,' he said turning to John.

John suddenly felt weak; his knees shook and threatened to give way. He placed an arm on the wall to steady himself.

Artullus looked back. 'They've got the Primary Key,' he said, 'which means they've severed John's connection to the yellow zone.'

Harry looked at the partially sealed opening. 'As soon as they see that, they'll know where we are,' he said. 'John, are you okay to move?'

'He'll be alright in a minute once he's adjusted to the lower energy levels,' said Artullus.

John took a step towards the stairs and fell to his knees.

'Jack, Elleria, help him down the stairs,' said Harry, 'and hurry, we need to put some distance between here and us.'

At the bottom of the stairs there was a doorway on the left which opened out onto a service tunnel. With light fittings that didn't do much more than glow every ten paces or so, the light level was poor. Running along the centre of the ceiling was a glass pipe which contained a single twisting dark violate plasma stream. The plasma gave off a little light, but it was no more than a glow across the ceiling.

Harry was the last to reach the tunnel; 'which way?' he asked.

'Right takes us to the centroid tower and left away from it,' said Artullus.

John had an arm over Elleria's shoulder and was leaning heavily on her. 'Left,' he said weakly.

'Why left?' asked Artullus.

'Because they know I've lost the yellow zone connection and they'll assume that I'm going to try and reconnect to another distribution crystal. They'll be waiting for us,' replied John.

Since Frank had been shot John had been having a long conversation with The Librarian. They'd been quantifying the problems and weighing up the options. With Elleria here to stabilise John they could return to Earth without him destroying the solar system. But then what? How long would they last without Amantarra? Amantarra and Scott both needed rescuing and if they left Valheel to go to Earth, they wouldn't be able to return. The solution therefore, must be found here in Valheel. The Librarian's voice had trailed off after John had lost his connection to the yellow zone.

'Left it is then,' said Harry. 'Jack, bring up the rear.'

With an arm around Artullus and Elleria's shoulders for support John looked down at his legs as they made their way down the tunnel. His legs just didn't feel right, he couldn't coordinate them; they were moving backwards and forwards but they weren't in synch with the floor. At least that's what it seemed like; the reality was that John was being dragged. John had stopped being concerned at how weak he was, he was past that now and had reached the point of not caring.

After about a hundred metres they reached a crossroads. Harry peeped cautiously round the corners of the junction before leading them through. They were in a patch of darkness between two of the widely spaced lights, about twenty metres beyond the junction when the threat came.

'Down,' whispered Jack loudly. John's legs crumpled beneath him as Artullus and Elleria dropped to the floor.

Jack got himself into position. Laid flat on his stomach he nestled the stock of the machine gun firmly into his shoulder and pivoted it slightly around the bipod. Five guards had appeared out of the opening to the stairs they had descended when they first entered the tunnel. Harry didn't think they'd been spotted because the guards seemed unsure of which direction to turn.

They held their breath in the darkness. If they moved they would be seen. Perhaps they would assume, as John had indicated, that the distribution crystal would be their target, and turn that way.

John felt remote, detached; as if he were watching the events unfold through binoculars. The Librarian was shouting something at him but he couldn't work out what he was saying, he just couldn't take it in.

Five more guards arrived. Now it was irrelevant what the guards assumed. They split up, four of the guards heading towards the distribution crystal and the other six heading straight towards them. They were halfway to the junction when Jack pulled the trigger.

Click!

John felt as though he'd been hit in the chest with a sledge hammer.

'Bollocks!' cursed Jack under his breath; ladies present and all that. He pulled the cocking lever back and tried again.

Click!

Again the blow to the chest, John struggled to catch his breath. The Librarian was shouting again. 'Tell him John, tell him,' John heard him say. Tell him what? John didn't understand. He felt so tired. Must focus! The tunnel seemed to recede further into the distance and then return. Focus... focus. With a massive effort of concentration John suddenly realised what The Librarian was trying to tell him.

'Don't pull the trigger again, the guns won't fire,' said John in a breathless whisper, 'I haven't got the energy. I'm down to the last of my reserves.'

Jack turned and looked at Harry. 'We're screwed,' he whispered.

30
CAT AND MOUSE

Amantarra was stood in a clear tube lit by white light from below. She counted fifty identical tubes arranged around the wall of a large circular chamber. She searched the chamber; if it wasn't here then she would be in trouble. The scan of her avatar was complete so she knew that the city would have the Primary Key and it wouldn't be long before the erasure procedure began.

The centre of the chamber was occupied by circular plinth which supported twenty spheres. The light shining up and reflecting off the inside of the tube made it difficult to see parts of the chamber and Amantarra had to press her face right up to the glass to get a clear view. Then she saw it. On the floor sticking out from behind the plinth was the leg of a prone figure. It wasn't moving. That had to be him.

Amantarra banged on the tube. 'Scott,' she shouted. There was no response. She tried banging again, this time with both fists. 'Scott!'

The foot twitched and then disappeared behind the plinth. Moments later Scott looked over the plinth at Amantarra and then immediately moved sideways to hide behind one of the spheres.

'This is no time to be shy Briggs. Get over here now,' she shouted.

Scott's faced reappeared looking puzzled. He stared at Amantarra for a few seconds and then stood and walked over to the tube.

'Who are you and how do you know my name? Actually scrub that. What are you and how do you know my name?' Scott stared at Amantarra taking in the strange features of her face. 'Come to think of it, I'm sure I've dreamt of you.'

Despite his initial reaction, Amantarra noted that Scott displayed absolutely no fear whatsoever.

'My name is Amantarra, but you have always known me as Frank.'

'Frank! I don't think so,' retorted Scott as he looked Amantarra up and down.

'Look Briggs, it's a long story and I don't have time to tell it. The city is still congratulating itself on regaining the Primary Key, but it's only a matter of time before they come across my records about you.'

'What?'

'I need to unlock your full potential before they realise how much of a threat you are.'

'You certainly talk like Frank, because I can't understand a single word you're saying,' replied Scott.

'Just listen to what I've got to say.' Scott opened his mouth to reply but Amantarra continued without waiting for his response. 'Amantarra sequence start… three... seven... four... one... one... five... nine... four...'

*

'What now?' Artullus whispered in the darkness. The five guards were almost at the junction twenty metres in front of them.

'Keep still, maybe they'll turn at the junction,' whispered Harry. He didn't actually think it likely; the best he could hope for would be that the guards split up. Perhaps they could over power two guards and take their weapons.

Elleria was laid on her right side looking at John with a concerned expression. She was clutching John's MG34 to her almost as if it was the only thing holding him here. John was laid flat on his back looking up at the roof of the tunnel watching the dark violet plasma dance in the pipe. He was trying to concentrate on something The Librarian was telling him but his mind kept wandering. As he watched the plasma, he thought, if there was as much energy in that pipe as there should be, then why isn't it glowing brighter than it is. Then The Librarian's voice, which was always in the background, would get louder and clearer, as if he were shouting from the window of a moving train, only to fade into the background again. John's mind would go back to the plasma;

maybe it was giving off energy in a different part of the spectrum from visible light. Yes, he thought, that must be it. It was taking more and more effort for John to remain focussed on the librarian's voice as it returned and faded. John was getting bits and pieces of what he was trying to say, but never the whole thing no matter how many times The Librarian repeated it. Then something clicked and all the fragmented part of the message fell into place.

With some effort he rolled onto his side to face Elleria. John smiled and placed his right arm around her in a sort of half embrace.

'Pack it in you two,' whispered Harry. 'This is not the time.'

'Wait here,' said John quietly.

'What?' Harry asked.

'Wait here for me. Don't let anyone wander off,' repeated John.

'Why, where are you going?'

John kissed Elleria on the lips and rolled onto his back dragging her and the machine gun on top of him.

'Oo,' said Elleria, followed by 'Oh,' when she realised that they were no longer in the tunnel. She blinked at the sudden brightness.

'You haven't got time for that,' said The Librarian.

'People keep saying that,' said Elleria as she rolled off John and placed the MG34 on the floor.

The Librarian looked at the weapon. 'Goodness,' he remarked.

'Hello again Librarian,' said Elleria.

John sat up and looked at Elleria curiously. 'You've met before?'

'Yes, it was The Librarian who sent me to you.'

'The one you met before was the original,' said The Librarian, 'I'm actually a copy; but my thoughts are synchronised with the original.'

'How do you feel?' Elleria asked John.

'Much better,' he said, 'I couldn't have supported four and a half avatars for much longer. It was draining me completely.'

Elleria looked puzzled, 'four and a half?'

'Jack draws half his power from the city,' said The Librarian.

'Help me up,' said John. Elleria stood and pulled John up off the floor and held onto him as he tested his legs. 'I had to use the last of my reserves to create the portal.'

Elleria looked round. 'Where are we?'

'We're in the library,' said John, looking up at the arched corridors that radiated out from each level of the vertical shaft.

Elleria took in the perspective effect down one of the arched corridors with the shelves seemingly meeting at a vanishing point and realised how long the corridor must be. Then she followed John's gaze up at the multiple levels. 'This place is huge,' she said.

'And this is, as you know, is The Librarian,' finished John.

The Librarian bowed his head slightly in acknowledgement. 'It's also John's core,' he said indicating the constantly changing shape in the centre of the chamber.

John felt stronger. He jumped up and down a couple of times to exercise his legs.

'So,' said Elleria, 'what now?'

'Let me summarise the situation,' said The Librarian; 'John has lost his connection to Valheel's energy supply and is now connected only to Earth. The Primary Key has been lost to the city. Amantarra and Scott have been captured. I have concealed the portal you used to come here by reducing its size, so that there is still a connection to the city but it won't be detected easily. What I think will be detected is Jack, when he becomes an avatar again. Once the city realises that he is drawing power it will be able to track him. The good news is that the Earth is safe now that you two are back together.'

'There is some good news then,' said John.

'Unfortunately, it's not good news that you can exploit. Returning to Earth would only result in its destruction at the hands of the council or the city if you prefer. I assume you've worked out that they are different aspects of the same thing?'

'Frank told me that the city had a multiple personality disorder,' said John.

'Yes, as far as I can work out there are six; the five councillors and the original being.'

'Oh,' said John, 'I've just thought of something. If I'm the same thing as the city, does that mean that I might develop multiple personalities?'

'Yes… hello,' said the librarian waving a clawed hand at John.

'Ah… I see what you mean.'

'Don't worry; we've been designed this way; whereas Valheel somehow evolved its personalities.'

'We need a plan,' said Elleria, 'because at the moment we are just running from one crisis to the next. Do you have any ideas?'

'I don't, but The Librarian has,' replied John.

'First things first,' said The Librarian. 'Elleria, connect John to the rest of Amantarra's nodes. That should give him enough energy to maintain all your avatars and sustain the fire power.'

Elleria placed a hand over her mouth in embarrassment. 'I should have thought of that! I'm so sorry John.' Elleria closed her eyes and the light level in the chamber rose and then slowly fell back again. John studied her face; in the changing light and with her eyes closed, he found her even more attractive.

'There, it's done,' she said as she opened her eyes again.

John leaned over and kissed her cheek. 'It's alright, this way is much better.'

'What way?'

'You'll see.'

'Next,' said The Librarian.

*

'Harry… Jack… Artullus… where are you?' Elleria whispered into the fog.

'Here, where you left us; I've learnt my lesson,' replied Jack, 'and there's no need to whisper, remember.'

'Sorry, I was just being over cautious,' said Elleria.

'What's happening then?' Harry asked.

'We've got a plan.'

'That'll be a nice change,' replied Harry.

'Not going to be much good if the guns don't work,' said Jack.

'The guns will work, The Librarian guarantees it.'

'Who guarantees it?' Jack asked.

'It doesn't matter. The important thing is that we need to get to the base of the centroid tower in about ten minutes.'

'Is John going to attempt to reconnect to a distribution crystal?' Artullus asked.

'In a manner of speaking,' she replied. 'Come on, we need to move quickly.'

Moving quickly through the fog was difficult, the problem being that the faster they moved the more they tended to drift through the tunnel walls. They'd been going for about five minutes when they passed the four guards that had set off towards the tower earlier.

'Stop,' said Jack, bringing them all to a halt. 'Why don't we each occupy a guard? That way we'll be able to see what we're doing.'

'No, we need to get to the tower base ahead of them. They'll find us soon enough,' said Elleria. 'Now quickly, let's move.' And they were off again leaving the shadowy guards behind them.

A few minutes later they came to a low wall across the tunnel. The glass pipe continued over the wall and on into the darkness beyond. There was a flight of steps on the right, without hesitation Elleria started to climb with the others close behind. The top of the steps came out in the short corridor that ran from the plaza entrance to the centroid tower and the distribution chamber. Elleria turned right and ran through the closed doors and into the distribution chamber.

'Gentlemen, when John moves back into these dimensions and we rematerialize, our task is to defend this chamber,' said Elleria.

'They'll never find us,' said Harry. 'We're nowhere near where we were before.'

'Yes they will, because now they can track Jack,' Elleria answered.

'Great,' said Jack, 'just what I need; a target painted on me.'

'Harry,' said Elleria, 'they'll be coming through that door. Get everyone positioned.'

*

The Librarian opened his clawed hand to reveal a ring set with a single large red stone. John took it and held it up to the light.

'It's not really my style,' he said. The Librarian gave him a curious look. 'I mean it's more of a ladies ring, like the sort my mother would wear.'

'It's a device designed by Artullus to disrupt the protective field around the Node Zero allowing you to access it directly,' said The Librarian. 'Why would your mother wear it?'

'Because it's jewellery,' answered John.

'Jewellery… jewellery;' The Librarian stroked his chin as he looked it up. 'Ah yes, yes, I see what you mean. You must forgive me, but the Ja'liem don't even wear clothes; so when I copied Artullus' design I had no idea that it might be gender related.'

'It's alright; nobody is going to see me wearing it.'

'Try not to allow the jewel to come into prolonged contact with your skin because any more than a few seconds will disrupt your protective field.'

'I have a protective field?' said John. 'You learn something new every day.' Being careful to avoid touching the jewel, John slid the ring onto the middle finger of his right hand.

'Are you ready?' asked The Librarian.

'Yes,' replied John. 'Are you ready? You're the one who's going to have to control this when I've made the connection.'

'Yes, it's just a matter of the sample rate and frequency. If we get it right we should be able to tap around twenty percent of Valheel's power without affecting any of the Zones. Once we've got that we can mount a direct challenge by increasing the amount of power that we draw until we have control. All you have to do is bring the ring into contact with Node Zero.'

'Librarian...' said John, 'I do have one question.'

'What is it?'

'I thought you said that you couldn't interpret or apply this knowledge to any problems; and yet you've come up with this plan.'

'I didn't say I couldn't learn from you.'

'Fair enough,' said John.

In the air in front of them both appeared a semi-transparent model of Valheel. It was accurate in every detail, with the red, green, blue and yellow zones and their associated centroid towers clearly visible. The sphere expanded enveloping them until they were stood next to a magnified Node Zero chamber. The image rotated so that the top of the blue centroid tower was at the bottom of the Node chamber. The Librarian indicated the framework around the top of the tower.

'You'll have to climb this to reach the Node,' said The Librarian.

John noted the blackness of the Node and the beam of energy passing through the framework on its way down the tower to where his friends should be.

'I'm still not entirely happy about using the others as bait,' he said.

'They've got machine guns,' said The Librarian. John didn't look all that convinced. 'They'll be fine,' he added. 'And you do agree that we need to distract the guards away from you?'

'Yes, but... well, it's the principle of the thing. Still, I suppose Jack will be in his element.'

'Yes, I think he will be.' The Librarian paused for a moment to make sure that John was happy and then indicated a position on the model. 'Open a portal here at the top of the blue stairs right next to the framework. As soon as you are through I'll close the portal. Remember you'll need to remain in Valheel until I tell you that I've established the power tap.'

'How long will it take?'

'Not long, give me five minutes at least though. And whatever happens, don't get shot. That will send you straight back to Earth without Elleria.'

'Let's get this over with,' said John, he was getting the same feeling he got in the dentists waiting room.

The model of Valheel vanished. John closed his eyes and thought about opening the portal at the position The Librarian had indicated. He'd never done it before and was expecting to fail, but when he opened his eyes, he found he'd already done it. With a final nod to The Librarian John stepped through the black doorway.

*

The fog transformed into the interior of the centroid tower base. Harry did a quick assessment of the structure and indicated the double doors they had come through. 'Is that the only entrance?'

'Yes,' replied Artullus. 'There is a short corridor that runs to the outside doors.'

'Better have this set of doors open so we can see this corridor. That way they can't rush us,' said Harry.

'Won't that mean they will see us earlier,' said Elleria.

'Yes, but it also means that the corridor will become a killing zone. Artullus nodded and looked thoughtful. The concept of a killing zone fascinated him.

Elleria ran and opened the doors, locking them back in position. As she returned Harry started to position everyone.

'Jack and I will take the central positions behind this plinth on either side of this energy beam. We are going to take out the bulk of them in the corridor. Elleria, you're down here behind this seat.' Harry indicated the bench on the left side of the plinth. 'Cover the left side of the door only, it's your job to stop them getting in round the side. Artullus, you do the same job on the other side of the plinth covering the right side of the door only. Does everyone know what they are doing?'

Everyone nodded.

'Right,' said Harry, 'everyone into position.'

*

As soon as John entered the Node Zero chamber he could feel the presence of the Node pushing him away, or was he trying to push it away, he couldn't quite decide. What he knew for certain was that he did not like being this close to Valheel's Node Zero and he suspected that the feeling was mutual. The black Node was directly above him, but then no matter where you stood in the chamber, it was always directly above you.

John turned to face the arched metal that formed a framework over the top of the centroid tower. The energy beam passing through the ring at the top made the air sing. John stared at it, hypnotised by its raw power until the sound of gunfire from the bottom of the tower reminded him why he was here. He started to climb. The four MG34's sounded impressive and he was glad he wasn't on the receiving end of them.

At about the six metre mark, the framework bent over and sloped up towards the ring through which the energy beam passed on its way down to the base of the tower. John looked down and wished that he hadn't. The staircase spiralled round the energy beam down the inside wall of the tower until it couldn't be seen any more. He stopped climbing. Going vertically up was one thing, but climbing along a slope over nothing was something quite different.

'Oh, bloody hell,' he said to himself.

Tearing his gaze away from the drop he forced himself to look up towards where the framework met the Node. There was still nearly the height of a house to go and the fear gripped him again drawing his gaze down. John's head spun making it feel like the framework had moved and he almost lost his grip. Closing his eyes he felt the metal in his hands and reassured himself that it was still there. Sliding one hand along the frame he could hear the ring scraping over the metal. He took a deep breath, held it and then slowly released it. Don't think of it as climbing away from the ground; he told himself; think of it as climbing out of a hole and up to the ground. He raised his head again and pointed it in the direction of the ring at the top of the frame. Then he risked opening his eyes again. Focus on the top of the frame, that's the target, it's the only thing you can see. Now climb.

The first step was the hardest, the second less so, after three and four he contemplated the fifth with a reasonable amount of confidence despite the fact that his target didn't seem any closer.

'Is that your mum's ring you're wearing Godbert,' said a voice behind and below him.

John froze.

'Actually no,' continued the voice, 'I don't think it is because I've seen it before. Why are you wearing Amantarra's ring? It doesn't suit you.'

The mocking tone was pure Burnston; even the sound of the voice was the same and John struggled to comprehend why he would be here in Valheel. He sighed; to look to see who it was he would have to take his eyes off his target and look down and he didn't want to.

'Is that you Burnston?' John asked as he lowered his head to look down and behind him. It wasn't Burnston. From the upside down view John was getting, the creature looked very similar to the councillors he'd encountered. It was stood about five paces back from the top of the stairs. John studied it for a moment. 'Who are you?'

'I'm Tyrus, although Burnston knew me as Martin Macadam.'

'Martin… Martin…' the name sounded familiar, 'Ah yes, Burnston's invisible friend?'

'Yes, that was fun influencing your large friend like that. The looks he got when he was talking to me were most entertaining,' said Tyrus with a look on his face that smacked of vindictiveness rather than amusement.

John took an instant dislike to the creature, even though there was no way he could ever describe Burnston as a friend. 'Was there something I could do for you? Only I'm quite busy at the moment,' said John.

'Yes… tut, tut, where are my manners,' said Tyrus. 'I'm curious to know why you are in the same position Amantarra was in when I saw her wearing that ring. If I recall correctly, that ring caused a lot of problems the last time it was used on the node.' Tyrus took a step to his left and raised his arms above his head. A ball of blue white energy formed between his hands. 'I would ask you to get down, but I know that you are likely to be as stubborn as Amantarra in this matter, so I've decided not to.'

Tyrus brought his arms forward and hurled the ball at the framework. It struck the support that John was on about halfway up evaporating a section of it instantly. John's relief that the fireball had not headed his way was short lived when the frame started to swing in towards the energy beam coming from the Node. John saw a brief flash of green construction lines as the lower part of the frame touched the energy stream and dissolved into it. There was only one thing he could do. John let go of the frame as it swung him towards destruction.

31

TROJAN

'... eight... four... two... seven... seven... Amantarra sequence end.' Amantarra finished the activation sequence through the glass of the tube. As the last number was spoken Scott went completely still. His eyes were staring straight ahead, his pupils dilated and focusing on nothing; it was as if he'd been switched off. Amantarra waited, patiently watching his expressionless face through the glass.

It was a full fifteen seconds before Scott blinked and looked silently up at Amantarra, his face still bearing no expression.

'Identify,' said Amantarra.

'Scott Briggs, Human / Enforcer Hybrid model 002, linked to the Node John Godbert.'

'Who do you accept commands from?'

'I accept commands from only the following; Amantarra, Artullus, John Godbert and Elleria.'

'List your power sources.'

'John Godbert; and I currently have a connection to Valheel which is providing more power.'

'Excellent,' said Amantarra. 'Now release me from this tube.'

Scott placed a hand on the glass. A pinpoint of brilliant light appeared on the palm of his hand and the glass was replaced by a grid of green lines.

Amantarra stepped through the grid and down from the plinth. Scott removed his hand and the glass reappeared.

'Thank you,' she said. Scott remained silent, his expression still blank. Amantarra looked at him as he stood waiting for her next command. 'And I think we had better have Scott's personality switched back on, would you reactivate it please.'

Scott blinked... and blinked again.

'Are you back?' Amantarra asked.

'Yes,' said Scott; losing the blank expression, his face taking on a look that was more familiar to Amantarra. 'What a revelation this is, I had no idea any of this was going on.'

'Yes, sorry about that, but the fewer people that knew the better,' apologised Amantarra.

'Including me?'

'Especially you, Scott Briggs.'

'So, what's the plan? I assume there is one.'

'There have been several,' said Amantarra. 'I have a good idea of what we should do, but experience has taught me that I shouldn't refer to it as a plan. The first thing we need to do is find a way out of this chamber.'

'There's a hatch over there, under that spikey thing sticking out of the wall,' said Scott pointing to the gap between the tubes.

'Good, let's take a look.'

On the other side of the hatch was a long round corridor with glowing green walls. There was a single glass pipe running down the centre which lit up occasionally as a pulse travelled down towards them and then back up. Amantarra stepped through the small hatch and started to float, there was no gravity here, there didn't need to be. They both used their hands to pull themselves along the connecting tube until they entered a large cube structure. Link tubes and glass pipes entered from each of the six surfaces; with the pipes terminating in a sphere in the centre of the chamber. Pulses of light were traveling up and down the pipes every few seconds.

'Which way do we go?' Scott asked.

Amantarra watched the pulses of light for a few seconds.

'That way,' she declared, indicating the hatch on the left.

'Why?'

'Because if you watch, all the pulses come down that pipe and then go back up it, regardless of which direction they take when they arrive.'

Scott watched the pulses. 'I agree,' he said.

*

Tyrus waved as John fell past him. He watched John fall down the tower with degrees of both satisfaction and disappointment. He had thought that John would have put up more of a fight, but this was so easy... too easy. What an idiot John was to have put himself in that situation. There was no way his avatar could survive a fall from that height. Thirteen point nine, two, four seconds, that's how long it would take before the impact destroyed John's avatar and removed his troublesome comrades from Valheel permanently. Tyrus counted off the seconds as he started to make his way down the tower.

'Three, two, one and dead,' said Tyrus out loud. He waited for the machine guns to stop firing. Any moment now, he thought. Tyrus stopped on the stairs to listen. The sounds of battle continued to rise up from the chamber far below. There was no way Godbert could have survived that fall, he thought; but he must have. Tyrus started to run down the stairs. He'd been running for seven minutes when the sounds of battle stopped. Tyrus slowed to a walk. John's protective shield had obviously prevented his avatar from expiring immediately; he must have been in agony. Tyrus smiled and relished the thought of the amount of pain John must have been in.

*

John stiffened as he fell. Who was it that said "the fear of something is worse than the thing itself"? Well they were wrong about falling. John saw last of the frame he'd been clinging to vanish into the energy beam with a flash of green. It was strange, but he relaxed a bit after he saw that. Perhaps it was the thought of a fate averted, he didn't know, but at least he started to think about how he was going to get out of this.

How high was the tower? How long would it take him to fall down it? The Librarian dutifully informed John that it would take less than fourteen seconds to fall the nine hundred and fifty metres; which while interesting, was of no help whatsoever.

The turns on the spiral staircase flashed past him at an ever increasing rate. John was too far away from the edge of the staircase to make a grab for one of the turns, and he noticed, he was getting further away from them. He could sense the energy beam close behind him. Turning his head he could feel it burning his cheek. It was less than an arm's length away and it was getting closer. He suddenly realised that he was being pulled towards it.

'Ten seconds,' said The Librarian helpfully.

Perhaps it was pure instinct, John couldn't say, but he made a fist and pushed against the beam. For a few seconds it was working and although the beam felt hot, John managed to counter its pull. Then his fist slipped passed the protective field guarding the beam and into the energy itself. A searing pain shot up his arm and he was thrown explosively towards the wall of the tower. John's own protective shield had repelled the beam. Spinning, John hit the wall with some force, slid round and down it until he struck the steps and started to tumble down them. Each contact with the wall and the steps slowed him down a bit more, but it seemed to take forever.

When John eventually came to rest, he was laid on his stomach with his head pointing down the stairs. He ached all over and his right arm was numb from the shoulder down. He propped himself up with his good arm and swung round so that his legs were pointing down the stairs. His right hand was blackened, burnt and twisted beyond recognition. The ring had not survived, the jewel was fractured, its deep red colour faded. John watched the smoke curl slowly off his burnt hand and he tried to gather his thoughts.

For a while all he could think of was, "this really hurts"; but then the sounds of battle from below interrupted his reverie. It sounded a lot closer and John realised that he must have fallen a long way. His friends; they were in danger now that the plan had failed. He must get to them and bring them to the safety of his own system dimensions. Then they could plan the next move. Plan, thought John, that's a laugh, nothing we've planned since we got here has gone right. No doubt Tyrus would be on his way down the stairs to gloat over John's demise at the bottom of the tower. Why was time always against him? Steadying himself with his left hand against the tower wall John stood and started to make his way unsteadily down towards the machine gun fire.

John stood looking over the edge of the stairs. He was one revolution back from the bottom. Jack and Harry were firing continuously to John's left. The flash from the muzzles lit their faces and cast flickering shadows behind them. Further away he could see Artullus behind one of the benches. He assumed that Elleria was below him on the other side of the plinth. He could certainly hear four machine guns which brought some comfort. Strange, thought John, that the sound of machine guns could be considered comforting.

The air was full of random energy pulses from the guards. The pulses were striking the lower part of the staircase where it dropped below the ceiling, the energy beam itself and, in fact, almost everywhere over the heads of their targets. They'd abandoned all idea of not firing near the beam which was absorbing the pulses without a problem. The guards seemed to have no concept of the idea of aiming, but at least it meant that his friends were relatively safe. Unfortunately it also presented John with another problem; how was he going to get down to the bottom without being hit? He decided to put the energy beam between him and the guards and then jump. That would leave him exposed for a short distance on the stairs until he got behind the beam.

John moved back to the wall and made his way round to the point where the stairs became exposed. He rocked backwards and forwards a couple of times and then ran for it. They spotted him almost immediately and a volley of shots followed him closely as he ran; so much for them not having any aiming skills. A couple of shots whizzed past in front of him and John dived onto the steps and slid the rest of the way on his stomach.

Now he was in the shadow of the energy beam John crawled to the edge of the stairs and looked over. It was much higher than he'd hoped. It was therefore going to hurt more than he'd hoped, but this avatar was finished anyway he didn't have the time or energy to repair it. With the shots continuing to rain either side of him, he pushed himself up and squatted on the edge. He took a deep breath and jumped. The floor of the chamber rushed up to meet him.

Landing heavily, he felt his legs buckle beneath him. He'd been right about the pain, but not about the intensity. John opened a portal to his system dimensions behind him. He could see that the guards were again firing over a wall of their fallen.

'Harry,' he shouted, 'get everyone out of here.'

Harry turned and saw John sitting on the floor in front of a black doorway with his legs twisted at odd angles in front of him and his right arm blackened and smoking. If the sight alarmed him, he didn't show it.

'Artullus, Elleria,' he shouted, 'through the door now.'

Elleria was the first to move as Harry and Jack laid down suppressing fire and she was already squatting at John's side when Artullus was hit. There was nothing they could do about it. Elleria moved behind John and placing a hand under each arm tried to move John towards the portal, but she was struggling.

'Jack,' shouted Harry, 'now!'

Together they both stood and continuing to fire, walked backwards towards the portal. Without pausing they each grabbed John as they passed and dragged him through the door, bowling Elleria over backwards in the process. As soon as they were through, John closed the portal.

*

It was twenty minutes before Tyrus reached the bottom of the tower. He was still smirking. John must have lingered nearly a full ten minutes before his avatar terminated itself. The elation that he felt was amazing; Tyrus had never experienced anything like it. This loathing of Godbert, and just about everyone else, must have been something that he had inherited from Burnston. What joy, he thought. Tyrus wondered what Burnston had inherited from him.

At the bottom of the stairs Tyrus found a group of six guards standing at the back of the distribution crystal. The rest of the chamber bore no signs of the battle. The fallen guards had vanished back into the system and any damage done to the structure had been repaired.

'Report,' said Tyrus to one of the guards.

'Sir, we only managed to get one of them.'

The expression on Tyrus' face was one of glee; 'the one that fell? Did he linger long?'

'One appeared on the stairs and he dropped down behind the feed beam. The others were observed dragging him through a portal.'

'They escaped?' Tyrus did not look pleased.

'Yes. The remains of the portal are here.' The guard, who was completely indifferent to Tyrus' emotional state, indicated the faintest of outlines where the portal had been.

Tyrus passed his hand through part of the outline. Where his hand had been the outline wavered and evaporated. Tyrus needed to know where this led, but he would need help. Closing his eyes he called the council and moments later they appeared in front of him. If the council had granted his request to be able to travel around Valheel in the same manner, he would have been able to finish John off before he had escaped. One day, Tyrus promised himself, he would not have to kowtow to any entity. But for the moment, Tyrus held his tongue.

'The human Node escaped through this doorway,' he said pointing to the faint outline.

The Yellow Councillor placed a hand close to the distortion which reacted to his proximity by bowing out towards his hand.

'I recognise the signature,' he said. 'It is the same as the energy tap that was on my distribution crystal.'

'Can you trace its destination?' asked Consulus.

'Yes,' replied the Yellow Councillor.

*

Scott and Amantarra looked down from the hatch that connected the last link tube to the tower at the centre of Valheel's system. Immediately above them was the spire that terminated the glass tube in the tunnel they were in. There was a constant stream of plasma linking the spire to a sphere above them; this in turn was linked to a large stretched sphere by another plasma link.

'That's where we need to be,' said Amantarra, indicating the stretched sphere. 'That chamber seems to be the centre of everything.' The perfect place for a Trojan gift like Scott; if only they could get into it. From this distance it was difficult to tell, but there were features on the top of the chamber that could be hatches.

'It's a long way down,' said Scott. 'Do you think that there's any gravity on the other side of this hatch?'

'There's only one way to find out.' Amantarra pushed herself through the hatch and into the inside of the tower. Holding onto the bottom of the hatch the rest of her body floated freely. 'No,' she said. Amantarra brought her legs round and braced them on the wall of the tower.

Scott joined her, holding onto the hatch with one hand and bracing his legs like Amantarra.

'Aim for the sphere,' said Amantarra grabbing Scott's free arm; 'on three; one... two... three.' They both pushed with their legs launching themselves into the vast void of the tower.

'Supposing we miss,' said Scott.

'We're bound to hit something at some point; so we'll just turn around and have another go. Keep hold of my arm.'

At around the halfway mark it was obvious that their aim was good, and they would land on top of the curved surface. The shapes on top of the chamber resolved themselves into the hatches that Amantarra had hoped they would be.

'So far, so good,' said Scott as they floated slowly towards their target.

As they got nearer the chamber the twisting plasma got closer. It was surprisingly broad and it gyrated around making it seem even larger.

'What happens if we touch that?' Scott asked.

'I don't know. I suspect that it's all data and that there isn't much energy in it, but I still wouldn't want to get too close.'

They weren't far from the chamber now, but instead of concentrating on where they would land, they were constantly distracted by the plasma. Once or twice it had twisted round and almost caught them. Scott looked down and noticed that the path they were on would take them close enough to be enveloped by the gyrating plasma. He pointed.

'What do we do?' Scott asked. 'Do we just take our chances?'

'Trust me,' she replied. Amantarra gently pushed Scott away releasing her grip on his arm as she did so.

Amantarra's timing was impeccable. The pair of them separated, avoided the plasma and then landed close enough to a hatch to allow each of them to grab hold.

Hanging onto the hatch with one hand, Scott leaned to the side and shouted round the plasma link. 'What now!'

'Let's get you inside and see what sort of damage you can do,' replied Amantarra.

*

Elleria was laid flat on her back, legs splayed with John's head resting on one of her thighs. She propped herself up on her elbows looking indignant.

'Sorry missy; but we…' started Jack. He stopped because he'd noticed his hands; they were old and liver spotted again. He looked at Harry who wore an expression that indicated that his haemorrhoids were back. Jack sighed. 'Well at least it was good while it lasted.'

'You got that right,' said Harry noticing where John had come to rest and that his avatar was now renewed. 'Looks like you got the best of this deal young Mister Godbert.'

John stood and tested his new legs. 'Don't worry Harry…' John paused; the face he was looking at wasn't the one he'd got used to calling Harry. 'Mr Fleming,' he corrected. 'I'm sure Jack will sort you both out again.'

Harry was looking round at the arched corridors that circled the tower. 'Call me Harry,' he said in a distracted manner. 'Where are we?'

'You're safe in John's system dimensions,' said The Librarian who appeared behind them from nowhere.

Harry and Jack wheeled round and pointed their weapons at the creature not sure whether to fire or not. Jack thought the thing looked like a cross between a bear and a garden gnome, whereas Harry noted the large teeth and the sharp black claws and didn't care what it looked like.

'Don't shoot The Librarian!' exclaimed Elleria.

Harry and Jack looked at each other. John and Elleria didn't see The Librarian as unusual in any way; so they relaxed and lowered their weapons.

'John,' said Jack, 'is that your mum's ring?'

'Don't you start,' replied John, noticing for the first time that the ring had repaired itself at the same time as his body. 'It's a device designed by Artullus to disrupt the protective field around the Node Zero.'

'Only it looks as though it might be worth a bit, that's all,' said Jack.

Harry shook his head, 'You can take the man out of the pawnbrokers, but you can't take the pawnbrokers out of the man.'

'Old habits,' said Jack.

'It would look better on me,' said Elleria. John took the ring off so she could examine it closely. She placed on her finger and held it up for everyone to admire.

'Congratulations on your engagement, I hope you'll both be very happy,' said Harry.

Elleria cocked her head on one side, gave him a disapproving look and then returned the ring. John smiled at her and placed it in his pocket.

'On a serious note,' said Harry, 'what went wrong?'

'Tyrus was waiting for me.'

'Damn!' said Jack.

'I was over the tower when he destroyed the framework I was on and I fell… a long way,' said John, remembering and swallowing hard.

'Eight hundred and seventy-three metres,' said The Librarian helpfully.

'Then I touched the energy beam and it threw me onto the stairs; otherwise… well I don't know; jumping that last little bit hurt enough.'

'Would it have worked? If Tyrus hadn't been there I mean,' asked Elleria.

'I think so,' replied John.

Harry scratched his head. 'Do we try again?'

John remembered the climb along the framework and the view down the tower, he thought about his fear of falling, and the fall, which was worse than the fear of the fall, and then he remembered his collision with the stairs after touching the energy beam. All finished off by his final jump into the distribution chamber; but above all, he remembered the pain. 'No,' he said.

'So,' said Harry, 'what now?'

The others were looking at John. 'I don't know, the last plan was The Librarian's idea,' he said turning to look at The Librarian. 'Got any more ideas?'

The Librarian scratched his belly. Harry looked at The Librarian and saw a simple animal. Why were they listening to a tree dwelling bear, surely this creature couldn't be the cleverest out of all of them.

'The original plan was to reunite John and Elleria so that she could stabilise John. This, despite everything, actually worked,' said The Librarian. 'When Frank was shot, John lost his connection to the Yellow zone and we were starved of energy. Without energy you cannot all even enter Valheel, let alone fight there. Elleria has now fixed that by connecting John to more Nodes, but it still isn't enough to compete with Valheel head on. Our attempt to steal energy from Valheel has failed.'

The Librarian scratched the underside of his muzzle with a single claw. Harry, who had been completely drawn in by the summary suddenly went back to thinking tree bear again.

'I wish you would stop scratching yourself,' said Harry. 'Every time you do I get the thought "tree bear", but when you talk I think "astute Librarian". It's very distracting.'

'Yes, that's what it's supposed to do. Clever isn't it,' said Elleria. Harry shook his head.

'Perhaps the attempt on Node Zero was a bit obvious,' continued The Librarian. 'So what we need now is something the city can't predict.'

They were all looking at him expectantly, but it was Jack who asked the question; 'what?'

'I don't know. Rescuing Amantarra, Scott and Artullus would be desirable, but it's very predictable.' The Librarian cocked his head on one side as if listening. 'There is something we might turn to our advantage.'

'What's that?' asked Harry.

'We have a visitor,' replied The Librarian.

*

Tyrus looked at his hands, they were human. 'Wherever this place is, I'm here in the form of Martin Macadam; even wearing the school uniform,' he reported. 'I never physically appeared in this form on Earth; this was what Burnston, and only Burnston saw. I must therefore be drawing power from Godbert, hence the change of avatar. I would speculate that I am in the system dimensions of the Godbert Node Zero.'

Tyrus was stood in an arched corridor lined with books. The lines of the shelves merged towards a vanishing point which was off to the left and hidden, indicating that the corridor was curved. The sheer number of books was staggering. Tyrus ran his finger along some of the books and pulled one out at random. There was no title written along the spine just a series of numbers; "004-5-999-0-012-04-07" which he assumed was some sort of index. Opening the book revealed it to be about the manufacture of primitive three dimensional photo-electronic components, known as the first hyper intelligences, the sentient forerunners of Valheel.

'This must be the technical data that Amantarra stole from the Great Library of Valheel.' The book was of no interest to Tyrus and he discarded it, letting it fall to the floor.

'We concur,' said the voice of Consulus in his head. 'Despite its alien format, this is the stolen information. As there is no obvious threat here, we will leave the portal open so that you can relay any useful information back to us.'

Turning, Tyrus looked past the portal and along the corridor in the opposite direction. As he expected, the vanishing point was hidden to the right. Tyrus about faced and started to walk in his original direction. The scene never changed, the books and shelves were identical except for the reference numbers on the spines. Occasionally he passed under what looked like a supporting arch on two piers which protruded out slightly from the line of shelves. He guessed their purpose was for separating sections of shelves rather than structural. He'd passed under ten arches when he noticed there was something different ahead. Looking up at the ceiling he could see two arches close together, with a third arch between them to the left. It was a junction with another corridor.

Tyrus peered left round the corner. Another long corridor, but this time the vanishing point was dead centre. This corridor was straight, not curved and there were junctions every few metres. If the corridor I'm on is circular, mused Tyrus, then this one must lead straight to the centre of this place and each one of those junctions must be another circular corridor; all full of books no doubt. This method of storage seems very inefficient.

In the wall to his right, facing down the straight corridor was a set of shelves. Yellow books lined these shelves, extending down from the ceiling to about waist height. With the exception of one book, each label along their spines started with the word "Index" followed by a number. The last shelf extended out from the wall and was obviously intended to be used to rest books on when referencing the index. One book was lit by an inner light that slowly grew in intensity, the colour changing to a more orange yellow, and then fading back to yellow again. It was titled "Recently accessed". Tyrus pulled the book out, placed it on the extended shelf and started to read.

The entries in the book were arranged latest first and at the top was a paragraph titled "Field Disruption Technology", it was about the ring he'd seen John wearing. To the right of the paragraph was a picture of a book and a reference. Tyrus touched the picture and the knowledge from it instantly entered his mind. He skimmed over the information and immediately passed it back through the portal to the waiting councillors. The next paragraph was titled "Saranythia". Accessing the book revealed it to be about Amantarra's missing sister. Tyrus read with growing concern that she had also set out to create a living Node. So the threat to us does not end with the destruction of Godbert. Tyrus quickly passed it back through the portal and moved onto the next entry.

*

'Isn't that our school uniform?' whispered Harry.

They were watching an image of Tyrus as he made his way along the book lined corridor towards the junction.

'Yes,' answered John.

'Who is he? I don't recognise him.'

'I think the only person that would recognise him is Burnston,' said John. 'I'm guessing here, but I would say that we are looking at Martin, Burnston's imaginary friend.'

Harry gave John a curious look. 'Imaginary friend; Burnston's a bit old isn't he? And he doesn't strike me as the sort of person who would ever have had an imaginary friend; even as a child. Mind you, he doesn't strike me as the sort of person who would have had a childhood.'

'That's what we said when Scott mentioned it. His real name is Tyrus and I suspect that he's been influencing Burnston in this form for some time,' said John.

'Explains the uniforms,' commented Harry.

'And this insurance scheme he's got going,' said John.

'Protection racket,' corrected Elleria.

'I don't know anything about this,' said Harry.

'No, well you wouldn't would you, being as how you don't need any protection from him. That's why we were on the stage,' said John. 'It was part of Scott's plan to win the money back with marked cards.'

'Good idea,' said Jack. 'The boy's got promise. You should tell him to come and see me when this is all over.' Jack thought for a second. 'No, he can't, can he, because I'm dead. What a nuisance.'

'And you say Briggs thought of this?' Harry couldn't believe it.

'Apparently,' replied John.

'Interesting that this system has given Tyrus a human avatar,' said The Librarian, refocusing their attention on the matter in hand; 'even though he never physically took human form on Earth.'

'What are we going to do about him,' said Elleria. 'Having Tyrus here can't be a good thing.'

'Me and Harry could sort him out for you,' said Jack.

'No,' said The Librarian flatly. 'The last thing we need is a fire fight here. Besides, I've had a better idea.'

Tyrus was at the index now. They watched as he pulled a book from the shelf and started to read.

'What's he reading?' asked John.

'Let's just say that by way of a distraction I've given him something he can't possibly resist; which should keep both him and the council occupied while we spring a little surprise.'

'What exactly is it that you've done?' asked Elleria.

*

Scott was the first to open the hatch.

'There'll be gravity inside the chamber,' warned Amantarra too late.

The drop wasn't that great, but Scott had got used to having no gravity and as soon as he swung his legs inside the chamber it grabbed him and pulled him inside. He attempted to hang onto the side of the hatch but the sudden force was too much and he fell. Halfway down, Scott struck the curved surface of a domed force field that had been thrown up around the core. Blue and white ripples flashed across the surface of the field as Scott slid ungracefully down it to the floor of the chamber.

'Bloody hell, that really hurt,' complained Scott, his face turning bright red with anger.

'Another human,' said Consulus. All five councillors were looking directly at Scott from inside the force field.

The field flashed again as Amantarra made a slightly more graceful entrance sliding down on her feet to a point where she could jump.

'Amantarra,' said Consulus, 'how pleasant it is to see you again. And we are so pleased that you are well. We were most concerned about you.'

'Really,' replied Amantarra sarcastically.

'But what are you doing here? Asked the Blue Councillor, 'You weren't thinking of attempting to connect to the core, by any chance?' Amantarra made no comment.

'You're wasting your time. There's no way you or your little pet can penetrate the protection around the core. We extended it to accommodate ourselves after the last human visitor,' said Consulus with some venom.

'John caused you a bit of difficulty, did he? Let's try a little experiment,' she said, 'your force field against a human-enforcer, hybrid. Mister Briggs, if you please.'

Scott held his arms above his head. A small white ball of energy formed between his opened palms. The light from the ball grew in intensity until it was as bright as a star. He brought his arms forward and projected the star towards the councillors. The star stopped just above the surface of the force field. A high pitched ringing sound filled the chamber as the star began to spin. The surface of the force field flashed with greens and blues as lines of force radiated outward from the star. Within moments the field started to buckle, forming a dish shape which took on a yellowish tint. The concentration on Scott's face was intense as the star started to move slowly into the field elongating the dish into a milky white tube that reduced the intensity of the light. Then with a bright flash the force field vanished and the star jumped forward only to be stopped by a second shield. As before ripples began to form on the surface of this unexpected barrier but the star had lost a lot of its intensity. Then the first shield reinstated itself and the star stuttered and vanished. Scott's legs buckled and he sat on the floor exhausted.

'I did try to tell you,' said Consulus. 'It's over Amantarra, we know about the technology you have used to penetrate our shields in the past and as you can see we can now counter it. We also know about your sister Saranythia, and soon we will destroy her little experiment.'

Six Guardians appeared on perimeter of the chamber to the left of Scott. The first shots missed him by fractions galvanising him into action. Scott rolled. In a single movement he sat up and swept his arm in a horizontal arc. A thin sliver of energy scythed through the air from his fingertips cutting the Guardians in half before they could fire again. Each inactive guardian fell to the floor in two pieces, their legs buckling under them as they fell.

More shots came from behind.

'Lie flat on the floor!' he shouted to Amantarra.

Spinning round onto his knees he dispatched three more with single pulses. More guards were being created. Now that Amantarra had taken cover, Scott scythed both arms through the air covering three hundred and sixty degrees. Without pausing he threw several balls of red energy up over the top of the forming guards. The balls exploded on contact with the ceiling showering the guards with thousands of sparks. The sparks didn't do much damage, but they did disorientate the guards long enough for Scott to take them out with another volley of single shots.

Amantarra watched the display with a mixed feeling of pride and dismay. All this way, all this time, such a long journey. She was almost within touching distance of her goal. For all Scott's heroic efforts, all that was happening was that they were being distracted. The council, safe behind their force field, were deep in conversation and not even interested in the battle.

The rate at which the guards were appearing was increasing, and more and more frequently some of them were getting shots off. More red sparks and two more scythe shots. Palms facing around twenty guards, Scott pushed both arms forward sending a wave that rippled through the air throwing the guards against the wall of the chamber. Another twenty had appeared behind him before the corpses had fallen to the floor. Scott dropped low and scythed their legs off as shots flew over his head.

As yet more guards materialised; there was a sound like stone grating against stone and Amantarra turned to see a portal opening up to her right. John, she thought, and he's walking straight into a fire fight, but it was The Librarian who ambled through it, walking with his hands behind his back like he didn't have a care in the world. Scott, let off a volley of shots at The Librarian as he made his way passed Amantarra.

'Don't shoot the Librarian!' shouted Amantarra, as the energy pulses hit a force field around the creature. The shield shimmered around him like a glass egg sending the shots off in different directions.

The councillors stared at The Librarian with some amusement.

'This is the creature that Elleria encountered prior to her activating the human Node,' said Consulus. He turned to Amantarra. 'What part...;' Consulus looked irritated as he was interrupted by one of Scott's volleys as it struck the shield around the core. 'What part does he play in you master plan? Does he do tricks perhaps?'

'Yes gentlemen,' said The Librarian, 'I do tricks; observe.'

The Librarian walked effortlessly through the shield and over to the core. The councillors moved to intercept him but were repelled by The Librarian's own force field. He placed a hand into the core and it ceased its writhing motion for an instant and then continued as before.

'I call this trick the Trojan Horse,' continued The Librarian. 'Although in reality I couldn't have done it without your help. Did you find those files useful?'

'So the files contained a Trojan, very clever,' said Consulus, 'but surely you did not think that we would not have planned for this possibility.'

Consulus, the rest of the councillors and the Guardians vanished from the chamber.

'I was enjoying that,' said Scott. 'Where did they go?'

32
FULL CIRCLE

There were memories that he desperately needed to keep secret. The entity was powerful and the barriers Artullus initially offered were no more effective than wet paper. He got a sense of the intelligence behind the probe, it showed him how little of its potential it had used to effortlessly sweep aside his resistance. This was not the council, this was something else. The council members were simple minded aspects of this entity, merely part of the interface it offered. Dark and secretive, this was the original consciousness that Artullus had created. He recognised some of the nuances as he tried to resist, but it had evolved beyond anything he could have imagined. This wasn't just multiple personalities in conflict with each other as he and Amantarra had first thought; this was a single intellect. Artullus got a sense of recognition; it was if the entity was acknowledging him as its creator.

Perhaps if he could resist enough the force would crush him, destroying his mind, wiping the memories before they could be read. Artullus met the force head on, blocking access to his mind with everything he could muster. The force increased slowly but relentlessly. Artullus pushed back, he could feel the pressure growing. It was working, soon the burden would be too much and his mind would fracture, shattering into nothing.

His thoughts strayed to his daughters. Saranythia... I should find Saranythia; my daughter has been gone too long. Artullus could only picture her alive. Alive was one thing, but he needed to picture where she was. It saddened him to think of her as missing, not being able to tie her image to a place. Where had he last seen her? It must have been three hundred thousand years before he'd said the same goodbyes to Amantarra; they were both there, both his daughters, in The Great Library of Valheel. "I wish I could take all this with me," Saranythia had said, indicating the data crystals that lined the walls of the library. Perhaps if she had... well, hindsight was a wonderful thing and the same mistake was not made with Amantarra. And how had that turned out?

Artullus realised to his horror that the increasing force was simply a distraction. The entity had crept into his mind like a morning mist. It was already learning about Saranythia. He tried to fight back, but it was too late; his mind was no longer under his control.

Then suddenly the entity was gone.

Awareness of the upgrade chamber returned to him. The lights were on, at a low level but at least there was some light. The tube he was standing in was dark and inactive. He felt as though he'd just been abandoned. The connection to the system was still open, but the intelligence was gone.

Artullus knocked on the glass of the tube he was standing in. He wasn't going to get out that way. Focusing his mind on the connection he searched the other side of it. There was nothing but automated systems. He pushed his mind through the connection and into the system on the other side. In the upgrade chamber, the form of Artullus vanished from the tube. He was in the system.

Valheel spread out around him, his being occupying both sets of dimensions. He was occupying the city in the same way that he occupied an avatar. In an instant he could see all the changes that had been made since its creation. He could feel the power flowing between the dimensions. He checked the rules that created the reality. They were unchanged. If the entity could have changed those base rules it could have done anything, even accessed the protected minds of the Bruwnan. The weapons of the guardians were the failsafe, the only means by which the city could access that protected space. Artullus had argued against the weapons at the time, but had been overruled. For all the entity's power, even possessing the primary key did not allow it to change the base rules. Artullus breathed a sigh of relief.

*

Harry poked his head through the portal. 'Is it okay to come in yet? Only that Tyrus character has disappeared.' The Librarian nodded and Harry, Jack, John and Elleria joined them in the core chamber.

'What's just happened?' asked Amantarra.

'We've won; or at least we've won this battle,' replied The Librarian.

'Won… yes, I can see that, but how have we won?'

'Well you gave me the idea of a Trojan horse, so I attached one that allowed me access to Valheel's core to some files that I knew the council would not be able to resist,' explained The Librarian.

'I thought Scott was the Trojan. Do you mean to tell me that we were just wasting our time?'

Scott made his way over to The Librarian.

'Well I suppose you were a sort of distraction, but in essence, yes, you were wasting your time,' replied The Librarian. 'Could you stop that please,' he asked Scott who was now stroking his head.

'Sorry,' said Scott pulling his hand back.

John and The Librarian looked at each other. 'Do you sense it too?' asked John.

'Yes,' replied The Librarian.

Amantarra looked from one to the other. 'What?' she asked.

'I've found Artullus,' said John.

'Where is he?'

'Everywhere; he is Valheel.'

'Yes, and it's amazing,' said Artullus. His voice was heard by everyone. 'I should have done this in the first place.'

'So,' said John, 'what happens now?'

The core chamber vanished and they found themselves in the plaza at the base of the blue centroid tower.

'Can't have you cluttering up my system dimensions,' said Artullus.

'What of the old council?' Amantarra asked.

'All aspects of those personalities have been completely erased. They no longer exist in Valheel in any shape or form,' replied Artullus, 'and neither does the controlling entity.'

'Controlling entity?' asked John.

'Yes, the councillors were just puppets.'

'Librarian, that Trojan you used was pretty thorough,' congratulated Amantarra.

'No I'm afraid it wasn't me. All that the Trojan did was allow access to the system. It was an attempt to even up the odds.'

'He's right,' said Artullus, 'the entity left of its own accord and I can find no trace of where it went.'

Harry cleared his throat. 'What if it comes back?' he asked.

'It won't get back in here,' replied Artullus confidently, 'but I suspect that it doesn't intent to.'

The first Bruwnan appeared on the plaza. Then another and another as the word got around that the portals were finally open. Soon the plaza was crowded.

'Full circle,' said Amantarra.

'Time to go home,' said John.

*

The stage was as they'd left it. John's place marker was still enveloped with arcs of electricity. The dark violet sphere was still in John's chest and it was still difficult to look at.

'What a mess,' said Elleria. She took John's hand in hers. The electric arcs vanished instantly and the dark sphere slowly diminished in size until it was no more. The stage, now lit only by the two low wattage bulbs, was dark and gloomy by comparison.

'You made that look so easy,' said John. Elleria kissed him on the cheek.

'What about Jack?' Harry asked.

'He'll be fine in Valheel,' replied Frank, 'Artullus will look after him. Now, are we ready to return to the real world?'

'Will I remember?' Harry asked.

'Do you want to?' Frank enquired.

'Yes.'

'Me too,' said Scott.

'You realise that I will still have to punish you,' said Harry.

'After all the effort we put in to getting off the stage?' complained John.

'Unfortunately, the others on the stage didn't see you leave, so that's where you'll have to remain,' said Harry.

*

'What are you boys doing in here?' Harry thought he had better repeat the question that nobody had heard last time. There was a clatter as one of their chairs tipped over backwards. 'Come on, out you come.' Harry made a mental note of each name as they filed past him. 'Can't have you on the stage lads; it's a bit of a health hazard.' He was feeling quite conciliatory and figured that perhaps a mild warning was enough. After all he hadn't had to break up a fight involving Burnston.

As the last of them went through the door, there was a noise on the stage.

'Who's that hiding in the shadows?' demanded Mr Fleming as he took a step back through the door for a better look. 'Step into the light boy so I can see you.' There was a scraping from some of the old scenery as the figure moved into the light. 'Martin Macadam!' Mr Fleming turned to Frank and John and whispered, 'Tyrus?'

John and Frank both looked at each other.

'Come on Mr Macadam, over here with the others.'

ABOUT THE AUTHOR

When I was a teenager I was fairly skilled at drawing. I produced some good pencil images which sadly have now been lost. There was a drawing of an engine from a Rolls Royce Camargue. It was large, and the shading of it used up three pencils. I remember the hours I spent on its production during the summer holidays, and the music I listened to as I worked. I was destined to go to Art College, but family circumstances meant that I never got there. Instead, I finished up getting a job.

My working career started in Architecture, where with ink stained fingers and an adjustable setsquare I turned the architect's concepts into technical drawings. Eventually the drawing boards were abandoned in favour of computers, which led me to forge a career using the dark arts of information technology. The technical world in which I found myself doesn't really cater for artists, and for a long time I didn't do anything creative. The artist in me had been well and truly suppressed.

Suppressed, but not forgotten, and certainly not gone. There was still a thread that connected us together. The artist called to me from the wilderness, whispering in my ear, subtlety altering my perception of things. He fed my mind when it needed to escape the tedium that work can sometimes be. Reading was the thread that bound us, and I don't remember a time when I haven't had at least one book on the go.

Sometimes though, reading isn't enough. There wasn't a specific point when I decided to write a novel. There was no revelation moment. One day I just started writing about how I had received the silver watch mentioned in Amantarra. I then attached a fantasy aspect to the gift, which led to the birth of Valheel, the creation of Elleria, Amantarra, and a puzzle surrounding all of them. The artist had escaped.

Several months after I published Amantarra on Kindle, I met someone I hadn't seen for thirty years. He was a friend of my father's and I've known him since I was four. At some point in the conversation I told him I was a published author. "You haven't changed," was his comment. He seemed disappointed that I still retained some aspects from my childhood. Things that he thought I should have grown out of. Quite what he was expecting me to have become I don't know, but I make no apologies for disappointing him. I have never lost my fascination with the imagery that good story invokes. I hope I never will.

www.ingramcontent.com/pod-product-compliance
Lightning Source LLC
Chambersburg PA
CBHW062017170626
46813CB00001B/193

*9 7 8 0 9 5 7 3 2 5 7 4 6 *